"You American men."

She pursed her lips and frowned. "What is the purpose of all this chewing and spitting? 'Tis even more revolting than the atrociously hasty manner in which you men eat and dress." Her eyes captured him again in their amber depths. "In England, a man would rather die than eat a meal with his hat on."

"You're not in England," he muttered, narrowing his eyes upon her. "We beastly American men manage to do a lot of things with our hats on." He leaned toward her, so close he could smell her warm, dewy scent, and couldn't resist a rather obvious dip of his gaze to the curve of her bodice before his eyes collided with hers. "And our boots."

For several moments she stared at him with unmistakable confusion. Then her eyes widened. "You . . . you have no decency."

"And no conscience, either, English. . . ."

Dear Reader,

This month we bring you the first book in a delightful trilogy by author Maura Seger. Set in Belle Haven, a fictional New England town, *The Taming of Amelia* is an adventurous tale of two people destined to forge new lives for themselves in the Colonies. It sets the stage for stories of the town's future generations—right up to the present day, with a tie-in book from Silhouette's Intimate Moments line.

Prolific newcomer Kit Gardner is sure to please with *The Stolen Heart,* a high-spirited romance between an aristocratic English girl and the Pinkerton detective whom she thinks is an outlaw.

New to Harlequin Historicals but certainly not to romance, Virginia Nielsen has written a moving story about a privateer and the Creole woman who rescues him in *To Love a Pirate.*

Knight's Lady, Suzanne Barclay's new book, features another of the irresistible Sommerville brothers. Introduced in *Knight Dreams* (HH #141), Gareth is the eldest sibling and heir to a fortune, yet the granddaughter of a lowly goldsmith holds the key to his heart.

Look for all four titles at your favorite bookstore.

Sincerely,

Tracy Farrell
Senior Editor

The Stolen Heart

Kit Gardner

Harlequin Books

TORONTO • NEW YORK • LONDON
AMSTERDAM • PARIS • SYDNEY • HAMBURG
STOCKHOLM • ATHENS • TOKYO • MILAN
MADRID • WARSAW • BUDAPEST • AUCKLAND

Harlequin Historicals first edition February 1993

ISBN 0-373-28760-7

THE STOLEN HEART

Books by Kit Gardner

KIT GARDNER,

a former C.P.A., lives outside Chicago with her husband and two young sons. When her busy schedule allows, she enjoys skiing, golf, travel and reading anything from romance to the latest in sensational thrillers.

Chapter One

Laramie, Wyoming
April 1876

The largest breasts west of the Mississippi pressed against his naked back. The longest red nails adorning the most talented hands he'd ever known snaked about his waist and rubbed with slow, suggestive promise over his belly. Her breath whispered hot and wicked in his ear, the languid rolling of her hips testing the squeaky springs of the bed.

And his mind wandered.

The faintest of spring breezes stirred the frayed lace curtain yet again, affording him another view of the dusty street below. His eyes narrowed upon his prey, the unmistakable black duster, the trademark black-and-white pinto and the black hat pulled low against the setting sun, though Blades wore it thus regardless of the time of day. His henchmen rode not quite alongside him but reverently several paces behind, their shadowed faces grimy, expressionless masks bent upon striking fear into the hearts of many. Experience, however, had proven that those duncelike countenances required little in the way of practice, for not one of the lot possessed an ounce of sense. Discharged Confederate soldiers, they were, continuing to live and die by the gun. Nothing but quick-triggered hoodlums who had boasted on more than one occasion of killing for pleasure.

His eyes flickered back to Blades, the one person capable of arousing some emotion in him. Vengeance, as full and potent now as it had been those three years ago. And now, at long last, he was so close, the revenge tasting sweet and good and just.

A bitter taste filled his mouth and he had to force himself to keep from shoving the soft woman aside with an impatient sweep of his arm. Her warm tongue darted into his ear and he scowled, catching one wandering hand firmly in his just before it delved purposefully into his loosened pants, seeking. She moaned, a fitful little sound, like a kitten stretching midnap, and snuggled closer against his back, her lips moving over his shoulder.

Again, his mind wandered.

Revenge. He was close enough to taste it, so damned close, and they'd ordered him back East. Back home. They'd taken no small risk resurrecting him from the dead for this mission, one that would prove the greatest challenge thus far in his career, though they couldn't know that. How could they? The identity they had imposed upon him for this time was not one he could hone behind a bar or acquire at some poker table over a bottle of whiskey. Nor could the cropping of his hair, the sporting of a beard or the donning of a dandy's fine silks accomplish the required transformation.

He'd assumed identities as casually as he put on his boots, a different persona with each hat, a new name and trade, yet the purpose remained the same. Justice. His eyes narrowed upon Blades. They were taking Blades away from him, giving his revenge to some operative who would rise nobly to the occasion and apprehend the bastard forthwith. Shouldn't justice be revenge enough?

The foul taste again invaded his mouth, bitter like gunpowder and burnt flesh. He wanted to kill the man, callously steal his life from him just as Rudy Blades had killed Aaron, with four shots fired at such close range that the muzzle blasts had burned away clothing, skin, hair.

How this lust for revenge filled him, bubbling up within him, aching in his chest for release. He'd given serious thought to refusing the order, though that would undoubtedly require some explanation, at least more than the black-sheep-of-the-family story he had been obliged to divulge those seven years ago. Not that he had lied, but there was far more to it than that. Far more. Things he hadn't thought about in years. Things he would have preferred to face on his own rather than being forced by an oath taken to confront his past, all in the line of duty.

He closed his eyes, dimly aware of the palms insistently kneading his belly. He was tired, he knew it. And worse yet, *they* knew it. Being tired meant the threat of becoming sloppy, a touch less astute, less cautious about covering tracks and disappearing with the wind. In this business, a man could pay with his life for that kind of mistake.

"Oh, Shane, darlin'..." Those breasts rubbed wantonly against his back, the nipples taut, insistent, impatient. "Why're you leavin' town so soon, Shane... sweet Shane, darlin'?"

He opened his eyes and scowled. *Shane*. What the hell kind of name was that to give a man? Almost as bad as Sebastian had been two missions ago. Aliases. Where the hell did they come up with them? Surely there were a few names that began with *S* that weren't so damned... *peculiar*. Names that didn't make his tongue itch. Decent strong names. Names with indubitable character. What the hell was the matter with those guys?

"Shane, honey, don't you want me tonight?" She licked his ear then bit down playfully as one well-rounded and very naked leg encircled his waist. Even if he didn't want her, she was bound and determined to change his mind. "Rudy's due back soon, darlin'. You wouldn't want him to find us together now, would you?"

An interesting idea he'd toyed with on more than one occasion.

Her breath was hot on the back of his neck, her pelvis grinding into his lower back. This time when her hand delved into his pants, he made no move to stop her.

"He wouldn't take too kindly to his girl bein' found in bed with the local barkeep, now would he?" Her voice was high and singsong and laced with plaintive appeal. "C'mon, honey, quit starin' out the window." Her girlish giggle sent a wave of hesitation through him. "I've got lots here you can look at... an' touch... an' squeeze."

He grunted and slid a hand slowly down the length of her leg, pausing to idly caress the curve of her hip. Rising, he toyed with the loosened button of his pants and peered out the window at Blades tethering his horse before the saloon directly across the street. He turned toward the bed and shed his pants with one swift movement.

Her widening eyes traveled over him, and she fairly smacked her lips with anticipation. "Oh, honey, I've never seen a man that can compare to you. Not even Rudy, and he's..."

"Shh..." He moved before her, pressing a finger to her lips and drawing her to her knees, full against him. "No more talk."

She evaded his kiss with an uncharacteristic twist of her head and a wary glance into the shadowed corner of the room. "Does that...that...*thing* have to watch?"

His eyes flickered to the pile of fur dozing peacefully in the shadows. "Trust me, he's not watching."

She shuddered delicately. "What is it, anyway?"

"Who, Sam?" He watched the look of revulsion sweeping across her features. Young, beautiful, blond and damned lusty. Blades had an eye for women, there was no denying that, though he obviously inspired little loyalty in them, in bed or otherwise. Then again, she was far too empty-headed to realize he'd been using her for far more than her eager body. His hands cupped her full buttocks then lifted her, spreading her legs as he fell upon her and entered her with one quick thrust. She clasped him close and moaned. His mouth found the pillow beside her head and he closed his eyes. "Sam's part dog, part wolf, part coyote..."

Just like him. All parts and no whole.

Identities. After ten years, the toughest of all would be becoming himself.

"Phoebe Sinclair, you're naked!"

Heaving an exasperated sigh, Phoebe glared into the dense foliage, now quiet and still, as if a terrified young man had not just a few moments past flung himself into those bushes with a yelp of fear to beat a hasty retreat. Phoebe bent a scowl upon her friend. "Not quite, Charlotte. As you can see, I still wear my shift, no thanks to you."

"What?" Charlotte Lambert parted the last of the bushes before her and stepped into the clearing. She drew her wrapper close about her against the chill and pursed her lips. "No thanks to me, indeed! Why, if I hadn't seen fit to find you, that Donnie Duncan would have..."

"Oh, poohey." Phoebe waved a hand and bent to retrieve her gown. "He wouldn't have done anything I wouldn't allow."

Charlotte raised a knowing brow. "That's precisely what I'm afraid of."

"Oh, cease, you goose." Phoebe stepped into her gown, thrust her arms into the sleeves and presented her friend with her back. "Here, make yourself useful and button me."

"You're not even wearing a corset, for goodness' sake," Charlotte mumbled, tending to the task.

"'Tis the middle of the night, silly. Besides, imagine poor Donnie attempting to maneuver his way about a corset." Phoebe shook her head and her blond ringlets tumbled about her shoulders. Idly, she caught one curl in her finger and twirled it thoughtfully then sighed again. "No... trust me. Donnie's just a boy and..."

"He's a score and two, hardly a lad, and three years your senior."

"I know, but... he just... he's..."

"Sweet."

"Oh yes, he is at that, but he's so..."

"Kind."

"Oh, that, too. Very kind, indeed. But he's so... so..."

"Handsome."

Phoebe spun about and lifted a brow at Charlotte. "Perhaps Donnie dallied with the wrong maiden this eve, hmm?"

Even in the pale moonlight, Phoebe detected Charlotte's blush, the dipping of her ebony head. "Oh, for heaven's sake! No! Oh no, Phoebe. I'll leave all the fun to you."

Phoebe couldn't resist another sigh. "If that it were in the least bit fun."

"Oh no, not again."

Phoebe threw up her hands in a helpless gesture. "Would you rather I lie to you? Tell you that I thrilled at far more than just the mere thought of a clandestine meeting with a beau? Let me tell you, I didn't. Or should I perhaps tell you that the entire time he fumbled and fussed and served up the response I expected, the response *I* controlled, I was thinking about how terribly boring I'm finding this Wellesley College, as terribly boring as I'm finding men." She crossed her arms beneath her breasts and shook her head. "Charlotte, something is dreadfully wrong with me."

Charlotte gave her a level look. "Forgive me if I don't feel the least bit sorry for you."

"You know me better than that."

"Do I? Phoebe, one cannot help but wonder what it is you seek from these ventures into the night, other than expulsion, of course. Donnie is what, the third to capture your fancy just this spring?"

"Well, for heaven's sake! A girl can seek a little fun, can't she, amidst all this drudgery of higher education? But you certainly don't expect me to remain enamored with a fellow if he's . . ." Phoebe frowned as she sought the perfect word. After a moment, her eyes flew wide and she gave a confident smile. "*Easy*. That's it! They're all far too easy."

"One might find oneself thinking the same of you."

Phoebe pursed her lips. "If *one* were a godawful prig who wore her bloomers too tight, perhaps. For goodness' sake, Charlotte, you certainly didn't harbor the ludicrous notion that I'd even considered for a moment *giving* myself to some panting and sweating schoolboy?" She shook her head with determination. "No, I intend to bestow my virtue upon my husband, a man, Charlotte, a big, powerful *man* whose experience renders him entirely beyond my control."

"Don't shiver too deliciously, Phoebe. I have a notion you wouldn't find that kind of man suitable husband material. I know *I* wouldn't."

Inclining her head, Phoebe wrapped her arms tightly about her and contemplated the starlit sky. "Mmm . . . I don't know. I'll tell you this. Just the thought of what a real man could do to a girl . . . the things he would make *you* want to do . . . Doesn't it just make you all hot and gooey and—"

"Please, Phoebe . . ."

Phoebe raised a wicked brow and grinned devilishly at her friend. " 'Tis a delectable thought, is it not?"

Charlotte looked entirely out of her element. "To be perfectly honest with you, it leaves me rather squeamish."

"Oh, for heaven's sake, you sound just like Priscilla Snodgrass."

Charlotte's eyes flew wide. "Oh, my goodness! Priscilla Snodgrass! Phoebe, blast you, you made me forget why I came looking for you!"

Phoebe couldn't resist a thoroughly smug look. "You see? All this talk of big, powerful men was getting to you, wasn't it, Charlotte?"

"Oh, hush up! We're in a dreadful pickle."

"Not Priscilla again. Surely that meddling busybody isn't resorting to blackmail again?"

"A lot of good that would do her and she knows it, too. We're completely out of money for the month."

"Already?"

Charlotte stared meaningfully at her friend. "If a certain someone hadn't chosen to bribe her in the first place, we would have at least a farthing between us."

"Don't look at me like that, Charlotte. She found me out. What choice did I have at the time?"

"True. You were wearing even less then and you were in the fountain." Charlotte closed her eyes and shook her head as if the notion were unthinkable. "No, even you couldn't have wiled your way out of that one."

"The fountain, that's right…with Jeremy. I must say, of all my beaux, he was certainly the most game of the lot and by far the best kisser and…"

"Phoebe, for heaven's sake, you're obsessed! Listen to me. Priscilla intends to present a full account of your illicit activities to the dean of students first thing on the morrow."

"Bitch."

"Phoebe!"

"Well, you know she is, even if you won't allow yourself to think it."

"Whatever are we going to do?"

"*We?* 'Tis painfully obvious even to me that this is entirely a problem of my own doing. I'll devise some plot."

"Phoebe, for goodness' sake, I'm your best friend. We've come all this way to Boston together, across an entire ocean, halfway round the world! We shall stay together."

Phoebe grasped her friend's hand. She would have done the same for Charlotte were the circumstances reversed. After all, theirs had been a remarkably successful collaboration, ever since their initial idea to embark upon their own version of a grand tour to America and Wellesley Women's College, prompted, on Phoebe's part, solely by the desire to postpone the inevitable drudgery of a teaching post. Besides, the mere thought of the legions of strapping American men simply awaiting discovery was a temptation a girl of Phoebe's adventurous inclinations could not resist. Convincing their respective fathers that the idea held merit proved somewhat of an obstacle, being that both had secured much sought-after teaching positions at one of England's most prestigious women's public schools. Broadening one's mind through the experience of living in America had merely served to raise one of her father's brows in a caustic expression until Phoebe had stumbled quite by accident upon the dramatic historical significance of the American Centennial celebration taking place in Philadelphia that May. Capitalizing upon her father's piqued interest in the subject, she was finally granted his consent to accompany Charlotte to Wellesley, along with his ominous promise that he and his wife, Elizabeth, would also attend the centennial if only to ensure that Phoebe was behaving. How often had she wished her father didn't know her so blasted well?

"Phoebe?" Charlotte timidly inquired of her thoughtful friend. "What about another bribe? We've our jewelry, you know. Lots of it."

"Are you daft? Give my precious jewelry to a...a...snot like Priscilla Snodgrass? Never! Money, yes. But jewelry? I'll choose expulsion, thank you. I've an idea."

"Oh, thank heavens!"

"We'll leave."

"We'll what?"

"We'll leave *before* they expel us."

"How on earth will we do that without rousing suspicion?"

"Why, Charlotte, our teaching services have been requested at several dreadfully exclusive schools...somewhere..."

"Where? Home?"

"Oh, for goodness' sake, no! All the way back to England after only eight months? My father would guess right off, and if *he* didn't, Elizabeth surely would. I've never been able to pull one over on her."

"Perhaps with the new baby, and she does have the toddler, as well."

"Just because she's borne two babies does not mean the woman hasn't a brain in her head." Phoebe tapped a finger against her lip. "No, England is out of the question."

"I rather miss it."

Phoebe's fair brows swept together in thought. "I'm always reading about those quaint little country towns in desperate need of schoolteachers. We're more than qualified. Enough of this further enrichment and broadening of our minds."

"But where, Phoebe? One doesn't simply set out with no destination."

"And even less in the way of a recommendation." Her finger tapped thoughtfully at her lip once again. "Too bad we haven't some long-lost relatives somewhere that we could visit for a while, some . . ."

"Uncle Carson! Why, of course!"

"Who?"

Charlotte could barely restrain her glee. "Uncle Carson McAllister! A second or third cousin on my mother's side, I believe. I haven't heard much of them since Mother died, but I'm certain he and his new wife and family live somewhere in northwest Pennsylvania. Buttermilk Falls is the name of the town. Such a charming name, and Mother always spoke so highly of Uncle Carson."

"Good. Then it's settled." Phoebe's amber eyes met those, very wide and dark, looming in Charlotte's pale face. "Whatever is the matter, Charlotte?"

"J-just like that? We're going?"

"Indeed. Just like that. But first we must send off a tidy little missive to your uncle, explaining that we are simply passing through on our journey west to the teaching positions awaiting us in . . . oh, someplace adventurous and wonderful like . . . Kansas!"

"Kansas? Where in the world is Kansas?"

Phoebe waved an airy hand in a westerly direction. "Oh, never mind. Leave the composing of the letter to me. With any luck, we'll catch the post before we catch our train."

"Train?"

"Why, of course! How did you think we were going to travel from Boston to this Buttermilk Falls? By boat? Really, Charlotte!"

"I . . . I've heard train travel in the States is not what it is in England."

Phoebe linked her arm through that of her friend and urged Charlotte in the direction of the dormitory. "How bad can it be, hmm? Though I do hope they have room for Mabel."

Charlotte stopped dead in her tracks. "Surely you're not considering taking *that* contraption?"

With a thoroughly disbelieving look, Phoebe replied, "Of course I am, you goose. I wouldn't think of leaving her behind."

A moment before it happened, he sensed trouble. Perhaps it was the sudden pricking of his mount's ears, accompanied by a nervous prancing that had been lacking in the horse's otherwise leisurely gait these past several miles. Or had the warning come from Sam, his abruptly halting stride, his mangy body rigid, unmoving save for the moist blue-black tip of his nose twitching, seeking, in the warm afternoon air.

Heeding the warnings, he pulled up on Zack's reins and instinctively reached a hand inside his coat to his waistband. He had but a moment to narrow his gaze upon the twisting path before him, directly at the spot where it climbed a sudden steep hill, rounded a thicket and disappeared. His ears strained. Yes, he heard it, too . . . something . . . creaking . . . and humming . . . a husky female voice. His finger eased one whit upon the trigger.

In an instant, whatever it was burst upon them. He achieved but a glimpse of brown and white and blond . . . yes, lots of blond, and some conglomeration of wheels and iron before an ebony mane blocked his sight as Zack reared with a terrified scream. Or was it the girl who screamed? For an instant, Zack's front hooves touched ground, or rather they all but trampled that conglomeration of wheels and metal before reaching skyward again.

With a curse and a fierce tug upon the reins, he spun the stallion about, though not before one back hoof landed soundly and with a decided crunch upon one wheel.

"Blast you! Look what you've done to Mabel!"

Another tug upon the reins brought Zack about just as he'd shown every sign of bucking in a rash attempt to unseat him. Another curse escaped his lips as he struggled with his skittish mount while assuring himself that the girl was safe.

She was as safe as one could be having landed soundly upon her rump in a clump of thick grass. He tipped his hat back upon his head for a better look and muttered under his breath for Zack's ears alone. His stare did not waver despite the horse's nervous snorts and the angry tosses of his black head.

His first thought came as no surprise. After all, thinking like that came naturally after seven years on the job.

Was she the contact?

His eyes narrowed upon her. Too young.

Maybe.

The sunlight caught at the white blond streaks in the otherwise honeyed tumble of curls peeking from beneath her brown cap and falling in complete disarray about slender shoulders. Too beautiful.

Was there such a thing?

She didn't even bother to shield her eyes from the sun as she glared up at him. Twin pools blazed amber fire above a tiny nose and a wide, full, pouty mouth. Much too beautiful.

Then again, those guys weren't dumb. What could be more potent than a beautiful, young female operative? His eyes dipped to the undeniable curve of her crisp white bodice and the slender sweep of silk-stockinged calf revealed by what looked to be brown tweed bloomers. Bloomers?

Definitely female and not that farfetched a notion. Though how she could have known he'd be coming this way, at exactly this time of day... She must be good. Very, very good.

He watched her as she scrambled to her feet and bent another heated glare upon him, as if she were expecting some response. What had she said?

He glanced at the jumble of metal lying at Zack's feet. "Mabel?"

A fair brow arched in his direction before she turned and proceeded to dust off her backside with painstaking care, presenting him with a delectable view of her rounded derriere snugly encased in those damned bloomers. He caught himself when those amber eyes sought his. "Yes, you ninny, Mabel. Just look what you've done to her!" She flung her arm in an accusatory manner at the pile of metal and pursed those pale pink lips. "She's ruined."

He cocked a brow and fought the smirk that threatened. If she was indeed his contact, she wouldn't take too kindly to anything in the way of a patronizing attitude. He'd be better off getting to the heart of the matter so they could cease this charade with this damned Mabel contraption. And *he* had complained about *his* aliases!

He contemplated the twisted pile of metal. Leave it to a woman to name a contraption like that. "Mabel. What was she, if you don't mind my asking?"

He received a look of such utter stupefaction that for the briefest of moments he felt decidedly chagrined. She strode toward him and his eyes strayed again. Much, much too beautiful.

Then, suddenly, there wasn't a doubt in his mind. She was the contact.

"Mabel was a bicycle."

"A what?" He stared down at the brown cap sitting at a rakish angle upon her head. Had she been hoping to pass for a lad? Again, his eyes strayed. *No way.*

Her eyes lifted to him and his chest grew tight. "A bicycle." She looked at him as if he were insufferably thick-headed.

Bicycle. His mind flew. *Bicycle?* Was it some kind of code? Had he left Laramie before they had communicated this to him? That had to be it.

He stared directly into her eyes, a stare full of meaning. "Of course. A bicycle." She glanced away before he could glimpse anything besides complete annoyance in her eyes. Oh, she was damned good. His eyes focused upon one long curl falling halfway down her back and he asked levelly, "And where did you acquire this 'bicycle'? Philadelphia?"

The blond head shook and she knelt beside the twisted metal, one hand tracing almost reverently over what had once resembled a wheel. "Every last one of the spokes is broken." Her fingers were long and slender.

His chest tightened again. If not out of the Philadelphia office, where?

"Chicago?"

The blond head shook again and he could have sworn he detected a soft sniffing. Lord, but she was good. If not Chicago...certainly not Denver? But it had to be. They had no other offices. So why hadn't he heard of her? Female operatives were a rarity.

"Ah, then Denver."

She presented him a tearstained visage. "No, you dolt! I procured my bicycle in London at Hydes and Wigfull's! And it seems that I shall have to return there to see to acquiring another, no thanks to you!"

London? She was from Scotland Yard! So her accent wasn't pretense. His chest tightened with something more than desire this time. Anticipation. They hadn't ordered him back East for some thinly disguised bout of rest and relaxation. No, indeed! This mission was of international importance, a joint operation requiring operatives from Scotland Yard, no less.

He closed his eyes with relief. Hell, he hadn't realized he'd been *that* worried. Then again, considering what was waiting for him, he was damned glad it would all be worth it. His mind flew. What could the mission be? His eyes followed her movements as she struggled to right Mabel.

What kind of mission would require a young, beautiful English girl? His heart almost stopped and his mouth opened with shock. Adam Worth, notorious international jewel thief and bank robber, known for his penchant for beautiful women. Who else could it possibly be?

A smile tugged at the corner of his mouth, a slow, confident smile, the kind that feels very good when one realizes one's importance in an organization. Feeling very good indeed, he slipped from the saddle and bent to lend this English operative a hand.

"Here, I'll take it," he offered, lifting Mabel from the ground and eyeing a stray wheel that rolled drunkenly into the bushes.

" 'Tis the least you can do," the English girl muttered, retrieving the wheel and unceremoniously thrusting it into his full arms. "Shall we? 'Tis quite a walk."

He lifted a brow at her impertinence, then, pausing but a moment to admire yet again the turn of her slender hips in those bloomers, he set off after her like an obedient puppy. With his eyes still fixed upon her, he stopped and scowled, muttering under his breath, then called after her. "Er...miss...my horse..."

She turned, frowning at him as if he were some damned nuisance, then strode past him to retrieve Zack. His eyes couldn't help but follow. She wasn't very tall, her head barely reaching to his shoulder, but she definitely possessed a commanding air, no doubt about that. A woman who knew her mind. What did he expect of Scotland Yard?

"Does your beast have a name?" she asked, breezing just as airily past him leading a docile Zack.

Of course! She would identify him by his horse. "Zack," he replied, extending his stride until he was in step beside her, then looking closely at her.

She wrinkled her nose and waved a hand before her as if to ward off a fly. "Peculiar name."

He stared at her. Was she expecting something else? His head swiveled about in search of his other "beast" and he gave a soft whistle. "Sam's with me, as well." As if on cue, the mangy creature emerged from the thicket and trotted along beside him.

The girl exchanged glances with Sam, a quick, assessing glance, before her eyes fixed once more on the path before her. "Peculiar dog. You're rather unimaginative, aren't you?"

"Pardon me?"

"Sam. Zack."

"Mabel."

She glanced sharply at him. "Mabel is a lovely name. What's your name? No, don't tell me. Something extraordinarily American. Like Billy-Bob."

He couldn't resist a smile. "Not quite." This was it. The time had come to cease all pretense. He drew a breath. "My name is..."

"Billy-Bob doesn't quite suit you, though, does it?" She pressed a finger to her bottom lip in so thoroughly enchanting a manner he almost missed the assessing sweep of her eyes over him. For a moment, he also forgot about the burning of the muscles in his arms. Mabel was getting damned heavy. "No, you're far too beastly a man to be a Billy-Bob."

Something in her tone and that look in her eye told him that "beastly" was far from a desirable state. He imagined his beard was as grimy as the rest of him.

"Train travel does not lend itself to cleanliness," he replied.

"Indeed!" she huffed, tugging relentlessly upon Zack's reins. "So cramped and stuffy and, dear God, the smoke! Thick oily stuff that fills the lungs!"

"So it's the same in London?"

She gave him *the look* again, the one that made him certain that she was some highly educated, supremely well-bred Scotland Yard operative deigning to assist him with the mission.

"*Those* kinds of trains in *London?*" She shook her head as if at a total loss with him. "Are you daft? My horrendous experience with American trains ended rather recently, thank God, once I arrived here from Boston."

His pulse quickened. Adam Worth was known to have a ring of thieves in Boston.

"Then again, you Americans don't all have such dreadful imaginations when it comes to names. Pine Grove isn't such an awful name. Yes, it's quite charming, indeed. A suitable name for an English country estate, even."

His step faltered. "Did you say Pine Grove?"

"Why, yes. 'Tis where you're going to deliver me. Oh, I don't live there, of course. Simply passing through for a visit, you see. I arrived several days ago and . . . oh, but it was dreadful. The house is in mourning, you see, and we hadn't a notion. Not the slightest. Of course, if we had, we never would have . . ."

"Mourning?"

"Oh yes, you see, Uncle . . . I mean, Carson McAllister passed away not six months ago."

The blood suddenly pounded so ferociously in his head, he momentarily lost his vision. He felt the weight around his heart, a load far more overpowering than that in his arms. The English girl's voice sounded very far away.

"Why, whatever is the matter with you? Don't drop Mabel, for heaven's sake!" Her hand was upon his arm. "What did you say your name was?"

His eyes found hers just as he realized she couldn't possibly be the operative. But that mattered very little at the moment. "McAllister," he said. "Sterling Jace McAllister."

The English girl stopped dead in her tracks and stared open-mouthed at him. "Carson's son? You can't be. He's dead."

Chapter Two

Sterling McAllister lengthened his stride, fixing his gaze before him as if his thoughts were indeed elsewhere. Under his breath he muttered, his voice deep and gruff, like his beard-stubbled face, "As you can see, I'm very much alive."

Phoebe hurried along after him. "Well, Madeline doesn't seem to think so, though the poor woman is all but overcome with her grief. In her state, one can't be too sure of her ability to decipher fact from fiction."

A sound not unlike a disgusted snort came from him and he shifted Mabel in his arms. "My father's wife honed that skill to perfection many years ago." Phoebe's eyes focused upon his mouth, which was pressed into a sudden fierce and feral line. She couldn't be certain but she would have wagered another Mabel that the word he spat under his breath sounded very much like "bitch."

"You don't appear to be a man grieving for his dead father."

His stride lengthened, his eyes staring off into the distance as if he hadn't heard her.

"Surely you were aware that he had passed away."

Nothing but the muffled thud of his boots upon the dirt path and the distant screech of a bird reached her ears. Peculiar man. Phoebe glanced at Sam trotting obediently in his master's wake. And a peculiar animal, indeed. The size of a large dog, he was, with a mussed coat of some nondescript color, short pointed ears and the face of a wolf. His tongue lolled out one side of his mouth and his black eyes were hooded, as if he were frightfully bored with all this.

As her eyes flickered over the tall man at her side, she couldn't help the slight wrinkling of her nose and a brief sniff. He looked as if he'd been dipped in grime from the top of that mangled excuse for a hat to the tips of those pointed black boots.

"You'll certainly prove something of a surprise," Phoebe remarked, tugging upon Zack's reins when the horse dallied at a growth of violets. "One can't help but wonder why you've allowed your family to believe you dead for seven years."

He grunted and trudged even more determinedly up the path. He obviously knew where he was going. "I have my reasons, English."

Phoebe raised a brow. "I have a name."

The corner of his mouth twitched. "Something extraordinarily British, no doubt. Alfreda, perhaps?"

Phoebe tucked her chin in and gaped at him. "I should say not. Alfreda, indeed! Why, I once knew of a girl whose father owned a cow named Alfreda!"

"Norma?"

Phoebe sputtered.

"Bliss?"

Her mouth spread in a slow, huge smile. "Bliss…why that's a perfectly lovely name. Where on earth did you hear of that?"

He hesitated, his eyes narrowing slightly for a moment. "Let's just say I also once knew a girl."

"Oh." Phoebe couldn't resist the distasteful curl teasing her lip. Her eyes darted over him again. "You look more the type to have had your way with at least one Alfreda and several Normas, if not a few Berthas, but never a Bliss. No, a Bliss would most definitely look the other way."

She detected the flash of very white teeth from somewhere beneath the shadow of his hat, amidst all that dark stubble. "This one didn't."

"Then I shall be eternally grateful that I was not given such a name," she sniffed, lifting her chin a notch. "Phoebe suits me just fine." She frowned at a sudden thought. "You don't know of any Phoebes, do you?"

"None. You're the first."

For some reason, that pleased her tremendously. She sneaked a glance at him, at that hawklike profile, the hollowed cheeks that looked as if the man hadn't had a good meal in many days. He was a big man, nevertheless, tall and broad of shoulder, though the thigh-length buckskin coat of the same nondescript color as his dog hid his torso from view. His buckskin-clad legs were inordinately long, his strides requiring two of hers to keep pace. Her eyes flickered over him again. The grime he had been dipped in was of one color: dinge. Still, he was a formidable-looking man. Formidable, indeed.

"And what of you?" she inquired, wondering at the sudden chill that chased up her spine. "Such a laborious name you bear."

"I never liked it."

"Why not? Sylvester isn't such a bad name. A trifle peculiar and more suited to an animal but . . ."

"Sterling."

Phoebe frowned at him. The poor man looked as if he hadn't bathed, eaten or slept in a week. Little wonder he was becoming delirious. "Silver? I thought we were discussing names."

She received a dingy-looking scowl from beneath the brim of his hat and his tone was laced with something akin to impatience. "My name is Sterling."

"Sterling? Oh, I like that much better, though 'tis a bit odd and doesn't quite suit you. Rather stilted."

"Call me Jace."

"Is that some American derivative of Sterling?"

He looked positively irritated. "No, it's my middle name."

Phoebe gave his profile a curious look. "If your mother wished you to be known as Jace, why on earth would she give you a godawful name like Sterling?"

"Because Sterling was her family's name." His voice was taut and drew Phoebe's attention to his profile yet again. When he swung a hardened gaze upon her, she felt her blush sweep to the tips of her ears and she knew not why. "You did manage to catch McAllister?" he uttered in an even tone not in keeping with his sarcasm.

Phoebe raised one haughty brow. "Forgive me, Mr. McAllister, but perhaps I am frightfully unused to people speaking as if their mouths were full of pebbles. I must say, this decided twang you Americans possess has caused me considerable distress, though *you* seem to have escaped that plight in favor of this...this..." She waved a hand as she sought her word, which required more than the usual amount of mind-searching, for his eyes had fixed upon her. "This rumbling sound you make very deep in your throat. Diction, Mr. Mc-Allister, is fundamentally important."

"You sound just like Miss Merriweather."

"Now *that's* a lovely name."

"I remember her as a rather lovely woman. In fact, I do believe she was my first love."

"Things could have been worse. Your first love could have been a Norma."

He stared directly before him and a frown creased his brow. "She broke my heart."

"Perhaps she didn't care for your name."

"I believe the problem lay in our ages."

"I see. You were a trifle too old for her?" He definitely looked the type that young innocents best avoid altogether. Especially a young innocent with a name like Miss Merriweather.

His frown deepened as if he were lost in thought. "Perhaps. I was always rather tall for my age and painfully mature. Then again, perhaps she didn't care for the apples I left for her." He shifted Mabel in his arms with a slight grunt and shot Phoebe a quick look. "Of course, who could blame the woman. I was only nine at the time, and desperately in love."

"As only a nine-year-old can be with his teacher." She couldn't resist a smile. "How charming." She felt his eyes upon her again, assessing, just as they'd been assessing her since the moment they'd collided.

"You remind me of her in many ways."

"Oh, heavens no! Teachers all possess that frightful habit of looking down their noses at everyone."

A smirk lifted one side of his mouth. "And here I'd thought you Brits had cornered that market."

For a moment, Phoebe considered losing her temper, then thought the better of it. "Bold words from a man just risen from the dead seven years past. How *did* you die, Mr. Mc-Allister?"

"I'm sure the rumors would be far more entertaining than the true story, English."

Phoebe bristled at his manner of addressing her. For some reason, she had the distinct feeling that he was mocking her. She lifted her chin a notch. "'Tis not so very odd that you are stock full of conceit, assuming that the townspeople have nothing better to do than discuss the likes of *you.* For your information, I have heard your name but once since I arrived two days past. In fact, 'twas Madeline who informed me that you had died in an Indian raid during construction of the Union Pacific railroad line in some godawful place..."

"Wyoming."

"Is that anywhere near Kansas?"

"Not really."

"Thank heavens. So you obviously didn't die."

"I came damn close."

"So why on earth didn't you come home?"

"I don't recall Miss Merriweather being so damned nosy."

"Inquisitive, Mr. McAllister. A sign of intelligence."

"Nosy. A sign of an idle, scheming mind."

Phoebe pursed her lips with exasperation, feeling the color flooding her cheeks. "You boorish lummox!"

His laugh was huge and genuine, reverberating deep within his chest. "Aw, c'mon, English, you can do better than that."

"Bastard!"

"Watch it. I'm carrying your precious Mabel, remember?"

Phoebe stopped dead in her tracks. "You brute! If it hadn't been for your dumb animal... Why, the gall!" She paused but a moment, for Jace continued on without hesitation as if he hadn't heard her, agilely climbing a rather steep grassy slope then pausing, finally. A breathless Phoebe followed, tugging with mounting irritation upon Zack's tether.

When she reached his side, she bent a heated glower upon him, which he chose to ignore in favor of the landscape sweeping before them. She bit her tongue, allowing her eyes to follow. From their vantage the Allegheny River valley swept before them, resplendent in its sun-dappled spring garb, all newly sprung pale hues of green, yellow and white. Hills carpeted with dense white and hemlock pines surrounded them on all sides, and nestled deep within the valley, tucked beside an oblong lake, not a mile from the river itself, lay Pine Grove. The main house was just visible through the trees, its three stone chimneys jutting majestically through the very top of the foliage. Majestic it was, made entirely of stone, as were the guest house and servants' quarters situated some distance back from it. A veranda wide enough for a coach and six flanked the house on three sides, and a cobblestone drive, but a thin pale ribbon at this distance, wound its way from the front of the house to the stable and a barnlike structure, then meandered some distance to the main road and beyond to the river.

"After so many years it must look a bit different," Phoebe mused, shielding her eyes from the sun as she swung her gaze to that imposing profile.

"Smaller," he muttered in a tight voice, his eyes narrow and his mouth set. He seemed to draw in a deep breath then set out at his determined pace, plowing through the deep grass with strides both sure and strong.

For several moments, Phoebe stared dumbfounded at his broad back. "What the devil are you doing?" she called after him. "The path is over here . . . Mr. McAllister?" With an exasperated sigh, she set out through the meadow after him. "You're rather in a hurry, aren't you?" she managed between huffs, forging her own path for several moments before wisely deciding to follow in his. "'Twould serve you well to consider tempering your disposition." She frowned at his back, noting how supremely arrogant he managed to look. "As you are, I would venture to say that you shan't receive too warm a welcome."

In reply, she received naught but a grunt.

Only when Jace reached the cobblestone drive did his pace slow. He drew a deep breath, allowing his eyes to sweep about, slowly, lingering, and the melancholy feeling washed over him again. The wind stirred in the trees, those huge elms; they were larger, much larger than he recalled, and the house seemed much smaller by comparison, and older. Very old and sad. His throat tightened and he looked away. Two men loitered just outside the stable and by their dress he guessed they were hands. As yet, they seemed unaware of his presence, their attention fixed upon a rusted tin can sitting not ten paces away. Rather suddenly, one of the hands erupted with a brownish orange stream of thick spittle that hit its mark with a decided *clang*.

This brought several triumphant, thigh-slapping whoops from the creator of said spittle and a decided intake of breath from the young woman at Jace's back.

He paused, glancing at her and noting the telltale wrinkling of her nose, that unmistakable indication that she was thoroughly repulsed. He'd already seen that look directed at him several times. Her amber eyes slid to his and he found himself longing for a bath. After five days, even his teeth felt grimy.

"You American men." She pursed her lips and frowned at the two hands again, though Jace found his gaze lingering upon the sheen of perspiration bathing the golden skin of her face. "What is the purpose of all this chewing and spitting? 'Tis even more revolting than the atrociously hasty manner in which you men eat and your careless modes of dress." Her eyes captured him again in their amber depths. "In England, a man would rather die than eat a meal with his hat on."

"You're not in England," he muttered, narrowing his eyes upon her. "We beastly American men manage to do a lot of things with our hats on." He leaned toward her, so close he could smell her warm, dewy scent, and couldn't resist a rather obvious dip of his gaze to the curve of her bodice before his eyes collided with hers. "And our boots."

For several moments she stared at him with unmistakable confusion, then her eyes widened and her mouth sagged open then snapped shut. "You . . . you have no decency."

"And no conscience, either, English."

"That doesn't surprise me. 'Tis a cold man that wanders to his father's doorstep after seven long years of allowing his family to believe him dead." She lifted her nose and sniffed. "You're despicable."

He stared at her for a moment, then with very little ceremony dropped all fifty pounds' worth of Mabel in a heap at her feet before turning on his heel and walking toward the house. Her huge intake of breath followed by an unadulterated scream of rage lifted one corner of his mouth, as did the string of language she hurled at his back, language not quite suited to a prim English miss.

He flexed his arms several times, absently rubbing each as if to massage the burn in his muscles, then proceeded around the house. His eyes flickered over the structure, drinking in every detail as if he were a parched, desert-bound soul, a soul thirsting for home...and finding memories that left only a bitter taste in his mouth. Had it really been ten years? Ten long years since he'd hastily stuffed a sack with what little he could rightfully call his own before fleeing, yes, fleeing beneath his father's murderous glower. He'd been a boy then, a sapling of a man, full of shame, confusion...

A movement further along on the veranda caught his eye, and he felt the blood pound suddenly in his ears. An apprehension like none he'd experienced in quite a long time welled up within him and his pace slowed.

He stared at the lad, ten-years-old almost to the day. His eyes narrowed. Lad? He took a step closer. The boy's hair was the color of honey, long and tortured into precise sausage curls down the small head. The child sat alone on the veranda, slumped in a high-backed chair, tiny hands plucking idly at the deep blue velvet pantaloons and matching short jacket. A severely starched, voluminous white collar rubbed against the child's chin and the matching cuffs all but hid the tiny hands from view. One foot dangling over the chair kicked rebelliously at a table leg. Jace would have done the same had he been forced to wear muslin stockings and high-buttoned black leather shoes on such a warm day. Or any day.

The staccato sound of heels tapping upon the veranda brought the child's head up with a snap and his back ramrod straight. A thoroughly meek smile affixed itself upon his pale face and he folded his hands docilely upon the table and his legs primly beneath his chair.

"Here we are, James. Some nice tea and cakes."

"Yes, Dearest," little James replied with a resounding lack of enthusiasm.

Dearest? Why not Mother, or Mommy, or even Mummy? Jace narrowed his gaze upon the woman. In that regard, at least, Madeline had not changed one whit. But time had definitely taken its toll. Then again, he would always view her in the harshest of lights, especially now...knowing that she had somehow managed to kill his father.

Black did not suit her, no matter how fashionable the gown. It sallowed the colorless skin of her face, a face pinched and lined with far more than the ravages of time. It dulled the gray-streaked dark hair twisted and coiled high upon her head, hair once a vibrant chestnut, the same color he remembered her eyes. And the current fashion, of which he would have bet his life she was painfully aware, did nothing for her figure despite her stature. The sleeves of her black bombazine gown were far too tight, the narrow lines of the simple dress accentuating the sag of her bosom, the excess in her belly, hips and thighs. Time had not been kind to her, and she looked several years older than her thirty-nine years. Was she only nine years his senior?

He felt a chill around his heart as he watched her tend to her son, the painstaking care she took tucking a primly starched linen napkin in his collar before fussing unnecessarily with his locks. She pursed her lips, the kind that implied she would never be quite satisfied with anything. Then, as if she suddenly grew aware of the intrusion of another, she raised her eyes to Jace.

He stared at her, a cold, hard stare that required little in the way of drumming up. It was all still there. All the scorn, all the contempt for the one woman who had destroyed their lives. He grew dimly aware that what little color her face bore drained instantly and she clutched a trembling hand to her breast as if she were gulping for air. The sight of a dead man obviously proved a trifle overwhelming for even the most cold-hearted of women.

Her mouth opened, trembling, and she clutched the table before her with uncharacteristic clumsiness. "Jace..." Her voice was unchanged, still full of a deep, throaty huskiness that no doubt had stirred many a man's imagination at one time. It certainly had his father's. It was not the voice she had longed for, that of some well-bred matriarch. It was the voice of a whore. And in her case, her voice was the window to her soul.

His eyes released her when twin blue orbs and an angelic face turned to him. His heart lurched and an ache welled up to the lump in his throat.

"Dearest, who is that man?" The lad's voice was as tiny as he.

She moved as if she hadn't heard the child, though she must have, for she managed an idle wave in his general direction before moving very slowly around the table to the wooden steps. With deliberation she proceeded, the only testament to any distress the white-knuckled hand clutching her skirt and the shining eyes she fixed relentlessly upon Jace.

He stood unmoving, watching her until she paused before him. With the same deliberation and purpose, her eyes traveled over his entire length before locking with his once again. He almost gave full vent to a scornful laugh. Madeline. Just as subtle as she'd been ten years before.

"My God, you're alive," she whispered.

He swallowed the dozen or more replies that ached to be flung at her lying face, words that had drummed relentlessly upon his mind since he'd left Laramie nearly a week ago, words seasoned by years of rage and humiliation. He set his jaw and hooded his gaze.

"My father's not."

"You didn't know?"

He glanced at James, at the thin leg kicking the table again. He shook his head.

"Would you have come?"

They both knew the answer to that. His eyes found hers again. She looked sad and stricken, yet revulsion welled within him. Carrying on some semblance of a conversation with the woman went against everything that he believed in.

"How did he die?" he asked, staring straight into her eyes.

She drew a breath and pressed a hand to her heart as if to still some ache. Deceitful bitch. "Fever. It lingered...very long. Finally...He was very weak...delirious." He felt the heat of her eyes all over his face. "Where in God's name have you been?"

"West."

"You've changed."

"You haven't."

She had the effrontery to blush, obviously misinterpreting his intent, though she'd always been a supremely self-confident woman. She had to be to pull off what she'd done. "You seem older."

He had no reply for that but he sensed where the conversation was going. He was right.

Her eyes dipped again, focusing somewhere on his chest. "You're awfully dirty and...bigger." She spoke as if half to herself, her voice low and husky, her eyes aglint with far more than mere shock. He'd seen that look before. Even after ten years, she wore her passion the same. "The beard," she murmured, "though I recognized you immediately." The hand over her breast gripped tighter. "Some things a woman can't forget."

He gritted his teeth and swept his gaze about. "The place looks like hell."

She drew herself up with a heavy sigh. "I know, but since Carson's death, the business has fallen off and..."

He clenched his jaw and stared hard at her. How could that be? Pine Grove sat on more than a thousand acres, densely covered with the finest stand of white and hemlock pine east of the Mississippi, smack in the middle of Pennsylvania lumber country. "You've no money?"

She gave a small, helpless shrug that seemed grossly out of character. It must have been some gesture she deemed entirely suited to one of station. "I've some, but I employ two hands and..."

"To do what? Fill cuspidors all day? Fire them."

She gaped at him. "But I need them to chop wood...haul goods. Poor Delilah can't do man's work and *I* certainly won't!"

"Fire them. Today."

"Jace, that will leave me with more problems than I have already. I don't suppose you've any solutions."

"I do."

"Of course, you always were one step ahead of the game, weren't you?"

He filled his words with but a drop of his rage. "Never ahead of you, Madeline, you can be sure."

Her mouth opened and she released a breath, her hand clutching at her breast. "You're staying."

He allowed his gaze free roam over the place, the memories now like an oppressive weight about his heart. No, he'd rather leave, never to return to all he'd managed to blot from his mind for ten years, even if this had once been the only home he'd ever known. Damn those orders. "I'm not staying long," he muttered.

"It's yours, you know."

He stared at her, at the quivering of her lips, at the glint of desperation in her eyes, ignoring the sudden leaping of his own pulse. A ploy or a dying man's hand in a quirk of fate?

"Your father's will," she continued. "He always believed you were alive and that you'd come back ... to manage the business, perhaps."

"I don't want it. Or the house. Like I said, I'll only be here a short time."

Despite her obvious distress, she felt some dire need to offer forth a brief chewing at her lip with mock indecision and several thoughtful sighs before peering over his shoulder. His eyes followed, and he almost smiled at the sight of a still-enraged Phoebe on her knees beside Mabel. "We've guests. Your cousin from England, Charlotte Lambert, and her friend Phoebe Sinclair will be with us for an undetermined time. Something about teaching positions awaiting them in Kansas. In any event, propriety dictates you not stay here at the house. The hands stay in the guest quarters. I'll send them packing now. It's yours if you want it."

"Fine. I'd prefer it." The farther he kept from Madeline and all those dark memories, the better. He didn't give a damn who rightfully owned the place. He turned and strode toward Zack, aware that she hurried several paces behind him.

"Jace. Why are you back ... now that your father's dead?"

The implication loomed painfully clear and he had to clench his fists at his sides to keep from strangling the woman. "I needed to come home."

"I'm glad you did." Apparently undaunted by his stoic silence or the unyielding breadth of his back, she continued, "I'll have Delilah put some stew on for you and ... Good heavens! What's that?"

He knew without even looking. "Sam. My dog."

"What an awful-looking creature. Perhaps we can convince the hands to take it with them."

His hands stilled upon the saddlebags but he didn't turn to face her. "If he goes, I go." Without pause, he grasped Zack's reins and headed toward the stable, with Sam following in his wake. He didn't turn around. He didn't have to. Madeline had retreated. This time.

Chapter Three

The moment Delilah appeared from the back of the house, Phoebe lurched from her chair and hurried across the veranda toward the servant. Her heels tapping along the whitewashed wooden planks seemed entirely too loud for so early in the day, but she gave that not more than a moment's thought. She had a purpose, one that would not wait for the rising of the sun any further in the sky.

"Delilah!" She smiled, a warm, sympathetic smile, gathered skirt in hand and, with nary a thought for her dress, hurried across the dewy grass to the young Negro servant. Reaching both hands for the tray, she offered, "Here. Let me."

Delilah looked positively scandalized. "Why, Miz Sinclair, I's bin doin' this myself fer goin' on fifteen years now an... Why, don' you look purty today! All dressed up fine an' so early, too."

"Thank you, Delilah, but 'tis far too lovely a morning to lie abed or wander about in bloomers." She glanced at her gown, a rich satin frock of creamy yellow dotted with sprigs of pale violet flowers. The neckline was high and prim, the bodice simple and so fitted to a point just below her knees that "hurrying" of any kind was indeed a feat accomplished. The gown was swathed at the hem and gathered just below the derriere, falling in an elegant drape and rather inconvenient train. Fashion! Who would have guessed several years ago, in the day of the crinoline, that trains would be chic even for day dresses.

Phoebe smiled again at the servant, and proceeded toward the guest house. "Thank you again, Delilah." She tossed the words over her shoulder, the servant all but forgotten as she fixed a determined gaze upon the door of the small stone dwelling. No doubt the beast still slept. She certainly hoped so. She had every intention of employing less than gentle methods to rouse him.

She banged but once upon the heavy wooden door before it was flung open. She could do naught but gape at him. *This* was no beast.

Incarnate, he seemed much taller than he had the day before, or perhaps it was the manner in which his faded denim pants fit snugly about impossibly long, muscular legs ... and those slim hips. Then again, the man wore no shirt, nothing but a towel slung carelessly around his neck. His solid wall of chest filled her vision, the bronzed planes sinewy, sculpted from sleek marble and covered with dark smooth fur, which narrowed over his taut belly and disappeared within his pants.

She gulped.

One brawny arm was braced against the door. The other was bent, the muscle flexing in the morning sun as he reached for the towel about his neck. Only then did her eyes sweep up to his face.

He had shaved ... and bathed. Her heart tripped along. His jaw was strong, hollowed, his chin square, with a cleft, and his eyes ... his eyes were the color of the sapphire earrings she wore. His hair was a tousled cloud of blue black, slightly long and roguish.

The man was so handsome she nearly died on the spot.

"English." He grinned, a dazzling version that crinkled his eyes and left Phoebe awash in her racing pulse, though she was quite certain he relished standing there, allowing her a good long look. When his eyes swept over her from head to toe, her legs all but dissolved beneath her. "You're looking awfully fit this morning."

Phoebe, temporarily bereft of speech, stared at him for a moment then at the tray she carried. "I brought you breakfast," she managed, thrusting the fare at him and watching his hand grasp it. It was a large hand, very large, with extremely long fingers. *He* was large ... and powerful. A big, powerful man.

Jace turned to place the tray upon a table and Phoebe's eyes fastened upon his backside. His pants were so tight she could see his muscled buttocks flexing when he moved. Phoebe licked parched lips then nearly died when he turned and his eyes fell to her mouth. Very slowly, her tongue slipped inside her mouth, but not before a blush flamed to the very roots of her hair. Hastily, she glanced away, her eyes finding the pile of dingy clothes lying in a heap before an enormous stone fireplace. Silence crackled, breaking the calm of this early spring morning. She lifted her eyes and found him looming before her again, not a handbreadth from her. So close, in fact, she could *smell* him, a clean, masculine smell, like nothing she'd ever known.

"Forgive me, English, but you don't strike me as the type to appear on my doorstep for the sole purpose of delivering my breakfast. Perhaps there's something else you needed?" His voice rumbled low and deep in his chest, the very chest she seemed incapable of ignoring.

She raised innocent brows, shook her head and managed a shrug. Why *had* she come? Her mind flew, sought and found nothing. She forced a wavering smile, suddenly assailed by an undeniable and thoroughly uncharacteristic urge to flee. "I—I see you're settling in comfortably."

"The place is filthy but it'll do."

She couldn't resist a peek around his shoulder, her nose wrinkling distastefully at the mere thought of that pair of heathen stable hands chewing and spitting their way about the place.

"Just three rooms, so it won't be too tough to clean. It's not much, but it holds tremendous sentiment for me, far more than that..." His eyes flickered over her shoulder toward the main house.

"One would think you'd rather stay at the main house. There *are* seven bedrooms."

"It's not for lack of bedrooms, English, trust me." His hand upon the door moved, almost caressing the heavy wood. Phoebe couldn't help but watch, noticing, as she did, that his fingernails were free of the last traces of grime. His hands were rough, callused and beautiful.

She slowly looked away, pretending to survey the building. "This structure seems much older than the others," she managed, her breath suddenly very short.

"This was the house my parents built before the main structure. We spent quite a few years in these three rooms." He folded his arms across his chest in a thoroughly masculine manner.

He was wonderful. To bloody hell with Mabel . . . Mabel?

She lifted her chin, summoning her ire, her purpose renewed. "I must speak with you regarding my bicycle."

"Ah, yes. Your contraption."

She bristled. "I'll have you know that 'contraption' is far more useful than the cleverest nag *you* ever bestrode. She consumes nothing but a little oil."

"And God only knows how I'll ever fix the damned thing." Before Phoebe could reply, he stepped away from the door, sweeping an arm before him. "Would you like to come in, or do you Brits prefer to linger in doorways?"

She stared at him. "You know very well that I cannot enter your dwelling. 'Tis not some godforsaken notion fostered solely by us *Brits,* Mr. McAllister. Indeed, I hasten to temper your rather boorish and narrow opinion of the English. You see, I have come to realize 'tis you Americans who are painfully determined to avoid committing a faux pas. Every living and dying move you make is carefully prescribed in your eagerly read books of etiquette. Why, Madeline must have twenty volumes! I've never heard of such a thing! One book goes to very painstaking lengths instructing one how to dress, how to eat and how to sleep, for heaven's sake!"

"I take it you've been doing some reading."

"Indeed, I have. And I anticipate doing a good bit more." She glared at him. "Now that Mabel is indisposed. Nevertheless, just listen to this, Mr. McAllister. Another book, that one by Mrs. Mary Elizabeth Wilson Sherwood . . . oh, Madeline simply adores that one . . . why, page after endless page is devoted to courtship."

A corner of his mouth lifted. "Thank heavens. What would we blundering Americans do without Mrs. Sherwood?"

"Indeed, though one has to wonder where the woman comes by her peculiar notions." She shook her head helplessly and frowned at him. "Did you know that if a lady permits a gentleman to spend money on her for pleasure, the lady thereby assumes an obligation to him, which over time may require some...repayment to him? The idea! Do you think Mrs. Sherwood is suggesting that the lady *pay her share?*"

Jace looked as if he tempered a smirk. "The implication is certainly there."

Phoebe nibbled thoughtfully at a finger. "I just may have to write the woman a letter."

"Undoubtedly she would appreciate your views on the subject seeing that we Americans derived every last one of our 'godforsaken' notions from you Brits." He crossed one leg casually over the other, leaned on one hip and thrust a hand into his pocket. "Perhaps you can forgive these poor Americans, English. Now that they've made their quick fortunes they aren't at all sure how to behave. The nouveaux riches haven't the benefit of an aristocracy to emulate."

"Nouveaux riches? Madeline? I find that a trifle difficult to believe. Why, the house itself attests to some great fortune and boasts only the most grand of furnishings."

"Merely the spoils of war. My family made their fortune from the lumber industry, English. Take a look about. You won't find richer timberland in all the East. Postwar reconstruction lined many a purse and still does."

"I should say so! Why, just yesterday a beautiful porcelain *bathtub* was delivered, and the day before that a lovely little birdhouse came, one for the sparrows, you see. 'Twas imported from Europe and obviously quite expensive."

"Ah, yet another testament to those marvelous Europeans."

"You're a cynical man."

"I prefer to think of myself as a realist."

"Arrogant, too."

"I think the word you want is *confident.*"

Phoebe lifted her chin a notch. "I deem a gross overabundance of confidence arrogance, Mr. McAllister."

His eyes narrowed to slits as he studied her. "And what would you deem a gross overabundance of self-righteous, self-impressed twittering?"

Phoebe gaped at him. "I have never twittered in my life."

He grinned. "Now what made you so certain I was talking about you, English?"

She gritted her teeth and clenched her fists against the satin folds of her gown. "You're insufferable."

"Watch it, English. Your Mrs. Sherwood may advise that a lady do her best to avoid losing her temper."

"To bloody hell with Mrs. Sherwood. To be perfectly honest, Mr. McAllister, after reading all her words of wisdom, I found myself nearly overcome by the urge to do something entirely scandalous."

"Your bloomers were a good start. And, of course, Mabel."

Phoebe waved a hand. "Oh, I wasn't seeking scandal there, you can be sure. Why, bloomers are the absolute rage in London. Mr. McAllister, how on earth did you think we women were supposed to ride our bicycles?"

"I hadn't given the matter much thought."

"Of course you hadn't. You Americans are so frightfully ignorant of certain things, aren't you? Bloomers...bicycles." She felt his eyes upon her and suddenly she realized how awfully long she had indeed lingered in his doorway. Propriety, however, had very little to do with her sudden distress.

"I'm sorry about Mabel."

"And well you should be. However, until I acquire another I shall endure..."

"Somehow."

She looked closely at him, at those clear sapphire eyes, which divulged not one whit of his thoughts. "Indeed. How long will you be staying on, Mr. McAllister?"

"You can call me Jace."

"You could call me Phoebe."

"I prefer English."

She wrinkled her nose. "I don't particularly care for that, but then again, you arrogant sorts usually do as you please, isn't that right, Mr. McAllister?"

"We try our damnedest. How long will *you* be staying on, English?"

Phoebe raised very self-important brows. "Oh, not too, too long. You see, Charlotte's and my services have been requested at an exclusive boarding school in Kansas."

He seemed thoroughly impressed. "I see. Topeka?"

She stared at him.

"Wichita?"

She gave a helpless little smile, hoping beyond hope that he merely thought her a trifle bad with names.

"Then it must be Dodge City."

Oh, she liked that name, though it sounded just a tad too American. She dissolved into a huge smile. "That's it! Dodge City. Have you been there?"

"I passed through once, some time ago." He fingered his chin as if deep in thought. "I don't seem to recall a boarding school in those parts, but then again, I wasn't there long."

"Oh, 'tis one of the very best in the country."

"Of course."

She glanced sharply at that too-innocent smile he bestowed upon her. "Of course," she repeated, wondering why she felt as if he knew she lied through her teeth. Had he been a gentleman she might have believed that he would feign complete ignorance of her lies. But he was far from a gentleman and a trifle too full of himself to allow her to get away with anything. Besides, any man who looked *that* good couldn't possibly be inordinately clever, as well. Why, a woman wouldn't stand a chance with a man like that!

She clasped her hands before her. "I shan't keep you from your repast a moment longer."

"It can wait."

A feeling like a fluttering butterfly began low in Phoebe's belly. She waved a hand airily and with a decided lack of conviction toward the house. "Oh, I've enormous amounts of..." She hesitated.

"Reading?"

"Oh my, yes! A veritable *mound* of reading. And I must assist Madeline in planning her little garden party. So much to do!" She gave him an overly sweet smile and a wave before turning on her heel. "Good day, Mr. McAllister."

He merely smiled in reply, a slow, sensual smile that burned its way shamelessly into her mind's eye to haunt her relentlessly for the rest of the day.

If a man had every intention of being as conspicuous as he could possibly be, yet bore some thoroughly sordid reputation, seasoned by death and fostered by ten years' worth of

wagging tongues, he would ride very slowly through the heart
of town. And that's exactly what Jace did, the entire five-block
length, before pulling the wagon to a halt before the General
Store. He jumped from his seat, Sam at his side, and checked
on the horse standing docilely before the wagon. He rubbed a
hand idly over the bay's nose, his eyes beneath the rim of his
hat darting about the busy street. Searching. For a mind-
numbing moment, he wondered if anyone at all would recognize him. What the hell would he do if they didn't? But then,
out of the corner of his eye, he detected several figures lingering upon the wooden sidewalk, staring . . . at him and his dog.
He shot them a quick look. His luck had not run out.

He tipped his hat at the ladies and moved slowly around the
horse toward Zack, who was tethered behind the wagon. He
almost gave in to his smile. He couldn't have planned it any
better. By the time he finished with his business in the General
Store, Henrietta Witherspoon and her daughter, Violet, would
have had sufficient opportunity to spread the news of his arrival all over town and into several counties beyond.

Out of habit, he tested Zack's tether, glanced at the twisted
heap in the wagon bed, then mounted the steps to the General
Store. Not more than a quarter of an hour later, he stepped into
the morning sun once again, swept his gaze about, then ambled down the steps and tossed his wares into the back of the
wagon. Narrowing his eyes, he glanced about as surrepti-
tiously as he could. The town had aged in ten years yet obviously prospered, many of the businesses he remembered well
still thriving in this community supported by farm and lumber, and fairly recently even oil and iron ore. His thoughts
wandered for a moment as they were wont to do since his arrival back home. Too many dingy memories lay in the foggy recesses of his mind.

Jace remembered a time when a speculator had all but
promised his firstborn to his father in an attempt to persuade
Carson to lease or sell a large parcel of Pine Grove. It was
widely rumored that a vein of ore lay beneath the surface. The
speculator had so fervently believed the rumors, he'd offered
Carson an unheard-of sum for the property or even a small
tract. He recalled his father's laugh as if the scene had occurred not a day past. It was the kind of laugh that swept aside

the speculator's false smile and brought the color high in his cheeks. The kind of laugh that leaves little doubt that someone thinks you a consummate fool.

Something swelled within Jace's chest, bubbling up in his throat, choking him for a moment until he cleared his throat so noisily that Zack jerked back upon his tether and Sam eyed him curiously. Jace murmured to the horse and scratched between Sam's pointed ears, directing his thoughts elsewhere and his eyes to the street once more. People ambled by, some meeting his gaze, others avoiding him altogether, and some giving him that "Oh my God, you're Jace McAllister!" look.

Where was the contact?

A man could linger only so long without looking as if he were lingering too long. Waiting. Perhaps he should leave and return later that afternoon. As if he had nothing better to do. Hell, he had enough work at Pine Grove to keep him occupied for three solid months.

"McAllister? Jace McAllister? It *is* you!"

His gut tightened with anticipation and he spun toward the booming voice. A tall man, of his own age, he guessed, sporting a snappy dark blue topcoat and matching pleated trousers, hurried toward him. A dapper hat of deep blue sat upon his head and a starched white cravat was tucked beneath his neatly trimmed red beard. When he bent a jaunty smile upon Jace, his heart fell. Whoever this snappy gentleman was, he most certainly was not the contact. Jace had never seen the man before in his life.

"I can scarcely believe it!" the gentleman boomed, grasping Jace's hand and pumping it heartily. "I was but taking a leisurely morning stroll when a rather flustered Henrietta Witherspoon nearly mowed me down right there on the sidewalk. Why, one thing led to another, and before I could utter a word the poor woman told me that Jace McAllister had risen from the dead and was in our General Store at that very moment. Of course, I couldn't resist having a good look myself."

Jace stared at the man. There was something about him... some vague familiarity that ten years had all but obscured. Again, he looked closer, at the twinkling brown eyes, the copper-hued hair, the smile, that toothy grin that lit up his face like...

"Pryce."

The gentleman pumped Jace's hand again. "At your service, my good man."

"Dalton Pryce, how the hell are you?"

"Didn't recognize your old buddy at first, did you?" Dalton Pryce tugged at his whiskers and patted his girth. "Ten years changes a man, but then again, look at you, all lean and mean with that black hat just shading your eyes. You do the tales justice. We all thought you were dead."

"A close call."

"It must have been. We heard every last Union Pacific worker was massacred."

"All save two."

"You and...?"

Jace lowered his gaze momentarily to his dust-covered boots. The same old feeling swept over him, the rage, that blinding rage at the unfairness of life. At that very moment, Rudy Blades roamed free while Aaron lay in his pine box, his body riddled with bullets. He clenched his jaw and raised his eyes to Pryce once again. "Just me and another guy... a friend of mine."

Pryce gazed thoughtfully down the street for a moment. A wagon rumbled by, its driver nodding to Pryce and giving Jace a stony-faced look. "Aaron was a good man. One of our finest operatives in the West," Pryce muttered, his eyes following the wagon's progress down the street. "It was he who recruited you into the business, if I'm not mistaken. I'm sorry, Jace."

Jace felt his hair stand on end as he stared at his old friend. "What the hell..."

Those twinkling brown eyes met his. "I know how it must have felt to leave Blades behind but you had to do it. There's no arguing with the boss, is there?"

"For God's sake, I don't believe it."

"Maybe we should go somewhere to talk."

Jace erupted with a hoarse laugh and contemplated his boots again, shaking his head. "Damn, I *am* tired, or maybe I'm just losing my touch."

"The legendary Sterling McAllister lose his touch?" Dalton gave a hearty chuckle. "Do the fair women of this town realize what that means? And the law-abiding men? We may as well hand the whole damn town over to the outlaws right here and now." Pryce slapped him on the back and chuckled again. "C'mon, Jace. Your horse looks like he could use a new set of shoes. The blacksmith is just around the corner."

Jace raised a brow as he grasped the bay's reins and set out with Pryce. "You don't look like the type of man to be seen associating with the likes of me."

"On the contrary. The first person a ne'er-do-well like yourself would seek upon returning home would be the local solicitor. Especially if said solicitor was a childhood friend."

Jace shook his head, closed his eyes and winced for effect. "You're a lawyer."

Pryce's chest puffed up and he bellowed, "The best in the county."

Jace couldn't resist an ironic lift of his brow. "Naturally. Those guys employ only the very best, don't they?"

"That they do, my friend. Just take Charlie here." Pryce pulled open the door to a large barnlike structure and indicated the blacksmith, who glanced up from his work and gave them a nod.

Jace narrowed his gaze upon the man. "Hell, you guys are everywhere."

"The eye that never sleeps, or so the advertisement boasts."

"Yeah, yeah." Jace tempered his grimace and shook hands with the blacksmith. He watched as Pryce muttered something to Charlie, who nodded again and moved around the wagon to tend to Zack. Tidy. Efficient. Ever so capable. Yet another link in the chain of operatives that connected the nation.

Jace followed Pryce to the back of the barn, around a corner and into a small dark room tucked into the shadows. Pryce lit a lantern and shut the door.

"Now we can talk." He rubbed his hands together, then indicated a chair for Jace before sliding one close for himself. His eyes studied Jace for several long moments. "It's damn good to see you."

"Why wasn't I notified when my father died?"

"You don't mince words."

"I never saw the need to." Jace studied his friend through hooded eyes. "Who do those bastards think they are?"

"They had a reason for not telling you, Jace."

"Give me one good reason. A damned good reason."

"You were chasing Blades across Colorado Territory at the time, if I remember correctly. Or was he chasing you?"

"He never knew I was on his tail. Does it matter?"

"Not to them. He's a wanted man, a murderer, a swindler, a bank robber and a butcher of innocent people. Slippery as an eel, to boot, and capable of driving fear into the heart of an entire county out there. Hell, there isn't a lawman between here and Laramie that would walk within a mile of that guy. They had to find the guy, Jace, and they wanted only the best man for the job."

"It didn't hurt that I had my own score to settle with the man, did it?"

Pryce looked him square in the eye. "Maybe it was too personal a vendetta, Jace."

"Yeah?" He felt the blood surge through his veins. "He killed my best friend. Point-blank range. And laughed about it like it was some damned joke."

"You were there?"

Jace sucked in his breath then hung his head, closing his eyes on the painful memory that loomed as vividly today as it had three years before. "They *used* me, Pryce. Used me to find the guy then concocted some two-bit reason why I couldn't just haul his ass in. Something about infiltrating the damned gang and confiscating all the loot."

"Sounds reasonable to me."

Jace snorted, his voice rasping with cynicism. "They always get what they want, don't they?"

"You know damned well they do everything they can to ensure it."

"Despite the consequences."

"You're a cynical man, Jace."

"You're the second person to tell me that in as many days. I'm starting to believe it, but I'll tell you this, my friend, you would be, too."

"Because of Blades . . . and your father."

"You're damned right, because of my father."

"If you'd known, would you have come back?"

Jace scowled and flung his gaze about the tiny room. He knew the answer to that and he hated himself for it. After all he'd accomplished, all the outlaws he'd apprehended, all the swindlers he'd double-crossed, all the bullets he'd dodged and those he'd taken, even after Rudy Blades, he was still a coward. That familiar acrid taste filled his mouth. The only reason he was back was because they had ordered him back. Bastards.

"How's Madeline?"

Jace glanced sharply at his friend. He knew. They all knew, or at least suspected. He'd never even had the courage to talk with Pryce about it. "The same. She'll never change."

"And James?"

Jace scowled again. "He looks like a damned girl."

"I know. It's a shame."

Jace shook his head, leaned back in his chair and crossed one dusty boot over his knee, shoving his thoughts aside. "So why the hell am I here?"

"I'll get to that in a minute." The manner in which Pryce waved his hand left Jace more than a tad suspicious that his friend was purposefully postponing the inevitable.

"But first," Pryce said, leaning forward, his brown eyes glittering, "I've just got to know how you did it."

"Did what?"

"Found Blades! How the hell did you know where to find him?"

Jace shrugged and contemplated his boots. A smile tugged at the corner of his mouth. "A tried-and-true method, my friend. His girlfriend wasn't too difficult to locate. Squeezing information out of her was even easier . . . and far more enjoyable."

With a shake of his head, Pryce leaned back and smiled. "You're far from losing your touch with the ladies, Jace, and that's why they ordered you back here."

Jace allowed that hint of cynicism back into his voice. How it ached in the back of his throat. "It better be a damned good reason."

He couldn't be certain, but Jace would have bet a hefty sum that Pryce swallowed in a somewhat nervous manner before raising his brows and nodding vigorously. "Oh, indeed, it's a mission of some importance. Yes, indeed."

"Who is it?"

"It's a jewel thief. Actually, the ringleader of a band of female jewel thieves."

Jace sat up straighter in his chair, feeling his heart thumping. "Adam Worth?"

Pryce shook his head slowly. "Not exactly."

"What the hell does *that* mean?"

"Well, this band of thieves has been linked with Worth's organization and the ringleader hails from England, or so we think. Upper class, the gentry, I believe. Titled. You know, the idle rich."

"Worth is based in England."

Pryce nodded. "But these thieves have been working the East Coast with tremendous success and we have reason to believe they're headed in this very direction. They don't go for the big score but they're shrewd, very shrewd. Swindled the mayor of Boston out of his entire purse all in a matter of two minutes. They'd somehow managed to switch his full purse with one stuffed with paper. And another heist, this one in Boston, as well, involved a drug-laced nostrum. Apparently, a rather wealthy member of Boston's upper crust, a diamond merchant to boot, found himself besotted with a young Englishwoman who had patronized his store on more than one occasion. Upon inviting her to dine after work one evening, he ended up with his chin in his soup and upon awakening discovered his bag of gemstones missing from his waistcoat pocket. It was three days later before he remembered that his wine had tasted rather peculiar. A small fortune, that one."

"So who is he?"

"She."

"She?" Jace gaped at his friend. "She? They took Rudy Blades away from me because of a woman?"

"She's very good."

"She'd damned well better be! Hell, I don't give a damn, do you hear me?"

Pryce gave a sheepish smile. "Loud and clear, my friend, and I'd wager Henrietta Witherspoon can hear you, too."

Jace scowled ferociously and slumped in his chair. "Damn those guys. A woman, a damned woman."

"She's supposedly a real beauty."

Jace averted his gaze and merely muttered in reply.

"Blond."

Jace scowled even more ferociously.

"The kind of body that drives men insane."

Only then did Jace's eyes slide to his friend.

Pryce grinned, a thoroughly wicked grin. "They call her Peaches."

Jace closed his eyes and groaned. "Hell, my career is over. I lost Blades because of a Peaches."

"A man could do far worse, let me tell you. Hell, I would have gladly taken this one, but they wouldn't let me. It seems I'm a trifle too much on the up-and-up. A woman like Peaches wouldn't give a lawyer the time of day." His eyes flickered over Jace. "But you? *You* and your generally disreputable character will prove all but irresistible to her if she's looking to fall in league with someone. And, of course, how could she resist the McAllister touch?"

Jace grunted, his eyes still closed, his head slumped back. "Peaches," he muttered.

"Yeah..." Pryce sounded dreamy of a sudden. "Peaches St. Clair. All she wears are peach-colored gowns, bloomers, even smells like a peach, or so they say. Kind of gets your blood all fired and—"

Jace sat bolt upright in his chair. "What did you say?"

Pryce stared at his friend then smiled. "I said a woman like that gets you all—"

"Her name, man! What's her name?"

"Peaches St. Clair."

Jace closed his eyes and slumped into his chair. "From England."

"So they say."

"Blond."

"Honey blond and amber-eyed and . . ."

"She's here."

"She's what?"

"She's at Pine Grove."

"What the hell are you saying?"

Jace opened his eyes and stared at the door. "Peaches St. Clair is staying at Pine Grove, only she's not going by that name. Her alias is Phoebe Sinclair."

Chapter Four

Jace slumped in his chair, stared at the ceiling and heaved a disgusted sigh, choosing to ignore his friend's thoroughly disbelieving laugh.

"Peaches St. Clair at Pine Grove?" Pryce guffawed. "Even *you* couldn't be *that* lucky."

"Call it what you will, but I've never been one to believe in coincidence."

Pryce seemed to ponder that, his bushy copper brows sweeping together for several moments. "Phoebe Sinclair. I must say, for an alias . . ."

"It's perfect." Jace shook his head with complete wonderment. "Think about it. The English pronounce St. Clair as Sinclair if I'm not mistaken."

Pryce rubbed his beard thoughtfully. "I don't know. We have no proof."

Jace scowled and leaned his head back against his chair. "You're thinking like a lawyer and not like an operative."

"And to my eye, you're far too suspicious, my friend. Did it ever occur to you that you just may jump too hastily to certain conclusions?"

"I've been at this a long time, Pryce. I know what the hell I'm doing." He flashed a confident smile. "Besides, I've never been wrong once in seven years."

"Yeah, so I hear." Pryce folded burly arms over his chest. "So convince me."

Jace gave a hoarse laugh. "She hasn't pawned off any jewelry to my knowledge thus far, if that's what you're implying."

"That's about what it will take to apprehend her. A far cry from two names that by happenstance sound alike. That means a lot of shadowing on your part, you lucky bastard."

"Some luck." Jace grimaced and regarded his friend through heavy lids, then allowed himself a sly smile. "Peaches."

Pryce dissolved into his wicked grin. "Aptly named?"

Jace allowed his thoughts to wander to earlier that day, to the image of a willowy yet undeniably curvy young woman poised in a ray of sunlight upon his doorstep. "I'll say."

Pryce cupped his hands and held them several inches from his chest, positively leering at Jace. "So?"

Unable to resist, Jace cupped his own hand, peered at it for several moments, then closed his eyes and leaned back in his chair. "Oh, more than a handful, without a doubt."

"God . . . Tell me more."

"Young, English, blond, beautiful . . ." He opened one eye and regarded his friend. "And she damned well knows it, too." He closed his eye once again. "Ripe. That's the word. She's ripe, has a certain look about her."

"Like a peach." Pryce let out a huge breath that sounded like an agonized groan. "I don't care. Take my practice from me. Turn me into a desperado, Rudy Blades's best buddy, I don't care. Just let me have this one, Jace."

With a genuine laugh, Jace sat up and slapped his friend on the back. "Sorry, my friend. I'm afraid they wanted me for this mission. Maybe I'd better thank them."

"Not two minutes ago they were bastards," Pryce grumbled, with his own version of a scowl.

"Yeah, and Phoebe Sinclair was but a spoiled English miss supposedly on her way to Dodge City to teach at an exclusive private school."

"Huh?"

Jace couldn't resist a smile. "No doubt it's her cover, though one would have thought she'd devise something a little more plausible. Don't get me wrong, she's educated all right and her accent seems genuine enough. Even though she could pass for a teacher she's obviously never been to Dodge City or she would know that would be the last place one would find a private school. She does seem bent upon Kansas for some reason."

"Maybe Worth has a connection out there."

Jace shrugged. "Or it could be a ploy, an out-and-out lie. That makes even better sense." His eyes narrowed at a sudden thought and his voice lowered, causing Pryce to lean a bit closer to hear him. "It could all be a ploy. The girlfriend, Charlotte . . ."

"Who?"

"Charlotte Lambert. My cousin from London. Our Peaches has somehow managed to hook up with a relative of mine."

"How the hell did she do that?"

"You said she was shrewd. They claim they've known one another for years, both wealthy little English heiresses. Supposedly they came by ship from London to attend Wellesley, the women's college." Jace looked squarely into Pryce's eyes. "In Boston."

"It certainly sounds like our Peaches." Pryce's look of amazement dissolved into a frown. "So this Charlotte's a member of the ring?"

"Maybe."

"Maybe?" Pryce gave Jace a mocking wide-eyed look. "How'd the girl manage to escape suspicion?"

"She somehow just doesn't look the part. Too innocent. Too wide-eyed."

"I like her already."

Giving his friend a sideways glance, Jace shook his head. "A bit preoccupied, aren't we, Mr. Pryce. No women in your life?"

Pryce drew himself up in his chair, puffing out his chest. "Oh yeah, lots of women. But a man can't have too many now, can he? Besides, I'm a part of this operation. There's no reason why I can't lend my hand, so to speak. This Charlotte may find me just a tad irresistible."

"How could she not? You're not the one they tell all the tales about, are you?"

"Disreputable though it is, your image could use a little bolstering. After all, short of pawning her wares, Peaches just may feel the urge to take somebody into her confidence. Who better than the town's back-from-the-dead bad boy, a gunslinger of the worst kind, a crack shot who kills squirrels at fifty paces, a mysterious bandit fresh from blazing a trail of thievery and swindling across the western frontier . . ."

Jace held up a hand. "Okay, I've got the picture."

"You also have a prodigious capacity for whiskey."

"There isn't an outlaw who doesn't."

"Oh, and you recently killed a man but it's never been proven."

"Thanks." His tone was flat.

"Well, Jace, you *have* killed before."

"I never liked it."

"In the line of duty, I'll wager, and there's nothing dishonorable in that. Tell me, if you dislike it so much, what the hell are you doing in this business?"

Jace studied the floor for a moment. "Good question."

"Really? You're one of the best."

Jace shook his head. "So they keep telling me."

"The pay's damn good."

"That it is."

"And I'd wager if I strolled over to that bank across the street and did a little inquiring, I'd find you've got a tidy little sum all tucked away. You could have spent that money."

"I thought about it. Came awfully close once. The local saloon owner in Laramie offered me half ownership of his place after I caught a couple of hoodlums cheating at poker. One of them drew on me, real fast, and I had no choice. It's like a reflex after a while. I didn't kill that guy but came damned close. After that, they were ready to pin the sheriff's badge on me."

"You see? You've had ample opportunity to give it all up."

"I couldn't. I'd just managed to find Blades." He lifted a gaze full of burning hatred, and the familiar sneer curled his lip. "I'll find him again and all the Peaches in the world can go to hell."

Pryce stared at him. "I don't doubt that for a minute, my friend, though I would think he's been duly apprehended by now, thanks to you, and is wiling away his time in some Wyoming jail, or maybe the lynch mobs got him."

"Don't count on it."

"You think he's that wily, eh?"

"I know he is."

Pryce seemed to ponder that a moment. "Well...to the task at hand. You'd best maintain a fairly high profile, ingratiate yourself into the proper circles, if you know what I mean. Lay pipe with the outlaws, my friend. And I know of just the place."

"Don't tell me, Buttermilk Falls's version of the Nymphs of the Prairie, the soiled doves and calico queens."

"What the hell are you talking about?"

"Women who do 'horizontal work,' my friend."

"I picked the wrong profession. And *you're* not satisfied."

"It takes a hell of a lot more than a good romp with an eager whore, my friend. A lot more. So, where's this place?"

"Gideon Goare's tavern, just down the block. Boasts of a pretty rough crowd and rumor has it there's a game to be had."

"All beneath the town solicitor's nose, eh?"

"We needed the lure. Besides, even though gambling's illegal, there isn't a town between here and Philadelphia that doesn't have a poker game going at any hour of the day you choose." Pryce raised his brows. "You could go over there right now."

With a quick shake of his head, Jace rose and moved to the door. "Not today. I don't want to look too eager. Besides, Peaches awaits back at Pine Grove, busily planning a garden party, I believe." He gave Pryce a thoroughly wicked, lopsided smirk. "And come to think of it, I miss the young lady."

"I'll bet you do. Just watch yourself, Jace. From what I hear, a woman like that could turn a man's head around. You don't want to wake up one day and find yourself in love with her."

Jace gave a short, caustic laugh. "*Now* you sound like a sentimental fool. In love? I'd rather spend the rest of my life chasing Rudy Blades." And with that, he flung the door wide and exited the room.

Phoebe was hot. *Dreadfully* hot and just as bored. She perched precariously upon the very edge of an overstuffed sofa in an overstuffed room, feeling a bit overstuffed herself, snugly swathed as she was in her reams of peach satin and silk, balancing a cup of very hot tea on her knee. Through the lace-draped window at her back, the midday sun beat down relentlessly upon her. She shifted, attempting to draw a clean breath, feeling a trickle of perspiration weaving its way down her spine.

Her eyes fell for what seemed the thousandth time upon the assortment of iced tea cakes sitting directly before her and her mouth watered yet again. Blast her appetite, her craving for sweets and goodies, which at times became nearly obsessive. If it hadn't been for a strength of will fostered by her dear stepmother, Elizabeth, she would no doubt be as puffy as a house, and dreadfully miserable. Shifting again, she drew in her belly and straightened her spine, then scowled at those lovely tea cakes.

If only the blasted room weren't so desperately in need of a good airing. She was of a mind to inform Madeline that a room required opening daily, not just when callers happened by. But then, of course, Madeline wouldn't sweep those doors wide with such grand aplomb and offer forth this parlor, this testament to refinement, this...

Phoebe's eye swept about the room, purposefully ignoring both Madeline and their guests, as well as their mindless exchanges of trivialities, which had long since degenerated into a dull buzzing. It took a strength of will to keep from wrinkling her nose.

This was refinement? *This* was culture?

Madeline's much ballyhooed parlor was stuffed from fanlight to floor with an eye-boggling collection of umbrellas and fans, plaster busts, wicker rockers, lamps, cushions, coat racks, china cabinets, small tables and too many showy objects of little or no value to count. Every shelf, dressing case and mantel was littered with these gimcracks. Multicolored fans, dragon candlesticks and vases with Japanese bird kites protruding from them covered the upright piano, Madeline's pride and joy. Turkish and Persian rugs bearing little or no relation to one another with regard to color covered the floor. Every chair boasted tidies, those intricate pieces of fancywork to protect the headrest from wear, and the lounges and sofas had embroidered cushions hidden under tidies. Indeed, the sofa upon whose corner Phoebe perched was all but uninhabitable due to the conglomeration of pillows and tidies. In one corner a crimson screen concealed the radiator, and fuchsia Arabian scarves attempted to conceal the screen. And every space that was not occupied by any of the above boasted a clock.

Phoebe simply gaped at first. And Madeline, beaming from head to toe with pride, had graciously and rather solicitously informed her that if there was enough room to move about without walking over the furniture, there was hardly too much in a room.

Phoebe simply had to wonder how she was going to extract herself from the place. Her eyes darted over the callers. And these blasted women.

She nearly jumped when the older plump one sporting a nest of dull-colored, tightly wound curls upon her head fixed a puckered mouth and assessing dull-colored eyes upon her. What was the woman's name? Henrietta something. Phoebe glanced at Henrietta's equally dull-colored, frail-looking daughter. Violet. Some violet. The poor girl looked as if she were about to wither up and blow away. That was it! Witherspoon! Henrietta Witherspoon!

"Splendid weather we're enjoying, is it not, Miss Sinclair?" Henrietta raised her brows as if she were inordinately curious as to Phoebe's view on the subject, then lifted her teacup, raising what she no doubt deemed one very pristine and elegant little finger over the handle.

Phoebe forced a smile. Wherever it was she and Charlotte were headed, they'd best be about it. She couldn't endure much more of this.

"*Splendid.*" Phoebe's very being reverberated as she spoke the word, hovering dangerously close to mocking the precise manner in which Henrietta herself melted into the word each and every one of the dozen or so times she'd uttered "splendid" just this afternoon. What had Jace said about the nouveaux riches? Splendid must be a word much advised by that etiquette queen Mrs. Sherwood. Then again, the English displayed a certain fondness for the word. These Americans. Ever at the ready to emulate. One could certainly have a bit of fun with them . . . if one were so inclined.

Phoebe offered her most genuine smile, seeking to erase the suspicious narrowing of Henrietta's eyes upon her. She summoned her demure tone, the one she reserved solely for her beaux when they sought favors she had little intention of granting. "A trifle warm." She pressed a hand delicately to her throat as if she positively ached to fan herself yet resisted solely for propriety's sake.

"Ah yes, you must be somewhat cold-blooded, being from London," Henrietta replied with a taut smile. "You've really no climate over there, only weather, and mostly foul."

Phoebe forced a tiny little gasp of delight. "Why, you've been to England!"

Henrietta's mouth opened and closed exactly three times before she spoke. "Well, in all truth, I haven't but . . ."

"Why, the manner in which you spoke left little doubt in my mind that you had."

Henrietta looked completely flustered. "Oh, my pardons, but I would simply adore visiting London. I've told my Walter many a time, I've said, 'Walter, we simply must see London this year. A splendid city, it is.' Yes, yes, I've told him precisely that. A splendid city."

Deliciously wicked excitement surged through Phoebe. This was becoming rather fun. Her mind raced on and the words tumbled from her lips. "Indeed! On the cool side, I'll grant you that, but 'tis known to experience extremely hot days. However, Englishwomen, with all their wisdom and centuries of breeding, have devised a rather unique manner of coping with the heat."

Henrietta leaned forward eagerly, her sweat-dampened brow glistening in the sun, her gown of heavy satin clinging rather obviously to her chest. Phoebe's eyes flickered to Charlotte, perched upon a chair directly across from her, then flickered away just as quickly. She had little trouble recognizing the warning in Charlotte's dark eyes, the trepidation, the irrefutable knowledge that Phoebe was up to something. Sometimes Phoebe wished Charlotte didn't know her so well.

"Oh, do tell!" Henrietta gushed, and Madeline nodded her head vigorously. How they ached for it! Hopefully enough to believe just about anything. And if they didn't? She nearly shivered despite the heat. The risk was well worth it.

She lowered her eyes and paused, drawing a breath as if with indecision, milking the moment for all it was worth. She could practically hear Henrietta's pulse thumping eagerly. No doubt the woman would hightail it from the room, tripping over furniture and umbrellas and fans and mounds of clutter in her haste to be the first to announce the news.

It had to be perfect.

Very slowly, Phoebe raised grave eyes and her most serious of expressions, as if she indeed divulged some deep secret. "'Tis rather new, you see, and practiced within only the most elite of circles. Even the queen herself . . ."

Henrietta's gasp ruffled the tendrils encircling Phoebe's face. "The queen?"

"Indeed. I've a dear friend who attends to the queen."

Charlotte groaned and hung her head in her hand.

"Out with it, girl!" Henrietta boomed.

Phoebe licked her lips. "Well, it seems that whenever the heat grows a tad unbearable, we women suffer the most, what with these heavy, restrictive gowns and the corsets and bustles. Of course, we must never look as if we're uncomfortable, and God only knows fashion must never suffer. Therefore, Englishwomen find relief from a rather simple notion. Perhaps you American women have thought of it yourself."

"I can tell you we have not," Henrietta replied with a flamboyant waving of one gloved hand before her face. "So what is this notion, Miss Sinclair?"

Phoebe stared into Henrietta's eyes. "Why, we simply go without our bloomers."

The woman's jaw fell just as her eyes dropped to focus upon Phoebe's hip area, as if she expected to see right through the fashionable peach frock. "You what?" she croaked.

Phoebe smiled. "We forsake our undergarments. We wear positively nothing beneath our skirts." Her smile widened in direct proportion to the color mounting in every one of the ladies' cheeks. "Nothing."

"Dear God," Henrietta gurgled.

"Mummy . . ." Violet gulped.

"Interesting," Madeline intoned.

And Charlotte merely groaned.

"More tea, Henrietta?" Madeline offered, lifting a sterling teapot from the ornate tray upon the table.

Henrietta managed a quick wave of her hand and a shake of her head then seemed to gather her wits. "No, thank you, Widow McAllister."

Phoebe's eyes darted to Madeline, to the undeniable wince that creased her features whenever she was addressed thus, though to date, Henrietta Witherspoon seemed the only soul to harbor such a predisposition. Phoebe certainly couldn't bring herself to even utter the word *widow*. Madeline always seemed so awash in grief. She couldn't help but think Henrietta wished to shove Madeline's situation down her throat at every opportunity.

"We've already lingered far too long as it is. But I simply had to come." Henrietta leaned forward and drew herself up, tucking her chin under in a very self-impressed manner. "I've got news."

"Is that so?" Madeline's tone was flat. "This wasn't merely a social call?"

"Not quite, though I believe we owed you a return call, did we not? In any event, you'd best prepare yourself, Widow McAllister. I've seen fit to bring some of my Lydia Pinkham's Vegetable Compound just in case." Henrietta patted the pocket of her gown and turned to Phoebe. "Cures any number of the female weaknesses, if you know what I mean."

Female weaknesses? Henrietta didn't look to be particularly familiar with the weaknesses elicited by big, powerful men.

Madeline held up a hand. "No thank you, Henrietta. I believe my tea shall suffice for today."

"Suit yourself." Henrietta folded plump arms over her lap and fixed a pinched look upon Madeline. "Widow McAllister, I wouldn't have believed it had I not seen it with my own two eyes. And thank heavens Violet here was with me or I would have swooned dead away on the spot."

Phoebe glanced at poor Violet. The girl wouldn't have stood a chance had her mother been so overcome as to swoon dead away.

Madeline sipped slowly from her tea and her tone seemed a trifle too casual. "What is it that you saw?"

Henrietta lifted her nose and widened her eyes. "A ghost."

Violet nodded frantically and stammered, "In-indeed! A ghost!"

Phoebe sat up straighter and couldn't resist chirping, "Oh my, how lovely!"

"And who is this ghost?" Madeline asked, pouring herself another cup of tea. "Anyone I know?"

"I should say so!" Henrietta huffed. "He's back!"

"Who's back?"

"Why, that good-for-nothing Jace, that's who!"

"I know."

Henrietta gaped then drew a noisy breath. "Widow McAllister! Do you realize what this means?"

Madeline's voice was low. "Of course. But I hasten to point out that he's no ghost. He's very much alive and living here."

"Widow McAllister!" Henrietta waved a hand frantically before her face and gasped for breath. "Why, I can scarcely believe it! How could you take him under your very roof?"

"He sleeps in the guest quarters."

Henrietta pursed her lips and shook her dull curls. "Even so, after what that...that...that *animal* did beneath this very roof? I realize it's all talk, but hardly idle, I should say! Why, the man cannot be trusted to control his...his...*temperament* any better than...than..."

Phoebe leaned toward Henrietta. "Temperament?"

Henrietta glanced quickly about then hissed between her teeth, "His animal desires."

Phoebe frowned and stared at Madeline, who had hastily averted flaming cheeks and appeared to be studying with much concentration the hideous pattern of one of the rugs.

"Widow McAllister, I cannot help but wonder what your dear departed husband would say were he alive to see this."

"He's not," Madeline stated flatly, lifting an anguished expression. "Though I can say with little hesitation that this is really none of your business, Mrs. Witherspoon."

Henrietta shifted uncomfortably in her chair. "Really! The talk, Widow McAllister, shall not be favorable. I hasten to point out that it's high time the truth be told, even these many years past. And you, Widow McAllister, are just the one to do it."

Madeline stared intently at the other woman. "The truth was told ten years ago, Mrs. Witherspoon. I resent your implication to the contrary."

"Humph!" Henrietta snorted, shifting yet again.

"Enough, Mrs. Witherspoon," Madeline said, reaching a slightly trembling hand for the teapot. "Violet, more tea?"

Henrietta pursed her lips even more fiercely and slowly swung her gaze toward the window. The knowing expression that slid across her puffy countenance caused Phoebe's eyes to follow.

There, upon the veranda in a ray of sunlight, sat young James, diligently bent over what looked to be a schoolbook. He wore his typical primly starched suit, this of stiff cream linen trimmed in pale blue satin and sporting a matching sash. Delilah hovered nearby, obviously prepared to temper any wayward notions the child might conjure. Phoebe's throat tightened at the sight of the lad, yet the blood seemed to pound with far greater urgency through her veins when Henrietta spoke again. What the devil was this all about?

"I can hear the talk now. That after ten long years spent plundering his way across the West, Jace the outlaw has returned a changed man, wishing to lay claim to his... Oh my God." Henrietta's words hung suspended in the thick, unmoving air. Her mouth sagged open as she stared out the window. Every eye in the room could do naught but follow.

It was Jace. Phoebe knew the moment she leaned forward and parted the lace curtain, though she couldn't see his face. No man but he could look like that. He stood upon a ladder leaning against the veranda, his head hidden well above the roofline, the rest of his body visible for all to see. He wore a thin white cotton shirt, the sleeves rolled high over muscled arms, the fabric straining and taut across his chest.

"Oh my..." someone murmured.

He still wore those faded denim pants, the ones that fit like a second skin. The ones that hugged his hips, shaped his muscled thighs, proved beyond a shadow of a doubt that he was indeed a man. One very big, powerful man.

Phoebe's insides turned to jelly. Indeed, she all but forgot the oppressive heat, the gaudy furnishings, those lovely tea cakes and her triumph over that pompous, self-righteous Henrietta. She even forgot the nagging sense of disquiet she'd felt when Madeline and Henrietta spoke of Jace. Indeed, for some reason she could not fathom at the moment, she was suddenly consumed by an overwhelming sense of destiny, the conviction that she belonged with that man. The force was magnetic, undeniable, something she could never even hope to control.

"Phoebe..." Madeline's voice, sounding as if from very far away. "Phoebe, where are you going, my dear?"

Phoebe turned as if in a dream, feeling a whimsical smile curving her lips. "Why, outside of course." And with that, she turned and floated from the room.

Chapter Five

If confidence was a virtue and arrogance a vice, one very blond and beautiful jewel thief had a stranglehold upon the latter. Or perhaps it was blinding stupidity. Then again, it could very well have been brilliant duplicity. Whatever it was, Jace's thoughts swam, his mind a confused and irritated muddle when he turned at the sound of his name, uttered in that voice just dripping melted butter and sweet cream. There she stood, ablaze in the afternoon sun, wearing a silk gown of the most astonishingly vivid shade of *peach,* a gown that clung to the full swell of her breasts, nipped her narrow rib cage and the slight curve of her belly, then swept sleekly over the slender arc of her hips.

His thoughts collided, his pulse raced and it was several long moments before he realized he stared at her breasts. And that his mouth was full of nails.

With a scowl, he grabbed them from between his teeth, stuffed them into his pocket, along with his hammer, and met her gaze. Wide amber eyes peered not so innocently up at him. Cat eyes, slanted and heavy-lidded, and focused right around his midsection . . . no, a little lower, upon his hips, his backside and his . . .

Good God . . .

He nearly fell off the ladder when she lifted her very frank gaze and smiled at him, a long, slow, sensuous curve of those full lips that galled him and sent fierce heat directly to the very spot she had ogled so thoroughly. Oh, she was a pro, all right. That poor sot in Boston, the diamond merchant, hadn't stood a chance with her. No doubt he'd have willingly handed her the bag of jewels, his house, whatever she'd wanted, if she hadn't drugged him first. Hell, but she didn't even seem to care that she'd been caught gaping. Of all the guileless, naive, asinine...

His eyes narrowed upon her. Then again, she was shrewd, very shrewd, and it could all be a ploy, her innocence a guise, that damnable way she looked at him...as if she dared him not to notice her dress, every last peach silk curve and hollow, offered forth like a sweet gift, an untouched virginal temptation...every man's desire. Could there be so shrewd a woman? A woman that had somehow managed to expose a vulnerability he had little notion he'd possessed? A vulnerability to innocence, to a seemingly guileless nature devoid of cynicism, as if she'd somehow managed to avoid the harsh realities of life? How she played upon it! His only solace was that the whole damned thing was an act. If it wasn't...

Gripping the roof with both hands, he blinked, mentally shaking himself, and found himself wishing those guys weren't always so damned on the mark. They knew him better than he did himself. He *was* tired, hideously tired, seven long years tired, so tired he could envision himself bungling this mission, this...this throwaway mission, this flimsy excuse to get him to come home and rest. His career, precariously perched upon a cliff of very warm, very round peach silk.

His eyes flickered over her and he longed for a drink.

Yeah, he could bungle it all right. Just a few more days of shadowing this Peaches, a few more days of sloe-eyed glances and soft smiles and full lips promising everything that ached to be released from that damned gown. The McAllister touch. Where the hell was it now?

"Mr. McAllister?" She smiled at him again, and bit her lip in a manner that made him want to taste her mouth, taste her skin, every last peach-scented inch of her.

The touch...the touch. A fine time for it to have deserted him.

On the wild and entirely inconceivable notion that perhaps the height had something to do with it all, he stepped down the ladder and faced her. Bad move. Her eyes were all over him, somewhere on his chest, and by God if he didn't suck in his breath, just enough to stretch the fabric taut. She licked her lips and he all but roared with frustration. Insanity, that's what it was. The smell of spring in the air. The blasted heat so early in the season. The sun flaming in her hair, those loosely coiled golden tresses.

"Mr. McAllister, what were you doing up there?" Her lashes were dark, too dark for one so fair, and long, sweeping to her fair brows, which hinted ever so slightly at a curious frown. Her cheeks were round, sun-kissed and covered with a soft blond down. Just like a damned peach.

He sucked in a breath and forced himself to look away, anywhere, and his eyes found the sagging roofline of the veranda. "The roof," he managed through a tight jaw. He put his hands on his hips and pointed toward the very end of the veranda. "See there, where the underside of the roof has sagged ... and there. It needs work." He scowled. "Lots of work, and the trim needs paint. The whole place needs paint."

"I see."

He glanced at her and felt a peculiar tightening in his chest when he discovered her eyes caressing the length of his arm. Almost self-consciously, which rattled him beyond measure, he balled his fist and lowered his arm to his side. She saw, ha! Hell, she probably hadn't even looked at the roof.

Ripe? Poor choice of words. *Hungry*. The girl hungered for it and he'd be damned if he was going to serve himself up with an eager smile as the main course. *She's a thief, a common criminal. Do your damned job!*

He cocked his head and summoned a casual drawl. "Have you had your fill of garden party planning?"

"Oh, yes ... well ... 'tis a trifle boring, if you must know." She smiled gamely and clasped her hands before her.

If his life had depended on it he couldn't have kept his gaze from her breasts, pressed wantonly together between her slender arms. A master, that's what she was. A master at the art of seduction, leading him by his pants with no more than this flimsy guise of innocence. He shoved a hand through his hair and wondered why he couldn't seem to get enough air with every breath.

"We have guests," she remarked, her eyes for the first time releasing him to glance over his shoulder. "Your arrival has indeed proven newsworthy. It seems the entire town is abuzz."

"How flattering."

"Hardly that, I can assure you. It seems you are somewhat of an outlaw, Mr. McAllister."

"Is that so?"

"Wanted, perhaps?"

"Perhaps." He watched her closely, waiting for that barely perceptible flinch, the sudden hesitation, the flame of fear and revulsion in her eyes. It never came. The spark was one of interest piqued, the flame of passions stirred, and the upward curve of her lip and the arch of a delicate brow hinted at much more than idle curiosity. The thief was baited.

"Indeed," she mused, eyeing him closely. "You're awfully secretive, Mr. McAllister. Ah, but you're a self-effacing sort, are you not?"

He had to smile. "Incredibly so. Very much like you, I would wager."

"Me? Shy?" She laughed, and her laughter was deep and husky and, to one less suspecting, thoroughly genuine. He saw it for what it was, for it stirred his blood and conjured sensuous images that had little to do with his job. She was a wicked little thing. "You jest, of course. Shyness has never been an attribute to which I have aspired, Mr. McAllister. It requires so much blasted energy and wastes oodles of time. All that delicate posturing and fluttering of one's lashes." Her grimace reminded him of a kitten painfully intent upon capturing the elusive mouse. "And all to achieve the same end that I obtain with far less exhaustion. I have no time for all that!"

Thievery did require meticulous, time-consuming preparation. "You are, after all, extraordinarily busy."

"Oh, dreadfully so. What with school and all our traveling about." She peered at him as innocently as a lamb. "Have you ever been to Boston, Mr. McAllister?"

He nearly started. Surely she wasn't contemplating divulging her identity already? She had very little reason to trust him thus far, her impressions gleaned solely from an earful of the town gossip, which had had only one very short afternoon to simmer and stew. No, this had to be but a mere testing of the waters.

"Never," he replied. "I've heard it's quite charming."

"Oh, charming, indeed. Why, it reminds me of London in some ways. Did you know that Boston has its own society of sorts, the upper crust, the *old* rich, Mr. McAllister, moneyed aristocracy. Society queens abound, ensconced in their turreted mansions, their jewels draped about them, their wigged footmen imported from England, I'll have you know. None of this nouveau riche rubbish.''

He gave her a thoroughly interested look, as if all that appealed to him in some peculiar way. No doubt it occupied her every traitorous thought. "You weren't there long?'' he asked casually.

"Oh, around eight months or so, but circumstances didn't quite turn out as I expected . . . I mean, I had a bit of troub—''
She actually blushed, an extraordinary shade of pink so captivating that for one ludicrous moment he marveled at her ability to conjure forth such a hue. She waved a hand and forced an airy laugh, which shook his convictions for a staggering moment. "Oh, 'twas nothing, really. Actually, I was quite overcome.''

The thought of imprisonment could certainly render one *overcome.* His eyes wandered over her hair, the delicate turn of her jaw, the diamond-and-sapphire earrings twinkling in the sun. She really was quite lovely.

"And once I realized 'twas a highly respected position, one which I had been recommended for by the very dean of students . . . well, you can imagine . . .''

Indeed he could.

"Oh, but we were discussing you, were we not, Mr. McAllister?''

"I wasn't aware that we were,'' he muttered, narrowing his eyes upon her.

She met his gaze, her eyes wide, fathomless pools. "Why did you leave Pine Grove ten years ago, Mr. McAllister?''

The question startled him. He had been expecting something else, some request for an excruciatingly detailed account of his escapades, of the men he'd killed, of the hearts he'd broken. Certainly not this.

She stared at him, her lips parted, her every breath visible within that dress. She looked cool yet she seemed to radiate heat, the sun caressing her, the wind teasing her hair, rustling her gown.

"Call me Jace," he found himself murmuring as he reached a hand to brush a stray tendril from her cheek, from skin softer than the finest of silks. His eyes dipped to the curve of her breasts. His throat felt thick and his voice coarse. "And I'll call you Peaches."

"Oh my..." The wind nearly snatched her soft murmur and she averted her cheeks, pressing a trembling hand to her throat. "I...I believe I like that much better than English, but I..."

He stared at her. She seemed genuinely distressed for some reason. Thoroughly embarrassed. He'd expected a knowing look, an affirmation of some kind, a casual nod, even. Certainly not this.

"I, well, I suppose the reasons are obvious..." she stammered, casting him an uncharacteristically shy look from beneath the fringe of her lashes, and his belly tightened. "But, I must say, Miss Burbridge...I mean Elizabeth, my father's wife, well, she always told me that if I get myself to bed early and rise early, well...that I would grow large bosoms."

"You heeded her advice, didn't you, lovely Peaches." He surrendered himself to her just for a moment, a fleeting, wonderful moment, so captivated was he by her guileless charm, her forthrightness even in the face of his blatant ogling.

"Oh my, yes! Of course I did!" She looked at him as if he were daft. "Wouldn't you? I had positively *nothing* at that time. Flatter than a board, I was, and dreadfully plump, to boot. A double tragedy. Every girl's nightmare! Can you imagine?" She shook her head with wonderment. "And then...poof! One day it seemed everything I ate went straight to my br—" Her eyes widened and she gulped, as if suddenly realizing that she was heading at breakneck speed directly down some forbidden path. Propriety and conscience and every last bit of all that English upbringing reared its head and brought the color flaming to her cheeks.

"Oh, dear God!" she wailed, pressing both hands to her face. "Oh my...I...Mr. McAllister, Jace...I...this is dreadful. I'm so sorry...oh, I've ruined everything! Excuse me...I...oh, blast!"

She turned so quickly she all but tripped over the train of her gown. With what sounded like a curse, she hoisted her dress to her knees with both hands and scurried toward the house, curls tumbling, leaving Jace to contemplate not the low-heeled peach shoes she wore but the slender curve of silk-stockinged calves.

He had half a mind to go after her, to drag her into his arms —though he had more than an inkling she would resist very little, despite her discomfiture—to sweep aside those wayward curls and tell her he wanted to hear more, wanted to know more about a dreadfully plump and despondent young girl who forced herself into and out of bed solely for the sake of acquiring a bosom. He ached to tell her that she needn't fret over propriety, that she could tell him anything that bubbled forth, anything she wished.

The thought that she was but a child, an innocent woman-child, caught him unawares. Off guard and completely vulnerable to her, he was. He closed his eyes and sought to rein in his thoughts, to achieve some semblance of logic. What the hell was the matter with him?

He opened his eyes to find James, still seated obediently before his schoolwork. The boy stared at him so solemnly, yet so transparently, he had to wonder what Madeline had seen fit to tell the child. Another victim. They were all victims.

As if he couldn't bear to look at the lad a moment more, he spun about and strode toward the barn. There, backbreaking, muscle-testing work no doubt awaited him, the kind of work that would temper those fires burning within him and, for a time, lessen the raw anguish of a shame that would prove by far his greatest foe.

Phoebe entered the room without pausing to knock or peek or announce herself in any way other than with the urgent tapping of her heels upon the floor. And the unceremonious banging open of the door. Without preamble, she proceeded in her purposeful manner to the dressing table, ignoring for the moment the flustered gasps emitting from the four-poster. With an exasperated sigh, she leaned toward the window and sent the shade snapping up with a flick of her hand, allowing late afternoon sunlight to spill into the room.

"Phoebe, what the devil are you doing?" Charlotte gasped from the comfort of her bed, rising up on her elbows and blinking sleepy eyes.

Phoebe tossed a hasty glance at her friend before flipping a gilt-carved jewelry box open and sifting a finger through the contents. She waved one hand and frowned. "I'm looking for that . . . that . . . thing you use in your hair."

"You could have knocked."

"Oh, poohey, Charlotte, you had no business being in bed at such an hour. Whatever is the matter with you?"

"I'm dreadfully hot."

"Take a walk," Phoebe muttered, intent upon her task.

"And my head aches from far more than the heat. Phoebe, what you said to Mrs. Witherspoon, 'twas *heinous*."

"Ooh! I've never seen *this!*" Purposefully ignoring her friend, Phoebe drew forth a three-strand pearl choker and held it up to her throat, casting an appreciative glance at herself in the mirror. "Why, 'twould be lovely with my violet silk . . ."

"Oh, no you don't, you little thief." Charlotte scooted from the bed with amazing speed and reached for the choker, which Phoebe relinquished with a pout.

"You're rather stingy for a best friend, Charlotte."

"And you're awfully full of yourself today, aren't you?" Charlotte tucked the choker into her pocket as if she didn't quite trust her friend. "You've your own jewelry." She folded her arms and peered closely at Phoebe. "In your own room. Go . . ." Charlotte turned and reached for the shade. "Go on and leave me to snooze the afternoon away and . . . oh, well, he certainly is an ambitious fellow, isn't he?"

"Who?" Phoebe murmured, seizing the opportunity to sift through the jewelry box while Charlotte mooned from the window.

"Jace," Charlotte replied casually, drawing the shade low.

"Jace?" Phoebe abandoned her task with a yelp and all but plowed over her friend in her haste to throw the shade up with a sharp snap. "Where?" She thrust the lace curtains aside and peered intently from the window. "Oh my . . ."

He was chopping wood, and doing a mighty good job of it, too. Shirtless, hatless, sun-bronzed and glorious amidst all those flexing muscles. Something raw and primitive stirred in

Phoebe as she watched him raise the ax high over his head before bringing it down with a mighty whack. His shoulders seemed miles wide, his waist impossibly narrow and sleek, his legs strong and powerful. He paused, retrieving a cloth from his pocket to wipe across his face, then threw his head back as if drawing deep breaths of air. Staring at the strong column of his throat, the expanding, fur-covered chest, Phoebe fell hopelessly and haplessly in love. Or lust. To her, there was little difference.

"Oh God..." she groaned, licking her parched lips and wallowing in light-headedness. "That man...that..."

"Outlaw," Charlotte muttered, before erupting with a groan that was brimming with despair. "Oh, dear God, Phoebe, don't even think about it."

"Trust me, Charlotte, I'm beyond thinking."

"For once, just once, use your blasted head."

"I can't."

"You must!"

"I'm in love."

"Oh God."

Phoebe rested her elbows upon the window ledge and dissolved into a dreamy sigh. "He's the most beautiful man...positively divine. I look at him and suddenly I'm lost...tongue-tied..."

"Will wonders never cease."

"Truly, I'm a blubbering fool."

"At least you have the decency to admit it."

"Stop making fun, Charlotte."

"I've never been more serious in my life, you goose."

Phoebe snuck a sideways glance at her friend then allowed herself yet another long, leisurely perusal of Jace. "He looks at me and I burn...here..." She pressed a hand to her lower belly and sighed. "The world spins and my legs quiver, my heart sings..."

"Perhaps you've an ailment."

"If 'tis that, I shall surely die happy."

"Mrs. Witherspoon left some of that atrocious vegetable compound, if you'd care to partake. I don't particularly like the woman, especially after she told me in no uncertain terms that

I would derive tremendous benefit from a heaping dosage of her Egyptian Regulator Tea."

Phoebe had to frown at her friend. "What the devil is that?"

Charlotte pursed her lips and drew herself up, though Phoebe detected a telltale pinkening of her cheeks. "'Tis guaranteed to bring a graceful..." Charlotte paused and bit her lip. "A graceful plumpness to us...flat-chested girls."

Phoebe grimaced and focused her attention upon wood chopping. "Poohey on Henrietta Witherspoon. You've a divine figure. So slender..."

"Bony."

"And stately. A regal bearing..."

"Gawky. I'm far too tall, my arms are too long..."

"You're lovely."

"I knew there was some reason why I allowed you to remain my best friend."

Phoebe sighed yet again, hopelessly awash. "Oh God, Charlotte, what am I to do?"

"Forget him this instant. He's bad, he's...I don't know. You heard Henrietta. He's got animal desires."

"Of course he does, just look at him. He stares at my breasts, Charlotte. Oh God, I feel all hot and..."

"Listen to me, Phoebe. Tear your eyes from that blasted window for one moment!"

"I can't."

"Of course, lest I forget, you've never attempted restraint in your life. You must! He's an outlaw! God only knows what he's done, how many men he's killed."

"I believe he's wanted."

Charlotte gasped with astonishment. "By whom? For God's sake, don't tell me that thrills you in some godawful way? You truly are perverse."

"He's done this to me...I don't know, he's possessed me."

"You've been possessed before, not a month past. Remember Donnie and Jeremy?"

"This is entirely different. They were boys and I...I was but a child. Jace is a man and I'm..."

"An addlepated fool. A raving lunatic." Charlotte knelt beside her and her words dripped with plaintive appeal. "If Jace is indeed wanted, someone will be after him. What am I saying? Someone *is* after him, and that gives me and *you* very good reason to doubt in the man's judgment. After all, the last place a wanted man should come is home.''

"Not if everyone believed him dead.''

"And that's another thing. All this secrecy, all these rumors. People are talking.''

"Oh, Charlotte, people always talk. They talk when something wonderful happens and they talk when something dreadful happens and they even manage to talk when nothing at all happens.''

"What about our plans? Have you forgotten about those truly wonderful positions awaiting us in Kansas? You still haven't told me where Kansas is.''

"It's not anywhere near Wyoming.''

"Thank heavens,'' Charlotte replied with deliberate sarcasm. "I was beginning to worry.''

"You always worry.''

"Dear God, Phoebe, someone has to! What the devil are we going to do now? Uncle Carson up and died on us. Madeline is so immersed in her grief she can only sit upon that veranda and stare. I doubt there's little she can do for us in the way of securing teaching positions anywhere, least of all in some godawful place like Kansas.'' Charlotte heaved a thoroughly dejected sigh and muttered in a tiny voice, "We should go back to England.''

"No!'' Phoebe spun from the window and grasped her friend's hands urgently. "No, we mustn't! If my father knew we had left school he would . . .''

"He'll do far worse if you dally with the likes of Jace McAllister.''

Phoebe sighed as that familiar dreaminess invaded her senses. "Did you know his name is Sterling? What a lovely name.''

Charlotte groaned and hung her head. "Why on earth do I ever allow you to talk me into things? We're lost, doomed. What the devil are we to do? We've no money . . .''

Phoebe gave her friend a reassuring pat on the hand. "We've our jewelry, which we can sell if need be, and we've our education. No one can take that away from us.''

"Little good it does us if you're in love with an outlaw. Phoebe, imagine the lewd women he's...he's...you know..."

Phoebe stared at her friend. "He's what?"

"Well, my God, a man like that would attract all sorts of heathen types, women of easy virtue, loose morals. Well, now that sounds painfully familiar to me. Does it to you, perhaps?"

Phoebe summoned a stricken look. "Charlotte, I shall never forgive you for that. My virtue has proven anything but easy."

"Forgive me, Phoebe, but you looked as if you positively ached to hand Jace your virtue from this very window not two minutes past." Grasping Phoebe's hands tighter, Charlotte leaned closer and set her mouth grimly. "You're right, Phoebe, he is different, in a very dangerous way. Be careful, dear God, promise me you will. Our very lives are at stake here."

Phoebe grimaced and peeked out the window at Jace, carefully stacking chopped wood. "Charlotte, when did you become so blasted melodramatic?"

"Me? *This* from the queen of melodrama!"

"Trust me, Charlotte."

"Oh God, I hate those words."

"Listen, just as soon as summer is over..."

"What?"

"Surely you didn't expect anyone to believe...oh, he's done...he's leaving...he's..." Phoebe thrust the curtains wide, flung the window up and leaned out so far Charlotte clung to her hips to prevent a complete disaster. "There he goes! He's heading away from the house...down the path, toward that growth of trees!"

"Far be it for the man to leave your very sight! No doubt he's headed toward the lake."

Phoebe spun to her friend. "The lake?"

"Yes, the lake. He bathes there every morning, I believe. Perhaps the man is hot and wishes to...oh God, no! Phoebe, quit smiling like that. I know what you're thinking and, blast you..."

"My," Phoebe all but purred, fanning herself with one hand and drawing the shade with the other. Her heart thumped wildly within her breast and it took a strength of will to temper her wicked smile. " 'Tis dreadfully warm, Charlotte. Indeed, I too seem to suddenly feel quite overcome."

"Phoebe . . ."

"Hmm, perhaps a nap." She urged her friend none too gently toward the bed. "Yes, why don't you just lie down, Charlotte."

"Phoebe, I swear it, I shall follow you."

"Now, Charlotte, whatever do you mean?"

"Cease! Oh, my head aches. Phoebe, you're depraved."

Phoebe surrendered to her grin. "Oh, incredibly so, and dreadfully in need of something to chase the heat away. Some cool lake water, perhaps."

Charlotte flopped upon the bed and drew a limp-wristed hand over her eyes. "Oh God, let me wake up from this nightmare. Anytime would be quite lovely."

Phoebe took great pains smoothing Charlotte's gown upon the bed. "Now don't stir too soon, and for heaven's sake don't follow me. God only knows your constitution would never manage the sight of a naked outlaw."

"Oh God," Charlotte groaned.

"Sweet dreams," Phoebe murmured, before spinning about and skittering from the room.

Chapter Six

Jace didn't even pause when he reached the grassy bank. Indeed, he strode without hesitation into the lake, pausing only when the water reached midthigh. Retrieving his crumpled shirt from his back pocket, he immersed the white cloth, then, without squeezing one drop of cold water from the garment, slung it over his face, across his shoulders and down his chest. The chilled water snatched his breath for a moment but he reveled in the feel of it all over him, soothing, cleansing, running in icy rivulets down his arms, his belly, and disappearing within his waistband. Dousing the shirt once more, he raised it over his head and squeezed. He sputtered, opened his mouth and tasted, drank, then shook his head vigorously and gave full vent to a shudder and a groan. Damn, but it felt good.

He flexed his arms, feeling the satisfying ache in his muscles, and dunked the shirt again. He ached all right, in places he didn't even realize he had muscles. But it was a good ache, an ache from honest toil, albeit prompted by rather dishonest thoughts—depraved was more like it. But, hell, a man had his faults. Jace squeezed the shirt over his head again, shook himself from head to toe, just as Zack did after a self-indulgent roll in the mud, then paused and allowed his gaze to roam.

A now familiar ache welled in his chest as he drank in the serene beauty of a spot he had known like the back of his hand at one time. How many times a day had he come here, sometimes alone, more often than not with his father? Before the war. Before Carson had enlisted so damned fast he'd been one of the first, securing the worthy assignation to the Washington Artillery and National Light Infantry group. So damned full of

Yankee fervor, his father had been, giving not a moment's thought to the young wife he'd left behind. Madeline, the wife he'd taken not more than three months after Jace's mother had died.

Trying to stifle the painful recollection, he swallowed heavily and swung his eyes to the house, that grand structure just visible above the treetops. His mother, Ann Sterling Mc-Allister, had envisioned the house and Carson hadn't rested until the last stone was in place. It was *her* house, it would always be, deserving the very best care, certainly not negligence and ill use from a woman who had no business living beneath that roof, a woman no better than a whore.

God, how he hated Madeline. That hatred curled and clenched his gut, wrenching, tearing at him and threatening to erase all those satisfying aches of honest toil. But how could he not despise the woman? A whore disguised in fashionable clothes and a husky voice. That's what she'd been those sixteen years ago, all of twenty-three, oozing sweet promises and thinly veiled grand delusions neatly packaged in a body that could render a man senseless.

He knew. He knew all too well.

And his father had swallowed the entire act, believing her tale of being orphaned as a babe and then misused by a lecherous uncle, her sole guardian. She'd plucked and played a siren's song upon a lonely widower's heart, tugging at his despair, every ounce of his compassion, and, in the process, slithering her way into his bed such that he believed her pregnant the very day he took her as his wife. Much to Jace's disgust, his father had mourned yet again not more than two weeks after the wedding. Of course, she'd somehow managed to lose the baby, the baby that never was, and even produced a tear or two herself. No doubt the thought of ensnaring the county's wealthiest man had prompted a celebratory watering of the eyes, tears she'd hastily brushed aside in her diligent pursuit to become the county's version of a duchess. The reigning queen of moneyed aristocracy, Madeline had absolutely everything she had ever wanted in her entire life.

Why hadn't his father seen through it all? Why hadn't he believed the rumors that this Madeline Sutton—Sutton, a name that by sound alone conjured up images of terribly old money—this Miss Sutton was none other than Mistress Maddie, a scheming little doxy, fresh from some high-class brothel in Philadelphia. And no doubt on the run from yet another foiled plot to capture a tidy fortune by way of a smitten husband.

Oh, Carson had been smitten all right, from the very start. Then again, he'd spent agonizing months watching Ann endure the ravages of consumption, the tender, loyal and painfully celibate husband forever at her side. Perhaps he'd felt some relief when she'd finally gone, relief amidst all those tears, all that grief. Jace had felt it, and that was no easy burden to bear, even now.

So Carson had proven relatively simple prey for Madeline, requiring but a few husky whispers, a glimpse of round shoulders and but one sultry look from those dark eyes, eyes that promised every last ounce of the passion that simmered just beneath her meticulously coiffed and manicured veneer. Oh, her eyes said it all, they always did.

And Jace had seen it coming from the moment his father had left for the war. Perhaps that was why he'd asked, no *begged* his father to allow him to enlist. After all, he'd harbored more than his share of patriotic fervor. But his father had forbidden him, all but ordering him to tend to the farm, the business, and, of course, to watch over Madeline. He'd been but a lad of fifteen then, a mere boy, not even of an age to serve the North. And in the five long years that his father was away, all that time he'd spent looking after Madeline, Jace had become a man.

Jace closed his eyes and squeezed the water over his head as if to cleanse himself of the memories, of that painful gnawing in his gut, the ache in his head. Would it ever cease to plague him? Would he ever be free of this...of Rudy Blades...of unfinished business...of duty and honor and all those damned oaths and allegiances that dictated his every thought, his every move? Would he ever look into a woman's eyes and trust her? Would he ever trust himself?

When he opened his eyes Madeline was there, looking older than she had when he'd first arrived, standing so close to the edge of the lake that the modest black ruffle along the bottom of her dress hung a good inch into the water. He found himself somewhat surprised that the pathetic creature didn't seem to care that her best bombazine could quite possibly be ruined. Then again, she simply stared...at him. The kind of stare that men all over the world fervently and with the utmost secrecy yearn for from a woman. The kind of stare that leaves very little in the way of conjecture as to the woman's motives or appetites. The kind of stare that would, even on his worst of days, prompt a tightening in his loins, a quickening of his pulse. After all, it had been a good week since he'd had Blades's woman, and he rarely allowed himself even that long a respite.

But all that the respites, covert male yearnings and heavy-lidded, slack-jawed stares from Madeline would ever elicit was disgust, revulsion...and, though fleeting, a very strong, cold-blooded desire to kill her. He could, very easily. He'd done it before with his hands placed just so around a man's neck...squeezing...

The woman took a step farther into the water, her dress beginning to float around her, and the bile rose in his throat. Jace all but growled at her then averted his gaze and strode with definite purpose toward the shore. She caught him, her hand clutching at his arm at first, then trembling as it slid over the length of his forearm, over his elbow and up...

He snatched her hand in a grip meant to bring a painful wince to her flushed face. If she had but known that he exerted tremendous control...that he ached to yank her arm from its socket, to slap that traitorous, adulterous passion from her eyes...

"Don't," he rasped through his teeth, aware that his mouth curved in a feral sneer.

Her lips parted, her eyes shone and her breasts heaved as if she drew in large gulps of air. "Oh, Jace...I can't help myself. You've no idea what it's like. I..."

"I've an idea," he growled, flinging her arm aside as if it were aflame and turning his back upon her.

"Jace, please!" She clutched at his arm, stilling his feet. "Please...j-just talk to me. Just look at me."

"I've had my fill of whores," he ground out, closing his eyes against the pain, all that damned guilt.

That silenced her for a moment, though she groaned softly before moving before him. "For God's sake, it's been ten years. Haven't we all suffered enough?"

He almost laughed. "Suffered? How have you suffered, Madeline? Do you even know the meaning of the word?"

She hung her head, affording him a view of the liberal streaks of gray in her meticulously coiled hair. Perhaps aging alone was torture for this woman. "I suffer every time I look at James." She spoke in a tiny voice, so meek, so unlike Madeline. Raising shining eyes, she whispered hoarsely, "Imagine what I suffer when I look at you."

"And well you should," he growled, his voice devoid of emotion, his heart cold and bleak and barren. "You killed my father."

"I loved him!"

"Bold words from an adulteress." He gritted his teeth and focused on the opposite shore. "What you did to him killed him."

"He forgave me!"

Something clammy gripped his soul and he swung a vicious sneer upon her. "The consummate fool. What did you do, Madeline, mewl and beg for a token few minutes before stripping the poor man's pants from him and employing every damned whore's trick you ever learned?"

"No!" she wailed, reaching a hand to him.

He gripped her arm, ignoring her painful whimper and the way she shrank from him fearfully when he took a step nearer. "Listen to me," he hissed. "I'm not my father and I never will be. No woman, do you hear me, *no woman* will ever again wheedle her way into my pants, into my bed, for the purpose of ruining my life."

"I never meant . . ."

"Save it for some local bumpkin, Madeline," he sneered. His eyes raked scornfully over her entire length as if he found her grossly wanting. "Even as old and sagging as you are, I'm certain a man well into his cups wouldn't find you too offensive in his bed. After all, you were once known to spread your eager legs wide for any drunken sot."

He should have anticipated the slap, knowing Madeline as he did. Then again, she bore the McAllister name, was indeed his father's widow and for that very reason deserved token respect and . . .

Hell, she deserved nothing. His cheek stung from the blow, throbbed with pinpoints of pain.

She gaped at him, horrified for a moment, then with a wail threw herself against his chest, sobbing. "Oh, Jace, I'm sorry...so sorry..."

He gripped her arms and flung her from him. "Stay away from me," he warned, clenching his fists with unabashed fury. "Don't make me exert my proprietorship, Madeline. The only thing that saves you from being thrown out is your son."

"Oh God, no!" Trembling hands rose in a pleading gesture and the tears spilled from her eyes. "No...don't...I need you. I need..."

"Don't fool yourself. I'm here to get the house in order and to tend to what's left of the business. Once timber season is over, I'm leaving. You, Madeline, don't matter to me in the least."

She wailed again, a mournful sound echoing upon the lake, but he had turned and was gone, plowing his way blindly through underbrush where there was no path until at last he found the path, or at least something that looked like the path through the haze of pain and...

That's when he bumped headlong into Phoebe...or Peaches.

"English." The word escaped him in a rush of air and his chest seemed on the verge of exploding. He found himself nearly overwhelmed by an unconscionable urge to crush her against his chest, bury his face in her tumbling hair, feel the beating of her heart against his own. Something about this girl...something in her eyes, in her voice, in the way she moved, the way the sun spilled over her peach dress.

Then he remembered.

"Ah, hell," he moaned, closing his eyes and shoving a hand through his hair. Duty and honor and oaths and justice...

"Did you enjoy your swim?" Her voice coaxed and plucked and swept away every last ounce of guilt and pain. And by God if he didn't want her, instantly, even before he opened his eyes.

"Yeah...yeah," he muttered, wondering at the girl's naiveté, the way she told him everything with her eyes. And he liked it. Hell, he loved it. He wanted her. To hell with his job.

Jace stared at her, *all* of her, his mouth curving of its own accord into the faintest smile, a smile he hoped she understood. Taking a step closer to her, he expected some retreat, some coquettish fluttering and twittering that never came. She simply gazed at him, her eyes somewhere on his damp chest, then on his mouth, and he nearly groaned.

The world stilled around them, the calm broken only by the humming of some very busy bees and the chirping of a bird nearby. He didn't even pause to consider her motives. He all but banished his duty from his mind. And Blades...and Madeline...and all his unfinished business.

He took another step and she seemed to sway toward him, her breasts lightly brushing his chest with every breath she took. He didn't breathe, so suspended in the moment was he, until she raised fathomless amber pools and parted her lips.

"You're going to kiss me," she said. It was a statement, spoken with absolute conviction, and his head swam with the implication.

Oh, he was going to do a lot more than kiss her. He was going to ravish her, plunder her, seek solace and warmth within her. He watched her lips part in soft, sweet temptation. The forbidden fruit.

Where were duty and honor now?

His hand found her neck, his fingers delving into her hair, his thumb caressing her throat when she gulped, the only testament to any distress she experienced.

"Your hands are cold," she murmured with a wavering smile.

He dropped his wet shirt and slid his other cold hand about her waist, urging her just another whisper closer to him until her breasts seared his chest like twin flames. He felt her hands fluttering uncertainly upon his arms as if she didn't quite know what to do with herself, and the flames shot through him. No...she couldn't possibly be a virgin.

He didn't pause, choosing to blatantly ignore every warning screaming through his mind. "You're warming me just fine," he said, tilting her face up to his. Such lovely skin she had...how soft and supple and incredibly desirable she felt beneath his hand. Banishing every last thought, he lowered his mouth to hers. He tasted slowly, employing every last ounce of restraint to brush his lips with painstaking softness over hers.

She was like a flower, sweet and warm, tasting of dew and in-nocence.

She trembled against him, her hands fluttering wildly upon his chest before he captured them beneath his hand, close against his pounding heart. She moaned, a breathless little gasp for air, and lowered her head. Fighting the nearly overwhelm-ing urge to tumble her back upon the soft grass, he pressed his lips to her hair, inhaling of her scent, then lifted her face and lowered his mouth to her temple.

She sighed and closed her eyes, swaying against him like a sapling willow beneath an urgent spring wind. Her palms spread upon his chest and moved, sliding over aching muscles and burning flesh, across his ribs to encircle his waist. Her lips were a firebrand upon his chest, a slow torture that swept his eyes closed and tightened his arms fiercely about her. He crushed her to him, painfully, though she did naught but press her cheek against his chest and cling all the more to his waist. His mouth found her hair, her ear, so slow and sensuous he felt as if he were in a daze. And then she tilted her face to his, her eyes smoldering with fires aching to be stoked, and every last glimpse of restraint fled.

Her lips parted beneath his even before the first thrust of his tongue. Jace ravished all right. He plundered her mouth, and when she gasped for breath, he crushed her closer and slanted his mouth over hers with even more intensity. Her hands were kneading his back and she moaned, rising up on her toes and molding her sweet body to his. He required no further encour-agement.

His hands roved over her back, slid over narrow hips and cupped a derriere as full and high and round as he could ever hope for. He lifted her against him, against the throbbing ache in his groin, knowing by her soft gasp that she felt him against the softness of her belly, then lower, against her...

He heard his own rasping breath as if from a great distance, felt her hot breath in his ear, against his face as he buried his mouth in the damp skin of her throat, against the prim lace at her collar. She didn't smell like a damned peach. She smelled like lilacs ... and jasmine ... and woman.

"English..." he groaned, his hands spanning her waist, her rib cage, reveling in the delicacy of her. She was so narrow, so lithe, yet so lush.

A soft, husky sigh escaped her lips when his hands cupped her breasts, and he nipped at her swollen lips as his thumbs brushed over the peaks. So responsive she was, her body swelling and blooming beneath his hand.

And then he heard it. The sound of damp black bombazine swishing through grass, and he hesitated, his hands stilling upon those full mounds, his head lifting. Hell, it would serve Madeline right to find them.

"What was that?" Peaches whispered, pushing gently against his chest and staring at him, wide-eyed. "I...I heard something."

He was in a pickle. A damned fine pickle. As if with a will of their own, his thumbs brushed against damp silk and taut, insistent nipples straining against the confines of layer upon layer of clothing.

His mind screamed. His body ached and burned from far more than honest toil or debauched thoughts. "An animal," he murmured, grasping her hips and lifting her against him. "Just an animal." His mouth found her neck for an instant before she pushed urgently against him.

"I don't know, I think it's—"

"Jace, oh, thank God you didn't leave me and...oh my God."

"Madeline!" Phoebe...or Peaches...sprang from his arms like a frightened rabbit. "Oh, Madeline! I...I...oh, Madeline! I...Delilah! Yes, Delilah wished me to tell you that supper...I mean dinner...or is it supper? Well, it's ready...finished and...oh my!" She hadn't even taken a breath yet, hadn't even looked at him, and all he wanted to do was sweep her into his arms and carry her off to his bed. The whole world could go to hell.

She clasped and unclasped her hands, bobbed up and down and blushed to the very tips of her delectable toes. She was a goddess. "I believe I hear Charlotte. Yes, yes, I do. Oh, I'm so glad I found you, Madeline...and you..." Finally her eyes flickered in his direction, not quite making it the entire way. Actually missing by a long shot. Well, not so long. She got all

the way up his legs to his hips before her cheeks flamed scarlet
and she all but dissolved before him. He watched with growing amusement as she opened and closed her mouth ineffectu-
ally several times before spinning and dashing away, clutching
her skirt all the way up to her knees.

"You bastard."

He ignored Madeline, ignored the voice dripping bitterness
and ten years' worth of humiliation. He didn't even look at her.
Retrieving his shirt, he strode toward the house, listening not
to the vile curses flung at his back but to the sound of gathering dusk. And his feet squishing in his boots. And his heart
thumping in his chest. All the way back to the guest house . . .
and well into the night.

She ate heartily, a welcome change from all the women with
whom he had shared a table over the years. And tavern food,
at that. What was it about food and drink that rendered the
most lusty and demanding of women naught but shy little
sparrows capable only of delicately picking at their food while
wearing atrociously disinterested looks?

English jewel thieves obviously knew better. He watched her
over the rim of his glass, then drained the whiskey in one gulp
and set the glass alongside three identical empty glasses on the
table. He'd shoved his clean plate aside two drinks ago, pushing his chair back and stretching his legs beneath the table the
better to peruse her from beneath the rim of his hat.

She'd bestowed that finely arched brow of disapproval upon
both him and his hat when he'd made no move to sweep the
thing from his head upon entering Goare's Tavern. He had
pretended not to notice. After all, an outlaw fresh from sordid
skulduggery paid little heed to manners and even less to delicately arched brows. He had to be believable, though he'd
found he couldn't resist pulling her chair out for her. Of course,
what better opportunity to observe her settling her plump little
derriere into her seat. Even outlaws employed chivalry as an
excuse for out-and-out ogling, especially if said outlaw knew
exactly what that plump little derriere felt like through reams
of peach silk.

He drew a hissing breath and, from force of habit, reached
for his empty glass, then scowled. This prodigious capacity for

whiskey was going to get him into trouble. He cleared his throat and hailed the barkeep, who nodded in that thoroughly expressionless and blasé manner in which all barkeeps nod.

Jace nodded his own blasé version when the barkeep placed another whiskey before him. He stared at the gold liquid, refraining for a moment, fingering the glass, then pulled his hat lower over his eyes and ogled Peaches.

She had just finished the last of her roast and potatoes, had cleaned her plate, in fact, and sat chewing very slowly as if she savored every last morsel. She swallowed, dabbed at her mouth, drained the last of her wine and looked as if she were about to smack her lips. She sent him a smile, obviously finding his silent regard disconcerting, for she blushed the exact shade of her dress and fiddled with her napkin. With a sigh, she glanced about as if seeking something, her eyes flickering over the scattered handful of other patrons toward the bar. Before he realized, he rather chivalrously motioned to the barkeep again.

"I hope they have something positively wicked for dessert," she chirped happily, her eyes brimming with anticipation.

Dessert. Of course. Self-indulgent little . . .

So refreshing, she was. Besides, any woman who could eat like that and still look like that—hell, as far as he was concerned, she could have all the dessert she wished.

"I'm awfully bad," she murmured, idly fingering the silly pink feather protruding from her silly pink hat. She clasped her hands in her lap and sighed. "I find restraint elusive, Mr. McAllister."

His kind of woman.

The barkeep paused beside their table and looked at Peaches in a manner that made Jace want to bloody his damned freckled nose. The fellow had wasted little time abandoning the casual facade. To Jace's eye, he so thoroughly feasted on the sweet pink confection before him that he all but foamed at the mouth.

Peaches cooed her way through ordering apple pie and curved those full lips such that the barkeep gaped at her and Jace downed his whiskey in one ferocious gulp. Without thought, he growled a request for another, scowling at the barkeep until the lad meandered away.

"You drink awfully much," Peaches murmured, peering at him closely.

"I'm a man of tremendous appetites," he replied in a low, even tone. He was baiting her, goading her, flirting in his own depraved manner with her. It annoyed the hell out of him. Worse yet, none of it had anything to do with his job.

And she wasn't biting. Not even a nibble.

Maybe that accounted for his decided surliness, a surliness four whiskeys had done naught but enhance. In fact, if that damned barkeep didn't cease his damned ogling, by God, he'd...

"Mmm," she sighed, and he found his thoughts scattering as he stared at her mouth opening to reveal a pink tongue, at her lips sliding slowly over her fork, at her languid eyes. "This is positively divine."

He grunted, averted his gaze, then found his eyes drawn to her again as if by some force beyond his control. So fleeting and elusive, his supposed control. He'd awakened renewed, refreshed, brimming with the worthiest, the most honorable of aspirations, a dedication reborn, only to feel it all slipping slowly, effortlessly out of his grasp.

His stride had been determined, his thoughts focused, his mind keen and primed. And then she'd appeared like a newly bloomed rose in the morning sunlight. And all his resolve had slipped a notch.

She'd requested to accompany him to town for some blasted reason, and he had more than a notion it had something to do with regaining Madeline's favor. She hadn't come right out and said it, but she seemed the type to trip all over herself to please her hostess. Being found in the arms of the local bad boy obviously dictated some recompense.

The clever enchantress had settled herself none too closely beside him and the ever present Sam upon the seat of the curricle, then, much to his astonishment, endured the ride in silence. A silence that, for a woman like Peaches, screamed with innuendo.

Duty, honor, keen and primed, had slipped again.

That was when the baiting had commenced—no, more like a hell-bent plunge into debauchery, fool that he was. He should have welcomed her silence. How often had he wished a woman would simply shut up? With Peaches, on this particular morning, he'd received nothing more than a few sniffs and a decided lifting of that pert little nose. And maybe one blush or two and a sideways glance, which no doubt accounted for him finding himself jovially accompanying her to the General Store and the milliner's and even a dressmaker's shop, shadowing her like the damned good operative he was, and thinking not once about his job or honor or duty or justice.

He'd simply watched the tumbled blond curls, studied the bob of that pink feather, the sway of her hips.

The notorious stoicism and composure threatened to slip again—more than a mere notch.

Captivated, he'd been, by the turn of her cheek, the sweep of her lashes, the full pout of her lips and all those damned breathy ooh's and oh my's, as if she'd never seen a hat shop in her life.

Once more it slipped and slid, perched precariously upon the very edge of sublime foolishness, one tiny step away from the end of his career. And then he'd spotted Goare's Tavern. In a valiant, last-ditch effort to salvage some measure of his worthiness, he'd grasped her elbow and propelled her toward the low-slung wooden structure, silencing her wails of hunger with a promise to buy her lunch. She'd squealed with delight and followed like a lamb being led to slaughter.

He filed her eager acceptance away. There was no telling when he might need to resort to bribery with her.

With the last crumb of pie gone, she sat back looking very much like a contented dove cooing and fluffing her feathers. Perhaps if he threatened to withhold her dinner, she'd join him at the lake for a little debauchery later on.

Debauchery, hell, he couldn't even get her to talk to him. Coquettish play wasn't her style. It was something else.

She gave him a tenuous smile, wistful in its hesitancy, and all he could think about was what he had done to inspire such a...cooling. That was it. A definite cooling.

He didn't like it one bit.

"About yesterday," she ventured in a small voice.

He started, sat up in his chair, opened his mouth to speak and...

"I'm awfully sorry." She stared at her hands, clasped in her lap, and looked every inch the spoiled English heiress she wasn't. "I truly had no idea you and Madeline . . ."

Damn. Surely she didn't think he and Madeline had . . . or were going to . . . What kind of lewd character did she think him?

He leaned his forearms on the table, pushing his whiskey glasses aside, acutely aware of a sudden urge to temper every last one of her misconceptions. "Listen, I don't think you understand."

"Oh no, Mr. McAllister, I do, and . . ."

"Jace," he found himself grinding out with sudden agitation. "Call me Jace, damn it. I'm not your damned schoolmaster."

She stared at him. "I'm sorry."

"Quit apologizing."

"I'm sorry, I didn't realize . . ."

"You did it again."

She bit her lip. "I did."

He stared at her mouth, gulped from his drink and summoned coherent thought. "Listen, what happened between us . . ."

"Oh, you needn't apologize."

"I had no intention of apologizing."

"Oh. I see."

For an agonizing few moments, he found himself completely befuddled. "Perhaps I should apologize."

"You should?"

He closed his eyes and wondered how such a mixed-up creature could endeavor to steal jewels and manage to avoid capture. Opening his eyes, he leaned toward her. "I apologize if I offended you."

She stared at him.

He gritted his teeth. "Did I offend you?"

"Oh no, heavens no!" She ducked her head and plucked at her gown. "I was rather . . . flattered."

Flattered. Not consumed or overcome or senseless or incapacitated. Not even shaken. Flattered. Flattered hadn't even entered his mind. He didn't know what to say.

"But 'twas terribly foolish of me to all but throw myself at you, and you caught so unawares what with Madeline and all and..."

"Peaches, listen..."

"Oh heavens, don't call me that."

He swallowed. "I thought you liked it."

She looked at her hands as if she couldn't bear the sight of him. "I do...I mean, I did but..." She bit her lip.

He was suddenly overcome by a fierce desire to take her hand, draw her onto his lap, cradle her in his arms and taste those bee-stung lips. His hand even reached toward her. "Peaches, Madeline and I..."

"No! Please don't. I...hic!" Her eyes flew wide and she gaped in horror. "Oh my goodness, I...hic! I've got...hic! I've developed hiccups and I...hic!"

He couldn't resist the tug at his mouth as he leaned toward her and suggested, "Perhaps you ate too much."

She looked positively mortified. "Oh, blast...hic! This always happens when I...hic!"

He searched the place for the suddenly absent barkeep. "Perhaps some water."

"Yes, water or...hic!" Her hand reached over her empty wineglass then fumbled across the table for his whiskey.

"I don't think you want to do that," he advised, his hand brushing hers as she snatched the glass from the table. He was still musing on the peculiar tightening in his chest at that briefest of touches, when she drew the glass to her mouth.

"You...hic!...bloody American men." She rolled her eyes and shook her head. "Chivalrous at the...hic!...most inappropriate moments. No doubt you...hic!...think this—" she waved the glass for effect "—this...hic!...more threatening to me than your bloody...hic!...hat."

"Suit yourself," he drawled, observing her with a lopsided smirk as she drained the last of the whiskey in one resounding gulp. Lest he foster her ill-conceived notions of bloody American men any further, he neglected to mention that Goare's whiskey was, without a doubt, the foulest brew he'd tasted since he'd stumbled upon an ancient and addlepated old goat of a prospector in the bleakest of Colorado Territory who'd offered him a weathered old jug of home brew. He could still taste the stuff burning a trail of flame to his breastbone, where it smoldered for the better part of the evening. Peaches looked as if she felt very much the way he had that evening, though she sputtered and wheezed and turned shades of scarlet he would never have allowed himself to turn no matter how foul the brew.

"You . . . you . . ." she sputtered, gasping for air and feverishly fanning her face.

"Perhaps some air," he offered smoothly, moving to ease her chair from the table and help her to her feet with a bloody American hand at her elbow.

The sound of the tavern doors swinging open with a bang obliterated her breathy reply, though she made her way quickly from him toward the exit. Of the two men that entered, Jace immediately recognized the older, red-haired, swarthy one as Gideon Goare. Indeed, Goare appeared unchanged, save for the increase in his girth attributable to age, though he still looked like a man capable of the rigorous work he'd accomplished under Carson McAllister's employ those ten years ago.

The younger man with the oily black hair, the one leering like a greasy little weasel at Peaches as she brushed past without pause, the one staring at her sashaying buttocks like a man starved—no, Jace didn't know him. So he knew damned well that his instant and profound dislike for the man stemmed from nothing more than this feeling that Peaches was *his,* and his alone.

A damned nuisance it was all becoming, especially since outlaws reserved what little sentiment they possessed for their horses. Their women they kept satisfied only to the extent necessary to render them just the slightest bit recalcitrant beneath the sheets, yet still brimming with philanthropic fervor lest said outlaw ever find himself behind bars and in need of a comely female to aid in his escape.

For the briefest of moments, Jace's eye followed Peaches through the set of windows as she made her way down the sidewalk. Then his eyes flickered to Goare, who had sidled up to the bar, his massive belly pressed against the mahogany, his eyes beneath the shade of his hat scanning about, then settling upon Jace. The look was shadowed and unreadable, and Jace found himself thankful that Peaches wasn't around to witness this initial meeting. Better that she wander into another store and yet another after that. With a full tummy, he could well imagine her capacity to browse was inexhaustible.

Jace shoved his chair aside and strode with deliberate lack of purpose to the bar, where he perched a good five paces from Goare. The barkeep materialized, peering over Jace's shoulder for some glimpse of a silly pink feather, no doubt. Jace thrust the necessary coin at him with a scowl and the fleeting thought that he was a damned fool to let her wander about the town alone. To hell with Goare and bolstering his damned reputation.

Just as he turned to beat a hasty retreat, Goare's voice boomed throughout the hollow room. "McAllister, that you?"

Jace nodded and pulled his hat lower over his eyes for effect.

"Ooo-eee! *The* Jace McAllister." The greasy weasel weaved his way around Goare toward Jace, a decayed, gap-toothed grin on his face, and smelling as if he hadn't bathed in weeks. He spat a brown goo into his palm, wiped his hand on his greasy thigh and extended it to Jace. "I never met no outlaw." The greasy head jerked sharply toward the door. "Nice piece o' woman ye got there, McAllister."

Jace leaned an elbow upon the bar and crossed one boot casually over the other. He cast a bored glance over the weasel before locking eyes with Goare, who was keenly observing at his five-pace distance.

The weasel's leer slid into a sneer as he lowered his ignored hand. "Why, you good-fer-nothin' damned mother..."

"Hawkins." Goare's voice crackled with a commanding air.

"Aw, c'mon, boss," Hawkins whined, before sneering at Jace long and hard and looking as tough and menacing as any greasy little weasel could, being that he barely reached Jace's shoulder. Hawkins turned, took two steps, then spun about. But Jace had seen it coming. And was ready. Hawkins's fingers had but brushed the cold steel bulge in his belt when he found himself staring with disbelief down the barrel of Jace's Smith & Wesson revolver.

What better way to bolster one's sordid reputation than drawing a revolver in a public tavern. For effect, Jace glared at Hawkins, a mean, nasty glare that belied his casual stance.

From somewhere in a shadowed corner of the room, Jace detected a slow, appreciative whistle.

"God..." Hawkins mumbled, holding his hands in the air and backing into a table.

Goare's chuckle filled the room. "Hawkins, give me the damned gun. Good God, man, get a hold of yourself. Then get your scrawny ass out there and water those horses. And no more guns, you jackass. McAllister..." Goare tipped his hat back, exposing a thatch of flyaway red hair that matched his bushy, handlebar mustache. His grin was just as Jace remembered. "Put that damned thing away, boy, and pull up a chair." He turned to the white-faced barkeep, who seemed captivated by Jace and his mighty revolver. "Hey, boy...yeah, you...I'm payin' you, remember? Get us some whiskey. No, no, not that rotgut crap. The good stuff. In the back." Goare leaned over the bar and produced two clean glasses. He shoved one in front of Jace. "C'mon, McAllister. It's on the house."

Chapter Seven

Once she'd regained her breath, Phoebe paused beside the curricle and absently stroked Sam's head, as he had seen fit to assume a rather lofty and no doubt cozy perch upon the vehicle's plush seat. Phoebe murmured to the animal, who merely closed his eyes and lolled his tongue in reply.

"I'm finding your master far more peculiar than you," she said, scratching between his ears. "Thank heavens you're not half as handsome as he or I would be twice besotted, indeed. So determined I was this very morn to practice restraint..." She grimaced. "God, how I hate that word." She sighed and inclined her head toward Sam as if he offered some advice. "God help me, but I care naught for histories and clandestine meetings at lakes—unless of course 'tis *I* that he wishes to meet. Madeline can take all her frosty glares and... you know something, Sam? I think there's far more to all this. Far more to Madeline and Jace, and a definite reason for all her cool looks. 'Twill require a little effort, but I shall discover all those tidy little secrets and ensnare one wickedly handsome outlaw before he even realizes." She shuddered and gave Sam a huge smile. "Ooh, the mere thought..."

She paused, bending her smile and a brief nod upon a tall, rather jaunty and frightfully dapper copper-haired gentleman passing by. He paused as well, tipping his top hat and returning her smile despite any reservations he might harbor regarding a young woman carrying on a conversation with a beast perched upon a curricle seat. His twinkling eyes captured hers and he leaned upon his walking stick. When he spoke, he became an instant friend, if not more, soaring to the very peak of

her list of gentleman friends. After all, Phoebe was as much in
need of flattery as the next girl.

"Miss Sinclair, I presume," he said with a dimpled smile.
"Of course, who else could you possibly be? Buttermilk Falls
is abuzz, my dear, positively abuzz with the news of your arrival, this enchantingly beautiful Miss Phoebe Sinclair."

Phoebe fluttered her lashes and blushed. "Why, yes, 'tis I.
And to whom do I owe this pleasure?"

"Dalton Pryce, at your service, my lady." He bowed,
sweeping his hat from his head, which endeared him to her
forever. "Are you enjoying your stay, Miss Sinclair?"

"Oh yes, very much. Such a lovely little town, Mr. Pryce."

"Dalton, my dear Miss Sinclair," he replied, his eyes twinkling so devilishly Phoebe could not resist another blush.
"Simply enchanting..." she heard him murmur before he lifted
a brow and glanced about as if he sought someone. "Do you
require any assistance, Miss Sinclair?"

"Oh no, I, actually, I am with a...someone...Jace Mc-
Allister. He's in that..." Phoebe waved a hand over her
shoulder toward the tavern.

"I see. Jace McAllister." He seemed to ponder that.

"Indeed, the man just rose from the dead. Do you perhaps
know of him, Mr. Pryce?"

"Miss Sinclair, I have known him many years, and for that
very reason you must heed my advice." Pryce glanced covertly
about then leaned toward Phoebe. "How can I phrase this
delicately?"

"You needn't," Phoebe replied, eliciting a sharp raising of
bushy copper brows followed by a deep chuckle.

"As you wish, though I must say a man finds himself
searching blindly about for the proper words in the presence of
such a lovely young lady." His eyes twinkled at Phoebe, though
he'd donned a rather grave look. "My point, Miss Sinclair, is
that perhaps you should seek other company while you're with
us."

"And whom may you be suggesting for such companion-
ship, Mr. Pryce?" Phoebe lifted her nose a notch to peer rather
coquettishly upon him. "Once I've had my fill of outlaws, of
course."

"Outlaws, my dear Miss Sinclair, can ruin a girl."

"Indeed," Phoebe mused. "He's awfully bad, is he not?"

"So they say. You've heard the stories, of course."

"Actually, Mr. Pryce, I've never harbored any fondness for gossip and take great pains to avoid lending my ear to such—" Phoebe waved a dismissive hand "—trivialities."

Dalton Pryce flushed beneath his whiskers and erupted with a short laugh. "Ah, indeed, well . . ." He drew himself up and leaned upon his walking stick. "Let me just say this, as a gentleman who wishes you well. One would certainly have cause to believe all that's being said about McAllister, since the man seems intent upon taking up with Goare's crowd in that tavern. My dear, that bodes nothing but trouble."

"Trouble does not appear to be something Jace takes great pains to avoid, Mr. Pryce."

"And the very reason you should achieve your fill of that outlaw forthwith."

"Such ominous warnings, and from a friend, no less."

"Hardly a friend, Miss Sinclair. I would venture to say Jace McAllister harbors rather jaded views of lawyers."

"A lawyer, you say?"

His burly chest puffed up. "The best in the county."

"Why, Mr. Pryce, it would please me greatly if you were to call upon me at Pine Grove some afternoon very soon. Yes, very soon indeed."

Dalton Pryce grinned from ear to ear. "I shall, Miss Sinclair." He tipped his hat and seemed about to depart.

"Mr. Pryce," Phoebe piped up, her curiosity proving the better of good manners. "What is it that Jace McAllister has done?"

"I'd rather think that was not for me to say." He paused, his manner hesitant as if he didn't dare tell her. "Though if you insist, I do believe a great many of the more sordid stories revolve around the man's notorious touch."

"His what?"

"His touch, the very livelihood of the safecracker and the gunslinger."

"Gunslinger? Oh my."

"Ask him, Miss Sinclair, about this legendary touch. I'm certain that his answer will prove enlightening." Dalton Pryce smiled, tipped his hat, then strode jauntily down the sidewalk.

Phoebe watched him amble off, feeling her heart tripping along and a warm, bubbling of delicious anticipation seeping through her limbs. A gunslinging outlaw! Why, the mere thought should have sent her fleeing for her life, not yearning, hungering for more. She drew a deep, steadying breath and felt a wicked smile curving her lips. The more notorious the man became, the more she wanted him, the more vibrant and alive she felt. How glorious to be in love, her life perched upon adventure, romance! No more would she have to be content with a staid and dreary existence, an existence broken only by her own mischief making and an occasional fumble and squeeze from some clumsy young oaf.

Ah, but ensnaring Jace McAllister would require every last ounce of her guile, every trick she'd ever employed, and more, all her daring and imagination. She chewed thoughtfully on a fingernail for a moment and glanced at Goare's tavern. God help her if *she* were to become too easy for him. No, she must take great pains to avoid it.

She thought about Dalton Pryce, the lawyer, a man who could indeed aid her when it came time to secure some type of teaching position, though God only knew the future she had in mind had little to do with teaching. No, Dalton Pryce was far too staid and urbane himself, far too dapper to be of any use in the plot she had in mind. He simply wouldn't do. She needed someone . . . devilish, just like Jace.

Her gaze flickered about the street, over wagons laden with goods rumbling by, over pedestrians moving briskly about, over the shop windows . . . And then she spotted it, in the shop window across the street, something that had been niggling at her since she'd arrived, and for a moment all other thoughts fled. Lifting her skirts, she set out across the cobblestone street toward the General Store, her stride purposeful, her mind muddling over exactly how she was to do this, when suddenly the heel of one of her not-so-sensible shoes caught in the deep groove between the cobblestones. She stumbled, then nearly fell, and no doubt would have, had it not been for the strong hands that steadied her and the breadth of chest that blocked her fall.

She glanced up, expecting Jace's savage countenance, then started and jerked upright despite hobbling about on one leg.

She opened her mouth, sputtered an apology and flushed to the tips of her ears beneath the man's unwavering regard.

"Ma'am," he drawled, his teeth flashing white in a devilish grin beneath a burnished golden mustache as he touched the brim of his black Stetson. His eyes were dark, narrowed upon her, his face shadowed, hollow planes and craggy sun-browned grooves, and his hair a wild untamed fall of sun-streaked gold across his brow and over his shoulders. He was dressed entirely in black, his faded denims, his shirt, the boots and the long black duster, which parted in the soft breeze to reveal slim hips... and a gun tucked into his waistband. A gun?

He smiled again. Wicked. Devilish. Ever so handsome. And perfect.

He bent to retrieve her shoe, offering one brawny shoulder as she steadied herself, then slipped the shoe onto her foot with hands that were rough yet gentle. An outlaw's hands.

Phoebe gathered her wits with characteristic speed and fluttered her lashes at him, managing, as well, to cast a hopeful glance in the direction of Goare's Tavern. Where the devil was Jace?

"My, but the gentlemen of this town are so gallant," she breathed, noting with some satisfaction that the outlaw seemed momentarily distracted by her bosom as he straightened to his full height. Not as tall as Jace but he looked strong. Very capable. A formidable adversary in vying for a woman's favors. Perfect, indeed. She raised a curious brow. "Have you lived here long?"

"Just passin' through, ma'am," he replied, giving her another grin accompanied by an appraising sweep of his eyes. Subtlety was obviously a virtue unknown to these outlaws. "I was thinkin' of movin' on, but now...well, ma'am..." His eyes fastened upon her breasts and he licked his lips. "I do believe I'll be stayin' on for some time."

"How lovely," Phoebe mused, lifting her chin into the breeze such that her hair fluttered in its most enchanting manner about her face. The outlaw seemed captivated. "I, too, have determined to lengthen my stay... interminably. Perhaps I shall see you again."

He grinned, and Phoebe found herself wondering if all outlaws were so blastedly charming despite their lack of couth. "You'll be seein' a lot of me, Miss . . ."

"Sinclair. Please, call me Phoebe."

"I will. You're not from these parts."

"No . . . England, actually. I'm in Buttermilk Falls visiting some friends. The McAllisters . . . Pine Grove. Perhaps you know Jace?"

"Never heard of him." He turned, affording Phoebe a view of his profile, the sharp hook in his nose, the granitelike jaw, the fiercest of countenances. Oh, he was an outlaw, all right. "I like your dog."

Phoebe's eyes followed his to settle upon Sam, still perched upon the curricle seat, and she found herself supremely pleased that this outlaw had apparently been watching her for some time. "Oh heavens, that beast? He belongs to a . . . friend of mine. Jace McAllister. A peculiar-looking animal, is he not?"

The outlaw appeared to study Sam for a moment, then shrugged and swung unreadable dark eyes upon her, and for some unfathomable reason, his look sent a chill chasing up Phoebe's spine. "I like dogs. Always have. Been thinkin' 'bout gettin' one." He paused, his eyes boring into hers then falling to her mouth. "Can I take you somewhere?"

Phoebe's heart fluttered. Her plan was working all right, almost too well! She had the blasted outlaw's attention, nay, she knew she had far more than that! Yet Jace was nowhere to be seen. Blast! Outlaws moved far too quickly for her . . . at least this one did.

"No . . . no, thank you. I've a bit of shopping to do, you see." She gave him a dazzling smile and lifted her skirts. "Thank you again . . . and I hope to see you soon. Perhaps at Pine Grove. Good day!"

Turning, she breezed airily along, not venturing one backward glance, and entered the General Store with all the sublime confidence of the young, foolish and unsuspecting.

Jace stepped into the sunlight, pulled his hat over his eyes and glanced about for some sign of Peaches. He scowled at Sam panting in his direction, an affectionate scowl, and made no move to sweep the beast from his lofty perch. His eyes darted about the busy street. Where the hell was she? He should have had the sense to keep her at least within sight, if not within arm's reach. What good did it do him to foster his bad reputation, gaining a spot at Goare's poker table, if Peaches wasn't around to witness it? A waste of time.

With a grunt of irritation, he set out down one side of the street, peering into each shop, his patience waning with every step. He crossed the street, started up the other side and skidded to a halt. She stood at the counter of the General Store, easily within sight of any passerby, looking as innocent as a pale pink lamb as she held out to the shopkeeper what looked to be...a jeweled necklace.

Something exploded in Jace's brain, rage, frustration and utter disbelief. With three long strides he reached her, roughly grasping her arm and spinning her about such that her pink hat slid from her head and golden curls tumbled about her shoulders.

"What the hell do you think you're doing?" he growled, gritting his teeth so fiercely his jaw hurt. He shook her arm as if he could jar some sense into her, yet this achieved naught but indignant sputters and gasps and a valiant attempt to pry herself free.

"What the devil is the matter with you?" she hissed, her amber eyes blazing upon him as if it were *he* who deserved to be hauled off to the nearest jail. "I was only bartering my necklace..."

"Good God," he muttered beneath his breath as he dragged her none too gently behind a stack of canned goods. "How easy do you want to make this for me?"

She jerked upright and stared at him, unbridled fear shining in her eyes. *"Easy?"* she whispered.

He stared at her, at the huge amber pools, at the parted lips, at the tumble of her hair...then glanced at the shopkeeper peering rather curiously in their direction. His pulse hammered in his ears, an insistent rhythm, the same staccato beat and pumping of adrenaline that spelled the end of a successful mission.

He clenched his jaw and found himself staring at her again. Damn, but he wanted her even now. When had he become so damned...weak? Never had a woman so affected him, in all the wrong ways.

"Give me that," he demanded, snatching the necklace from her and thrusting it into his pocket.

"Why, you...give me back my..."

"Shut up," he growled harshly, too harshly, and roughly turned her about and drew her to his side, ignoring her gasps of outrage. "Just follow me out of here like a good girl."

"What?" she shrieked, yanking her arm from his and planting her feet. "You pompous oaf! You can't tell me what to do!"

For the briefest of moments, he gave serious consideration to turning her in, to tossing her impudent little derriere into a rank and dingy cell. With one swift movement he grasped her arm and twisted it behind her, drawing her perilously close against him, so close he could feel her sweet, warm, traitorous breath upon his cheek and the fullness of her bosom crushed against him. "I'll tell you what to do all right, my little Peaches, and you'll listen. Unless, of course, you'd prefer the hangman's noose."

She gulped and gave him her wide-eyed look. "What the devil are you talking about?"

He shuddered with frustration, at her insolence in the face of her crime. Gritting his teeth, he muttered under his breath for her ears alone. "Just follow me out of here and to the buggy. I'm quite certain you don't want to pawn this necklace."

"But I do!" she cried, and he closed his eyes, wishing he weren't such a damned fool, so easily captivated by the turn of a cheek or the tumble of hair and an innocent guise. "I want to purchase that..."

"What?" he demanded with a disbelieving shake of his head. "A train ticket to Kansas? You wouldn't get to the next county."

She frowned at him. "Perhaps one day but..."

He groaned, releasing her, and hung his head for a moment. "So damned unconcerned," he murmured under his breath, his hand rubbing tired eyes, which found hers again, and he wondered if her success thus far was due entirely to her ability to render a man senseless. It certainly had little to do with cunning. "What is it that you wish to purchase? Something frivolous and selfish and..."

"That." She rose up on tiptoe to peer over the stack of cans and jabbed a finger at the store counter. "A scooter."

"A scooter." He scowled at the small wooden contraption. "Why the hell do you want a scooter?"

"For James."

His heart leapt and lodged in his throat. She looked up at him, her lips curving ever so softly, her eyes shining. If he had been any more of a fool he might have believed her. He reined in his wayward thoughts, his carnal desires, which seemed to have gotten the better of him, all his wits, and in the span of a heartbeat determined that she was indeed crafty. The wiliest criminal he'd ever known. What better way to confuse him, to leave him adrift in a decade of turbulent emotion such that he could never be entirely certain of her motives.

"For James," he found himself repeating dumbly.

"He needs toys. A child has to play."

"Yeah...yeah." He thought about the shambles she'd made of his career, of his life, and how he'd let her. He thought about giving it all up, heading west, building something of his own, working the land and eating heartily, rising before the sun, bathing in a Colorado stream... and sleeping next to a warm, soft, yielding woman who would bear his children and make sweet, passionate love to him.

"Go outside," he muttered, nudging her in the small of her back. When she hesitated, he nodded. "I'll take care of the scooter... and don't wander off."

He watched her take her leave, watched her smile airily at the shopkeeper, a sweet, winsome smile, and the shopkeeper smiled back. She'd captivated them all.

He paid for the scooter, then hesitated, eyeing the shopkeeper and wondering why he felt it his duty to protect her. "You'll have to forgive Miss Sinclair. They barter their children over there in England."

The shopkeeper gave an understanding nod and Jace touched the brim of his hat and strode from the store, the weight of the necklace in his pocket a grim reminder of that around his soul.

* * *

"Would you cease your staring from the window," the woman seated opposite him grumbled softly, and for the briefest moment his dark gaze flickered over her as she stabbed a fork disinterestedly at her meal. He drew on his cigarette and watched her sigh irritably. With a quick glance about the small saloon, she adjusted the wide-brimmed straw hat lower over her face, the better to conceal it and the cloud of peach-colored hair beneath. "What the devil do you find of such interest out there, anyway?"

He grunted, swung his eyes to the curricle parked across the street and exhaled the smoke in a rush. His eyes narrowed on the tall man, the man he recognized even without the beard. The man who had called himself Shane Morgan in Laramie. Steely eyes shifted to the woman in pink. The beautiful young Englishwoman with the accent. An accent like that of the woman mewling in his ear.

"Why on earth did I have to meet you in this godforsaken town?" she grumbled. "Adam said we'd rendezvous closer to Laramie."

"Worth don't always know what he's talkin' 'bout," he replied, drawing deeply on his cigarette.

This seemed to irritate the woman. "Adam Worth has never led me astray in the five long years I've been with his gang. 'Tis the very reason I agreed to disappear for a time. Had I known he would send for some heathen outlaw to escort me..."

"Worth an' me go back a long way, Peaches," he drawled wickedly, eyeing her closely. "Relax. Ol' Rudy knows how te take care of a lady."

"Relax?" She leaned forward and hissed between her teeth. "Half the bloody county's after me. Those Pinkerton agents are everywhere, trust me. In places you don't even suspect! Adam knows. By God, he's all but best friends with one of the Pinkerton sons. The longer I remain in one place, the better their chances of finding me! And I've still all the jewels!"

He erupted with a slow chuckle that brought the color high in her cheeks. "Just relax. Keep that hat on an' git yerself some more clothes if you plan te leave the hotel."

"Leave? Pray, to do what? Shop? By God, an Englishwoman is too bloody conspicuous in a town like this! 'Tis far too great a risk to remain." She glared at him. "I plan to leave town tonight."

He chuckled again and shook his head. "Oh, no ye don't. Not without me. We'll be stayin' on for a time."

"Why the devil would we do that? We've got to disappear! Have you forgotten that you're a wanted man?"

He scowled at her and flung his gaze to the window again. "Peaches, Peaches, trust me. I ain't plannin' on robbin' the damned bank. Besides, the only guy who knows who I am ain't gonna say a word."

"How can you be so certain? Dear God, we're talking about my life here! What is so bloody important in this godforsaken hovel of a town?"

He grunted, his eyes homing in on his prey as the curricle moved off down the street. "Revenge, Peaches honey. Sweet, sweet revenge."

"Ah yes, honor lies in honest toil. My dear friend, you're looking less and less like an outlaw every day."

Jace pounded the nail several more times than was necessary before bending a scowl upon the natty top hat, the silk embroidered waistcoat and immaculate black topcoat of the gentleman below. "Go away, Pryce," he muttered, presenting Dalton Pryce with his back as he turned to repair yet another loose shingle.

"Surly, eh?" Pryce remarked, chuckling in much too self-assured a manner to suit Jace. "It's too damned hot a day to labor on a roof. Get the hell down here and join me in some lemonade. I believe the lovely Charlotte shall fetch you a cool glass."

"Go away, Pryce," Jace grumbled, pounding with renewed fervor. True, the late-afternoon sun beat relentlessly upon his bare back, a back that ached and yearned for a good stretch. Sweat glistened upon his brow, on his arms, running in irritating rivulets down his belly and into his lashes, momentarily blurring his vision. His throat felt parched, his mouth watering at the mere mention of the drink. Yet something kept him on that roof, pounding away.

Pryce's voice drifted up to him when he paused in his hammering to shift position. "They're wondering why you haven't filed any kind of a report. It's been a good week since you took this mission."

"Nothing to report," Jace muttered between the nails in his teeth.

"Aw, c'mon, Jace, she must have said something incriminating at least."

"She hasn't said or done anything worth reporting." The hammering resumed, echoing off into the distance. With a last mighty whack, Jace paused, drew a heavy breath and eyed his friend. "The lady keeps an unremarkable itinerary, Pryce. She's ventured to town but once, with me. The only things she managed to steal were the hearts of the barkeep and that old man at the General Store, and she's..." His eyes found her then, the way they always did, with remarkable ease, as if with a will of their own. She sat on her rump, her legs spread wide in a most unladylike manner, in the shade of a mighty oak, her hair a tumbling blond cloud, her face as smudged as her gown, her hands, as well as James's beside her, immersed in the thick goo of the enormous mud puddle before them.

"What the devil is she doing?" Pryce asked.

"I believe she calls it playing," Jace muttered.

"With James?"

Jace gave a short, hollow laugh. "Not with me, my friend."

Pryce leveled a wickedly raised brow upon him. "If only that she would, eh?"

Jace scowled and flung an arm toward the mud-splattered pair. "Hell, she's a child. Just look at her! All day long making those confounded mud pies or climbing trees or scampering about, wearing flowers in her hair, stealing cookies, running from Delilah..." He drew a breath and gave a caustic laugh. "Do you think they'd want a full accounting of all that?"

"Maybe she's not Peaches."

Jace stared at his friend, at the cool, even look he received in return. "The hell she's not!" he bellowed, shoving his hammer into his pocket and swinging down from the roof in one easy movement.

"Adelaide Prescott's ball is but four weeks off."

Wondering what Pryce was up to now, Jace eyed his friend warily. "Should I care if that old dowager chooses to squander her dead husband's fortune on meaningless frippery?"

"Indeed you should. I'm quite certain our Peaches would be inordinately interested in the Widow Prescott's jewel collection. Perhaps you should ask her to this event."

Jace's mouth snapped shut with a click. "Hell no! You take her."

Pryce puffed up his chest. "I do believe the lovely Charlotte has agreed to accompany me. Besides, I'd never move in on another man's woman, no matter how fetching she may be."

Jace gritted his teeth and narrowed his eyes on his friend. "What the hell are you talking about?"

Pryce shrugged innocently. "Oh, one has to wonder, you know. I haven't seen you in town much."

"Listen, Pryce. Pine Grove is a shambles. The business is . . . hell, Madeline's let the business go. Thank God it's been so dry. We still have time to cut timber before the first flood. Hell, there's more than enough to keep me busy here besides shadowing a damned child."

Pryce turned to look at Peaches. "She looks like one hell of a woman to me."

"Yeah, well . . ." Jace paused, his attention suddenly riveted upon Peaches as she scrambled to her feet. *Her* attention seemed focused upon the mud pie she cradled gingerly in her palms, so much so that she seemed completely unaware that her gown had somehow caught high about her bustle such that her stockinged legs were revealed clear to the tops of her garters. Like a man starved, he feasted upon the delicate curve of her calves, the slender length of her thighs, the white lace garters that brought forth images of rumpled sheets, passion-swollen lips parting beneath his and slender arms beckoning him . . .

Jace sucked in his breath, hating her at that moment for what she'd done to him.

"Yep," Pryce drawled, giving Jace a wicked wink. "Looks like one hell of a woman to me."

Jace turned sharply away, intent upon finding God knows what among the tools strewn about the lawn. "Shut up, Pryce, and get the hell out of here."

Pryce merely chuckled as if he found it all somehow amusing. "My friend, I do believe you're in love with her."

Jace spun about, a hot retort burning on his tongue like the flames shooting through his brain. "The hell I am!"

And then she screamed, a terrified screech, and before he could think, before he could ponder the right move under the circumstances, before he had a moment to consider the icy chill that had descended about his heart when he'd first heard her, he flung his hammer and nails aside and ran blindly toward her.

And then he stopped. And laughed. Roared with laughter that he hadn't allowed himself for too long a time. When he finally looked up, she glared at him as best she could, a hateful glare that summoned another hearty chuckle. For there, in the center of that deep puddle of goo, she sat, immersed to her waist, with James frolicking about her, clapping his hands with glee.

Chapter Eight

Had Phoebe known that falling into a mud puddle would capture Jace's undivided attention, she would have thrown herself face first into the nearest goo seven days before and happily foregone his blatant ignoring of her, which had commenced the day she had purchased the scooter. Since then, he'd but grunted and nodded brusquely in reply to any of her attempts at conversation, his eyes never once meeting hers, his manner distant, bleak and so bloody efficient, as if his very life depended on patching the stupid roof. Or mending a fence. Or painting the porch.

Each and every day she'd brought him cool lemonade and had lingered, of course, allowing him ample opportunity to notice her painstakingly constructed coiffure, her crisp, pale summer dresses, newly nipped and tucked beneath Charlotte's practiced needle, the better to squeeze herself into the narrow sheaths. Yet for all the time spent at her toilette, all the muffins and tarts she'd foregone in favor of a seventeen-inch waist, all the teasing smiles and sloe-eyed glances she'd practiced in the mirror to the point of exhaustion, he hadn't paid her any attention.

He drank his lemonade so bloody fast he never failed to spill a good portion of it, leaving Phoebe captivated on more than one occasion by the trickles of cool liquid weaving their way through the tangle of smooth dark fur covering his bare chest. The relentless sun had darkened his skin to a molten bronze and set his hair aflame with burnished copper such that he seemed like some pagan god, all brawn and sinew, all simmering hooded looks, hollowed, stubbled cheeks and clipped responses.

Phoebe was getting desperate.

She'd immersed herself in play with little James, or Jamie, as she preferred calling him. At first she'd coaxed, presenting him with the scooter, then disappearing, leaving him to discover the thing on his own. When he'd finally ventured in search of her, she'd hidden in the branches of the mighty oak, swinging down with a cheery "Hullo!" which elicited a squeal of delight. Next, the construction of the mud puddle had commenced innocently enough—it was Jamie's idea. Phoebe had managed to locate two small shovels in the barn with the intent of digging in the dirt. After all, she'd reasoned, all children loved dirt. What she hadn't anticipated was Jamie's total commitment to the project. The only problem then was getting Jamie away from the thing. And laundering his clothes. And avoiding Delilah's clucking tongue and shaking head. And, of course, Madeline's frosty glares, though today Phoebe would be spared. Today Madeline had ventured to Titusville to pay her weekly call upon a dear sick friend, and wasn't expected back until late that evening. The woman hadn't forbidden Phoebe to play with the child . . . yet.

Madeline had, however, asked on more than one occasion when Charlotte and her friend planned to leave. Not how long they planned to stay. When they were leaving.

Phoebe, indeed, was getting desperate. Her plan to ensnare her outlaw had failed miserably to date. This extraordinary teaching position awaiting her did not exist. She couldn't return to Wellesley—dear God, they'd have to drag her back—and she couldn't return to England, beloved home that it was, yet a life as full of rigors and trials and routines as poor little Jamie's.

Thus, despite her immediate annoyance with Jace for laughing with such carefree abandon in the face of her mishap, despite the fact that her dress was ruined and her hair a dreadful mess, she summoned a thoroughly helpless look and raised doe eyes upon him. This was rather easily accomplished, for simply looking at him towering above her rendered her hopelessly overcome with tremulous emotion. And yearning for far more than a warm bath.

"Jace, I..." She'd no more than breathed the words and she was in his arms, whisked neatly and soundly from the muck and clasped roughly against a chest that felt just as she'd dreamed it would. He turned, shifting her in his arms so that one was beneath her knees, rather intimately situated under her gown—how he'd managed that, she'd never know—and the other about her waist. And then he proceeded, pausing only to mumble something to Dalton Pryce, who bent to tend to a much confused Jamie while sending an undeniably sly look toward Jace's back.

Her outlaw strode silently and with definite purpose across the lawn, over the cobblestone drive, around the barn and through the tall grass.

"Where the devil are you taking me?" Phoebe asked, clinging as if for her life to his shoulders. His sun-baked flesh was warm, heated with an enticing masculine scent. It took a strength of will she didn't realize she possessed to refrain from melting all over the man. She wanted to knead all those flexing muscles, taste his skin and those lips forever pressed into a grim line, kiss away the scowl that hovered mercilessly over his brow. He'd been laughing not a moment past, yet the brusque manner had somehow intruded itself upon them yet again, his silence an impenetrable fortress. Her heart beat a frantic rhythm, a timeless, incessant reminder. Her palm moved over his shoulder, softly, slowly, and then the other palm moved, her fingers slipping over wet mud and sinewed muscle. His profile loomed above her, as if chiseled from rock, his gaze fixed before him, and Phoebe sighed. She cared naught where the man was taking her. She only hoped he took his time.

And then dense brush engulfed them, jagged branches clutching at Phoebe's gown, no doubt scratching Jace's bare torso, yet he didn't so much as flinch. Phoebe's heart took flight and her lids lowered. A secluded clearing. What better place to strip away her soiled clothing, with soft grass to lie upon. So much for plans gone awry.

A little teasing, a little enticement, a kiss or two and then a firm no. She'd achieved resounding success with that plan countless times in the past. Why not now?

Yet he continued, and the angst plagued at her. She cast that unreadable visage a wary look. "Jace, where the devil..."

And then he emerged upon the shore of the lake, strode four, maybe five paces into the water, just about hip-deep, and before Phoebe could do anything but utter a disbelieving cry, he unceremoniously dropped her into the cold water.

She surfaced, sputtering and spewing tangled hair and water, struggling to gain her footing despite the sodden weight of her gown. Through a curtain of mud-caked hair, she watched him stride in his nonchalant and thoroughly infuriating manner toward the shore. Fire exploded in her brain.

"Y-you're not *leaving* me here?" she shrieked, gulping for breath, and stumbling as her gown caught beneath her foot. The garment all but sucked her beneath the surface. "Damn you!"

With a rage heretofore unknown to her, she watched him disappear without pause into the thicket. "Oooooh, you bastard!" Without another moment's hesitation, she tore at the front buttons of the gown, freeing some and completely tearing others from the sodden fabric. She cared naught for the rag, for her shoes, for decency and propriety or ensnaring an outlaw. She was bent upon vindication, so much so that she abandoned her garment with a victorious cry and scampered from the lake with resounding energy, clad only in a thin shift, garters and ruined silk stockings.

Into the thicket she plunged, heedless of the branches clawing at her hair, or of the path, and suddenly found herself lost in dense foliage. With a shriek of frustration she spun about, plowed through the brush and stumbled upon the path. And then she saw him, directly ahead in the shadowed clearing, sauntering along as if on an afternoon stroll. With a cry of unadulterated rage, she surged toward him. She was aware that he had turned, that his eyes had widened ever so slightly at the sight of her, that for the briefest of moments his lips curved in an appreciative smile... and then she was upon him, intent on clawing the self-satisfied gleam from his eyes, scratching bare skin, kicking those strong legs... all to no avail. With one sweep of powerful arms he caught her, rendering her struggles useless.

And then, with remarkable agility, he twisted her about, pinioning her arms across her chest, his breath a hoarse, angry rasping in her ear.

"Had enough, little Peaches?"

She heaved against the pressure of his arms, her anger snatching her breath for a moment. She felt the solid wall of his chest imposing itself against her back, the strength in his arms wrapped about hers, yet somehow this served as further provocation.

"You beast!" she hissed, gulping for breath and struggling anew. "I would claw your bloody eyes from your head if I could!"

His beard-roughened cheek rubbed against her jaw, so close was his mouth to her ear. "And the very reason why I won't release you, little wildcat."

Phoebe seethed with her frustration. "How I wish I were a man so that I could match your strength! Indeed, I would be certain to best you!"

"A man doesn't have half the weapons you possess, Peaches love. Now cease your squirming. I'd like a better look at you."

With a shriek, she wriggled from his grasp. Whether she'd caught him unawares or whether he'd allowed her to go free, she'd never know. What she did realize, as she whirled about, was that a wet, clingy, transparent shift was a lethal weapon indeed. And a muscled, bare chest doubly potent. She swallowed the hot retort poised upon her lips, hating herself for the blush she felt to the roots of her tangled ringlets. For the sake of her pride, she resisted the urge to spin about and cover herself. Let the oaf have his eyeful. She was still bent upon vindication. She drew a heaving breath, achieving some measure of satisfaction when his eyes feasted upon her breasts, then opened her mouth to vent her rage.

He took a step toward her, his eyes a smoldering deep blue, like a troubled ocean. "Peaches . . ." His voice was a sensual murmur that threatened every last fiber of her resolve. "What have you done to me . . . ?"

"Indeed!" Phoebe huffed, taking a wary step backward. Not ten minutes past she would have sold her firstborn child to see this look in his eyes. Now . . . "How dare you ignore me, treat me like some spoiled child!"

"I was a damned fool," he muttered, drawing a step nearer, looming before her like the most virile of beasts. She felt his eyes all over her, and it sent a shaft of white-hot heat to her core. "Just look at you... every inch a woman."

An uncontrollable trembling seized her and she managed yet another step away from him. Her pulse thundered in her ears, hammered in her breast. It was anger... anger. "Why do you treat me so? What the devil have I done to you? I..." And then she backed right up against a very sturdy tree. And Jace smiled, a wicked curve of his lips that set his eyes aflame.

"I don't want to talk, Peaches," he murmured, stopping directly before her, and her eyes skidded over the planes of his chest. With every shallow breath she drew, her breasts gently brushed his skin, yet the contact could not have been more palpable.

Her eyes met his, and for the life of her, she didn't know why she didn't simply throw herself into his arms. "I don't like you very much," she whispered.

His mouth twisted wryly. "I don't like you, either." His eyes fastened upon her mouth, and she suddenly yearned for him as she'd never before yearned for anything in her life. Even if he didn't like her. Even if he had little manners. Even if he treated her shamefully, embarrassed her, made a mockery of her. Perhaps she wanted him all the more for those very reasons.

"Then again," he drawled, raising his hand to brush a stray curl from her cheek, "liking doesn't have much to do with it." His eyes probed her soul, his powerful arms hanging at his sides. She wished he'd use them, by God. All thought escaped her. "So what do you want, little tease?"

Her eyes flew up to meet his and her lips parted with an indignant gasp. "I... you... you think I..."

"I *know*, Peaches. You want it. Bad."

She didn't even hesitate for the sake of coyness. "And you don't?"

"What man wouldn't?" One hand slipped about her waist to ease her gently against him. He buried his mouth in her hair, his voice sounding hoarse and rasping. "You're a witch."

Her hands somehow found his ribs, trembled with uncertainty, then clung, and she closed her eyes, laying her cheek against his chest, wondering why she wanted this man so desperately. She was afraid to move, yet somehow she molded herself to him at naught but the gentle pressure of his hands upon her back, easing unhurriedly over her waist, then lower over her hips, before stilling possessively upon the curved underside of her derriere.

"Flee from me, Peaches," he rasped into her ear, his hands urging her hips against his, cupping her buttocks and lifting her high against his solid length. "Flee... or I will indulge your every whim and more."

Phoebe's heart fluttered like a frightened bird. She couldn't have left him now if her life had depended upon it. "I... I cannot," she whispered. She pressed her lips to his skin, inhaling of him, tasting of the salt, nipping at the smooth dark hairs. "Indulge me, Jace..."

He groaned, drawing her tightly against him and burying his face in the curve of her neck. "I'm not going to apologize...ever," he muttered, his mouth working an age-old magic down the length of her throat then across her delicate collarbone. "And I'll tell you right now, it'll never work between us and... good God..." His mouth paused at the ribbon of her shift, his breath hot upon her skin, his hands cupping her breasts, his thumbs brushing over the sensitive peaks that strained against the damp cloth for release. Phoebe clung to his shoulders, her head falling back against the tree with the sheer pleasure he gave her. And then she felt his mouth upon her nipples, teasing, nibbling, his hands making quick work of the shift until it slipped easily over her shoulders and sagged from her bosom. "Ah, Peaches..." His hands moved over her flesh and his mouth followed. "So beautiful..."

"Oh, Jace... please..." She closed her eyes and shuddered.

"Don't get shy on me now," he murmured, his mouth teasing the curved underside of her breasts, his hands spanning her waist. "Your skin is so smooth, so damned soft." And then he was on his knees before her, his hands at her waist, sliding over her hips, holding her against the tree. Her knees had given way long before. Her fingers caught in his tousled hair when he suckled her... slowly, leisurely, the peaks of her breasts swollen, tender, yet thrusting impudently for more. And he gave more, as if it were his birthright to do so at his pace, until it all became a torment, the waiting for God knows what... some release that would satisfy the hot pulse throbbing between her legs.

Yet he denied her, prolonging the agony until she was only dimly aware of the breathless moans escaping her parted, parched lips. His mouth worked magic over her softly curved belly, her skin quivering beneath his masterful touch, and she wondered vaguely how many women he'd known, how many he'd given such pleasure, how many yearned for him as she did.

She felt his palms upon her buttocks, lifting her, spreading her legs, and then his fingers brushing, delving, seeking, and she gasped at this most intimate touch. He groaned, a strangled growling, and she jerked, stiffening against him for the first time when she felt his mouth at the tangle of blond between her legs and the suddenly painful pressure of his fingers . . . there.

"Ah, sweet virgin," he rasped, spreading kisses over the insides of her quivering thighs. "How you tremble, sweet innocent, but I'll never regret this."

And then he rose before her, as powerful and mighty a man as she could have ever conjured forth in a dream, and tore the shift from her with one movement. With a savage growl, he drew her hard against him, his mouth claiming hers for the first time, his tongue plunging relentlessly, plundering her soul, robbing her of her will, all strength, all sense. She sagged against him, all too aware that this was beyond her, that she'd been a fool to think she could ever control this man. And then she felt the naked length of his swollen manhood against her belly, and her hands moved lower, over his parted waistband, and she knew. . . .

With one swift movement, he lifted her against the tree, parted her legs with a thrust of his knee and surged into her. She cried out against his mouth, knowing that he had to have torn her asunder, knowing that he was far too big for her, that this pain seemed endless, and then, in a matter of moments, with the slow rocking of his hips against hers, it all changed. Her legs were suddenly about his waist, her arms clutching him tighter, and she returned his savage kisses with mounting fervor, the coil of molten heat escalating within her, and she cried out again, this time with a raw passion. The bark of the tree bit painfully into her back and she welcomed it, welcomed the torment, and wondered if he could take her any higher.

And then, suddenly, he paused, his hips stilling against hers, and her eyes flew open to meet his, a breathless, anguished cry escaping her parted lips. His face loomed close above hers, and for some reason she experienced an atrociously inappropriate shyness in the face of her abandon. She bit her lips and clutched plaintively at his shoulders.

"You want more," he murmured, his passion-glazed eyes hooded. His mouth lowered and brushed with an infinite tenderness over hers, his tongue gently probing, igniting the flames yet again.

She whimpered against his mouth, as helpless to control herself as she was the tides. "Jace...please...if you know what it is that I yearn for, you must...oh...Jace..."

With slow, languid strokes, his hips moved against hers, his face buried in her neck then lowering to her bosom. "I want to tease you, witch," he rasped, spreading feverish kisses over the high, full curves. "Tease you, torture you as you've tortured me...and will again."

With a helpless groan, Phoebe sagged against the tree, wallowing in the pressure building within her, cradling his head to her breasts. And the pressure mounted and peaked, and she prayed he wouldn't stop, that her cries of delight wouldn't deter him. And it peaked again and again, until she knew she would gladly die at his hand to achieve release. And then, with a strangled groan, he surged against her, thrusting deep within her, finally driving her over that threshold for the first time into a fathomless sea of swells and flows that washed over her then receded like the most gentle of tides.

With a shudder she sagged against him, feeling his arms wrapping protectively about her, aware that his breath was shallow, almost labored, upon her breasts. She buried her face in his hair and her palms moved over the relaxed muscles of his back, feeling the thin sheen of perspiration that covered them both. A bird called nearby. The sun peeked through the trees overhead, dappling the secluded clearing. The late-afternoon air was warm and sweet with the fragrance of spring. All was in keeping with Phoebe's supreme sense of peace. Of completeness. The incomparable sense of serenity that she had found the man she'd forever dreamed of. With a contented sigh, she snuggled closer against him.

Jace's mind swam with the ramifications, the enormity of the situation, though for the life of him he couldn't stop nuzzling the full mounds pressed to his face. He inhaled her scent deeply, as if to commit it to memory, and tasted her dewy skin—a warm, womanly taste unlike anything bottled or manufactured. His lips brushed over one nipple, delectably large, of the palest pink imaginable, and he couldn't suppress a groan as it swelled and blossomed beneath his mouth. With a moan of despair, he felt his manhood swelling within her, within the tightest, warmest sheath. His hands moved over her buttocks, lifting her, and she cried out—perhaps because of the tree, certainly not because she wished him to stop, for she was a wanton witch.

With one swift movement, he pulled her into his arms and tumbled her back upon the grass.

"Jace!" she gasped, even as she clasped him close. "Do you want to . . . again?"

"Again," he breathed against her mouth, plunging deep within her. There would be time enough for recriminations later. "I want to again . . . and again."

The pale peach-and-purple clouds of dusk streaked the sky overhead when Jace finally rolled onto his back and stared through the branches overhead. He was acutely aware of warm, soft woman curled against him, and that his hand seemed intent upon the curve of slender leg draped wantonly over his hips. His first coherent thought surprised him. He still wore his pants. And his boots. He'd been so damned consumed.

She was as naked and rosy and round as the day she was born. Her shift lay in tatters somewhere amongst all those aged, exposed tree roots, her stockings and garters within arm's reach, exactly where he'd tossed them after peeling them from her quivering limbs.

He closed his eyes, nearly groaning aloud beneath the onslaught of a guilt and self-disgust he'd never thought possible. Oh, he could brush this all off as simply doing his job to the best of his abilities, laying pipe with the outlaws, all right! He knew of some operatives who would have reasoned thus, completed the mission and slept like a baby. He couldn't. He'd taken her lustily, snatched her virtue without a moment's hesitation. Hell, for a man who had avoided virgins like the plague, he'd experienced a certain ... delight, no, a self-satisfaction in being the first. Good God, he'd reveled in it. And not once had he thought about her as anything but the one woman he had to have, for no reason other than he wanted her.

The frustration welled in his chest, nearly choking him on acrid bile. How could he have been so damned weak? He knew well the answer to that and it made him momentarily crazy. Indeed, the answer and all her irresistible charms burrowed closer with a soft little sigh that made him suddenly yearn to taste her breath...except that her mouth was buried in his chest and she was kissing him with swollen lips and a wicked pink tongue, licking him, and her sweet hands were roving all over him, and if he didn't put a quick end to it, they wouldn't make it back to the house until morning.

"Peaches," he muttered, catching her by the arms and lifting his head to direct a stern, authoritative look at her. He summoned nothing akin to stern and authoritative. One look at her all tumbled blond and flushed pink above him, looking ravished, her lips begging to be kissed, her eyes hooded, her breasts resting in the most excruciatingly provocative manner upon his chest.... He managed a strangled groan through the tightening in his throat and his head fell helplessly back upon the grass. "Peaches, honey, I can't ..."

She laughed, husky and deep, and slid her supple length against him. He closed his eyes and cupped full buttocks that seemed to curve perfectly in his hands. Her breath played sweetly upon his face, her fingers delved into his hair, her lips played a siren's song upon his forehead, over his brow, his bearded jaw, and nibbled at his mouth. "Oh, Jace," she breathed into his mouth, her tongue slipping hesitantly over his. "I want to do it again ... please."

For one wondrous moment, he thought about spending the rest of his life with this woman, this wild, wanton creature. Of feeling her beneath him as often as he wished, of making beautiful babies with her...

"This is crazy," he growled through clenched teeth, catching his hands in her hair to still her seeking mouth. He found himself staring into enormous pools, wide with sudden confusion, an unabashed display of conflicting emotion. Thank God he'd learned to conceal it all a long time ago. "Listen to me," he muttered, his voice sounding far too harsh and callous even to his ears as he struggled to right himself and set her away from him. And then she bit her lip and seemed to draw great gulps of air and his insides melted like creamy butter. His hand slipped about her neck, his fingers brushing her nape then drawing her to him. His lips lingered on hers until he drew her into his arms and across his lap, if only to still the trembling in her limbs.

What the hell had he done? He'd bungled it, all right, and with an astonishing lack of foresight. The more immediate problem, however, appeared to be his flagrant inability to function—except in the most primitive sense, of course—with this delectably naked jewel thief all over him. Hell, how could a mere man be expected to think with her doing all the things she was doing?

"Peaches...now, c'mon." He captured her wandering hands beneath his, yet couldn't resist the tug at his mouth when her sloe eyes met his. "We've got to get back."

"I don't want to," she murmured, rising up against him. She was all languid and warm and so, so eager. "Jace, I love..."

"Shh..." he muttered, pressing his fingers to her parted lips and hastily drawing her to her feet. He forced a smile he didn't feel and shoved a hand through his hair. "I...uh..."

"Let me tend to your pants," she said, her eager little fingers flying to the task until he caught both her hands in his.

"I'll...uh...take care of that. Now you, you..." He swallowed when he looked at her standing before him like Eve herself beneath a canopy of lush green. "You're too damned beautiful, Peaches."

She swayed toward him, her lips seeking his, until he caught her shoulders and all but shook her. Forcing a laugh, he cleared his throat and swiftly buttoned his pants. "Where's your dress?"

"In the lake."

He stared at her a moment then glanced at the tattered shift. "Wait here," he muttered, then set off toward the lake.

He retrieved the sodden gown, wrung it out as best he could and returned to find her indeed standing in the exact spot, proud, naked and glorious. Before he gave in to instinct and tumbled her again, he assisted her into the gown and had just regained his faculties when she turned toward him with a sweet, tremulous smile.

"I...I fear I cannot tend to these buttons." She indicated the double row adorning the front of the gown. "My, I'm shaking for some blasted reason."

With a scowl, he set about drawing the fabric over her bosom and tending to the buttons. This required slipping his fingers beneath the fabric and against her skin more than a few times and he soon wondered if his fingers wavered even more than hers.

"Your dress is too damned tight," he muttered, shifting uncomfortably within his own tight pants.

"Perhaps 'tis the water," she replied softly, giving him a knowing smile. The girl was too dangerous.

"They're all too damned tight, water or not," he grumbled. "That'll do." He scowled then brushed past her as if she were suddenly aflame.

"But these down here and..."

He paused and rubbed his eyes where a dull ache pounded. "It's almost dark. No one will see you."

She didn't reply, in fact didn't say anything the entire way back to the house, moving slowly through the grass just ahead of him. When she reached the porch step, however, she turned and placed a hand upon his chest. He wondered if she could feel the skin tighten at her touch or the fierce pounding of his heart.

She gave him a wistful smile, which he knew was borne from her disappointment that this interlude had ended. He couldn't tell her that there were to be no others, that it had all been a gross error on his part, that he would see her behind bars one day if it were the last thing he ever did. Yet these thoughts fled as speedily as dusk gathered, replaced by an overwhelming urge to crush her against him and bear her to his stone dwelling, to his crude mattress, to cradle her in his arms until dawn streaked the sky.

"Good night," he muttered, then turned and strode down the path to the guest house, intent upon retrieving his wits with the aid of a full bottle of whiskey.

Had Jace been less consumed by his thoughts, his instincts might have detected the presence of another, a shadowy dark form lurking amongst the wildflowers along the side of the house. The shadow lingered, still and unmoving, until Phoebe closed the door behind her, then, with a grunt of satisfaction, turned and disappeared into the night.

Chapter Nine

A week can seem like an eternity when one anticipates something...that never happens. Day after day of the same cloudless blue sky, endless, dry, hot afternoons stretching into moonless nights spent staring from an open window in the hopes of gaining some respite from the oppressive heat by way of even the faintest of night breezes...which never came. And hoping beyond hope that *this* would be the night he stole through the darkness, climbed the trellis of morning glories and slipped silently, sensuously, into her room and beneath her sheets, where she lay, trembling with her passion and naked as the day she was born. Jace never came.

In that entire seven-day period, Phoebe saw him but twice, both times in the wee hours of the morning when she'd awakened to the sound of wagon wheels upon the circular drive and men's voices still coarse and gruff from lack of use. She'd scurried from the bed, oblivious to her state of undress, and perched at the window, her eyes straining through the eerie gray morning light, seeking his familiar silhouette. How well she knew the breadth of shoulder, the particular set of his blasted hat upon his head, the manner in which only he could move about, prowling, stalking, all long legs and flexing buttocks. How she ached to beckon him to her, to ask him why he hadn't spoken to her, why he hadn't come to her since...since... A lump of dread lodged bitterly in her throat whenever her thoughts strayed to that glorious afternoon when she'd become his. Thus, she held her tongue in favor of simply watching him mount Zack and accompany the wagonload of men, with their saws and axes, all the way down the cobblestone drive until they'd disappeared into the morning mist.

From an ever-so-helpful Delilah she'd learned that Jace had hired on a score of industrious lumbermen to clear an enormous parcel of land choked with aging timber. And with these men he departed every morn, returning long past dusk, if then, such that Phoebe, who lingered with obvious intent upon the veranda for a good three hours after dark, knew all too well he did not spend his evenings in the blasted woods.

What sleeping with a man could do to a girl. After one day spent nibbling nervously at her nails, pacing about her room with her pulse drumming as insistently in her ear as Charlotte's scoldings, Phoebe realized with horror what she was fast becoming. After two days, desperation gave way to unbridled self-loathing and she indulged herself with three helpings of Delilah's gooseberry pie. After three days, she hated Jace. After four, she hated herself, again, and claimed to hate Charlotte for bringing her to such a godawful place. After five, she threw caution to the wind and, late at night, clad in naught but a sheer chemise, sneaked into Jace's bed and waited, in vain, for his return. After six, she packed her bags and got as far as her bedroom door before sinking in a teary heap upon the floor. After seven, she determined, finally, to get him back. And she knew precisely how she was going to do it.

Her device, the black-clad, scruffy blond outlaw, had just tethered his black-and-white pinto before Goare's Tavern. He turned, of course, at the singsong voice of the little man perched upon a wagon bed before the throng clogging the street. In the exact center of the crowd between Jamie and Madeline, a grossly bored and overheated Phoebe raised up on tiptoe, summoned a breathtaking smile and waved at the outlaw.

The steely character saw her immediately, gave her that charming grin, adjusted his black hat upon his blond head and set out in her direction. Her spirits soared until she spotted a pudgy arm waving frantically from the edge of the crowd, directly in front of the outlaw. The arm disappeared and Phoebe saw her salvation hesitate, as if his path were momentarily blocked by a rather large and imposing figure, and then, sud-

denly, a flushed and flustered Henrietta Witherspoon erupted
through the crowd with a mighty "Whoosh!"

"Widow McAllister!" Henrietta breathed, heatedly fanning her mottled, sweat-streaked face and gulping for breath.
Her heavy muslin gown clung to her damp chest, her feathered
hat sat slightly askew upon her colorless hair, yet she managed
to purse her lips with self-righteous indignation. "Why, you're
in mourning, are you not? To be *seen*, Widow McAllister. Tsk!
Tsk!"

Phoebe glanced at Madeline, at the heavy black bombazine
gown, at the severe black hat and mourning veil, which swept
well past her chin. No doubt Madeline fared worse than all of
them beneath the oppressive heat and unrelenting noonday sun,
yet her manner remained cool, her voice as chilled and clipped
as it had been this fortnight past. "Mrs. Witherspoon, one need
not closet oneself within one's home for more than six months
for fear that the proper homage not be paid to the dearly departed. I believe you are the first that has not offered kind
words this day. Perhaps the heat overcomes you?"

Henrietta dabbed at her beaded upper lip then pressed a hand
to her heaving breast. "Indeed, it does. Why, my poor Violet
took to her bed not three days past and hasn't yet risen. I, of
course, being of more stout character, have managed to bear it
all." Her lips twitched into a grimace of a smile and she leaned
toward Phoebe, who attempted to peer over the woman's
shoulder for some sign of her outlaw. "Miss Sinclair, I must say
that I find your Englishwoman's method of coping with the
heat rather... uplifting." Henrietta suddenly burst forth with
a tumble of high-pitched giggles, which seemed to surprise even
herself, for she hastily snuffed them beneath a gloved hand.

The thought of Henrietta Witherspoon waddling about sans
undergarments brought an amused smile to Phoebe's lips and
she couldn't help but raise a wicked brow. "Our men have yet
to complain."

Henrietta giggled again, then, as if she were struck by the full
import of Phoebe's words, her mouth sagged in a gasp of
shock. Before Henrietta managed more than a blustery reply,
Phoebe waved an airy hand to the gaily dressed man upon the
wagon. "Yon medicine man promises cures for any and all ailments. Indeed, he touts remedies for chronic fatigue, aching

muscles, dyspepsia—which cure I myself intend to sample—and even claims to hold within his grasp an elixir to combat a lack of..." Phoebe fingered her bottom lip thoughtfully then offered Henrietta a sympathetic smile. "Well, you know, a lack of feminine allure."

Henrietta drew herself up with a resounding huff. "Well! Widow McAllister, the manners of those you harbor beneath your very roof, why—!" Her eyes widened and her face twisted into a self-satisfied smirk as if she'd been all but overcome by a truly delicious thought. "As a matter of fact, word has it that your outlaw Jace has been seen *every night* this week, even Sunday, if you can believe it, at that...that thirst parlor." Her dull curls drooped over her forehead and her hat slipped yet another notch as she jerked her head toward Goare's saloon. With an acrimonious pursing of her lips, she announced, "Supposedly he gambles like a demon, all but inhales his devil's brew whiskey and has taken up with that floozy Flossie Dawson."

Phoebe's heart leapt to her throat and she forgot all about her blond outlaw struggling through the crowd toward her. Gambling, drinking, gunslinging...these caused her not a moment's pause. But who the bloody hell was this Flossie Dawson? Clutching her reticule with trembling hands, she bit her lip until it nearly bled and averted a suddenly cloudy gaze. Where the devil was Charlotte? No doubt off with her beau, Dalton Pryce, behind some lilac tree, rubbing noses or some such nonsense. Little wonder Charlotte had of late displayed not one whit of interest in leaving this godforsaken hovel. She and all her priggish notions had managed to ensnare a beau, a fine upstanding beau who whispered sweet and tender words of adoration, whose very smile promised years of a cozy, secure existence in some tidy, whitewashed little home, a veritable brood of children, a dog...

Phoebe heard the grinding of her teeth and blinked back the tears. How many times had Charlotte proclaimed that men, at least the men worth marrying, wanted for their brides women who made the going a touch difficult, women who weren't... Phoebe closed her eyes and swallowed over the lump in her throat. Women who weren't *easy*. Women who weren't like

Flossie Dawson or Phoebe Sinclair. Women like Charlotte. Why the devil hadn't she listened?

Because I'm not Charlotte.

Something vibrant and powerful welled within her breast and filled her with a grim determination. With a confident smile playing upon her lips, she turned toward Henrietta in time to hear the woman's query.

"So, my dear Miss Sinclair," Henrietta began, lifting a self-satisfied brow over her smirk. "Have you an escort to Adelaide Prescott's annual event? It's but two weeks away. If you haven't been asked by now, well, you'd best plan on spending that evening alone at Pine Grove darning socks, hmm?"

Phoebe erupted with a delightful giggle and even managed to lay a gloved hand in an ever-so-friendly manner upon Henrietta's plump arm. "Oh, my heavens," she crooned with a soft shake of her head. "Me? Miss an annual event? Why, Mrs. Witherspoon, how frightfully simple of you to think me the type! Of course I'm attending! Why, I've been planning my gown for weeks! Oh, and the luck! Oh, darling!" With a less than gentle shove, Phoebe pushed Henrietta aside and slipped her arm through that of her tall, charming, tousled blond outlaw looming at Henrietta's back. Much to her delight, his hand covered hers upon his arm and his dark eyes glittered mischievously above the amused curve of his lips. Summoning a coy smile and a blush, she allowed her gaze to flicker confidently over an openmouthed Henrietta, wondering as she did so what the devil his name was. "Mrs. Witherspoon, Madeline, you do know my new beau, do you not?"

"Ma'am," the outlaw drawled, extending a beefy hand to Henrietta, and Phoebe all but dissolved with her relief. "Shane Morgan, ma'am, late of Laramie, Wyoming. But here to stay." His eyes found Phoebe's beneath the rim of his black hat, and a cold tremor shuddered through her. "Yes, ma'am, here to stay."

Jace set his empty glass upon the bar, responding to the barkeep's raised brows with a subtle shake of his head. He'd had plenty. A day of toil beneath a sun that baked a man's skin, back-breaking work, indeed, a belly full of roast beef and potatoes, three whiskeys, and he was more than fit for bed. As was the red-haired woman at his side, though her purpose had little to do with sleep.

"Flossie, honey," he muttered, catching her wandering hands in a viselike grip. She pouted, something she had become awfully adept at over the past week or so, since she had yet to coerce him into the sack. Not that she lacked for determination or charms. She gave him a dimpled smile, fluttered her green eyes and leaned against him such that her generous bosom, daringly revealed by the low cut of her gown, quivered against his chest, just inches from his hand. His eyes flickered over her tumbled hair, the full curve of her cheek. No, it had nothing to do with her. The problem was with him. He was obsessed, still, after seven days of shoving it all out of his mind again and again, only to have the visions loom at the most unexpected times and set his pulse hammering. Visions of tumbling, golden blond curls, of skin the color of peaches and creamy milk, of fathomless eyes and full, parted lips, of achingly full breasts, pale pink...

"Flossie, honey, I'm tired," he muttered gruffly, itching to extricate himself from her hands, which were clutching much too possessively at him. She reminded him of all the other women he'd ever known, all those outlaws' girlfriends, all the whores he'd taken to his bed and eased himself upon, only to be forgotten with the next day's sunrise. They melded in his mind like the towns, the saloons, the bawdy houses and the outlaws, all but a fading memory. Yet this gnawing in his belly, this heightening sense of disgust—no, he'd never felt *this* before, no matter the woman. For some reason he had more than an inkling the way he felt had to do with Peaches. He suddenly couldn't stomach the clinging touch, the cloying, musky smell, the feel of this woman. Or any woman, except...

Hell, he *was* possessed.

"Jacey..." Flossie mewled, running a razor-sharp fingernail over his chest, parting his faded denim shirt with an insistent hand. "Yer always tired, Jacey. C'mon, honey. How 'bout a quickie upstairs? Ye don't want me thinkin' yer one o' them queers?"

She squealed with a giggle that prickled along his spine and brought a deeper scowl to his brow. "Now, there's a thought," he muttered half to himself before sliding from the bar stool and drawing her hands to his lips. "Flossie, honey, not to-night. Sorry." He gave her what he hoped was a charming smile and headed for the back of the tavern.

"Aw, Jacey..." Her voice calling after him sliced through his mind with all the precision of a very dull knife. The twang, the high, squeaky pitch, the painfully obvious lack of education...it all grated upon him. And that was another thing. When had he become so damned particular? When had his ear grown so fond of a rich, cultured voice, a fine British accent, a voice dripping of private schools, and very old money?

He shoved open the door to the gaming room with far more force than he would have liked to display. It was too damned early to return to Pine Grove. Her lantern would still be aglow, and if he dared look, he'd be able to see her moving about through the thin curtain, or hear her husky voice. He'd be far too tempted to succumb to this obsession, to climb that trellis of morning glories and slip into her room, into her bed, to give in to a weakness that threatened his sanity at times, so powerful was its hold upon him.

He'd been wrong for the first time in his career. Not about her, for he knew she was indeed Peaches, the thief who intended to pawn all her wares and evade capture. No, he'd been wrong about himself, about his flimsy excuse for a commitment to his duty and honor and justice, a commitment that had dissolved in the face of a wet, transparent shift molding lush curves and sweeping hollows.

He'd failed. Miserably. Seven years of honest work that filled him with a sense of pride and had managed to dim the memory of that day ten years ago when he'd left Buttermilk Falls a broken, embittered young man—seven years of building a reputation as the best in the business, seven years of steadfast commitment in the face of all danger. Seven years ... and here he stood, a virtual prisoner of his obsession with a thief he should have thrown into jail two weeks ago. And he didn't know what the hell to do about it.

"Si' down, McAllister," Hawkins slurred, leering from behind his cards and gulping from his glass.

Jace complied, easing into a chair opposite Hawkins. The only other man at the small table appeared to be dozing behind his cards. At the steady drone of his breathing, Jace rubbed weary eyes. He harbored scant desire to engage in an exchange of pleasantries with an imbecile like Hawkins, much less to rob the man of what little he had left to his name.

"Where the hell is everybody?" he asked.

Hawkins belched and scratched his belly. "Today's Pithole day."

Jace stared at the vile man and couldn't resist asking, "Pithole day?"

"Yup." Hawkins belched again. "Me 'n all the local boys all ride up Titusville way with Goare once a week. He has a sick friend or sumpthin' up there in Titusville that he goes te see, ye know. But we don' want te see nobody sick, ye know. We wants te see ol' Ben Hogan in Pithole City, the wickedest man on earth. Operates a damn fine bawdy house up there in Pithole with ol' French Kate an' her soiled doves." He gave Jace a leer and a greasy wink. "If'n ye know what I mean. You can go with us next week. How 'bout it?"

"Thanks," Jace muttered wryly.

"Yup. We jes' got back. A lot o' the boys is plum wore out, but not me, nope. I's got me a real cutie today, with real big..."

"Great," Jace muttered again, rising from his chair. "I guess I'll talk to Goare tomorrow."

"Oh, I wouldn'a do that if'n I were you. Goare's, uh...well, ye know...kinda mad an'..." Hawkins licked his lips and cast a wary glance at the dozing man. Gingerly, he pulled the man's hat lower over his eyes then leaned greasy elbows upon the table and raised bleary eyes to Jace. The whiskey had obviously loosened his tongue. "Ye remember that fella from Philadelphia passed through here last week? Real fancy dresser. Big gambler. Well, it seems Goare got into the whiskey one night with this fella over a game an' the stakes got real high an'...well..."

"Goare lost."

"Lost big."

"How big?"

"The saloon."

"The *what*?"

Hawkins dissolved into a mewling, smarmy heap right before Jace's eyes. "I tol' him time an' time again not te gamble. He's got bad luck. You seen it. But he had te go play big shot an' now we's in big trouble. Not like the kinda trouble we bin in before. This is worse. Aw, the boys 'n me, we's always sayin' how Goare's got some rich friend somewhere, ye know. He always comes up with the money, ye know. But this time's different. We need te come up with the money te pay off this debt within the month or we lose the saloon.''

"You're partners?" Jace couldn't temper the note of disbelief in his voice.

"Naw, but he was promisin' me real soon we was gonna be." Hawkins licked his lips. "That's why I thought o' this plan."

"Plan?" This ought to be good.

"Yup, an' a real good one it is. We jes' need yer help."

"My help?"

"Yup." Hawkins leaned forward nearly out of his chair with eagerness. "It's a ransom plot."

Jace scowled at the weasel. "Who the hell are you going to kidnap and ransom, for God's sake?"

"Yer little English heiress, the blonde."

Jace felt the blood drain from his face. "No."

"No?" Hawkins squeaked. "Why the hell not?"

"Because..." Jace shoved a hand through his hair and glared at Hawkins. *Because she's no heiress! Because I wouldn't let you lay one slimy hand on her.* "Because her family is in England." Lame excuse, but worth a try.

Hawkins leered. "I's already thought a' that. Takes ten days te' git from England. I's figurin' on holin' up with the lady 'bout three weeks er more till the ransom comes. Ye can be in on it, McAllister. I know ye could use the money and I'll need someone handy with a gun. Jest in case, ye know. All's ye gots te do is set the lady up."

Think like an outlaw, not like an operative in love with... The thought settled with cataclysmic force upon Jace such that he almost groaned aloud. He wasn't in love with her. He wasn't.

Think like an outlaw...

He narrowed his gaze upon Hawkins and summoned a casual tone. "Let me think about it. I trust Goare knows nothing about this."

"Nope." Hawkins puffed up his scrawny chest. "I thought of it all myself. Pretty damn good plan, don' ye think, McAllister?"

"Damn good," Jace replied, even as he marveled at the man's stupidity. Stalling shouldn't prove too difficult. "We've some time to think on this. Maybe even to devise another plot. Just give me a couple weeks, eh?"

Hawkins's decayed grin twisted into a sneer. "Don' ye go stealin' my plan, McAllister."

"Hey, would I do that?" Jace swallowed his revulsion and clasped the weasel upon the shoulder. "Ease up, Hawkins." And with that, he turned on his heel and set out for Pine Grove, realizing that he now had to shadow Peaches for an altogether different set of reasons.

And somehow, it made his heart soar.

"Do you think Delilah will find us?" Jamie whispered, peering anxiously through the cloud of fragrant cherry blossoms toward the house.

"Oh, heavens no!" Phoebe replied with a giggle, adjusting herself upon the branch, her eyes riveted upon the gooseberry tart balanced precariously in her palm. "She'll look for us in the barn, and in the rhubarb patch, under the porch...the usual places. No, she'd *never* think of looking for us in a tree."

"Of course she wouldn't. I've never before climbed a tree!" Jamie's eyes, wide with the adventure of it all, met Phoebe's. His smile broadened and his cherubic face, smudged, newly freckled and aglow with delight, tugged at her heart. She'd grown enormously fond of the child, perhaps too fond. She found herself forever bristling at Madeline's manner with him, the starched clothes she chose for him, as starched and rigid as her mode of parenting, which allowed for nothing in the way of fun. Hence, Phoebe had taken it upon herself to remove the child from beneath that mourning cloud, which permeated the house and his very existence. What she hadn't anticipated was the child blooming before her eyes, and, more important, the effect this would have upon her. She reined in her wayward thoughts and drew the tart beneath her nose. "Mmm...this smells divine! Far too good to waste on tossing at some poor unsuspecting soul, eh, Jamie?"

"And it's still warm. You don't suppose we shall ruin our appetites for supper?"

A warm, fragrant breeze teased his blond ringlets, tumbling in an adorable excuse for a coiffure. "Oh, indeed! We shall both suffer tremendous bellyaches but 'twill be worth it, Jamie dear. Delilah's tarts are without match!" Phoebe nibbled at the crust and smacked her lips. "I shall gladly forgo supper."

"And I," Jamie breathed, examining his tart as if he sought the perfect spot to venture his first bite. "Today I'm not going to eat any supper. I'm going to be with Jace at the lake."

Phoebe nearly fell out of the tree. "Jace is at the lake?"

Jamie nodded vigorously and took an enormous bite, which sent a glob of gooseberries down the front of his white linen shirt. "Yep. Right at suppertime, until it gets dark. He was there last night, and I know he'll be there tonight."

Phoebe knew very well what Jace was capable of at the lake, and the thought of him and that Flossie Dawson in the clearing . . . "Is he alone?"

Jamie nodded and took another bite.

Phoebe dissolved with her relief. "What the devil does he do there all alone?"

Jamie took his sweet time chewing and chewing and chewing, until Phoebe thought she would squirm out of her bloomers with anxiety. "He's fishing."

Phoebe wrinkled her nose with distaste. "Fishing? Whatever for?"

"I don't know. Maybe he eats them. My daddy did." Jamie swallowed noisily, apparently oblivious to Phoebe's groan of disgust. "Do you fish, Phoebe?"

Phoebe gaped at him. "Heavens no! Do you?"

"Oh no, but I would love to learn with Jace, except Dearest always makes me come in and wash my hands and eat supper. I hate washing my hands. I've told Dearest that I hate washing my hands but she scrubs harder until it hurts. I've told Dearest I want to go fishing with Jace and she says I can't because he doesn't like me."

"Why on earth wouldn't he like you? You're his little brother."

"Dearest says he's mean and nasty and shoots people with guns. She says nobody likes him because he's mean and that he doesn't like nobody. She says I should stay away from him." Jamie raised fair brows at an astonished Phoebe and nodded his head for emphasis. "He might shoot me with a gun."

"Your mother told you that?"

Jamie nodded and popped the last of his tart into his mouth. "But I told her he wouldn't."

"Well, good for you! And what did she say?"

For a moment, Jamie's blond head dipped and he clutched his fingers together in his lap. "She punished me."

"For disagreeing with her."

The small head nodded vigorously. "I was a bad boy."

Tears sprang unheeded into Phoebe's eyes, tears of rage and pity and love for a little boy mistreated by an overprotective, twisted mother, a boy all but ignored by a brother he feared, longing for a daddy taken from him too soon.

Her hand found his, sticky and grimy, yet she squeezed nonetheless. "You weren't a bad boy for thinking Jace wouldn't shoot you with a gun, Jamie. You know he wouldn't do that, don't you?"

Again he nodded vigorously, then raised enormous blue eyes to hers, sending a tremor through Phoebe's soul. His bottom lip quivered with his words. "I—I'm afraid of him . . . a little, I guess. B-but when he's near, I'm not scared of anything anymore. He makes me feel safe. Like my daddy did. Even if he doesn't talk to me."

Though she knew not the answers to the child's unspoken questions, Phoebe searched for the proper words. "Jace is very busy, Jamie. Sometimes too busy," she muttered half to herself. "He's not mean and nasty, and even if he has a gun, he would never shoot little boys like you."

Jamie stared at her. "Even if I'm a bad boy?" His tiny voice sliced with deadly precision through Phoebe's heart.

She swallowed the lump in her throat and squeezed the small hands. "No, sweet Jamie. Not even if you were a bad boy all the time, which you couldn't possibly be! Jace is kind and generous and he works very hard, just like your daddy did, I'm sure. Every morning he goes off to cut down those big trees and haul off the lumber. He loves your home! It's his, as well, and he wishes the business to thrive and—"

"Dearest is going to sell the business."

Phoebe stared at the child, momentarily confused by his abrupt statement. Forcing a hollow laugh, she ruffled his curls. "Jamie, wherever would you come by such a notion?"

Twin blue saucers, wide and innocent, met her gaze. "I heard Dearest talking to a man."

"What man?"

Jamie shrugged, his eyes devouring the tart Phoebe had long since forgotten about. "Are you going to eat that?" he asked, licking his lips.

Without hesitation, Phoebe gave him the pastry. "What man was your mother talking to, Jamie?"

Jamie shrugged. "I don't know. Some man with whiskers."

Whiskers? Nearly every American man she'd met, save Jace, sported whiskers. "Do you know his name?"

Jamie shrugged again, intent upon his tart.

"And you heard your mother tell this man she intended to sell the business."

Jamie shook his head. "No, I don't think she wants to sell the business. She was crying, like she used to cry when my daddy was here, and shouting at him like she sometimes shouts at me when I'm bad. Was he a bad man?"

Phoebe chewed thoughtfully at her lip then gave him an encouraging smile. "No, Jamie, he wasn't a bad man. He and your mommy were just having an argument."

"I don't like that man."

"He's been here before?"

Jamie nodded vigorously. "He comes at night when I'm supposed to be asleep. But I stay awake sometimes and I see him . . . with my mommy. And one time he was in the kitchen with Delilah and she was crying and . . . Where are you going?"

Hoisting her skirts unceremoniously to midthigh, Phoebe turned and shinned with startling dispatch down the tree. Drawing a deep breath, she rubbed her grimy hands against her skirts and glanced up at Jamie. "To the lake."

Jamie gaped at her wide-eyed. "Are you going fishing with Jace? I want to come." He stuffed the remainder of the tart into his mouth and started down the tree.

Phoebe caught him just as he reached ground. "Oh no you don't, little goose. I believe 'tis almost suppertime and Delilah shall be looking for you. Be off with you! I promise I shall fetch you afterward and then we shall both fish."

Jamie whooped with joy and scampered to the house, where a sound scolding no doubt awaited him. The tongue-lashing Phoebe was bound to receive would have to wait. Swallowing every last ounce of her pride and squaring her shoulders determinedly, she set out toward the lake. If *she* couldn't capture Jace's attention, what she had to tell him certainly would.

Chapter Ten

At first, Jace thought it was a very large fish, a huge black bass arcing out of the placid waters to strike at some unsuspecting lure. He heard the splash and watched the ripples fluttering his line, like the poignant and familiar ripples fluttering in his belly. A damned faded and dusty feeling, it was, like all those memories of ten years past, filling him with the anticipation of a young boy on the verge of hooking his first fish. Yet he stood waist-deep in the water, alone, with no father at his side barking instructions and lending a skilled hand, his gaff hook within easy reach of Jace's catch.

Except today he had no catch, not yet, at least, which was why he alternately scowled at his lack of skill in selecting the proper spot to cast, then scampered as quickly as he could to shore, reeling in his line and tempering his excitement. He reached shore, knocking over his empty wicker creel, such was his impatience to recast just beyond the growth of brush...just beyond the enormous elm that seemed on the verge of teetering into the lake...in the exact spot where the bass had jumped.

He moved stealthily, his heart hammering, his feet squishing noisily in his boots with every step. Shoving the brush aside impatiently, he took one step into the water and froze.

It was no fish. And this pleased him far too much for a man who liked to think of himself as a sportsman. Then again, some would say women were the grandest sport of all.

She looked like a nymph, willowy and blond, created by Neptune and Aphrodite and, yes, Lucifer himself. The divine temptation rising from the depths of fathomless blue, silhouetted in all her rosy naked splendor against a lush, fragrant green landscape, arching her back and thrusting herself like the most exquisite of offerings to a setting sun. To him. *This* required no lure, no delicate casting skill, no angling intuition of any kind. This was primitive, instinctual.

Without further thought, or perhaps with but one thought, he dropped his split bamboo pole, the very best bamboo pole money could buy ten years prior, the bamboo pole that he cherished, that had brought tears of joy to his eyes on more than one occasion. With a careless flick of his wrist he dropped it and the tangle that was once his line and waded into the water toward her.

His eyes feasted on tumbling blond locks, cascading in tousled disarray the length of her slender back to sway hypnotically over the high round curves of her derriere. His mouth went bone-dry. With rapt fascination, he watched the water lapping the full, plump underside of her buttocks, then devoured the narrow sweep of her hips, the sleek length of her back. He paused, suddenly aware of the drumming in his ears as she immersed herself to her shoulders in the cool water. She rose with a breathless gasp, seemingly unaware of his presence not three quick strides behind her. Like the possessed man he most certainly was, he watched her raise slender arms to run her fingers in a most languorous manner through that golden mane. Then she turned ever so slightly, her lips curving winsomely, perhaps at some distant sound, affording him a profile that caught his breath in his throat.

His gaze flamed over the soft curve of her belly, the sweep of her ribs, to the exquisite fullness of her breasts. Pale, sun-kissed peaks thrust impudently from the swelling mounds, and he watched, mesmerized, as droplets gathered then fell unheeded from the very nipples he so wished to feel beneath his mouth. And then he must have groaned, for the sight of her thus proved too much for him to bear in silence, and she turned to him, and he drew a step nearer.

For one joyous moment he glimpsed pleasure—no, a certain satisfaction—flicker across her lovely features, only to be quickly masked behind a gasp of unmitigated horror as she raised her arms to cover herself and sank shoulder-deep into the water.

"Jace!" she breathed, blushing and flustered such as he'd never before seen her. Nor had he ever again expected her to behave thus with him. They had, after all ... in the clearing ... not a week past. So why the devil did it seem like decades since he'd held her in his arms, tasted her skin?

He swallowed thick and heavy, wondering why his legs felt like lead, *knowing* why he felt on the verge of splitting his pants at the groin. It was almost too much to bear. Her eyes flickered over him once or twice, over his naked torso, then darted about like a frightened rabbit, skimming over his hips, widening slightly, glancing away, then fastening upon his groin and widening further ... and he took another step closer.

"Peaches ..."

And then she was twittering and fluttering and waving her hands, shooing him from the water, from *her,* and by God if he wasn't complying like a fool. He found himself upon the shore with that confounded peach gown clenched in his hands, and he almost tore it to shreds, such was his torment. She bade him turn his back, which he did, again like a fool, and he listened to the soft splashing, the sounds of long, naked, female legs moving through cool lake water.

"My gown, if you please," she murmured from just over his shoulder. All he had to do was turn around.

He gazed at the crumpled satin he held, an unwelcome smile playing at one corner of his mouth. "And if I don't?"

"You are no gentleman."

"I never claimed to be." He closed his eyes and *felt* her behind him radiating a heat all her own. He imagined that she crossed her arms over her breasts, that she rose up and down on tiptoe in an impatient and spoiled manner, that her hair tumbled gloriously about her. "You're not wearing anything else."

Her answer surprised him, and he came within inches of abandoning any gentlemanly aspirations he'd ever harbored for the sake of this woman. " 'Twas so bloody hot all day, I simply chose to forsake my bloomers and chemise."

He swallowed again. *Naked. She'd been frolicking about all day entirely naked beneath her dress.*

"Now, if you would kindly allow me my dress, I've a matter I wish to discuss with you. What a coincidence to have bumped into you."

A sudden bitterness invaded his mouth and he thrust the dress at her with a force he instantly regretted despite his anger. Yet he knew not why. He knew nothing of himself with this woman. She'd preyed upon him like the most cunning of thieves, and had stolen that which he'd forever thought would belong to no woman. Perhaps that was the very reason he didn't simply tumble her upon the grass and silence any resistance with the force of his mouth.

He shoved a hand through his hair, took a step away from her, then realized his boot had become entangled in his line. Gritting his teeth, he freed the line, scooped up his pole and strode with grim determination away from her. He heard her behind him and wondered if her needs were anywhere near as *pressing* as his.

"Jace! For bloody hell's sake, a word is all I seek!"

His scowl deepened and he muttered and grunted to himself like a wounded bear. "Words, words." And then he paused and whirled upon her. "Nothing more, woman? Nothing more?"

She skidded before him, wide amber eyes peering curiously up at him, one hand clutching her parted gown over her bosom. "Just a moment of your time, is all," she murmured with a frown, as if she were nowhere near comprehension of the state in which she rendered him.

He gritted his teeth and ignored the itching of his hands to sweep hers aside to tend to those buttons. "Then speak," he growled, even as he turned about and continued on his way.

"I see all your mighty felling of timber has done little to improve your disposition," she remarked in her highbred tones, which made him want her even more. "Oh, perhaps I failed to mention that I happened upon an outlaw the other day. Perchance you know him, hmm?"

He grunted in reply, wondering what the hell she was babbling about, wondering why he had ever decided to fish today.

"Shane Morgan is his name. Late of Laramie, I believe."

Jace stopped dead in his tracks, an icy chill descending upon him. How damned easy it had been to forget who she was, *what* she was, that this was all going to come to an end one day very soon, if not by his hand, then by Pryce's or some other operative's. Yet his first thought shocked him, galled him and spurred his rage. Amidst all that had passed between them, all that had conspired to muddle his mind, to fog his brain, to render him naught but a love-smitten fool, *she* had obviously managed to retain her wits, her guile and cunning. No wonder she had proven so damned elusive for so long. He'd never met another outlaw or woman, for that matter, like her.

She knew who he was.

He closed his eyes, feeling his rage roaring in his ears. She knew. She knew about the alias in Laramie. She knew that he hadn't thrown her into jail when she'd most certainly deserved it. She knew that he had betrayed his oaths. She knew that she had him, literally, by his pants.

Or did she?

He turned toward her. Something gnawed at his conscience. Perhaps the look of utter innocence playing upon her face, the seemingly unstudied guilelessness, which he'd once thought no woman capable of. He almost couldn't bear the thought that this was all part of the facade. Good God, he'd nearly forgotten who she was.

"Shane Morgan," she said with raised brows and perfectly parted lips. "Do you know him?"

He took a chance. "Yeah," he muttered, studying her so fiercely his eyes hurt. "Yeah, I know him."

This seemed to please her, for a hint of a smile curved her lips. "I see," she breathed, and hell if he didn't glimpse a devilish twinkle in her eyes.

She was toying with him. Then again, perhaps she knew only that he'd maintained an alias, something quite unremarkable for outlaws of his notoriety.

Doubts and more doubts. Were they born from a seasoned, razor-sharp mind, a keen intelligence, a skilled operative's intuition? Or were they merely the nonsensical delusions of a love-struck half-wit? Merely excuses to prevent him from facing the truth about her...and himself?

No fool would bet on a love-struck half-wit. Not even him. He took another chance. He narrowed his eyes upon her, allowing his lips to curve ever so slightly into a wicked grin, his voice to gather the smooth drawl of one very game outlaw ever at the ready to fall in league with another. "What did you have in mind, Peaches?"

A frown scurried across her brow before she offered forth a tenuous smile. She looked as if she had no idea what the devil he meant. "What? Oh, nothing. I..." Her gaze dropped to his pole and to his empty creel and he felt his face burn with profound embarrassment. What the hell did he care if she thought he was a lousy fisherman?

He was utterly at a loss with her. And himself.

"Have you caught any fish?" she asked, turning her back to him, no doubt in order to tend to her buttons. He wondered if the question were gratuitous.

"I, uh, just started," he found himself grumbling in reply as he scowled at his tangled line. Muttering to himself, he squatted and set about untangling the damned thing, all too aware that the curve of her hip was but a handbreadth from his face.

"To my eye," she was musing, still intent upon her buttons, "the inflicting of pain on living creatures in the name of sport is naught but a bloody sacrilege."

His laugh erupted hollow and short. "My dear Peaches, it was your bloody countrymen who endeavored from the very start to make it a gentleman's sport."

She turned about, ablaze in the rosy hues of the setting sun. "Sport, ha! I'm of a mind to call it loafing."

He shook his head and studied the twisted line, yet he couldn't seem to temper the mirth in his tone. "We anglers are a contemplative lot, seeking communion with nature, nothing more. Our triumphs are not the heroic events one might well imagine but happy interludes, leisurely enjoyment of simple pleasures." He gave her a sideways glance, noting the sudden horror when her eyes fell upon his bait. "Worms," he informed her in a cheery tone that surprised even him.

"Ugh," she shuddered, averting her face and looking as if she were about to retch. "You men and your creatures. 'Tis instinctive, to be sure." She frowned at him, perplexed. "What on earth do you use them for?"

"Bait," he replied, rising agilely to his feet with that satisfied feeling one has when one untangles a particularly frightful knot. Without hesitation, he scooped a rather plump worm from the pile and dangled it inches from her prim little nose. She paled. "I simply shove the hook right through the middle..." In went the hook. "Then coil this little fellow around and through the hook again and..."

She had closed her eyes, her hand upon her breast, her throat working against the bile that rises when one is particularly disgusted. His lips parted with his smile, and for some damned reason his heart was suddenly light. Perhaps it was the day, the way the damned breeze blew, the way this woman beckoned him at every turn. He leaned toward her, his eyes upon her mouth, his free hand rising to the back of her head to press her to him.

She opened her eyes and blinked several times. In that span of a heartbeat, he was assailed by an irrational and overwhelming urge to tell her he loved her. As if she were suddenly ablaze, he spun from her, nearly treading over the fine bamboo pole he didn't seem to care a whole hell of a lot about lately. Clenching his jaw and his fists and willing his stupidity to heel, he scooped up his pole and strode into the lake.

"What are you doing?" she asked from too close behind him, even though she was on shore.

"Casting," he muttered without turning around. "And unless you'd like to be stripped bare of that damned dress, you'd better move."

She yelped and scurried away, returning once he'd cast. "Why don't you simply purchase a net?" That imperious tone had returned. "I'm quite certain you would catch far more fish with that than you will with one of those dreadful worms."

"That's not the point," he said, moving his line slowly, gently, ever so delicately through the water.

"What did you say?" she asked.

"There won't be a damned fish within a half mile of here if you don't shut up." He tossed the words over one shoulder.

"You're rather impertinent," she huffed.

"Simply determined to fish fine and far-off," he replied, oddly thankful for the diversion his line furnished.

"I can't hear you!" she all but bellowed, and he twisted about, his brow fiercely raised.

"If you plan on talking your way through the evening," he growled through his teeth, "you'd better hoist your damned skirts, woman, and get your shapely little backside into the water."

To his surprise she actually blushed, perhaps at his left-handed compliment, then did as he instructed with all the naïveté of an innocent babe. To midthigh, *bare* midthigh, she hoisted her dress, then managed to secure it there with the expertise of a woman who had spent the last several weeks climbing trees and over shrubbery and into haylofts in these damned dresses. She waded into the water, stopping at his side to peer closely at his rod and reel then gazing down the length of his line.

"For what, precisely, are you waiting?" she whispered.

"A bite."

She seemed to ponder that. She looked about, waved off a bothersome gnat, then heaved a sigh. "How long will it take?"

He had to smile. "Getting hungry?"

She gasped with a burst of indignation. "You think I eat too much!"

"Quiet," he muttered, his eyes never leaving his line.

"You're insufferable!" she rasped in a hoarse whisper.

"And you're thwarting every effort I'm making to enjoy this and . . . hell, I don't believe it." Despite her twittering, her damned shuffling about and his gross lack of concentration, he had a bite. A big bite.

He braced his legs, gave one quick jerk on the line to set the hook and started reeling, easing up, then reeling again. "Damn, he must be nine pounds."

"What?" Peaches squealed with obvious delight, something he found odd for a woman who'd proclaimed the sport a sacrilege not five minutes past. "Oh, Jace!" She hopped up and down, clutching at his arms, rubbing against his side such that he gave a good moment's thought to abandoning the fish and his rod and sweeping her into his arms. "Oh, Jace, you got one!"

"A damned trout!" He shook his head with disbelief, lifting the fish by the hook embedded in its mouth. "I thought the lake would be too warm for trout but . . . look at the size of him."

"Oh, Jace . . ." Peaches was all over the poor fish, attempting to stroke the silvery skin, peering into its gaping mouth, then raising huge pleading eyes. "Oh, Jace, the poor thing."

Jace stared at her with disbelief then hoisted the fish for good measure. "This is the biggest damned fish I've ever caught!" he bellowed. "And I'll be damned if I—"

"Let it go."

He scowled at her. "We'll build a fire and I'll fry him up for you. Trout are delicious, Peaches."

"Dear God, I couldn't *eat* the poor thing! Besides, how do you know it's a he? It could be a mother with young babies! Oh, Jace, please, let it go!"

"No."

"Oh, I can't bear it! Please, you must!"

"No." He turned and headed for shore.

"Jace! Dear God, please, for me, would you let it go?"

He paused, turning back to her, his eyes narrowing upon her. "For you, Peaches love?" He stared at her, at the cloud of blond curls and eyes that a man could lose himself in, at the dress all bunched up over her bare knees. With a helpless shake of his head, he braced the pole between his legs and grasped the fish. "For you," he muttered, removing the hook then gently placing the fish back into the lake. He watched it swim happily away then took up his pole and waded to shore.

He hadn't even reached the grassy bank before she was all over him, her arms wrapped about his neck, her lips pressing sweet, sisterly kisses all over his sun-darkened face, kisses that never came within two inches of his mouth. "Oh, Jace, thank you so! Thank you."

He didn't even hear the splash of his pole meeting water. But he heard her. The gasp and then that sweet little moan in the back of her throat when his arms swept fiercely about her and his mouth swooped over hers. He crushed her to him, mindlessly, his tongue plundering the recesses of her mouth, tasting her, and he was consumed, such was his need for what lay beneath that gown.

Capturing her tongue between his teeth, he tore her gown open, groaning at the torture of her breasts spilling against his naked chest. And then he tasted them like a man starved, tasted the lake on her skin, breathed her in and suckled her with strokes that were far from tender. Yet she arched her back, drawing him closer, and merely whimpered when he shoved the gown up around her hips and roughly grasped her buttocks for a moment before his fingers delved lower and found her, wet and wanting.

His fingers slipped easily within and out, again and again, and he felt her trembling against him, felt her fingers clutching at his waistband, felt himself full and heavy, straining against all that contained him. She gasped and rotated her hips in so slow and languid a manner that he knew a momentary insanity. And then he tore at his pants with one hand, the other still stroking with a fluid patience he hadn't known he possessed. He fumbled with his buttons and then he was free, and all he could manage for a moment was groaning and breathing like a man possessed, and she was panting and moaning, spinning higher and higher, and then she shuddered and contracted around his fingers with delicate waves and ripples that sent white-hot flame through him.

Without thought, he grasped her beneath her arms, lifting, spreading, and surged into a sheath so hot he nearly lost his mind. She cried out and clung to him, and he buried his mouth in her neck, his hands beneath her buttocks lifting her, guiding her up and down. And then he moved—how, he would never quite remember—until he was waist-deep in the water and she was almost weightless in his arms, still impaled. He guided her and then she moved of her own accord, rotating her hips, delving her fingers into his hair then brushing her lips over his, tempting and teasing.

His hand caught in the tumble of her hair, forcing her eyes to his. She wore her passion like the wanton seductress she was, all full-lipped and heavy-lidded, drawing swift little gasps of air with his every thrust.

"Do you like it, little witch?" he murmured, his gaze dropping to her breasts swelling against his chest. He gritted his teeth and stilled her hips momentarily.

"Oh, Jace . . . no . . . don't stop." Her nails dug into his back and her breasts rubbed brazenly against him, urging him.

"You learn fast," he muttered, his voice rasping upon her throat before his mouth claimed hers, ferociously, and he surged deep within her, hearing her impassioned cries until he couldn't bear it a moment longer. He thrust so deep he thought he tore her asunder, achieving his own climax, and she arched against him with a hoarse shriek that sliced into his numb conscience, instilling a mindless fear made all the worse when she dissolved in his arms and started to weep. Uncontrollably.

He felt like an oaf, a dolt, a host of boorish lummoxes, and worst of all, like an animal incapable of controlling himself.

"Oh God, Peaches," he ground out, hating himself for the man he was, for scores of reasons. He shifted her in his arms, cradling her, and made his way to shore. He felt her forehead damp with perspiration against his jaw, felt her arms around his neck, heard the soft sobs, yet his mind was filled with but one thought. "God, Peaches, I hurt you. I'm so sorry I hurt you."

She blubbered something he couldn't decipher and hiccuped and sniffed and sobbed all over again, and he sank to his knees on the grassy bank with her still nestled in his arms.

"I was too rough. I..." He closed his eyes, allowing his head to fall back, and swallowed heavily over the lump in his throat. "You make me too crazy for both of us. It won't happen again."

"Noooo!" Her wail rent the stillness of dusk and she turned in his lap, lifting tearstained cheeks and trembling lips. "No, I...I mean, it wasn't you. I..." She bit her lip and lowered her eyes. "I believe I liked it. 'Tis simply that I..." She shook her head as fresh tears sprang to her eyes. "I...I know not what the devil's wrong with me. I just want to cry."

Awash in confusion, he stared at her, at a loss for what to do, yet finding her tumbled state stirring passions he thought had cooled for at least an evening. He pulled her back into his arms and rested his cheek against her hair, then spoke the first thought that entered his mind. "Was it the fish? Is that still upsetting you? Listen, I had no intention of keeping the damned thing. He was too big. Too fat. Fish aren't good eating when they're fat."

"What?" Suddenly she reared up before him, claws bared and eyes dry. "You tricked me!"

"No, Peaches, I was just teasing and..."

"Ha!" She shoved him in the chest and stumbled to her feet, apparently unaware that her breasts were enticingly revealed by the parted bodice, that her legs were bare from midthigh to ankle. "You plotted and schemed the entire scene! You wanted me to believe you would sacrifice something for me if I asked, even a bloody fat fish!"

"Hey!" he barked, lunging to his feet and tending to his trousers with remarkable efficiency. "You want to talk about sacrifice? I'll give you sacrifice." He shoved a hand through his hair and glared long and hard at her. "What the hell's the matter with you? I won't deny that had I known the response I'd get out of you, hell, yeah, I would have somehow schemed my way into your damned dress through a fish." He couldn't help the sardonic lift of one brow. "Tell me, Peaches, do you honestly think a lummox like me would waste time scheming to get you into my bed?"

Her eyes flew wide open. "How dare you insinuate that I am but an afterthought!"

"Hardly that," he muttered, suddenly unable to keep his eyes from her bare bosom. "We bumbling oafs simply take what we want without a thought." He took a step toward her, knowing that his eyes gleamed with his every devilish thought, and reached a hand for her. "Stop looking at me like you're going to skewer me and come here."

Those amber pools simply stared and then filled again, the tears spilling to her flushed cheeks, her chin trembling. Without hesitation he moved, crushing her in his arms, murmuring soothing words in a tone he'd never thought himself capable of.

"You think I'm unbalanced," she sobbed into his chest.

"I think you're a woman."

"Ugh!" she sniffed, sounding somewhat vexed, though her hold upon him didn't lessen. "The universal answer you men cling to whenever faced with a woman you believe unbalanced. Or perhaps you believe every woman unbalanced." She shook her head, sniffed and eased slightly from him, her trembling fingers moving clumsily over the buttons of her dress. "I must get back. I promised Jamie I would take him fishing." Her eyes lifted to his and he glimpsed something more in their depths, a sudden accusatory glint. "Though he would much rather you took him."

Jace heard the gnashing of his own teeth and fought the urge to turn away, flee, the way he'd done ten years before. "I've too much to do," he muttered, turning his full attention to her buttons.

She pushed his hands aside and glared at him like no woman had ever glared at him a scant few minutes after he'd... And in a damned lake, at that. " 'Tis painfully obvious to me that you avoid the child,'' she stated boldly, looking as if she expected him to burst forth with a reason. "He's your brother.''

Jace studied her through hooded eyes, wondering why a jewel thief would even care, then drummed up a reason. "I've never been good with children.''

A pained look swept across her features so suddenly he was caught off guard. "You mean you don't want children of your own?''

He came very close to scratching his head, such was his befuddlement. "I've never given the matter much thought. Why, do you?''

"Oh my goodness, yes!'' She all but gushed the words. "*Legions* of them, or more!''

And at that moment he envisioned her with her tumbled blond brood, some scattered at her feet, others scampering about as she was wont to do and a tiny one at her breast. His chest tightened, ached with a feeling of poignant melancholy, yet he couldn't fathom why. He found himself staring at her belly, wondering what she would look like pregnant, what a swollen belly and swollen breasts would feel like, knowing how damned easy it would be to keep her in that state.

"Jace?''

His eyes snapped up, his thoughts scattering.

"Did you hear me? I said you should try to display more affection with Jamie. He's an adorable little boy. If anything, 'twould serve you well to know what goes on in that house.'' She paused, as if with sudden indecision. "Believe what you will, but I gathered from Jamie that some man with whiskers is forcing Madeline to sell off part of the business.''

"What?'' White-hot flames surged through Jace such that he didn't even pause to wonder why he believed *her*, Peaches the thief, without question. "Who is he?''

Peaches spread her hands and shook her head. "Jamie knows naught of the man other than he's come by several times and . . .''

He couldn't simply stand there a moment longer, no matter how ravishable Peaches was.

"Jace!" she called out frantically from somewhere behind him. "Jace, wait! You cannot simply barge into Madeline's house like an ox and demand..."

He spun about so quickly, with a look of such ferocity, that Peaches skidded before him with a horrified expression. "That house is mine," he ground out through teeth clenched as fiercely as the fists at his sides. "And as long as I breathe, this will all remain as it was."

He turned again, yet she clutched at his arm, her tone beseeching. "Jace, please, listen to reason! Would you *please* stop all this angry stalking about and brooding and grumbling and listen to me! Besides, I believe Madeline is in Titusville this evening and shan't return until very late, so it won't do you any good to storm in there and..."

Something clicked in Jace's mind, clicked like the hammer of a pistol, with deadly intent. He stopped midstride, spun about and gathered a startled Peaches hard against him. His lips found hers in a smacking kiss before he paused, his gaze sweeping over her widening eyes, his lips curving ever so slightly. "Peaches, love, remind me to thank you for making my day, will you?" And with a last, lingering kiss, he turned to seek Zack.

Chapter Eleven

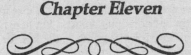

The crickets had just commenced with their evening song when Jace tethered his horse before Goare's Tavern. He adjusted his hat low over his eyes, then, almost by rote, ran his hand along his waistband, reaching for the reassurance only cold steel could provide. Except tonight he wasn't carrying his gun, and he felt too damned vulnerable of a sudden to suit himself. Hell, he should have worn his buckskin coat, despite the heat, and carried his gun and to hell with playing roles and laying pipe and all that.

Yet the role he now sought to assume had nothing to do with outlaws and beautiful blond jewel thieves. It had to do with family honor and all his unspoken grief over his father's death; of maintaining all that had meant so much to his family, and still meant to him. He gave a wistful grunt and shook his head. With Peaches at Pine Grove tucked snugly in her bed, nothing could distract him this evening.

Pushing the tavern doors wide with all the force of a man bent upon erasing his frustrations with a bottle of whiskey, he paused, his eyes darting about. Goare was having a good night, even though the business had slipped through his fingers. There wasn't a table to be had in the place. The air hung thick with smoke, unmoving, full of the raucous sounds of revelry from the men and, every so often, a high-pitched squeal from one of the few women.

Flossie Dawson perched flamboyantly at one end of the bar, looking rather stale and unkempt, as was her wont, and positively poured into a hideous red-and-black lace dress better suited to a lamp shade. He found himself studying her with a

cool, assessing and completely disinterested eye, the one he reserved for appraising horseflesh. A scant three weeks ago, a
woman like her would have struck something in him, some
spark of desire—no, far more than that, enough to make him
hoist her over one shoulder and tumble her upon some
squeaky-springed mattress in a threadbare hotel room. All it
would have taken was one inviting curve of those too puffy lips
or one jiggle of those enormous breasts. Yet here he stood, entirely unmoved except for a nagging contempt for the man he
had been three weeks prior, and even more for the man he had
become, a traitor to the only oaths and allegiances he'd ever
made, and all because of his weakness for one little thief.

He closed his eyes, willing Peaches from his mind, and when
he opened them again, they locked with Flossie's from clear
across the tavern, through hats and smoke. She smiled, scooted
off her little stool and swished and swayed her way toward him.
His heart sank deep into the pit of his stomach and bile rose in
his throat. She would smell cloying and musky and he would
gag on it.

He caught her against him, running one hand brazenly over
her hip then alongside one pendulous breast, which felt like a
mound of puffy dough. His mind recoiled yet he continued,
giving her his best devilish look and urging her toward the bar
with a muttered, "I need a drink."

She was all over him, and this drew an unusual number of
"You lucky bastard" looks from the more lewd and despicable of the male patrons, those who obviously fancied Flossie's
charms. Jace offered his hooded glare in response, keeping one
arm firmly about Flossie's waist. He ordered up two whiskeys,
drained them and ordered two more.

"Jacey, honey," Flossie crooned, her attention apparently
focused upon the vee of his shirt. "You're in some foul mood,
ain't ye?"

He grumbled like a wounded bear and gulped from his glass.
"Yeah, damned Madeline . . . no money . . ."

"Madeline?" he heard her murmur against his chest, her
tongue dancing feverishly upon his skin and making him yearn
for a bath. "There's talk 'bout you 'n Madeline."

"Is Goare around?"

She groaned and shimmied up against him, raising a pout and soundly grabbing his buttocks with both hands. "Why can't ye ever want me, Jacey, huh?"

"Oh, but I do, Flossie honey, and that's what makes the waiting worth it. Now, where's Goare? In back?"

She gave a reluctant nod and seemed to study him closely, as if weighing his response. "Can I come with you?"

He gave in, solely for the boost to the state of mind he wished to display. Thus, with a good four whiskeys dulling his senses and a hand draped casually over Flossie's shoulder such that his fingers toyed with her breast, Jace sauntered into the gaming room. And stopped short.

"An' this English heiress is stayin' at the McAllister place an'...well, doggone, if'n it ain't ol Jace hisself!" Hawkins all but tipped the poker table over, so forced was his enthusiasm to leap to his feet when his bleary eyes met with Jace's stormy glower. "An' Flossie, too. Hell, come on in."

Jace gritted his teeth against the nearly overpowering urge to level Hawkins with one sweep of his arm. What the hell was he doing blubbering on about Peaches to a damned stranger? If that little weasel still harbored some ludicrous notion about kidnapping her...

Jace's eyes narrowed upon the back of the only other man present, the man seated opposite Hawkins, the man wearing the dirty black Stetson, the black duster. A dull, angry buzzing descended upon him like a swarm of locusts over a Kansas prairie, obliterating all thought, all sensation save for the urge to summon every last ounce of strength, every last shred of vengeance, and kill. And then the man turned, and Jace looked deep into the eyes of Rudy Blades.

"Jace..." Hawkins's voice sounded as if he were trapped in a well. "Jace, this here's Shane Morgan. Late of Laramie. Maybe ye' know each other."

Shane Morgan? That was my alias! He knows! Need to think...get Pryce...notify Pinkerton's that Blades got away! No. A better idea...

Jace shoved his hand at Blades and muttered, "McAllister. Jace McAllister. I don't seem to recall us ever meeting before."

Blades remained impassive, though his handshake met Jace's strength for strength. Those black marble eyes narrowed, and Jace stared back, marveling at his utter stupidity to have left his revolver behind...and to have allowed his uncharacteristic fondness for a damned dog to make him traceable. How easy a time Blades must have enjoyed tracking him. When the hell was he going to realize emotional attachments always got him in trouble?

"Nope," Blades muttered. "Never met ye." His gaze shifted and settled long and leisurely upon Flossie, who seemed to quiver anew against Jace. No doubt she found Blades arousing. Most women did. The dark skin, the long blond hair; tall, strong, with a wicked smile and all the charm of the most savage of outlaws. He even managed chivalry, tipping his hat at Flossie with a smoothly drawled "Ma'am."

Hawkins's scrawny voice sliced through the silence, crackling like a tangible thing. "We was jes' talkin' 'bout that English girl. The one livin' at Pine Grove. Ooo-eee, that woman makes a man glad he's a man an'... Oh, sorry, Flossie." Hawkins flushed scarlet. "You's mighty purty 'n all but...that English girl, I's got it hot fer her. Maybe she's gonna need a man te take her te that highfalutin party that ol' Prescott bitch is fixin' te have."

In a scant instant the words poised upon Jace's tongue, eager to burst forth in a torrent of God knows what. Given the chance and the circumstances, Jace probably would have proclaimed his undying love for the girl, that she'd already agreed to accompany *him* to the damned ball, even though she hadn't, that "hot" wasn't exactly how he'd put it... And then Blades's voice cut with deadly accuracy into his conscience.

"The lady's comin' with me."

"Party?" Flossie squealed, tugging upon Jace's sleeve and squirming against him. "Jacey, aren't ye gonna ask me te go, too?"

"Yeah," he found himself muttering through the haze of rage and frustration engulfing him like a shroud. He barely heard her triumphant shriek, barely felt the hot smack of her lips against his cheek. "Yeah...sure." His mind filled with the enormity of it all, the implications, the motives. It was too much. Why had *his* Peaches gone and done such a thing? And where the hell had he been? Fishing . . . and making passionate love to the most deceitful, conniving and twisted of women.

"You lucky sumbitch," Hawkins muttered, clasping Blades upon the shoulder and offering a gap-toothed grin.

Blades flashed a grin that dared Jace with its arrogance. "Yep, she's somethin', all right," he drawled. His eyes, narrow and glittering devilishly, found Jace. "Yep. All round and soft and . . . ye know, gets ye thinkin' 'bout doin' all kinds a things with her. More than just holdin' her for some ransom, I'll tell ya. Let's jest say I'm lookin' forward to that party."

White-hot anger exploded behind Jace's eyes, blinding him with its ferocity. Blades was taunting him, baiting him, as if he knew damned well that had he stuck a knife in Jace's gut, the pain would have been less. And Hawkins . . . Jace almost spat, such was his revulsion and contempt for the wily yet abominably stupid little man. He shoved Flossie aside, ignoring her startled outburst, and would have lunged at Blades, so consumed was he, when a sudden realization struck him like a fist, all but driving the breath from him and stilling his movements.

Blades had followed him, but not because he knew he was a Pinkerton operative—after all, even as arrogant a bastard as Blades wouldn't purposefully seek out the law. And not because he'd known Jace had been on his tail for close to three years. No, Blades had followed him bent upon meting out his own brand of justice because Jace had slept with Blades's girl, that . . . What *was* her name? And it hadn't been only once or even twice.

Blades looked smug, all right, and confident, as if he did indeed relish the thought of Peaches beneath his callused hand. As if he, too, ruminated over the possibility of kidnapping her. And it was all directed at Jace. Revenge for the sake of some two-bit floozy. That had to be it.

Jace drew a steadying breath and slid a chair from the table, settling himself comfortably in it and pulling his hat low over his eyes. Nodding to Hawkins to shuffle the cards, he willed the whiskey-induced fog from his brain. He could hear his pulse thundering in his ears, a deafening roar, but it wasn't because he was so damned close to Blades, to meting out *his* own justice. Hell, one word to Pryce and Buttermilk Falls would be swarming with operatives, eager to ensnare the Colorado Territory's most wanted desperado. But Jace wasn't about to let them bungle it again. This time, Blades was his.

And suddenly he realized the thundering of his pulse had very little to do with exacting a three-year-old revenge, and almost everything to do with the nature of Blades's relationship with Peaches.

Jealousy was as foreign an emotion to Sterling McAllister as love. And neither sat well with him.

"How 'bout three whiskeys, Flossie," he muttered, flashing her a crooked smile that wiped away the last vestiges of her brooding little scowl. She shimmied off, jiggling in places that Blades seemed to find perversely fascinating. Jace observed his foe with a cynical eye. No doubt Blades had very little trouble rationalizing his own lack of fidelity while seeking revenge for that very crime. Outlaws, a twisted lot. Jace experienced a certain comfort knowing that of late he couldn't manage to think like one.

"So, yer in lumber, McAllister?" Blades observed without glancing up from his cards.

Jace glared for a fleeting moment at Hawkins, who appeared blissfully unaware of the bodily harm Jace would indeed do him. "Family business, though it's fallen off in the last few years."

"Jace was out West," Hawkins piped up. "A real outlaw, he is. Gunslinger an'...oh, uh, sorry Jace. I s'pose ye don' want that spread aroun' an'..."

"Never heard of ye," Blades rumbled, his glittering black eyes shifting over his cards.

Jace met his gaze. "I moved around a lot."

"The law on your tail, eh?"

Jace shrugged. "Pinkerton's."

"Pinkerton's," Blades spat, his lip curling in a feral sneer. "Goddamned bastards. I had te call off a couple jobs 'cause o' those guys." And then he laughed, low and decidedly evil, and cast Hawkins a glance that pinioned the little weasel to his seat and snuffed any and all inclination to spread this particular news about town. "Almost got me once. Came real close. But I got one o' them, instead." His mouth twisted into a self-impressed snarl that made Jace want to strangle the man.

"Some young kid, he was. All alone, thinkin' he was gonna take me himself. Stupid, too. Didn't even try te draw on me. I got him, right between the eyes."

Jace gritted his teeth, attempting to focus on his cards, his vision blurred by the memory of Aaron, his hands in the air, his head shaking, frantically... and Jace running so hard, so fast, his lungs burning with his every gulp for breath, trying to reach his friend, his own gun... and then the shot.

"They ever come close to catchin' you, Jace?" Hawkins's squeaky voice sliced into his conscience.

Jace shook his head and scowled at his cards, which slowly came into focus. "Uh, no, I... you know. Different towns, different jobs, different aliases."

Blades's upper lip twitched. "Different women."

If revenge were indeed what Blades was after, he would surely get his. Jace curved his mouth in an ever-so-satisfied manner. "Yep. Kind of makes a man wonder why he ever came home. Someday, remind me to tell you about this lusty little blonde in Laramie. She had the wickedest set of hands and the biggest..."

Blades was quick, almost too quick, but Jace, without a revolver, was even quicker, and smarter. Just as Blades's hand disappeared into his coat, his fingers reaching for cold steel and his eyes exploding with rage, Jace slipped his booted foot behind the leg of Blades's chair and tugged, hard, whisking the chair out from under Blades just as Flossie careened through the door balancing a tray laden with three whiskeys. As Flossie was a rather top-heavy girl and somewhat lacking in grace, she stumbled over Blades, sending whiskey and glasses tumbling to the floor, though most of the liquid managed to land squarely in the outlaw's face.

He sprang to his feet, agile as a cat, teeth bared, fists clenched, his vengeful glare sweeping over a dumbstruck Flossie to fix with murderous intent upon Jace. A sound not unlike a low, menacing snarl escaped Blades's twisted lips, yet he made no move toward Jace or to wipe away the whiskey trickling into his mustache, down his neck and into his open collar. Flossie, on the other hand, took it upon herself to coo and flutter around Blades, blubbering out her apologies while attempting, unsuccessfully, to dab up the liquid with the black lace hem of her gown. Jace busied his itching fists by shoving one hand into his pocket and hoisting a near-empty glass to his lips, glaring in his own dark and menacing manner at Blades. For one long moment, he thought Blades would attempt to draw on him again, Flossie and Hawkins be damned, and then a bulk filled the doorway and Goare's bellow echoed into the next room.

"What the hell . . . ? What's goin' on here?" Goare's bushy red brows drew together and he grasped Flossie by the arm. "Enough, Flossie. Get out front where you belong. Now."

With a flustered little cry and a longing glance at Jace, Flossie complied, and much to Jace's surprise, Blades followed close at her heels with nary a grunt.

"New guy in town," Jace offered, jerking his head after Blades. His gaze lingered on Goare, noting the shadow of doubt flickering across his ruddy features, the beefy hand rubbing his beard-stubbled jaw as if in thought.

"I could have sworn I've seen that guy . . ."

"He's a reg'ler outlaw, Goare," Hawkins piped up. "Shane Morgan's his name."

Goare's brows met, then swept upward, and he shrugged, obviously dismissing the idea, though Jace knew well that Goare had seen Blades before. The man's wanted posters were spread thick over every town from Philadelphia to Wichita and Blades damn well knew it. At times, arrogance in an outlaw bordered dangerously on stupidity. Then again, Blades had managed to avoid capture by Pinkerton's agents, the nation's finest, on more than one occasion. A certain amount of arrogance could be expected, though Jace was left to wonder, yet again, at the man's lack of conscience, at his insanely twisted sense of justice. He could boast of the cold-blooded murder of a defenseless man without any sign of remorse, yet risk capture and journey more than two thousand miles to avenge himself for a two-bit floozy's lack of devotion. No doubt that boded disaster for any outlaw's reputation, especially for a guy like Blades, who thought himself well above the law, well above Pinkerton's . . . a man living up to the legend. Jace had to wonder what had become of that girl in Laramie.

"So, McAllister, how's yer luck?" Goare's eyes suddenly narrowed upon Jace as if he studied him awfully close. Too close, as had been his wont of late. His tone, too, was curt and testy, as if Jace's mere presence struck some discordant note in Goare. During the past several weeks, Jace had, on more than one occasion, attributed Goare's foul mood, the lingering stares and a bristling manner barely held in check, to his financial distress. Now Jace knew better. It was the money, all right, but so much more indeed, though Jace had but an inkling. Enough, however, to sufficiently dim Jace's fond memories of Goare working as head hand for Carson McAllister all those years, even during the war, when Goare had remained behind, unable to enlist due to some childhood ailment that left him nearly blind in one eye.

Jace scowled, tipping his hat back upon his head and slouching in his chair. "Luck?" He erupted with a caustic grunt. "Damned work from sunup to sundown. Madeline can barely pay me enough to live on. Yeah, I could use some luck, though I was thinking..." He shot Hawkins a curious look and fingered his glass. "Tell me more about this Pithole day...."

"We've got a problem."

"We?" Pryce chuckled and recrossed one boot over the other upon his desk, then leaned back in his chair and puffed on his cigar like a man content. He gestured to an empty chair and chuckled again when Jace stalked about, offering naught but a grunt and a glower in reply. Pryce waved his cigar. "My friend, the world is a mighty fine place when you're a man in love. Ah, Charlotte. The name alone ..."

Jace stared at his friend, his hands on his hips. "God, look at you."

Pryce grinned from ear to ear. "Yep. And I feel good, too. Sit down, man, you're making me nervous."

Jace closed his eyes and shook his head. "My oldest friend is a lovesick pup. What the hell am I doing here?"

"Maybe you were about to file a report on Peaches. You *are* on a mission, remember?" A mischievous twinkle lit Pryce's dark eyes. "If you don't, they may start wondering what the hell you're doing with the girl."

Jace scowled and rubbed a hand over his weary eyes. "Listen to me, lover boy. There will be a hell of a lot more to report if Hawkins doesn't shut the hell up."

"Hawkins? What's he got to do with your Peaches?"

Jace gritted his teeth. "She's not *my* anything, Pryce. Goare's in financial trouble and Hawkins cooked up some flimsy scheme to kidnap Peaches and hold her for ransom."

Pryce's brow knit with thought. "Not bad for scum like Hawkins. Her father is supposedly one of the wealthiest men in England. Owns that shipping conglomerate..."

Jace couldn't temper his disbelief. "I don't believe it. Lovesick *and* gullible. You've been listening to Charlotte's lovely British voice for too long, my friend. You're starting to believe her. For all you know, she could be in on it with Peaches."

Pryce's feet found the floor with a solid thump. "The hell she is!"

"Damn it, man! Peaches is no heiress! She's a goddamned thief!" *Heiresses don't pawn their jewels, my friend!*

"You're the only one who seems to think so."

"I'm the only one around here with any sense!" With a disgusted snort, Jace resumed his pacing about the dimly lit office. "She's good, I'll give her that. Very good. In fact, almost too good." He paused, contemplating the wall of floor-to-ceiling bookshelves bulging with law books. His gaze found the framed diploma on the wall opposite. Harvard Law School. Pryce had far more than an operative's intuition behind him. And Jace had...what? A lumber business fallen into disrepair, Madeline, Jamie and bookshelves full of sour memories. When he spoke, the sneer in his tone surprised even him. "But I'll be damned if I'll be deceived by a woman."

"Then again, it might not be so bad. Think about it. After all, you *are* in love with her."

Jace swung about, his fists clenched at his sides. "The hell I am!" he bellowed. "You and your damned smug looks...get the hell out of here, Pryce."

Pryce looked as if he tempered a smirk. "You're in my office, remember?"

"So I am," muttered Jace.

"Sit down, Jace."

"The hell I will," he grumbled, taking several paces about, then indeed settling himself in the straight-backed wooden chair. He yanked his hat from his head and shoved a hand through his hair. "What have I become to seek advice from a love-smitten fool like yourself, Pryce?"

"You could start by inviting her to the Prescott ball."

Jace studied his hat, the hat he all but crushed in his hands beneath the force of a rage held tightly in check. "She's already managed to find herself an escort."

"Who?"

Jace shrugged. "Some guy. I don't know him."

Pryce let out a low, smooth whistle. "You lost your chance, buddy. Then again, maybe you're losing your touch."

"What the hell are you talking about? I don't have to take the girl to a damned dance to shadow her, do I?"

"It'd make it a hell of a lot more enjoyable." Pryce lifted a wicked brow. "A little spiked punch, a little stroll in the garden beneath a midsummer moon could make a man forget he's with a thief."

"You're besotted."

"Indeed, I am." Pryce's whimsical sigh oozed contentment and grated mercilessly upon Jace's nerves. "So, you're going anyway, eh?"

Jace gave a purposefully curt, almost imperceptible nod and rose from the chair. He knew his friend well enough to anticipate his next question. "It's too damned late to be sitting around here with a love-struck half-wit."

"So, who is she?"

"I'll see you." Jace got only halfway to the door.

"Jace, damn it, who are you taking?"

"Flossie Dawson, that's who!" Jace barked, feeling an uncharacteristic heat climbing up his neck when Pryce threw back his head and roared with laughter. "Shut the hell up, Pryce."

"Hey...wait, Jace." Pryce covered his mouth then coughed in an attempt to muffle his chuckles. He moved around his desk and clasped Jace upon the shoulder. "Sorry, buddy. That Flossie..." Pryce shook his head and grinned wickedly. "She'll make a great cover. And about Hawkins..."

Jace's eyes met his friend's. "If it comes down to it, I'm going to tell him the truth."

"You're what?"

Jace donned his hat and pulled it low over his eyes. "Maybe an idiot like Hawkins will believe me." And with that, he spun on his booted heel and strode purposefully from Pryce's office.

"Phoebe, you're looking for trouble." Charlotte's voice rang with the same thwack of finality as the slamming of the barn door in their wake.

Lengthening her stride, Phoebe flashed a saucy grin and patted Zack's sleek neck. "My dear Charlotte, I have deemed it high time to forsake trouble and adventure for a man. A glorious, magnificent..."

"Oh, spare me," Charlotte groaned, drawing a wheezing breath as she hastened after Phoebe. With a tremendous huff, she hoisted her heavy muslin gown with one hand and draped the other over her glistening brow. "I've got news for you. All that's glorious and magnificent shan't be too pleased when he discovers you've been dallying with his horse all day, every day while he's out felling trees and...ugh!" Charlotte skidded to a breathless halt, closed her eyes and gulped with revulsion.

"Watch your step," Phoebe breezed airily, casting a smirk at the pile of dung not one pace in front of Charlotte.

"I can't bear it," Charlotte moaned, delicately lifting her skirts and picking her way around the manure. "Blasted animals...ruining my shoes...too bloody hot for anyone."

"Cease your jabbering and resume your post, Charlotte. I plucked you from the jaws of all that mindless needlework for a reason, remember? You're my scout. Look smart." Phoebe's eyes purposefully avoided her friend's ominous glower and swept to the dirt road leading from Pine Grove and the distant sloping horizon. "He'll be coming soon. I just know it."

Pushing the paddock door wide, Charlotte grumbled and swatted at a pesky fly. "He's going to string you up and quarter you."

Phoebe grimaced. "Oh, hush, Charlotte. You're beginning to sound very much like a grouchy old shrew. What sort of wife will you make for your beau, Dalton Pryce, hmm?" She shook her head with mock disgust and looped the reins about Zack's neck, idly rubbing his seeking nose. "You'd best lean on the fence there, Charlotte, lest you swoon dead away at the mere mention of his name. Tell me, has he managed to kiss you yet?"

Charlotte flushed scarlet and averted her cheeks with a breathy, "Oh, Phoebe!" to which Phoebe could only heave a sigh. "I certainly hope he's tried, for heaven's sake. A girl should know what she's getting."

"Phoebe! The man hasn't even proposed!"

"Charlotte, you're too much of a bloody prig for your own good." She raised self-important brows. "How the devil will you know if you like it? Loosen up a bit. 'Twill do you worlds of good. Trust me."

"*Me* listen to *you*? Ha! Strange, isn't it, that you feel compelled to orchestrate some blasted scene in the hopes of ensnaring all that's glorious and magnificent, while I simply perch upon yonder porch..." Charlotte waved an airy hand, indicating the veranda, where Madeline sat, as was her wont, immobile, staring into the dry, dusty heat of late afternoon, rocking mindlessly in her creaky chair. Phoebe had more than a notion that that dull gaze settled upon the paddock from time to time. "Dalton calls every evening just after supper. Six o'clock sharp. *Every day.*" Charlotte flashed her own grin. "And I do naught but sip my lemonade and flutter my lashes."

Phoebe snorted, smoothing her starched white blouse into her bicycle britches, then patting her tummy. "Jace McAllister is a different breed from your Dalton Pryce, Charlotte, requiring more than simply posing prettily...though you do that awfully well, mind you. 'Tis just that with Jace, a girl must employ a certain skill..."

"Foolishness."

"And cunning..."

"Childish game playing."

"A coquettish flare and..." And then she heard it. The distant rumbling of wagon wheels churning upon cobblestones, the sounds of the men returning from a day's work, the same sound that had, for many days past, sent her fleeing into the barn hauling a mutinous Zack, lest she be discovered. Only today it was indeed her intent to be discovered, and more, by Jace, a shirtless, hatless, bronzed and glorious Jace, who would leap from that blasted wagon and rescue her before all those rough-and-tumble lumbermen, before Madeline... Phoebe's heart leapt into her throat. So relentlessly had she drummed the trick into Zack over the past week, she harbored not the slightest doubt in her ability to carry it off. Then again, one couldn't be too sure.

"Oh, dear God, here he comes! How do I look?" With trembling hands, Phoebe smoothed her britches and tugged at her coiffure, a tumbled excuse indeed, though one she had spent hours torturing into a studied disarray, which, to her eye, looked positively wanton.

"Your hair is a mess," Charlotte graciously remarked.

Phoebe scowled, sucked in her tummy and thrust out her bosom.

"And your britches are awfully...why, they're positively taut. And with those silk stockings it's all rather...revealing."

"Precisely."

Charlotte's discerning eyes settled upon Phoebe's bodice a trifle too intently, her dark brows meeting in a look of utter befuddlement. "Why, Phoebe, if I didn't know better, I would think I could see your...through your blouse. But surely you've at least a shift on under that or something." Her dark eyes flew wide and she erupted with a gasp of utter horror. "Phoebe, no!"

Phoebe couldn't resist the wicked curve of her lips. "Oh yes, Charlotte."

Charlotte gulped and clutched one hand to her breast. "You're evil."

"No, you goose, I'm smart and I know my man. Besides, 'tis so bloody hot and I was wondering what it would feel like...you know." The sultry tone invaded her voice, the tone that paled Charlotte's skin beneath her rosy glow and widened those enormous dark eyes. "You see, Charlotte, the feel of the cotton against my...well, it makes them thrust."

"No!" Charlotte shrieked, clasping trembling hands over her mouth as if that would still Phoebe's tongue. "Oh, dear God, to think I have put my fate in your hands! I am doomed!"

"No you're not, silly," Phoebe quipped, agilely mounting Zack and grasping the reins in a firm, practiced hand. "You're in love. Just like me. Now be off with you...no, not that way! My, but you are all atumble about this." Phoebe had to smile as her friend spun about exactly three times before hightailing it to the house. "You might want to try it, Charlotte! Your Dalton would love it, I would think!"

In reply, she received naught but a terrified wail as Charlotte scurried up the steps of the veranda and through the front door without looking back. Phoebe's gaze settled for a moment upon Madeline, who had risen from her chair to perch at the steps, her attention riveted by the wagon rumbling down the long drive. To Phoebe's eye, one hand seemed to clutch as painfully to her chest as the other gripped the banister. And then Madeline's gaze locked with Phoebe's...a long, even stare, and Phoebe raised her chin a notch before swinging Zack's head about and gently nudging him into an easy lope that took them around one side of the barn and out of sight of the drive.

Her thoughts did not linger long upon Madeline for the wagon had reached the circular drive, so close now she could hear the men, and she knew that once she swung Zack about and around the barn they would be able to see her. Her pulse thundered gloriously in her ears, her skin tingled with excitement, her mind filled with thoughts of Jace, and she barely felt the splash of the first raindrops upon her skin, barely noticed the roiling mass of blue-black clouds stealthily advancing from the west.

With a throaty "Giddup!" she dug her heels into Zack's flanks.

Chapter Twelve

Zack was a fast horse, suddenly too fast. The wind blurred her vision, or maybe the rain was to blame. Rain? Yet somehow Phoebe knew they'd rounded the barn ... at breakneck speed. Odd, in all the times they'd practiced the stunt, Zack had never responded quite as ardently. They must have reached the middle of the paddock ... it was difficult to tell ... everything was a blur.

As she'd practiced, she hauled back on the reins, so hard the wet leather sliced across her palms. Her legs braced in the stirrups, just as she'd done countless times over the past several days, then surged upward, spurring Zack again. He should have skidded to a halt, then reared up on his hind legs and dramatically pawed the air while she did her best to slide ever so gracefully from his back, wearing a thoroughly terrified expression, and fall in a very rescuable heap. This was not, however, what the crazed animal chose to do. A mind-numbing terror engulfed her at the precise instant jagged lightning sliced through the air, momentarily blinding her. And then came the thunder ... a tremendous crackle and a horrific boom, sending a shudder through her. A piercing scream rent the air, whether it was she or Zack, she knew not, for she suddenly clung with all her might to that pumping neck, her vision blurred by the sting of an ebony mane, her tears and the rain, as the stallion pitched and weaved, bucked and stumbled, then bolted. Her belly flipped into her throat and they were airborne, the muffled thud of hooves upon parched earth but an echo in her mind. They landed lopsided and she nearly fell over the stallion's neck, crying out hoarsely as the reins were torn painfully from her grasp, all but yanking her arms from their sockets, yet she managed to retain her seat by clutching at the thick mane. And then she knew naught but the merciless drumming of hooves beneath her, of torrential rain and brilliant, blinding flashes, of deafening thunder and the acrid taste of raw terror in her mouth.

The steed's horror-filled wheezing matched the thundering of her pulse, the pounding of his hooves, and she clung low over his neck, murmuring as much to herself as to the blasted animal. His pace intensified and she grew dimly aware that the crazed stallion navigated an erratic path through thick brush then open field, where the lightning engulfed them, and Zack screamed and plunged headlong into dense woods. As if from outside herself she moved, straining for the reins, which dangled uselessly just beyond her tremulous reach. She cried out with frustration, with terror, with pain at the sting of branches, and rough bark biting into her flesh. Her tears mingled with the rain and she thought of Jace . . . and how ironic to need his aid so very much now.

And then she felt it, slippery leather in her grasp, and she lunged forward, half out of the stirrups, and hauled back with every last vestige of her strength. And he slowed, perhaps because of the density of the brush or from sheer exhaustion. Phoebe collapsed over his neck and sobbed with relief, willing logic to triumph over her fear. She tasted blood and realized she must have bitten her lips at some point. Logic . . . rational thought. They were so very far from the house, they had to be, and Zack was naught but delirium temporarily under control.

And then she heard the thrashing of brush, the muffled thuds of horse's hooves fast approaching, and Jace calling her Peaches. Her heart soared and she swung Zack's head about, perhaps a bit too fast, her reply poised upon her lips. At that instant the world exploded before her eyes with a deafening roar and she was falling, slowly, hypnotically, landing once upon the softest of cool beds, and she marveled, as if in a hazy dream, at her stupidity. Then pain seared her skull and all was dark.

The tree literally exploded before Jace's eyes, such was the accuracy of that lone bolt of lightning. The air crackled and hissed, his skin crawled with the electricity, yet he cared naught except to reach her. Without thought, he dismounted and plunged through the brush, offering barely a murmur to Zack, who danced about in a skittish frenzy and showed the terrified whites of his eyes. To his knees he dropped beside her, into the swollen mound of grass on which she lay, flat on her back, and he instinctively reached for her wrist. His trembling didn't surprise him, his vision blurred, and he nearly cried out, so great was his relief at the insistent thumping in that delicate wrist. His hands moved over her arms, gently probing, then down her legs, so long and slender, saved from splintering by this uncommon tuft of wild grass that cradled her as if she were a wee babe. Jace cupped her face, his thumbs tracing over delicate jawline, high cheekbones eerily pale in the dim flashes of lightning. She was so still, her eyes closed. He cradled her head, his fingers probing through her hair. No blood, though the sizable lump forming at the back of her skull attested to a sound crack against some gnarled tree branch. She'd have one hell of a headache . . . he hoped nothing more.

His chest tightened, gripped by a sudden overwhelming pain, and his vision clouded again. Without thought, he swept her fiercely into his arms, pausing to press his lips to her temple, to breathe in her scent, to feel her warmth, perhaps to ease the grip fear had upon his very soul. He buried his face in her neck, only dimly aware that he muttered unintelligibly against her skin that the rain had begun to fall again as if poured from the sky, and he tasted the rain and salty tears, felt the water seeping into his skin, and drew ragged breaths. And then lightning splintered the air again and Zack screamed, a piercing sound followed by the thrashing of hooves through tangled brush, which faded beneath the roar of the shower.

The thought that his steed could quite possibly be lost to him caused Jace but a moment's pause. Rising to his feet, he cradled her close against him and set out through the brush.

Smooth, warm skin beneath her fingertips. The sinewed curve of shoulder. The flexing of a powerful arm. His scent, clean, woodsy, enveloping her. A heartbeat, insistent and strong beneath the furred chest pressed close to her ear. Hands, callused and huge, stroking along her back, over her shoulders, into her hair. Lips pressing against her forehead, her cheek... Then she heard his voice and she moved. Though her head was so heavy and all remained dark, yet her mouth tilted and sought.

His lips played upon hers, languorously, as if tasting of her for the first time, and her world spun crazily until the pain sliced through her, startling her to full awareness with a groan.

She buried her face in his chest and willed the ringing from her ears. His voice, resonant and deep, soothed her, though his words remained obscure. Opening her eyes proved far less painful than she expected, though focusing through the damp tangle of her hair seemed momentarily beyond her realm. She was very much aware, however, that she lay nestled in Jace's arms, that he sat upon some rough wooden floor, leaning against some rough wooden wall, in a dank and musty excuse for a dwelling. The air was thick, the light meager, and the insistent drumming upon the roof served as a grim reminder that the storm still raged.

Her joints rebelled as she shifted ever so slightly to nestle closer against him, and she reveled in the untested strength of the arms encircling her. Hers managed to loop themselves around his neck, her fingers delving into his damp hair, and she sighed, then winced, as pain shot like quicksilver through her skull.

"Why were you running away?"

Her eyes flew open and one hand found his bearded jaw. "I wasn't."

His hands stilled about her waist, all but spanning it, then began to move, slowly, in a rather torturous manner, up and down her rib cage. Flames shot to her core and she thought she would go out of her mind with longing if the pain didn't kill her first. "Come now, Peaches, the time for pretense has long gone," he murmured into her hair. "You were nearly killed out there. Another two paces and you would have gone up in flames with the tree."

She shuddered and grew very much aware of the dull ache at the back of her skull, a constant throbbing despite the intermittent flashes of pain. "I think I hit my head," she managed to slur, attempting to push herself up against him. And then he lifted her, settling her such that her breasts were flattened high against his chest, and their eyes met.

He looked haggard, his hair tousled, his beard-stubbled face taut, and she longed to ease the permanent crease between his brows, to soothe whatever plagued him, whatever it was that tortured those smoldering sapphire eyes. Her fingers traced over one dark brow, only to be soundly encased in an unrelenting grip.

"Where were you planning to go?" he muttered, his eyes narrowing to slits. "You wouldn't have gotten far on a stolen horse, not even close to Kansas."

Frowning was pure agony yet Phoebe somehow managed it. "What the devil are you talking about? Perhaps 'twas you who received the knock on the head."

This seemed to irritate him, for he scowled at her, though he made no move to set her from him, his arm wrapped like a steel band about her waist. She, of course, harbored not the slightest urge to leave this cozy spot, though she bristled, headache and all, at his manner and the grip he had upon her hand.

"So tell me, Peaches, why the hell were you on my horse? I didn't know you rode."

Phoebe lifted her chin a notch. "I'll have you know my father keeps a stable from which I've had many a mount to choose since before I could walk." For one very fleeting moment, she considered telling him the truth... that it was all a ruse, a ploy for him. "I simply wished to teach him a trick."

"He knows many."

"He didn't know this one." She met his raised brow with her own. "'Twas relatively simple, you see, getting him to rear."

"Rear?" He glowered at her as if he wished to do her bodily harm. "Damn it, woman! I've spent the last five years trying to get that animal to keep all four feet on the ground and you were teaching him to rear?"

"He was becoming rather good at it."

"Oh, for God's sake."

"I suppose you would have had me ask your permission."

"I would."

"To ride some dumb beast who shies at a few raindrops? I've never heard of such a thing!"

"He's afraid of storms!" he bellowed, his arm tightening like a vise.

Phoebe could only stare at him. "Why the devil would an outlaw want a horse like that?"

His gaze darted away then fixed relentlessly upon her. "I got him cheap."

"I would certainly hope so." And then she erupted with a gasp when he crushed her against him, almost painfully, as if he were consumed by far more than frustration.

"Listen to me, you spoiled little..." The words hissed between clenched teeth, momentarily shocking Phoebe with their ferocity yet stoking her ire just the same. "You know nothing about loyalty and bonds, do you, Peaches, about drifters with no home and a horse with a damned quirk that had him fated for nothing but fodder. Well, I do." His voice rumbled deep and ominous and sent a shudder through her. "That 'dumb beast' saved my life once...three years ago." He glanced away again, and a flicker of something softened his brow and swelled the lump lodged in Phoebe's throat. "It was because of a storm then, too." His tone deepened, lost a whit of its cutting edge, as if he immersed himself in some memory, and Phoebe held her breath lest she break the spell he wove. "He spooked and I wasn't ready. Hell, I didn't even know why I'd picked him up so cheap...until that day. Before I realized, I was sitting in tumbleweed and Zack was nowhere to be found. I went to look for him and..." He drew a ragged breath. "Aaron, my...friend, went on ahead and was ambushed by a..." The scowl descended upon his heavy brow and Phoebe experienced a fleeting disappointment at his hardening visage amidst her horror at the tale he told. "He was alone. By the time I got close enough, they'd just finished him off."

Phoebe thought he shrugged with that forced nonchalance men employ when they seek to conceal some deeper feeling. Yet she glimpsed so much more, the pain in his eyes, the stoic, ever-so-tough set of his jaw. Her outlaw, a tortured soul. Thus, despite his callous words, the brooding manner she found so infuriating yet so blastedly alluring all the same, she surged against him, wrapping her arms fiercely about his neck and cradling his head to her bosom. For one awful moment she thought he would resist, suffering some untimely attack of male ego, and then he crushed her to him and she nearly sobbed with relief.

"I'm sorry, Jace," she managed in a tight voice, mindlessly stroking his hair, feeling the crisp strands curling through her fingers. "I'm positively dreadful at times...speak without thought..." And then, as if with a will all their own, her palms slid over his shoulders, kneading the back of his neck and lower, where the muscles knotted and bunched. "I'm sorry," she whispered into his hair, inhaling his scent, knowing he couldn't possibly hear her. "Dear Jace..." Her whispers were barely audible to her own ears. "I love y..."

"Peaches..." His voice rasped against her skin, his hands moving, sliding over her hips then cupping her buttocks. "You've made my life a damned mess."

A faint smile curved her lips. How this pleased her. Never had she been so supremely overjoyed at rendering a man's life a bloody mess! She closed her eyes, willing the moment to expand and fill all time. Forever she would feel his breath upon her skin, his hands lying possessively upon her, as if she were his for all eternity, feel the vibrant beating of his heart against hers. Never had she so wanted to simply wallow in the feel of a man against her, as if she would breathe him in...

He, however, was of a soundly different mind of a sudden.

He moved and she uttered a gasp when his hands swiftly cupped her breasts, his thumbs brushing over the peaks straining against the damp cloth of her shirt.

"Peaches..." He eased away from her, and she had to close her eyes with profound chagrin when his gaze flamed over her bosom, no doubt brazenly revealed through the sodden garment. "What do you want of me? I'm only a man." He drew her nearer with a whisper of pressure against the small of her back, until his mouth poised over one thrusting peak, and Phoebe knew she would die of this sweet agony. "You frolic about in a half-dressed state, somehow managing to keep yourself just the slightest bit damp..." His mouth closed over one nipple and tugged, gently, and she surrendered to it all, sagging against him. "You don't wear anything under your clothes, which are all too damned tight, anyway." His eyes found hers, and he looked almost tortured. "Do you realize what you do to me? I can't think..." Unheeded, his fingers moved with certain skill over the buttons of her shirt and then cool air assailed her bosom, but only for a fleeting moment.

And then his mouth was upon her heated flesh, gently nibbling, suckling her with tender strokes that nearly brought tears to her eyes. Oh, how she wanted him . . . in ways she'd never before dreamed of.

"You're too damned sexy." His voice rose above the din mounting in her ears, his hands like firebrands upon her pulsing skin, stroking with a tenderness she'd never expected in him, with a leisure perhaps born of their circumstances. After all, the storm could rage for hours.

Her head swam from far more than a sound crack and she released a ragged breath when callused palms slid over her waist, his thumbs exploring the sweeping valley between her ribs.

She swayed toward him, clinging to his shoulders, luxuriating in the sensations coursing through her as his mouth worked its magic. His hands spanned her waist and he lifted her almost entirely from the floor, such was the strength in his arms, and his mouth branded the tender undersides of her breasts, her ribs, before he settled her soundly astride him.

The contact, even through at least two layers of damp clothing, sent a tremor of embarrassment shuddering through her, such that she pressed her forehead against his chest in a meek attempt at retrieving her wits. He wouldn't have any of it.

"Shyness doesn't become you, Peaches," he rasped, his hands stroking the sides of her breasts, pressing them, molding them wantonly to his chest.

Surrender was so easy . . . perhaps *she* was. Blast, she knew she was, and cared naught. She lifted her eyes and found his mouth hovering but a scant breath from hers. "Jace," she whispered, and his lips brushed like thistledown over hers. "This is too much for me. I . . . I cannot bear it."

He drew a ragged breath and pressed his lips to her forehead. "Don't even try to understand it. Somehow I think it's beyond our control."

She gulped past a parched throat. "'Tis all I am able to think of. 'Tis all we do when we're together."

"We still don't do it enough," he murmured, nuzzling her neck, her collarbone, the high curves of her bosom.

"'Tis an affliction."

"You're not half as afflicted as I." He raised eyes of the deepest, smoky blue, tortured eyes, yet his lips curved ever so slightly. "And you're complaining?"

She swallowed again, her gaze riveted upon his muscled expanse of chest, the smooth dark hair covering him then disappearing into his waistband and lower, where he strained against his trousers. The bulge she felt against her. He had possessed her. Indeed, this was more than love. Something entirely unexpected, and far too powerful.

"I want to know you," she murmured, her palms moving unhurriedly over his ribs, caressing lean sinew and muscle corded upon muscle. "I want to know everything about you."

"You know me well enough." His voice sounded hoarse, as if he spoke from the depths of a parched throat. He grasped her buttocks and guided her pelvis, sliding her up and down the length of that swollen shaft.

She bit her lip to stifle the gasp, her eyes locking with his, their words left unspoken, such was their understanding of this mutual need. Any yearnings to know more of this man, to discover all the emotional scars, the haunting memories—for there must be legions of them—were banished beneath the flame of desire curling deep in her belly. Later...she could learn all the rest later, for they had so much time.

His hands buried in her hair, pulled her mouth close, and his teeth caught at her bottom lip. "I want a bed," he muttered hoarsely against her parted lips. "A soft bed where I can lay you down."

She shuddered against him, her limbs aquiver with delight. A bed...so simple a request.

His fingers eased open the clasp of her britches and she felt warm hands caressing her belly. "A very large bed...so I can make love to you all day...all night."

"Will we sleep?" she breathed, her mind filled with the image his words inspired.

"A little..." Her britches slipped past her hips.

"Will we eat?" Their eyes locked, and with as much derring-do as she could muster, she trailed a finger down his ridged belly to the top of his trousers. She licked her lips and ran her finger down the entire length of his manhood through that one layer of faded denim. "I'm a woman of lusty appetites, you know."

"That's what I love about you," he growled. And then, before she could retrieve her soaring heart, for it had indeed taken flight at the mere mention of the word *love,* he swept her beneath him with a savage growl, shedding his trousers with an agility upon which she chose not to ponder.

He crushed her beneath him, pressing her mercilessly into whatever was rough and wooden and no doubt filthy upon that floor, his hips poised above hers, his mouth a breath from hers. "All day...all night. Maybe then you'd keep away from other men...men who aren't any good for you. Ah, Peaches...always so ready for me."

He had but slipped inside her, filling her the way she yearned to be filled, when she heard it, the muffled yet unmistakable clopping of horses' hooves upon rain-soaked earth, riders' shouts slicing through the still that follows a violent storm. And then Jace was above her, his fingers stroking the damp tendrils from her cheeks.

"You know I don't care if they find us." He buried himself in her and his lips brushed over hers with infinite tenderness. "The whole damned town could march through that door."

Possessed, adventuresome, splendidly in love but certainly not without conscience. Was he? "Jace...Jace, please..." She wriggled for all of a moment, then stiffened when Madeline's voice rang shrilly just outside the door.

"Check in here! Jace knows of this place, Mr. Pryce. It was a tenant's house at one time."

Before Phoebe could draw a breath, Jace uttered a muffled curse and sprang from her, unceremoniously hauling her to her feet. He shoved a hand through his hair and glanced about, retrieving her clothes and thrusting them at her with a sweep of his eyes that spoke volumes of his frustration. With two sharp tugs, he donned his trousers, then lent a practiced hand in repairing Phoebe's disheveled state.

"It doesn't matter," she whispered, willing the trembling from her limbs, the painful longing that still burned deep within her. "They'll know...dear God, they'll know when they look at us."

"I think they already know," he muttered dryly, catching her to him, and she was left to wonder if he meant to kiss her or perhaps say something that would render her a heap of melted butter, because at that moment the door burst open and a rain-soaked Dalton Pryce skidded through the portal.

"Jace!" he boomed, then grinned like a devil and doffed his water-logged excuse for a hat from atop his head. "Miss Sinclair. Well, what a surprise to find you both. The luck!"

Fingering her hair self-consciously, Phoebe ventured a wavering smile and cast Jace a sideways glance, startled by the ferocious scowl he directed at their rescuer.

"Bad timing, eh?" Pryce quipped cheerily, raising a wicked brow at Jace as they moved past him.

Though she heard Jace growl under his breath, Phoebe shot Pryce a frigid look despite the heat of her sudden flush, pursed her passion-swollen lips and strode from the shack and past an icy Madeline with head held high.

Even in the shadows cast by a lone candle, he could see that the ceiling needed paint. Hell, the entire place was crumbling in disrepair around him and all he could think about, all he could envision as he lay upon his crude mattress, begging for sleep, was Peaches, the self-proclaimed embodiment of refinement and centuries of fine English breeding, his Peaches, prone and passionate upon a filthy floor in a rank and dreary shack in the middle of the woods.

That, more than anything that had come to pass, proved beyond a shadow of a doubt that she had never been, nor could she ever be, a fine English miss, an heiress to some damned fortune, a woman who knew well the purpose of undergarments, the daughter of some shipping magnate who kept a stable of horses for her leisure.

He closed his eyes for the hundredth time and willed the tension from his jaw, the searing flame from lapping at his loins. He could never allow himself to believe any well-bred woman capable of such an unbridled passion, a raw sensuality just begging to be stoked and tamed. God, but he ached for her, thief or not, and she was certainly that, for only those women with little or no inhibition, no respect for right and wrong, could so wantonly lose themselves to all that was raw and primitive, could so brazenly, so impudently hunger for it and keep *him* hungering all the more, even afterward.

The night air hung heavily despite the afternoon's storm, yet he knew the sweat upon his brow had far more to do with the flame engulfing him, that hot, all-consuming need to have her... just once more... before Blades got to her, before she escaped, and God only knew, he'd let her go. Then again, he could go with her.

He shot out of the bed and rubbed a shaking hand over his eyes. What the hell had she done to him? Had he, even for a moment, considered giving it all up, everything worthwhile in his life, his career, even a crumbling heap of stone and a poor excuse for a lumber business, all of it, for one woman? And a scheming, deceitful, wanted woman, at that?

He sat upon the bed, cradling his head in his hands, and studied the uneven plank floor between his bare feet. The hell he would give it up. Lusty to a fault he might be, but never weak, never emotional, though he'd made a mockery of that when he'd told her about Aaron. What the hell had prompted him to do that? He should have been warning her about Blades. He should have been filling her delicate little ear with tales so grisly, so unconscionable she would have flung herself in a teary-eyed heap into his arms, begging him to protect her, begging him...

Or perhaps she would have found it all too interesting, too much of a temptation. He knew her well enough. Notoriety and sordid reputations set the girl's blood churning in her veins, those amber eyes glittering, her delectable little body squirming in all those reams of taffeta. And for one chilling moment he wondered if perhaps her attraction for him stemmed almost entirely from his trumped-up excuse for an alias. No...

Yet she'd taken up with Blades. Why hadn't he warned her?

"Because she's a damned foolish woman," he grumbled aloud. "Because she'd think you were some jealous fool— which you are—or she'd wonder why the hell one notorious outlaw would find another particularly dangerous... and then you'd be awfully tempted to tell her who the hell you really are." He stared at the low flame of the candle upon the table beside him. "And then she'd flee, because you're the embodiment of justice and upstanding values and she wants no part of that in her bed. You'd lose Blades—again—and she'd flee from you, and you'd..." He closed his eyes. "You'd follow her, you dumb bastard."

He released his breath in a rush and hung his head. Affliction? Hell, a life sentence, that's what it was. What the hell else could it be? Certainly not... To hell with Pryce and all his damned notions. Pryce needed to bed a woman, fast, to cure his ailment.

And he...he needed Peaches.

The stillness of the night loomed around him, the moonlight illuminating his path as he moved stealthily toward the main house, around the back, to the trellis of morning glories. With an agility honed by long days wielding an ax, he climbed the trellis and paused at her darkened window. A faint smile curved his lips when he found the window partially open. Silently he slid the window up and slipped into the room. It took him but two strides to reach the bed and shed his trousers, and then he slipped beneath cool, white sheets and reached for her, that sylph, that warm, fragrant, naked woman. She turned, half-rising, uttering a confused and sleepy little moan, and he swept her beneath him, capturing her parted lips with his.

"Oh, Jace," she murmured dreamily, her slender arms slipping around his neck. With wanton intent, she rubbed her breasts against him and parted her legs with but the softest of sighs. "Are you a dream?"

"I'm real," he murmured into skin and hair and woman he could never get enough of.

"Oh, Jace..." She molded herself to his hands, his mouth, his hips, and breathed and moaned as if still in a dreamlike state. "Jace...I love you so."

His breath caught and he stared at her, at the delicate beauty beneath the light of a midsummer moon, the whimsical smile curving her lips, the lashes resting upon the smooth cheek. This would all be some dusky dream, unfathomable to her tomorrow.

His thumbs traced over high cheekbones, caressed the sweep of her delicate jaw, and the words caught in his throat. "Peaches love, why do I need you so?"

His question went unanswered, for she drew his mouth to hers and lifted her hips, seeking, urging.

By morning's first light, he'd discovered that the bed upon which he slept and made love to Peaches was a very large bed, indeed.

Chapter Thirteen

The embroidered linen handkerchief swept again over Phoebe's brow, then lower over her temple, before she drew it to her lips and found her teeth tugging mindlessly at it. She sat upon her dressing table stool, swathed in her white cambric wrapper, and gazed from her bedroom window at Jace below in the paddock, saddling his mutinous stallion, that same stallion who had managed to find his way back to the stable after the storm not six days prior.

Jace moved about with a fluid, pantherlike gait, his muscular legs snugly encased in faded denims that hugged lean hips and flexing buttocks. His shirt, of the same faded denim, stretched taut across his back, over the high, muscled plains of his chest. He'd gotten more muscular over the course of the past several weeks, from days spent wielding an ax and hauling felled timber, and Phoebe knew well the feel of sun-baked sinew beneath her seeking fingertips, of finely tempered steel pressing unabashedly against soft, supple breasts. Her belly fluttered with a flurry of butterflies and suddenly the world spun before her eyes—again, blast it—so light-headed was she.

The heat. And lack of sleep. A wave of sensual delight coursed through her, and slowly her world refocused and her bed loomed in the mirror before her. There, upon those tumbled sheets still warm from the night, Jace had made love to her ceaselessly for the last six nights, the hours dissolving beneath a haunting yellow moon, the memories dusky, each night blending with the next... and the next. His lovemaking was skillful, tender, mindlessly passionate and unrelenting. Like a phantom lover, he slipped into her room even before Delilah or

Madeline doused the last candle in the rooms below, magnificent in his daring, consumed by his desire. And she welcomed him, supple and pliant beneath his hand until the first eerie gray of morning invaded their dusky cocoon. He left her then, with a lingering kiss warm upon her lips, with the brand of his body, his mouth, his tongue, upon her...everywhere. Only then, for a few swift hours, did she find a dreamless sleep.

She loved him with a recklessness never before known to her, the words themselves whispering through her mind like ghostly mists lifting from the moors of England. Perhaps she even uttered them, she knew naught. He rarely spoke, save for those passionate murmurs in the deep of night, words that threatened to drive her very sanity from her. How he teased and tormented, gave and received, then gave more...and more, until he'd delved where none had gone before, effortlessly exposing her vulnerable soul, which she would have given him, had he but asked.

She watched him spur Zack and disappear down the dusty cobblestone drive. Strange, how he took Zack today instead of riding along with the other men as was his wont. He would work all day. And tonight, again, tonight he would come to her. She closed her eyes and the liquid flame bubbled low in her belly, stirring her, and her breasts throbbed with the memory of his bearded skin, the nipples swelling against the cool linen...

"Phoebe, for heaven's sake, are you ill?"

Clutching the dressing table with both hands, Phoebe drew quick gasps and shook her head. Such dizziness...and she was suddenly sweating. "No, Charlotte. 'Twill pass. It always does. 'Tis the heat."

"The heat?" Charlotte appeared beside her, concern etched upon her brow. "'Tis a cool morning, Phoebe. And you've never been one to boast of a delicate constitution. Perhaps you've some ailment. Too much of Delilah's gooseberry tarts, I'd wager."

Phoebe blanched and drew the hankie to her trembling lips. She cast her friend a sidelong glance and wondered if she looked half as ravished as she felt. If so, Charlotte would know Jace had left her bed not a scant half hour past. Ailment? Ha! It was love, and it had possessed her. "In all truth, I haven't been indulging of late. Delilah's food has suddenly taken on a rather offensive odor, and I cannot bring myself to eating it, but, dear God, don't tell the poor woman.''

Charlotte clucked and smoothed the tumbled mass of blond ringlets over Phoebe's shoulder. ''You're ill, there's little doubting it. Blast, but I was so looking forward to us going to Titusville with Madeline today.''

''We are?''

''We *were*. I thought we could do a little shopping, you know, something new and wonderful for the Prescott affair. You're still going with that Shane fellow, aren't you?''

Phoebe closed her eyes and stifled a groan. ''Oh…him. Yes, yes I am.''

''Then you'll want something special and… What am I saying? We haven't a farthing between us.'' Charlotte seemed to contemplate this.

Phoebe drew the hankie over the pulse beating at the base of her throat. ''We could browse.''

''Indeed, we could.''

''Or we could barter some of our jewels.''

''What? You *are* suffering from heatstroke. Well, it doesn't matter now. You're ill. Go to bed. Blast, but I summoned every last whit of my courage to ask Madeline if we could join her. You know, she journeys all that distance to visit her sick relative every week. She's so very kind, don't you think?''

''You're afraid of her.''

Charlotte tucked her chin under and drew herself up. ''You'd better believe I am. And you should be, too.'' Charlotte all but wagged a finger. ''She could toss us out on our ears without a moment's notice and what the devil would we do then?'' She clutched a hand to her breast. ''Dalton would be lost to me.''

Phoebe scowled and bent closer to the mirror. She pinched her sallow cheeks, grimaced anew and took a brush to her tumbling hair with something less than a vigorous stroke. ''She won't.''

''You sound so bloody certain.''

''That's because I am, Charlotte. She won't toss us out because Jace won't let her.'' With skilled fingers, Phoebe swept her hair high to the back of her head, securing the locks with a fashionable comb and allowing artless curls to tumble down her back. "I'd wager she'd do just about anything for Jace."

"For an outlaw?" Charlotte gave a hollow, disbelieving laugh and peered from the window. "Why the devil would she?"

"Because she's in love with him, you goose." Ignoring Charlotte's huge intake of breath and her flustered, "She what?" Phoebe moved to her armoire and flung the doors wide. With a quick, discerning eye, she selected a high-necked, pale peach silk sheath, replete with swag upon swag of ruffles caught just below the bustle and extending the entire length of the train. It fit her like a second skin, *and* she had the perfect hat, the perfect shoes to match, and even a bloody parasol. If she timed it properly, Jace would achieve a wondrous peach eyeful upon returning from his day of toil. She shed her wrapper in a heap at her feet.

Charlotte's second gasp rent the air. "Phoebe, have you no shame? You're naked!"

Phoebe couldn't resist a soft smile as she tugged her shift over her head. "Charlotte, I seek not to embarrass or offend you. We *are* both women, are we not? 'Tis high time you get comfortable with your body."

"If I had a body like yours, perhaps I would." Charlotte settled upon the dressing table stool, studied her primly clasped hands, then lifted a wistful expression. "You've breasts the size of overgrown melons, hips that curve where they should, a derriere that requires no bustle. You're perfect. And I'm..."

"Perfect, too." Drawing her silk stockings to midthigh, Phoebe pursed her lips and frowned sternly at her friend. "Surely your Dalton tells you this?"

Charlotte flushed the exact shade of the red rose upon Phoebe's dressing table. "I...I...he does, but he doesn't know...I mean...he hasn't seen..."

"You're a goose, Charlotte." Phoebe scowled at her corset and left it in the bottom of her armoire. Stepping into the dress, she eased it up over her hips and thrust her arms through the sleeves. "The man has told you in how many different languages that he's in love with you. And you love him, as well, don't you?"

Charlotte looked as if she were about to swoon. "Oh, yes."

Phoebe's fingers flew over the tiny pearl buttons adorning the front of her gown. "I suppose you think that once the man glimpses what you conceal so fervently within your gown, he'll want nothing more to do with you, eh?"

Charlotte gulped and looked horrified.

"Has it ever occurred to you that a man's eye is capable of all but seeing through a blasted dress, if he so chooses? And I'd wager your Dalton has chosen, dear Charlotte, on more than one occasion to grace your lovely, willowy form from head to toe and back again. He knows well what size your breasts are, knows that your waist is lithe and supple, knows that you move like a graceful willow beneath a gentle wind. So stop your mooning." Phoebe plucked her feathered hat from a nearby chair and adjusted it fashionably low over her forehead. "I'd wager you've got the poor man as close to apoplexy as a suitor could be. He must want you desperately." Phoebe couldn't resist a shiver of delight as she sifted through the contents of her jewelry box. She fastened pearl-and-diamond teardrops at her ears and, unbeknownst to Charlotte, tucked several other weighty pieces into her pocket. "Ooh, Charlotte, give in, girl! If not for your sake, then for poor Dalton's. Now." Flashing her reflection a self-satisfied smile, Phoebe hoisted a stricken Charlotte from her chair and linked her arm through her friend's. "Shall we? Madeline awaits."

The moment Hawkins and his buddies disappeared up the creaky stairs of Ben Hogan's establishment, their respective fallen angels in tow, Jace extricated himself from the whore's clinging arms with a muttered apology, nodded to a lingering and rather weathered-looking French Kate and strode purposefully from the place. The smell alone was enough to make him gag. Why the hell Hawkins felt so compelled to visit the place... Not one of the women looked the slightest bit clean, much less palatable. Desperate men.

Then again, they didn't spend their nights with Peaches.

He made his way along the crowded, makeshift sidewalk toward his horse, the air about him heavy with the rank smell of oil from the wells littering the countryside the entire five-mile stretch to Titusville. Indeed, it seemed as if the town had sprung up and burgeoned overnight, fast on the heels of the discovery of oil in the hills. Oil . . . the sole reason Pithole City even existed. Jace knew Ben Hogan's bawdy house whores weren't the reason.

He untethered Zack and swiftly mounted, spurring the steed with a grunted command and reining his head about in the direction of Titusville. If his mount would have of it, he'd reach the city not long after Goare and his wagon, now empty of the dozen or so eager young men soundly clasped to quivering bosoms in every room French Kate had to spare. Goare hadn't lingered. He had a sick friend to see in Titusville.

Perhaps his "friend" and Madeline's "sick relative" were the same individual. Jace had more than a notion no such individual existed.

He settled Zack into a comfortable pace and allowed his thoughts a moment to roam. And roam they did to the memory of peach-toned limbs swathed in tumbled white sheets, of honey-blond curls cascading over the pillows, over him, of trembling thighs and impassioned little whispers. Hell, he should have been bending his brain to the tortuous task of unlocking Goare and Madeline's little secret, which he hoped was something more than a sordid liaison. How long had it been going on? Months? Years? Ten years? Madeline had never been anything but a whore, and he, Jace, her fool.

He scowled and flung those thoughts aside in favor of Peaches. Never had he behaved so foolishly, so recklessly, so without conscience, so damned lustily, at an astronomical risk to his own life, and it hadn't been only once. Or twice. And he'd do it again, fool that he was. Never had a woman so mindlessly enslaved him to his own raging desires. Never had a winsome smile, a hesitant stroke of delicate fingers, an innocent gaze ever set him instantly ablaze as if he were the driest timber. He had wanted her in ways he had never before dreamed he would want a woman, and he had had her, again and again, and still he wanted more. Her soul . . . he wanted that which she had preyed upon and stolen from him, and would continue to steal with every sweet thrust of her hips.

She'd made a mockery of his life.

There were times, during the long days beneath a scorching sun, his every muscle burning from lifting an ax, when he thought he hated her more than he hated himself. Hell, he had every reason. Hadn't he vowed never again to be made a fool of at the hands of a woman? Yet every night, just after dusk, his pulse pounded incessantly in his ears despite his physical exhaustion. His blood fired in his veins despite his every wish that it wouldn't, and his desire was so fierce, he thought he would go mad. And earlier and earlier each evening, he'd climb that trellis, slip into her bed, into her warmth, and let her make a damned fool out of him again.

It was madness. It had to stop.

And then he saw it. Goare's wagon parked directly before Titusville's finest hotel. Fool's luck, to be sure.

He guided Zack down a narrow alley and tethered him behind the hotel. Pulling his hat low over his eyes, he sauntered along the wooden sidewalk, tipping his hat to the ladies as they sashayed past. Hawkins and Company would do a hell of a lot better in Titusville, but Goare wouldn't abide by that.

He entered the hotel and paused, allowing his eyes to grow accustomed to the dim lighting. It was a posh establishment, with gilt chandeliers and a curved oak balustrade adorning the sweeping, red-carpeted stairs leading to the rooms above. The ceilings were high, the moldings polished oak, the furniture an overstuffed, gaudy mixture of red and gold. A hotel well suited to a woman of Madeline's tastes. A fitting locale for sordid affairs.

His mouth twisted wryly and he cast another quick glance about. Only a few lingering patrons, but no Goare. Shoving his hat back upon his head, he approached an enormous oak desk, behind which perched a tiny, silver-haired woman who eyed him keenly above her spectacles. He felt her long, cool assessment, found himself growing acutely uncomfortable, and by God if he didn't sweep his hat from his head and shove a hand through his hair. He flashed her a smile and felt like a school kid called to discipline before his teacher. A discriminating woman, no doubt. The clientele had to be right.

Her gaze released him and she reached for a leather-bound book. "A room, mister?"

"Not today. I'm just passing through." His brows drew together in a puzzled frown and he indicated Goare's wagon through the lace curtains. "I saw that wagon, the one with the red wheels, and I thought to myself, 'No, it couldn't be.'" His eyes found hers, dull and coolly assessing, and he grinned. "I used to know a fella that owned a wagon just like that one. He was from around these parts but I lost touch with him over the years. I thought, on a whim, of course, if it was him, what a hell of a surprise, eh?"

He eyed her closely and she eyed him back, her lips pressed into a thin, unyielding line. She was tough. He drew a breath. "A tall fella, big, bushy red hair and mustache. Name was..." Jace hesitated for a fleeting moment, knowing the chances were slim that Goare would use his real name, yet this old woman wouldn't even budge to breathe. The silence grew unbearable. "Gideon," he blurted as if he'd had a difficult time remembering.

For one painful moment she stared at him, then her wrinkled old face broke into a gap-toothed grin. "Mr. John Gideon, all right. Do you know him? A fine man. A mighty fine man."

Jace chuckled and shook his head with no small measure of relief at his lucky guess. "Doesn't that beat all?"

"Should I tell him you're here, Mr.—"

"Sterling, and, uh, no." Jace leaned slightly over the desk and gave her a wicked wink that brought the color flooding to her parchmentlike cheeks and a twinkle to her lackluster eyes. "I'd rather be one hell of a surprise. Maybe you could tell me which room he's in."

Her hesitation was so fleeting he thought he'd imagined it. "Two-thirteen, though I wouldn't go expectin' a hero's welcome." She shook her silvery head. "Poor man. But fine, I tell you. And his sister, too. Arrived just 'fore he did. Mighty fine folk."

"Of course, his sister, Miss . . ."

"Oh, she's married now. Sutton's her name. Madeline Sutton. Comes all the way from Clarion County, she does. Alone, God bless her heart, every week for goin' on two months now, and he from somewhere out East." She cast a furtive glance about and spoke in hushed tones. "It's the matter of the other sister."

Jace couldn't help but raise his brows. "The *other* sister, you say?"

The old woman tapped her forefinger against her temple. "Touched, or so they say, and livin' out at the sanitarium. Ever since that ol' rat of a husband of hers went off an' left her with ten kids an'..."

Jace listened with half an ear, knowing damned well how easy a cover like that had been to come by. Gossip, especially about a woman driven mad by a philandering husband and ten children, abounded in a city the size of Titusville. The women no doubt whispered about it in shops and markets, the men loose-tongued when well into their cups.

"An' Madeline took all ten of the kids..."

No one would dare question such devotion, such self-sacrifice. And then something moved out of the corner of Jace's eye, so fleeting yet so palpable he felt his blood surge. His eyes darted from window to window and back, and then he saw it, or perhaps felt it, the shimmy of a peach bustle and the bob of a peach feather moving into and out of his vision as she passed before the hotel windows.

He shoved his hat onto his head and raised a devilish brow at the old woman. "Well, what do you know? My wife's finished shopping already. Is this my lucky day or what? I'll be back, and not a word to Mr. Gideon, eh?"

The woman nodded and looked awfully pleased to harbor his secret. Jace tipped his hat and strode determinedly from the hotel, pausing only to assure himself that the bustle and the feather indeed belonged to Peaches. This required but one lingering sweep of his eyes. Only she looked like that from the rear, her hair a wild tumble down her back, her dress so damned tight he knew by looking she didn't wear a corset. Not that she needed to, by any means. Good God, but the way her hips moved aroused every primitive male instinct he'd ever possessed, and he found himself glowering at each and every male above the age of thirteen who ogled her unabashedly as she swept by. And by God if the little chit didn't sashay along as if entirely unaware of the confusion she left in her wake. Entirely unaware, as well, that Jace followed not ten paces behind. What the hell was she doing here?

His eyes flickered over Charlotte, as willowy and dark and elegant as Peaches was lush and blond and sexy. He watched his cousin, studying her movements, fluid, graceful, yet with an innocence and naiveté that Peaches probably hadn't known since childhood. With a sudden unwavering conviction, he knew Charlotte was no thief. Pryce would get his girl, after all. Happily ever after and all that.

They parted, Charlotte wandering into a millinery and Peaches continuing for several paces then pausing, drawing one peach-gloved finger to her lip as if in indecision. And then she turned. And Jace all but dived into the milliner's simply to avoid detection.

He knew a tremendous relief when she darted across the cobblestone thoroughfare, weaving with some expertise through a crisscross confusion of wagons and buggies and even a stagecoach. He followed, achieving something less than her startling success when his foot managed to find itself beneath a passing wagon wheel and several rather feral-looking fellows astride rather feral-looking horses filled his ear with as colorful talk as he'd heard since leaving Laramie.

Upon reaching the relative safety of the sidewalk, he paused, his eyes seeking her. She'd disappeared. Gritting his teeth against the frustration burning in his chest and the pain throbbing in his foot, he took two paces and skidded to a halt beneath a large, rather squeaky sign swaying in the hot breeze. He stared at it, his blood running cold for one fleeting moment before his anger burst within him, a fiery tempest that would not be denied.

Pete's Pawnshop.

He closed his eyes. She wasn't in there. She wasn't... He turned, his eyes straining through the thin-curtained glass door. She was.

Fire exploded before his eyes and he gripped the twin doorknobs as if he would tear them from the wood. Wasn't enduring this once in a lifetime enough? Would he again have to admit his weakness, his cowardice, for it was indeed that, his flagrant inability to do his damned job because of an obsession that held him ruthlessly in its talons? Sleeping with a known criminal was something he'd managed to justify. But how could he justify *again* his careless shirking of his oaths, his damned duty, everything Aaron had believed in and died for?

Someone tapped him on the shoulder and he spun about expecting anyone, Goare even, but not that weasel Hawkins.

"Ha! I found ya!" Hawkins leered at him through long, oily strands of hair.

Darting a quick glance at Peaches, still poised before the counter, Jace tempered his scowl and cocked a brow. "That you did. Had enough of women and whiskey already? C'mon, Hawkins, I thought you'd be there until midnight, a stallion like you."

Hawkins shuffled his feet and dipped his head. "Naw, I'm ... ya know, kinda ... quick."

"Ah, the efficient type."

Hawkins looked as if he liked the sound of that. "Yeah, real efficient, like. I came downstairs an' ol' Kate said ya'd took off Titusville way. How come?"

In spite of himself, Jace's eyes flickered again over Hawkins's shoulder to the female form fishing something out of her pocket. Hawkins spun about and all but flattened his greasy nose against the glass.

"Ooo-eee, lookee here! We gots us an heiress!"

Jace gripped the man by the shoulder and jerked him about. "Hey, now wait a minute ..."

"You ol' dog." Hawkins's fist glanced off Jace's shoulder in a familiar, friendly gesture that made Jace's skin crawl. "Why didn't ya tell me ya wanted in on it?" As if struck by a sudden thought, Hawkins suddenly squinted and leaned close to grace Jace with the fetid stench of his breath. "Ya weren't thinkin' of nabbin' her on yer own, were ya?"

Jace gnashed his teeth. "I think you're confused."

Hawkins drew himself up with a hissing breath. "What, ya think I'm stupid, don't ya?"

"Confused," Jace muttered, his gaze finding Peaches. "I'm going to let you in on a little secret, Hawkins. And I don't think you ought to spread this one around." Jace assumed his most menacing tone and glared icily at the little man. "If you do, I think I might have to cut off your ..." His eyes dipped to Hawkins's groin area. It helped immensely that his reputation was so damned vile, for Hawkins's Adam's apple bobbed as uncontrollably as his head. "Good," Jace muttered. He leaned close to Hawkins, his voice low. "She's not an heiress. She's a jewel thief. And at this moment she's pawning some of her take."

Again, Hawkins spun about and flattened his nose against the glass. "Well, I'll be. A damned jewel thief."

Jace grunted in reply.

"So what the hell are *you* doin' here?"

Jace's lips curved in a lopsided grin. "Hawkins, I'm losing faith in you, buddy. I would have thought you were one step ahead of me."

Hawkins stared at him a moment, then, with mouth partially agape, began to nod ever so slowly. "Oh . . . yeah. You were . . ."

"Tailing her."

"Yeah . . . tailing her. Why?"

"C'mon, Hawkins. Use your damned noodle."

Hawkins scowled and scratched his head, then displayed his atrocious lack of dental hygiene in a foul, gap-toothed smile. "Yer gonna get in on the take."

"And you're going to help me."

"I am?"

"Hawkins, who the hell do you think gave me the idea?" He clasped the offensive little man on the shoulder and drew him farther down the sidewalk. "I need you to get the hell out of here and fast."

"You do?"

"Hell, yes. If Peaches . . ."

"Peaches?" Hawkins gaped at him. "That's her name?"

Jace nodded. The name rolled like honey over his tongue. "Peaches St. Clair. If she sees you here, she may get spooked. You know thieves, they're generally a skittish lot, and a female thief doubly so. Trust me, Hawkins. I'll take care of it."

Jace watched Hawkins hightail it down the street. Something prickled the hair along the back of his neck, something that felt too much like a warning. He would usually bet on these feelings. Perhaps he shouldn't have told Hawkins about Peaches. God knows it was a risky thing to do. Then again, the thought of a share of a jewel thief's spoils should keep Hawkins's tongue in check. It had better. Jace was counting on it.

Phoebe had but taken two dainty steps from the pawnshop, a self-satisfied smile on her lips, when her arm was ensnared in a viselike grip and someone very tall and dark pressed solidly against her back and propelled her down the sidewalk. She stumbled and shoved an elbow into her captor's side, which elicited a grunt, a familiar grunt, and she wrenched her head about for some glimpse of the man's face. She froze.

"Jace!" Confusion surged through her, tempered only by her unabashed joy. "Jace...what...? Let go. You're hurting me!"

"Surprised to see me?" he snarled, his grip upon her only tightening. Indeed, he seemed intent upon lifting her clear of her feet as they stumbled along the sidewalk, drawing something more than curious stares from passersby.

She twisted and hissed, dislodging her hat and half of her coiffure. "What the bloody hell is the matter with you?" she shrieked, her temper flaring, suddenly beyond control. This...this beast was not *her* Jace, the man who came to her night after night. She locked her knees, attempting to plant her feet, only to stumble anew. "You beast! Release me! How dare you exercise your male whims upon me, you clod...you..."

"Hell and damnation," she heard him growl as he attempted to entrap her swinging fists. "Maybe this will shut you the hell up."

And then her feet left the ground and she was spun, turned in his powerful arms and hauled rather unceremoniously around a corner and into a shadowed, deserted alley. She sputtered, her limbs flailing, only to be driven roughly against the side of some wooden structure. Her head snapped against the wall at her back with a dull thud, yet she was only dimly aware of this, for the uncompromising length of straining male thighs pinioned her to the wall. She hadn't even a moment to gasp for breath when his mouth crushed hers, sweeping like fire over a parched plain, his tongue plundering, his chest flattening her breasts beneath him. She whimpered deep in her throat and clung, her palms moving over his back then lower, to the high-muscled curve of buttock. He murmured something against her mouth and shoved her harder against the wall with the insistent pressure of his hips. He was going to take her here, beneath the midday sun, in some dusty alley...and, by God, she'd let him.

"Thieving little witch," he rasped against her ear, his hands roving over her hips, claiming her breasts with bold strokes. "This is madness and it has to st— Oh God."

With an impudence even she'd never known, Phoebe flattened her palms against his belly, then, without pause, delved between them to gently cup that which swelled and strained for release against his denim trousers. She whispered lusty and wicked murmurings in his ear, and then suddenly he uttered a growl and clasped her seeking hand in his iron grip.

"Witch," he growled, his eyes a blazing sapphire tempest, the lines around his mouth etched and deep. "You've driven me mad . . . and it's going to stop."

She blinked at him with confusion, her heart sinking into the very pit of her belly, her traitorous body swelling and molding against him despite the cutting edge to his words. She knew a sudden horror. "Jace . . . no . . ."

His jaw tightened, his manner so ferocious she nearly shrank from him. Yet his eyes grazed her mouth, pouty and trembling just inches from his, and the scowl furrowing his sable brows seemed tortured. "What the hell are you doing here?"

She drew a gasping breath. "I came with Madeline. She's visiting her friend. Jace!"

And then he turned, and for a moment she thought he'd abandoned her . . . flushed and panting and wanting, slouched against some bloody wooden building. But he'd grasped her hand soundly in his and yanked her along behind him. She stumbled once, clutching at her poor hat, and hurried to keep pace with him.

"Damned foolish woman," he grumbled under his breath, his mouth unyielding. "I'll have to keep you with me just to keep you out of the damned jail."

Phoebe glowered at him. "Jace, you speak in riddles."

"Save it for some poor sot in Boston, Peaches," he growled, yanking her hand again. "You'd do well to remember I'm no fool. Just don't push me."

She bit her lip against the flurry of outrage that poised instantly upon her tongue and settled with grumbling and wondering what foul brew he'd recently imbibed as he hauled her across the cobblestone thoroughfare without the slightest hesitation. She gritted her teeth against the tears that suddenly threatened at the thought of his careless words, his cruel proclamation that it was going to stop . . . all without warning or explanation.

Yet had she ever been able, even during their most passion-ate moments, to completely dismiss her deepest fears that this would all come to some dreadful end? That he would indeed utter those very words, in that same clipped and cutting tone, with that same harsh glint in his eyes? Why now? Why not years from now? A hundred would do quite nicely.

And then she saw it. A hotel. A rather fine-looking hotel, no doubt brimming with big brass beds and fluffy pillows.

With a lightening heart, she ran her palm the entire length of his muscled arm and drew it close against the side of her bosom. She slanted him a beguiling look beneath a dark fringe of lashes and he merely scowled at her, yet kept his arm firmly against her. To bloody hell with proclamations. One sloe-eyed glance, a few lingering sweeps of her fingertips, and the man had succumbed. When was she going to realize that she'd in-deed ensnared him? She had little reason to doubt.

A soft smile teased her lips and she linked her arm through his, then blissfully accompanied him into the hotel.

Chapter Fourteen

Jace paused just inside the hotel and slipped one arm about Phoebe's waist, drawing her close against his side. Her every fiber tingled with anticipation and her eyes rose to his chiseled profile, ominous and shadowed by his blasted hat. Her brows quivered. When the devil was he going to learn to take the bloody thing off?

She pressed her palm against his belly, her fingers splaying over taut denim, softly caressing, until his hand captured hers and flattened it against his heart. And then he moved, drawing her toward the tiny old woman behind the massive desk. Phoebe felt a flush stain her cheeks despite the seductive lure of those beds upstairs and the enigmatic man at her side, a man with whom all propriety dictated she not venture into hotels...or brass beds.

"Mr. Sterling." The crone nodded at Jace and Phoebe's heart plummeted to her toes. Dear God, the woman knew him! He'd marched through yon door with easy women before!

"And this must be your wife."

Phoebe blinked and snapped her mouth shut with a decided click. Something about that word...*wife*...brought a rosy flush to her cheeks and a bubbling warmth to her soul. Blast it all, but that's what she wanted! To be his wife, his mate, to awaken with him, to sleep next to him, to linger all bloody day in bed with him. To bear his children...to belong to him.

Thus, she found it awfully easy to melt all over him when he flashed a grin and drawled, "Yep."

Yep?? Phoebe's smile grew forced and she ventured a wary glance up at him. He grinned from ear to ear like a devil and looked years younger, as if he were unaware that his voice sounded a trifle uneducated, lacking every last ounce of its rich resonance, the smooth, undulating tone that set her blood churning in her veins. He was up to something.

He leaned one brawny forearm on the desk. "I was wonderin', do you have any rooms available?"

Again, Phoebe's heart took flight. Whatever he was up to, she liked it.

The crone gave Phoebe a knowing, crooked little smile and disappeared beneath the desk, rummaging and mumbling and affording Phoebe every opportunity to snuggle closer against tall and lean, laying her cheek upon his chest. Liquid heat weighted her limbs when his hand caressed her backbone, gently pressing her closer, and she trembled against him, lush softness against poised steel. She lifted her eyes to his, her lips parting, only to encounter a visage so chilling and fierce her blood momentarily ran cold. His eyes, like an icy blue ocean flecked with blue-black shards, sliced through her soul.

"Two-fourteen, perhaps," he muttered to the old woman, though his eyes never left Phoebe's. Actually, they did, dropping to her mouth and her tongue sliding slowly over her full, pouty bottom lip. His arm flexed and crushed her almost painfully against a rock-hard thigh. And then he leaned toward her, his mouth hovering not a breath from hers. "You don't know when to stop, do you, my little wanton."

"Yup. Here it is." The crone appeared from beneath the desk and triumphantly waved a large brass key. "Two-fourteen. Right next to two-thirteen, your friend Mr. Gideon's room."

"Good," Jace muttered. "Perhaps we'll stay on tonight, though . . ."

His hesitation sent Phoebe's heart plummeting to the pit of her belly. He frowned and rubbed his jaw as if in thought, his gaze fixed somewhere upon her hat, as if he momentarily studied it, then he looked at her knowingly. "Darlin', ya know we can't leave all the kids with yer ma fer another night. She'll skin me alive, an' ya know it."

Phoebe gaped at him and squeaked, "The kids?"

Jace grinned devilishly and winked at the old woman. "Got us a real brood, we do. Four boys, all 'bout nine months apart." His twinkling eyes captured Phoebe's and his thumb traced the line of her jaw. "We keep busy, don't we, darlin'?"

Phoebe gulped, trying desperately to deny the fluttering in her belly, the weakening of her limbs, and only dimly aware of the old woman's cackling laughter.

"Ya musta married her awful young fer her te have whelped four babies, Mr. Sterling. She's but a baby herself."

Jace chuckled and drew Phoebe so close against his side her feet nearly left the ground. "She was fourteen, a right fine age to wed. Well, can ya blame me? Look at her? All dressed up in her Sunday best. I've kind of a mind to..." He leaned over the desk and muttered, "I'd appreciate if ya could hold that room there for us...that two-fourteen. Ya never know when the little lady here'll get herself all hot an'...well, ya know, a man don't make babies all by hisself an'...*ow!*"

He erupted with a forced laugh and then another, and clutched at his booted instep, which Phoebe had targeted with the pointed heel of her peach shoe.

She smiled sweetly in the face of his ferocious glower and batted innocent lashes, summoning her best imitation of a smooth, local drawl. "Is it your dyspepsia again, darlin'?" She leaned toward the old woman and gave a curt, knowing nod of her head, lowering her voice. "Drinkin's his problem, an' gamblin', 'course. Though I s'pose my cookin's not the best, but what can he expect? Took me from my mama 'fore I could boil water. Hands up my skirt every spare minute, but ya know what that whiskey'll do to a man." Phoebe gave Jace a sideways glance and had to suppress an overwhelming urge to giggle. He was glaring at her as if he meant to skewer her. Her pulse raced in her ears. "Too much drinkin' an' a man can't...well, ya know, ain't a whole lot'll get up on the man, if ya know what I mean. Poor fella."

The crone hadn't a chance to reply, for Jace unceremoniously grasped Phoebe's elbow and hauled her toward the stairs. "I think we'll just call on Mr. Gideon." He tossed the words over his shoulder through gritted teeth and headed for the stairs with determined strides.

Phoebe matched his gait, despite his viselike grip on her arm, and achieved some measure of satisfaction from his stormy glower fixed upon her. "Who's Mr. Gideon?" she chirped, pausing beside him at the top of the stairs and attempting to wrench her arm free.

"Quiet," he growled, looking as if he meant to give her a good thrashing before glancing up and down the dimly lit hall.

"You really are too much!" she scolded. "Abducting me before I could even have lunch—and I'm famished, I'll have you know—only to subject me to some...some horrid sham of a dressing-down."

"You could use a hell of a lot more."

Phoebe pursed her lips with exasperation. "You play mindless games and expect me to play along!"

He leveled a scowl at her from beneath the shadowed rim of his hat, looking so very much like an outlaw she thought she'd swoon. "You did a hell of a job playing along. Tell me, Peaches, where did you come by such an accent?"

"I have an excellent ear," Phoebe sniffed.

"Yeah, right," he muttered, starting slowly down the hall and tugging her along. "Just another prerequisite, eh?"

"You're becoming addlepated, Jace. Thoroughly so."

"No kidding. It's been my whole damned problem. Now quiet."

"No! Not until you tell me why the devil you brought me here and who the devil is this Gideon..."

And then he yanked her hard against him, his mouth inches from hers, his manner sending a chill through her. "Listen to me, you little hellion. Unless you'd rather I haul your plump little derriere down to the local jail, keep your damned mouth shut."

"Jail?" she whispered hoarsely, her confusion knowing no bounds. "What the devil have I ever done that's illegal?"

He looked positively pained, closing his eyes and rubbing a hand over his forehead as if to massage some great ache. He drew a deep breath and graced her with a bold sweep of his eyes. "In these parts, it's illegal to walk around in clothes that make you look like that, Peaches. Try a size bigger next time." He held a finger against her parted lips. "Now quiet."

That pleased her immensely, and she couldn't help smoothing her gown over her hips. So, he'd noticed. She followed at his heels, treading softly along the carpeted floors and studying his back, in particular the breadth of shoulder...

And then a door opened somewhere farther down the hall, accompanied by voices and heavy footfalls. Jace moved so quickly she'd barely realized until he shoved her against the wall and his lips swooped over hers. This was more like it! Her arms slipped around his neck and she was barely cognizant of the footsteps moving past them, of the hushed voices and muted giggles at the sight of the ardent lovers. She burrowed against him, rotating her hips against his in a slow, teasing motion she knew would render him senseless, and it was working ... until his mouth released hers. Her eyes flew open to meet smoldering, smoky blue ones.

"God, but I've never known a more hungry woman," he rasped, as if the words pained him, and then his hands moved upon her hips and she molded herself to him, parting her lips beneath his. "The whole damned world could go to hell and I wouldn't care. It's like some drug ..."

"Let's get the room, Jace." She nibbled at his lips, breathing against his mouth, her palms roving over his ribs. "Now, Jace ... please ... I can't wait until tonight. Forget this Mr. Gideon."

With a muffled curse, he released her and strode several paces up and down the hall. "Crazy ..." he muttered, his eyes pinning her to the wall. "You've made me so damned crazy I can't do my job, I can't sleep, I can't do anything." He paused before her, hands on lean hips, his denim pants hugging his legs like a second skin.

She drew a deep breath at the sight, her breasts heaving against her gown and drawing his narrowed eyes. Yet he seemed angry, frustrated beyond measure. "Jace ..."

He grasped her hand so roughly she cried out, then dragged her along behind him until they'd reached Room 214.

"Give me your hat pin," he muttered, and she complied without hesitation, clutching the hat to her bosom as he applied the pin to the lock.

"But your Mr. Gideon is in two-thirteen, Jace," Phoebe whispered, watching his long, skillful fingers maneuvering the hat pin into the keyhole like the proficient outlaw he was.

"So he is." In a matter of seconds, the door swung wide and he nudged her in the small of the back into the room's shadowed interior.

All she saw was a very large brass bed.

Jace, however, seemed far more intent upon the window. He parted the drapes and shoved the window open, then, much to Phoebe's astonishment, swung one leg through the opening, and then another, and disappeared.

"Jace!" With a careless toss of hat and gloves, she flew to the window and leaned out, saved from teetering over the sill by the mere weight of her bustle.

"Are you ever quiet?"

She gasped and spun her head about. He perched upon the narrow window ledge so blasted casually that Phoebe had to muse momentarily on his sanity. With a scowl, he lifted a finger to his lips and jerked his head to the opened window of the room next door, through which came the muffled sound of voices. Room 213.

Jace, the outlaw, was spying, and on his friend, this Mr. Gideon. What did he plan? To steal from or brutalize innocent people? *Her* Jace?

She opened her mouth then snapped it shut, her heart leaping and lodging somewhere near the base of her throat. The voice—the woman's voice—sounded like Madeline, very clear and shrill, as if she stood at the window with that drawn, strained look about her.

Phoebe's eyes locked with Jace's. "But Madeline's on the other side of town visiting her sick..." Her hoarse whispers died in her throat as Madeline's words carried clearly through the lace curtains.

"I refuse to argue about it. You simply can't come to the house anymore. We can't risk it."

"The hell we can't." The man's voice was deep and gravelly, one Phoebe didn't recognize, but laced with a suppressed rage. Mr. Gideon? "It's Jace, isn't it? Damned son of a..."

"We could never fool him!" Madeline cried. "He would suspect immediately!"

"He never suspected before."

"He's different now! Much too quick. Much smarter than those two little English chits. All they do is eat and sleep and moon about. Such a nuisance that Phoebe, spoiled little bitch in heat. I wish she'd just pack her damned bags and leave."

"Yeah, I know what's eatin' at you, Madeline. Ya still want him, don't ya? Jes' like ya did ten years ago." There was a harsh scraping of boots upon the wooden floor, a gasp and the man's voice, low, ominous and threatening, and much closer to the window, as if he stood very near Madeline. "An' he don't want nothin' te do with you, jes' like ten years ago. Ain't I right? From what I seen, that little English girl's been leadin' him 'round by his pants. An' he'd never let ya throw her out, would he? Ya know it, too, don't ya?"

"Stop it!" The muffled sounds of struggle floated out the window.

"Can't stand te hear it, can ya?"

"You're vile. You're hurting me."

"I thought ya liked me this way. Ya always did, 'til yer Jace come struttin' into town. *Now* I can't come te the house. *Now* ya don' want te even come here no more. *Now* I ain't good enough fer what ails ya, like yer Jace is, huh? Like he's always been."

"Jace has nothing to do with it. I told you . . ."

The man's laugh was harsh and short. "Yeah, sure. It don't matter, Maddie honey, 'cause yer mine, ain't ya? Ya always been, even when ol' Carson was around. An' I don't have te remind ya that I gots me a bag of tricks if ya start playin' tough with me. Don't I, Maddie, Mistress Maddie from Philly, from a mighty classy whorehouse, raisin' a bastard child . . ."

"Stop it!" Madeline shrieked. "You're heartless! You'd think you had nothing to do with . . ."

"Come here, Maddie, an' please me like ya always do. Come an' show ol' Gideon how much ya need him."

"I . . . I won't be blackmailed. I . . ."

Gideon chuckled amidst the squeaking of bedsprings. "Don't ya think it's a little late fer that, Maddie? Yer a high 'n mighty widow with a plum of a reputation to protect. I'd reckon if it all got out 'bout little James an' who his daddy really is, you'd lose it all, wouldn't ya? Yer house, an' maybe even James himself, eh?"

"That's enough! Please . . ."

"Now, that's more like it, Maddie. Come here. Oh, an' make sure ya leave the cash on the dresser over there. Ya know how much I need it, an' I wouldn't want te go an forget it, now would I? Seein' as how I always fall asleep after we..."

"Enough." Madeline's footsteps echoed upon the wooden floors, hollow and dull like her voice. "If Jace were to find out that I've sold off those parcels, my God, he'd..."

"He ain't gonna find out. An' if he does, ol' Gideon'll take care of everything. Don't ya worry, Maddie, beautiful sad Maddie, ain't never gonna have what she wants."

The muffled sounds of grunts and the squeaking of bed-springs brought the color to Phoebe's cheeks with startling dispatch and she ducked inside the window without venturing a glance at Jace. She trembled with some unknown emotion—confusion, perhaps—and shame at eavesdropping so fla-grantly, or perhaps it was fear that shivered through her bones. Fear of the answers to questions she'd never dared ask, an-swers she never wanted to hear.

She hugged her arms to her and stared at the wooden floor until she heard Jace behind her, moving stealthily as a cat to close the window behind him. Her eyes flickered hesitantly over his profile, noting the almost feral curve of his lips. "Is Mr. Gideon Madeline's sick friend?"

Jace erupted with a caustic grunt, swept his hat from his head and stared blankly from the window. "Yeah, I suppose you could say that."

"They're lovers." Phoebe watched him so closely her eyes hurt. The sun slanting across his face deepened the lines along his mouth, shadowed his lean cheeks, enhanced his brow with much more than mere concern. His was the face of a tortured man. An empty, raw feeling welled in Phoebe's belly.

"They're lovers," he repeated, his voice devoid of emotion. He crushed his hat in his hands so fiercely Phoebe had to won-der if he even realized the force of his own restraint. How this seemed to plague him.

She swallowed heavily and contemplated her words. "He's the man Jamie spoke of, the man with the whiskers. He's blackmailing her, isn't he? Forcing her to sell off parcels of Pine Grove and taking the spoils. Why the devil is she allowing this? Why are you?"

His eyes narrowed upon some object in the distance yet he remained passive, stoic and too silent.

"If Carson wasn't Jamie's father, who was?"

"I don't know."

Phoebe closed her eyes and summoned a breath. "Are you?"

"I don't know."

Her eyes flew open and locked with his, cool, impenetrable, like the fortress he'd erected about his blasted heart, a fortress she'd penetrated only at night, only when she held him in her arms and listened to his hoarsely murmured love words ... passion words ... words even a girl like her couldn't believe entirely. Yet that all seemed a faded, dusty memory a hundred-years-old, the feelings he aroused suddenly doused beneath the blunt force of his words. Bells rang in her ears and something exploded in her mind. Blinding rage? Jealousy? The inconceivable notion that she'd been played for a fool, an *easy* fool? What had Jace said? He'd never met a more hungry woman ... she didn't know when to stop. Hungering and wanton ...

She gulped for breath, deep, wheezing breaths, clutching one hand to her heaving breast, holding the other outstretched before her as he took one step closer. He could be Jamie's father. That meant he'd ... with Madeline ... his father's wife.

Raw bile welled in her throat. "Oh, God," she groaned, nearly doubling over as anguish gripped her belly. Tears spilled to her cheeks before she even realized, unspoken sobs gathering to an agonizing ache in her throat, begging for release. And then steely arms engulfed her, clutching her nearer, until Jace buried his hand in her hair and yanked her head back, forcing her eyes to his.

"You want the truth?" he growled, and somewhere deep inside her, she knew his fury had nothing to do with her. Yet the tears slipped from her eyes, streaming down her cheeks, over trembling lips that refused words. "The truth...something I've been running from for ten damned years." His eyes flickered over her face and softened slightly. "God knows why I'm telling you this."

She gulped, a sob escaping her parted lips, and pushed against him, needing release from those too familiar arms, knowing she couldn't bear the truth without some distance between them.

Yet his arms merely tightened, pinning her against his entire length. "I'm not letting you go, Peaches, not now . . . not until you hear this. The truth, the whole damned story . . . though there's not much. Just one night, ten years ago, when my father was still at war and I was home with Madeline, watching over her like a good son." His lip curled in a snide twist, as if the memory tasted bitter. "I was twenty, newly strapping, full of myself, longing for my first good taste of whiskey. I should have seen it coming, should have known by the looks, but I didn't. Too green, I suppose, not enough women, and she knew it. So Madeline opened a bottle one night and asked me to join her. We drank the entire bottle, even more, I don't remember. But I do remember Madeline that night, and the things she said, and the look in her eye when she took off her dress, and . . ."

"No," Phoebe sobbed, her head shaking frantically. "No, I can't . . . please."

His hand gripped the back of her head, forcing her eyes to meet his. "That's all I remember," he rasped. "Nothing more."

"Oh God . . ." A wave of nausea surged over her and she slumped against him, her legs dissolving beneath her, and he caught her, then somehow cradled her in his arms and sat upon the bed. He held her so fast struggles were useless, yet she could only manage to concentrate on drawing breath, her ears straining for his words.

He spoke into her hair in a voice hoarse with emotion. "About that time, my father returned from the war. Madeline tried to fool him, waited a couple of months until she couldn't hide it, then proudly announced she was expecting his baby. Only my father wasn't at all pleased. He'd contracted some damned ailment during the war, mumps, I believe he called it. Anyway, the doctors told him he'd never father another child because of it. So he knew, right off, Madeline was lying. That's when she told him that the child was mine. I left, before he could throw me out, and haven't been back since."

All that responsibility he'd denied, the child he'd denied. And now she understood his aloof manner with Jamie . . . more denial. Phoebe listened to his heart beating against her ear, to the sound of his words dying in the musty room, wondering why she felt so dreadfully empty and in need of a cool glass of water. She pushed her elbow against his stomach and attempted to ease from his arms. "Jace...I...let me go, please. I need some air."

"Peaches..." The sole word, borne on a rasping whisper. And he released her, allowing her to rise to unsteady legs, then he grasped her hips and buried his face against her belly. "Peaches..."

She swayed, clutching at his shoulders as another wave of nausea swept over her, and then another. Her lips were so parched, her throat... "Jace, I...I need to lie down. I need..."

And then he must have lifted her from her feet, just as her legs dissolved beneath her, for she found herself upon her back amidst the softness of the bed, fervently praying that she wouldn't retch. She felt tender fingers smoothing the hair from her damp brow, heard the soothing murmur of his voice. And then he left her, momentarily, only to return with a cool glass of water, which he held to her lips. She gulped from it, then collapsed against the pillows, flinging one arm over her eyes.

"So bloody hot all the time," she murmured, and offered token resistance when she felt his fingers upon the long row of buttons adorning the front of her gown. He spread the silk and eased it over her shoulders, over her arms, and she groaned as cooling air assailed her skin. His fingers poised upon the top button of her chemise, lingering upon the high curves of her bosom. In spite of it all, that familiar yearning sputtered to life deep within her, yet she caught his hand beneath hers and merely pressed it to her.

"Please, Jace."

His lips brushed over her brow. "I'm not that much of a beast," he muttered, though his other hand had managed to venture down the row of buttons to pause and spread wide over her belly. "Perhaps you need to eat."

She groaned at the thought and shook her head. "No...no...'tis the heat. I simply need to rest."

In response, he rose from the bed, and for one telling moment she feared he'd left her. And then the bed dipped and she felt his lean length against her side, his breath against her temple, his hand possessively upon her belly.

She opened her eyes to find his dusty boots alongside her stockinged feet, faded denim legs resting against hers. "You're going to wrinkle my dress," she murmured.

"I would have anyway," he replied huskily, the warmth of his hand seeping through her skin, igniting sleeping flames, banishing nausea and jealousy and bile. His lips pressed against her ear, and lower, warm upon her neck. "Don't hate me, Peaches."

She stared at the ceiling, knowing he watched her. "I don't," she replied, and then he loomed above her, his features wearied, plagued, and she couldn't resist running her palm against his bearded cheek. If only a touch could soothe... Tears welled again, wetting the pillow beneath her head, blurring the vision of him so vulnerable... aching. Her heart swelled. "Oh, Jace, I don't know what to say. I..."

"Don't say anything." His lips brushed with infinite tenderness over hers, caressing, gently loving, and she trembled beneath him, suddenly all aching and wanting at his touch, as vulnerable as he, and wishing desperately she were not. She could no more deny him than she could stop the rising of the sun, and merely gasped with poignant pleasure when cool air assailed her naked breasts, then heated palms and lips, and his hand cupped her womanhood and delved.

He may have loved Madeline once, may have fathered her child and denied it, may have fathered a legion of illegitimate children, but Phoebe still loved him with a boundless passion, and managed to prove it to him that afternoon upon that very large brass bed.

Rudy Blades rapped twice short, once long, then twice short again. After a muffled scraping of heels upon the floor, the door opened a fraction of an inch and a mussed cloud of peach hair appeared. He smirked and shoved against the door. "Lemme in. I got some big news."

"Where the devil have you been?" Peaches rasped, closing the door soundly behind her and drawing her peach silk wrapper tight about her as if to shield herself from his narrowing eyes.

"Goare's Tavern." Blades surveyed the room with a hasty sweep of his eyes, peeked from the shaded window and studied the myriad crystal bottles atop a nearby dresser. Callused fingers lifted one flask to his nose and he grimaced. "Where the hell do ya get this stuff? Smells like a damned peach."

Peaches sniffed haughtily and snatched the perfume from his grasp. "Keep your bloody paws off my belongings," she snarled, her teeth baring in a sneer. "When the devil are we leaving this hovel? I'm becoming an addlepated fool cooped up in this dusty excuse for a hotel while you drink and wench your days and nights away. I can't shop, I can't go out to dine. God knows someone would recognize me. I can't..."

"Shut up."

Peaches gasped, and would have struck at Blades had he not caught her flailing hands in his and wrenched them behind her back, then hauled her roughly against him. For a fleeting moment, something hot and titillating raced through him at the feel of squirming, silk-swathed woman, but it eluded him after a moment. Perhaps it was the sweet smell, that peachy smell, he couldn't stomach, or the harsh lines creasing her heavily powdered face, or the fact that he'd never much cared for seasoned women, women who knew the score. He liked his women innocent as lambs and eager, and maybe even a little stupid. Yeah, that always helped, though stupid women could also be unfaithful, like that blonde, the one in Laramie, the only woman who'd ever needed another man...that Jace McAllister.

He yanked her hard against him. "Ya want te get outta here, Peaches? Then listen, and listen good, 'cause I gots us a plan."

Peaches recoiled from him with an unchecked grimace of disgust. "Plan? *You?* And where did you come upon such a novelty? In this tavern of yours, amidst all the drunken rabble?"

Blades glared at her, his lips twisting in a sneer. "Rabble talk mighty fine when ya buy 'em a drink or two. It's a hell of a plan, Peaches, an' it'll get rid of all our troubles. No more Pinkerton's on yer tail...*ever*. I can guarantee it." He raised a brow at her sudden change in manner, the fleeting glimpse of interest flaring in her eyes. "Sounds good, don't it?"

"Too good," she muttered, giving him a wary look and shoving at his arms, which encircled her waist like a vise. "Forgive me, but even Adam Worth has never spoken of guarantees."

Blades flashed her a wicked grin and couldn't resist thrusting his hips against hers. "That's 'cause Worth ain't Rudy

Blades, now is he? Yep, I can jest 'bout guarantee that we'll be able te walk right through the middle of town—oh, 'bout three days from now—an' you could wear your peach dress and smell like a damned peach an' ya could probably hit the mayor himself up for his gold watch an' nobody'd be the wiser. They'd all jest tip their hats and smile real nice and wave when we get on that train fer Dodge City.''

Peach-colored brows trembled and met over narrowed eyes. "You're half-mad, that's what you are. The Pinkerton's will recognize me immediately!''

"Not if yer in jail.''

"You bumbling oaf!'' Peaches struggled anew, hissing and swatting at his arms. "Jail? *Me?* I'd rather die. I'd rather...''

Blades chuckled deep in his chest and shook his head with wonder. "Not you, Peaches.''

"Then who?''

"You ain't the only English lady in these parts. An' I jest so happen te know that there's some talk 'bout this other girl. I gots me a friend at Goare's, ya see, an' he likes his whiskey. He also likes te make friends with guys like me. Mean guys, Peaches, not those fancy guys like Worth. Thinks by tellin' me all his secrets, I'll be his friend.''

Peaches rolled her eyes. "You neglected to mention he was a fool.''

"That he is, but the man knows a hell of a lot 'bout this town. Ya know what he tol' me, Peaches?''

Peaches closed her eyes and heaved an agitated sigh. "Oh, please, do tell, and be hasty about it. You stink like three-day-old whiskey and that beast you ride and you're ruining my silk wrapper.''

Blades chuckled with supreme self-assurance and leaned closer to Peaches until his lips barely touched her cheek. "Don't ya like gettin' dirty, Peaches? Ya ever think 'bout doin' it with a guy like me? Eh, whad'ya say?''

Peaches wrinkled her nose and averted her face. "How very gallant of you to offer, but no, I must say the thought of *doin' it* with the likes of you hasn't ever crossed my mind. Now, if you please, your plan, so I can get the bloody hell away from you.''

Blades released her with a chuckle. "Yer gonna want it one day, Peaches, trust me." He heaved a sigh and folded powerful arms over his chest. "Ol' Hawkins tol' me that this little English girl, this Phoebe Sinclair, the one visitin' at Pine Grove, he tol' me she's no heiress. She's really a jewel thief. An' her name's Peaches."

"What? Who the devil . . . ?"

"Hawkins ain't the only one who thinks she's Peaches. Jace McAllister does, too. Wants te get in on the take. An' that's just fine. Too fine. 'Cause it makes it almost too damn easy, ya know? No tellin' what they'll do te her when they catch her. Hangin' maybe, dependin' on the crime. Lynchin' would be better." The blood pounded in his ears at the thought. Revenge, sweet and simple. Jace McAllister losing his woman to a hangman's noose, or a lynch mob bent upon their own grisly justice.

From deep within his consciousness, Peaches's voice gnawed at him. "I'm not following you. Just because someone believes this girl is me doesn't mean anything. She's certainly not going to pull off some job at the proper moment so that we can make our graceful escape."

"Peaches, Peaches." Blades shook his head slowly. "Didn't Worth teach you nothin' but how te pick a pocket er two?" He flashed a devilish grin that felt very good indeed. "Listen close, Peaches, 'cause yer 'bout te learn the art of the sting."

Chapter Fifteen

Phoebe stuffed the wet rag into her mouth and bit down, hard. It was no use. Hot tears slipped from her eyes and splashed to her lap, to the damp chemise covering her roiling belly. And again the nausea welled, looming like an evil thing all the way up the back of her throat to lodge and torment. Her mouth watered and she fell to her knees over the porcelain bowl once again with a choked sob. She closed her eyes and ran a trembling hand over her brow. *Not again. Dear God, let it pass. Not again...*

All the praying in the world wouldn't have helped.

"Dear God, Phoebe!" A rustle of taffeta, the staccato of heels upon a polished bedroom floor, the faintest waft of Charlotte's perfume and tender hands upon Phoebe's back.

With a groan, Phoebe waved a dismissive hand at Charlotte and slumped against the dressing table stool, burying her head in her arms and sucking like a starving babe on the damp rag. "Go away, Charlotte," she croaked.

"My God, Phoebe! You're not even dressed! And they're here...I mean, well, yes, Dalton's here and your...er...your Mr. Shane Morgan. They're both downstairs looking at each other and not saying much. It's really most embarrassing. But, dear God, you're ill, and on the very night of the Prescott ball!"

Phoebe didn't even glance up. "Stop wringing your hands, Charlotte. I'll be fine. It shall pass... now. It always does after I...you know..." She bungled an attempt at swallowing her tears and erupted with a choked sob. "God, how I hate to retch. The mere thought makes me cry. Dear God, this ailment has plagued me for at least a week now. I can't bear the sight of food..."

"'Tis all this blasted heat. Phoebe, we're delicate English-women, bred for fine dewy springs and gentle moist winters. None of this blazing sun! Our constitutions are..."

Phoebe raised bleary eyes and grimaced. "Constitutions be damned. Go fetch Delilah. Perhaps she's a cure for me. Oh, and would you tell Shane I'm...indisposed for a time. Lie to him, Charlotte, but tell him I'll be right down."

Phoebe managed to get her feet beneath her by the time Delilah rapped softly upon the door. She bade the servant enter and assumed a rather tenuous perch upon the bed, avoiding her pale and drawn reflection in the mirror.

"Delilah, thank heavens. I'm feeling a bit... well, I've happened upon some foul little bug and could use one of your remedies."

The Negress folded her arms over her ample bosom, cast a knowing look about the room and eyed Phoebe. "This have sumpthin' te do wit you not eatin' my food?"

Phoebe hung her head wearily in her hand. "Oh, Delilah, do forgive me. 'Tis just that the mere sight of food sets my belly churning and I'm so blastedly hot and...I just feel so, you know, funny."

"Funny? Mmm-hmm."

Beneath the woman's all-knowing gaze, Phoebe shifted uncomfortably upon the bed. "Yes, you know, tingly and weak and like I'm about to swoon, God knows."

Delilah raised one very knowing brow. "You gots a man frien', missy?"

Phoebe's head snapped up. "What the devil does that..."

"Oh, ya don' have te tell me, no, ma'am. I's gots no ears on my head, no, ma'am. I's don' know why those morning glories on your trellis is all mashed and hangin' like a man done put his big foot in there. Mmm hmm. No, ma'am. Stand up."

Phoebe hesitated a moment, wondering why her cheeks burned so flagrantly at the woman's words, then decided to comply. She nearly jumped when the housekeeper laid a large hand upon her belly. "What are you..."

"Mmm-hmm, mmm-hmm. Ya says ya feel tingly. Like here?"

Before Phoebe realized, Delilah pressed her hands against the tender sides of Phoebe's breasts, breasts that had never before been so sensitive, so taut. "Delilah! How dare you? I mean, how did you . . . ?"

The older woman folded her arms over her bosom and gave a wide smile. "Missy, I's never bin wrong 'bout this. I's thinks ya gonna have a baby."

"Punch, Mr. McAllister?"

Jace started, unceremoniously drawn from his muddled thoughts by the white-jacketed servant looming at his elbow with a silver tray full of tiny crystal cups brimming with pale pink punch. Muttering his thanks, Jace scowled into the tiny cup then ran a finger inside his high stiff collar for the hundredth time that evening. He swallowed and drew a much needed breath, feeling supremely out of sorts and damned overheated, all trussed up in formal black attire and severely starched white shirt, balancing a dainty little cup in his callused palm. He shifted his shoulders within the confines of his topcoat, his jaded eyes sweeping over Adelaide Prescott's grand ballroom.

He gave a sardonic snort. A fine night for a ball. Hot, thick air hanging heavy with the scents of elaborately coiffured and elegantly dressed women in their fluff and froufrou, and men doing their gallant best to sweat the evening away in their finery. Only the orchestra could benefit from any balmy breeze that happened to sweep through the terrace doors, bringing with it the pungent scents of Adelaide Prescott's famed rose garden. His eyes lingered upon the musicians. Only the Widow Prescott could manage to drum up a damned orchestra in Buttermilk Falls. Then again, this was her annual event, something dowagers like her plan for months and upon which nubile young innocents pin their every heart's dream. Speaking of which . . .

His eyes narrowed and swept about the crowded ballroom. Peaches still hadn't arrived and he'd been here for hours, it seemed, waiting like a punch-drunk fool, nodding and smiling graciously and even managing to waltz with Flossie, a feat indeed. He ground his teeth and nearly crushed the cup in his palm. While he sulked about, achieving naught but bruised toes and profound agitation, Peaches dallied the evening away with Rudy Blades...somewhere. He clenched his fists, itching to put them to use. What a damned fool he was to have allowed Blades near her. Something very vital and possessive welled in his chest, tightening his belly beneath the fine linen of his shirt. She was his, and his alone. To hell with shadowing Blades and seeing him shackled in jail, to hell with avenging a friend's death, to hell with allowing another man within fifty paces of the woman he loved....

He slammed the cup upon a nearby buffet table, startling the insipid creature seated behind it such that she shrank from his stormy glower. He muttered something to her and shoved a hand through his hair, wondering what the hell had happened to him. He should have been pondering the fate of the family lumber business —his business— or what would be left of it if he didn't fell enough timber before the next flood. No timber felled, no goods to transport by way of a swollen, fast-flowing river to Pittsburgh or Kittanning. No barges to sell farther down the Ohio. Only rotting timber and diminishing acreage, thanks to Madeline. In a scant month's time he'd actually begun to feel a deep pride in running his own setup; it would be hard to leave behind once Peaches was taken care of.

He should have been pondering the shambles of his life.

Tempering his scowl, he nodded briefly to a nearby passel of giggly young women who looked as if they wished to make a meal out of him. Not a bad-looking bunch, to be sure. A man could do far worse. Then again, when one dined with startling regularity upon fare such as Peaches...

He closed his eyes and kneaded the ache in his forehead. Why hadn't those damned Pinkerton's, with all their solemn wisdom and volumes of investigative procedure, warned him just once about wild, wanton women? Women who could lay claim to a man's very soul such that he forgot who he was, could indeed sacrifice everything of worth in his life, everything that had ever held some import for him. He couldn't let her do this to him. He wasn't some sot in Boston. He wasn't a fool. It had to end—God, how many times had he told himself that, only to abandon his every conviction at the mere sight of her? Tonight. It would end tonight, damn it all. He could immerse himself in Pine Grove, dally his evenings away with the ever eager Flossie, keep miles away from Peaches.

And then for some reason he turned to the doorway, because of some commotion that caught the corner of his eye. Or perhaps instinct set his every fiber alive and vibrant, aware, even as he was not, that she had entered the room. And then, for one crazy moment, the room spun about him, tilting and careening amidst a deafening roar, until his eyes locked with hers and desire set him aflame.

She moved beneath an enormous crystal chandelier, all smooth, warm, peachy skin and a creamy silk that begged to be ripped from her supple curves. He found himself anticipating her slightest misstep, certain that she would walk away without the damned dress, so precariously was she poured into the thing. No froufrou for Peaches. A simple, ivory silk sheath that shimmered and beckoned, mocking his state with its brazen display of luxuriant curves and willowy hollows, rising to just barely cover the lush swell of her breasts. Bare arms, bare shoulders, a tumbling mass of golden ringlets, diamonds at her ears and a cream satin ribbon at her throat.

He wanted to see her in nothing but the diamonds and that damned ribbon. The thought shot hot flames to his loins. Painfully swollen beyond proportions suited to any trousers, his blood coursing through his veins, hammering in his ears, he yearned to get her out of this place, to throw his coat around her and toss her over his shoulder. He took two steps toward her.

"They make a lovely couple, do they not, Sterling McAllister?"

His world righted. "Widow Prescott," he managed in a voice that sounded utterly strangled to his ear. He suppressed a snort of self-disgust and nodded at the tiny, amply powdered elderly woman at his elbow. She gave him a tenuous smile from somewhere amidst that cloud of snowy white hair, pale pink taffeta and diamonds. And a dazzling array they were. Enormous emerald-cut pieces strung together to form a necklace that seemed to threaten to wither the poor woman beneath its weight. Matching earrings, bracelets, rings. The woman dripped with it. A veritable feast for even the most discreet. A temptation too tantalizing to deny for thieves so inclined.

His gaze found Peaches . . . and Blades, looking far too enigmatic, far too noble, far too civilized garbed in evening black. He'd even managed to wield a comb to his advantage, though it was the manner in which he all but loomed over Peaches that threatened Jace's sanity, a rather predatory looming to Jace's eye, a looming that spoke volumes of the man's intent, starched evening finery be damned. It was all Jace could do to keep from killing the man with his bare hands.

"A handsome couple, indeed," the widow mused softly. "Don't you agree, Sterling McAllister?"

The words caught in Jace's throat and he had to force his gaze to the older woman. "Handsome," he managed, wondering as he did so as to the source of the glint in the woman's eye. She'd known him since he was a boy. No doubt she had heard the tales. A shriveled finger waved directly before his nose.

"A woman like that needs a husband."

Jace lifted a brow. In spite of the murderous rage engulfing him, and forced his lips to curve in a smile. "Something tells me she'd be a handful."

Adelaide Prescott's dark eyes glittered mischievously above primly pursed lips. "And you're just the man to do it, Sterling McAllister." That shriveled finger wagged wildly and she plunged on before he could draw a breath. "Oh, don't puff up and try to tell me otherwise, damned fool that you are, just like your father. That fellow she's with..." Widow Prescott darted a quick glance over Jace's shoulder and shook her head with grim finality. "No, he won't do. Something about the way he leers at her. No, no, he won't do. But you..." Gnarled fingers plucked at his sleeve and she gave him a secretive little smile. "You look at her the way a man's supposed to look at a woman. Yes, yes, I saw you. I saw her, too, God help the girl. Call it what you will, I'm a meddling busybody and I always have been. No children of my own to fret over, I suppose. But trust me, Sterling McAllister, you would do well by marrying this English girl. Now, off I go. The servants never get it quite right, do they? Now where did I leave my punch? I'm always losing it, you know. Never quite remember where I left it. Oh, and you might want to see to your Flossie Dawson. I believe a line is forming behind her in the ladies' salon. Enjoy!"

With a wave of her bejeweled hand, she floated into the crowd, a drifting cloud of pink taffeta. Odd old woman, though something about her touched Jace. Perhaps she knew him better than he knew himself. Marriage. To a jewel thief.

His eyes sought Peaches. He didn't have far to look, for she stood almost directly before him, wearing what could only be described as a radiant smile, her eyes fastened steadfastly upon him despite Blades's meaty paw lying possessively at her elbow. Something hollow ached inside Jace, standing so close to her, her scent enveloping him, yet unable to touch her. He could feel her heat, a palpable thing, like so many words unspoken between them. God, but he needed her, so much so he forgot about Blades and must have murmured her name, for her lips parted and she seemed about to reach for him. And then her eyes darted away, widened and darted to his, and a chill swept over him just as Flossie's musky scent permeated his consciousness.

The woman looked as if she would burst at the slightest pinprick, oozing, as she was, from every tightly stitched seam of her frothy lemon yellow gown, a shade ill-suited to a woman of her coloring. Her lack of an eye, however, proved the least of Phoebe's worries. She struggled to maintain her balance when the woman melted all over Jace, plump arms encircling his lean waist, her red talons sweeping possessively over a breadth of white linen that had not moments before kindled the flames deep in Phoebe's belly. She couldn't for the life of her suppress the vision of those talons threading through Jace's tousled mane, over lean hips snugly encased in black trousers, over his forever turgid manhood...

And suddenly she couldn't bear it a moment longer, she needed air, yet her feet refused to move, and Shane Morgan seemed very intent upon Jace and his...his...

The father of her unborn babe had a doxy.

"Evenin', Mr. Morgan." Beady eyes beneath a tumbled mass of auburn hair swept with a dismissive finality over Phoebe before the doxy managed to melt anew. "Jacey, the other day I heard the cutest thang."

Phoebe couldn't help but raise a lofty brow despite the fierce gnashing of her teeth. *Thang?*

"Save it, Flossie," Jace muttered, his hand stilling the progress of one very long fingernail as it traced boldly down his chest. Phoebe knew him well enough to detect the frustration plaguing his brow, and the ominous glint in those sapphire eyes fixed relentlessly upon Shane Morgan.

"But, Jacey, it's the newest thang from England. And accordin' to ol' Henrietta Witherspoon, all the ladies in her quilting circle is doin' it." Flossie graced Phoebe with yet another brazen sweep of her eyes, and Phoebe countered with a haughty lift of her chin and the merest thrust of her bosom, something she knew Jace would not miss. Her efforts were instantly rewarded, for twin sapphire flames devoured her with such bold aplomb she had to press a slightly trembling hand to her burning décolletage.

The man was not enjoying this in the least. Best to let him squirm. Phoebe slipped her arm through Shane's and idly stroked his fine broadcloth sleeve with one finger.

"Yer that English heiress Henrietta was talkin' 'bout, ain't ya?"

Phoebe lifted her chin yet another notch. "Indeed, and you must be the woman I've heard so much about from so many... well, you know, small towns and gossip. It *is* Floozie, oh, so sorry, I mean Flossie Dawson, is it not?"

A frown scooted across Flossie's brow for a fleeting moment before she rested her head against Jace's shoulder, her palm flat upon his belly. "Seein' as yer from England, ya must know all 'bout Englishwomen copin' with the heat." Flossie jiggled and squirmed inside her hideous dress as if the mere thought were too much to bear. "No pantaloons," she whispered, then erupted with a piercing giggle that sent a chill racing up Phoebe's spine. "I ain't even wearin' any right this minute, Jacey." She slanted wicked eyes at him. "Wanna see, Jacey?"

Phoebe shot Jace a chilling glare over the top of Flossie's head and erupted with a gasp of unmitigated horror that brought Flossie's head about with a snap. "Oh no, not at night!" Phoebe cried, then pressed a hand to her throat. "You mustn't at night... but... oh no, never mind."

Flossie looked positively stricken. "What? What the blazes is ya babblin' about? What about at night? Henrietta didn't tell me nothin'..."

Ignoring the wicked, knowing lift of Jace's brow, Phoebe drew a finger to her lips, her brow knit with genuine concern. "I fear I may have neglected to mention to Henrietta about the night...*creatures*."

"Creatures?" Flossie squeaked.

Phoebe gave a little shrug. "Oh, they're nothing really, just tiny little things, actually, so small you can barely see them. But they're about, trust me, and on the hottest of evenings I believe they bite the worst. Why, I've seen them swarm around some poor girl who...why, she was just like you, Flossie. She hadn't heeded the warnings, either."

As if suddenly possessed, Flossie began fidgeting, then squirming as if she itched in a hundred places, until she let out a terrified howl and fled from the room without a backward glance.

Shane Morgan released a rumbling chuckle and covered Phoebe's hand upon his arm, his fingers stroking softly over hers. Despite the nearly overwhelming urge to snatch her hand from beneath his and flee, Phoebe stiffened her spine and peered haughtily down her nose at a very ominous, much-too-silent Jace.

"You'd best find yourself another tart, Mr. McAllister," she quipped, reveling in the feral gleam in his eye, the clenching of his mighty fists. "'Twill be a dreadfully long evening for you if you do not. Shane..." She slanted tall-and-blond a coquettish glance. "Dance with me, love, will you?" And with head held high, she moved onto the dance floor, her struggle to suppress her tears obliterating any and all satisfaction gleaned from stripping Jace of his whore.

"Who is that guy?"

"What guy?" Jace raised a brow at Pryce and did his very best not to look at Peaches and Blades moving about the dance floor. Damned outlaw even knew how to dance.

Pryce frowned and his eyes narrowed, a suspicious narrowing that quickened Jace's pulse. "That guy with his hands all over your Peaches, and don't tell me you haven't been watching them. He looks familiar to me, somehow, though maybe it's the clothes . . . or the hair. Something doesn't fit.''

Jace doubted Blades had ever been photographed for a wanted poster garbed in evening black with combed hair. Yet Pryce had a discerning eye, and Jace couldn't risk his suspecting that Peaches' escort was indeed the much wanted Rudy Blades. Another foiled plan he didn't need. ''I don't know him.'' Jace felt Pryce's eyes all over him. He mindlessly gulped some punch, grimaced and found himself staring at her again. His belly tightened from far more than the sickly-sweet liquid. She looked too damned flushed and rosy to suit him, far too ripe, spilling out of her gown, as pleased as a kitten in cream. Blades didn't even warrant a glance. ''I don't know him.''

''The hell you don't.''

''Go find Charlotte, Pryce.''

''A grand idea, my friend. The best you've had all month. Ah, Charlotte, a fairer maid I've yet to meet, and one I intend to make my wife.'' Pryce winked, then leaned closer to Jace and muttered under his breath, his voice laced with mirth, ''Now there's a notion. Marriage, hmm? Oh, one other thing, has your Peaches pawned any of her spoils yet? Or have you been keeping her occupied with more pleasurable pursuits, eh?''

Jace kept his gaze fixed on Peaches and his voice low and menacing. ''Go away.''

Pryce would not be denied. ''Why don't you just go out there and steal her from that guy? You look like a man possessed. Anyone with eyes in their heads can see it. Go on. The orchestra's just struck up a new waltz. I've a sneaking suspicion she won't deny you, though her escort might.''

Jace gritted his teeth against the frustration welling in his chest. Her denying him was the least of it. ''I'll see her in jail before I face her on some dance floor.''

''You're obsessed, my friend. So obsessed you wouldn't see the truth if it bit you in the ass. I hate to be the one to tell you, but women like Phoebe Sinclair don't wait around for anybody. You may lose her.''

''Damn it, man, she's not mine to lose!''

''Enjoy your evening, Jace.''

Jace scowled after his jolly friend, so damned dapper and full of himself. So infernally upstanding and secure next to his

Charlotte, a fine woman whose destiny screamed of hearth and home, children, good hearty cooking and warm embraces. A woman who knew well her place as a wife, supporter of her husband, care giver, lover. Everything Pryce could want, or any man, he supposed.

Marriage. To a woman like Peaches. His eyes narrowed on the slender sweep of her back and hips, probing the depths of that ivory sheath as she waltzed gracefully past. She probably had never boiled water or made a bed, sewn a stitch or mended a sock. She was selfish and stubborn, utterly childish and irrepressibly vain. No doubt she spent money as quickly as she could steal—on frivolous frippery and hairpins and stockings. His life would be a tangled mass of silly plumed hats, shoes and gloves in every imaginable shade, and dust balls gathering under every stick of furniture.

They could hire a maid.

He'd either starve or exist on charred meat and watery soup.

They could hire a cook, as well.

With a grunt, he searched about for a servant and, spotting one, requested a very tall whiskey. He leaned one shoulder against a doorjamb, uncaring that he was being unsocial.

She would grow bored, long for adventure, a little thievery to chase away the hours she spent alone while he felled and hauled timber.

He'd keep a baby in her belly until they had a legion or more, and then he'd just keep her in bed. She'd never have a moment to be bored.

Peaches was a snob, thief and all. Too damned full of herself and all her high-flown ideas.

She'd made love with him in a lake, against a tree, in a rank and dirty hovel, on a squeaky brass bed in some gaudy hotel in Titusville...and something about that prim lift to her nose, that haughty tilt to her chin, fired something deep and eternal within him. Something about the woman—far more than her passion, her spirit—had indeed possessed him. She was in his blood, his soul, a part of him he could no longer deny.

He drained his whiskey and set the glass upon a nearby table, intent upon sweeping her from that dance floor, from Blades—who could go to hell, for all Jace cared at the moment. He took two steps and skidded to a halt. They'd disappeared, swallowed by the surge of the crowd.

Jace spun about, shouldering his way through the mass toward the terrace, anticipating Blades's intent, and in his haste bumped roughly into a woman who seemed bent upon her own quest, such was her flight. She murmured a fleeting apology and something about the ladies' salon, averting her face and brushing past him with nary a pause. He gave her not another moment's thought and hastened toward the terrace doors, though he could have sworn the scent lingering in her wake smelled distinctly of a peach.

Phoebe gave Shane Morgan a tenuous smile of thanks and sipped the punch he'd retrieved. Grossly sweet, tasting very pink indeed, but chilled and refreshing, precisely what she needed to chase away the heat. The faintest of summer breezes ruffled the tendrils against her cheeks, cooled her pulsating skin even as it stirred her senses with its elusive rose scent, a sensual awakening despite her decided lack of feeling for the man looming silently beside her upon the shadowed and deserted terrace.

Her thoughts wandered with the breeze, sweeping through the well-tended gardens of Adelaide Prescott's estate, over hills and lush valleys of tall, fragrant pine, tripping along the banks of a moon-dappled lake. Jace. The name alone weakened her limbs, kindled the flames in her belly and drew the peaks of her breasts taut with desire. He'd rendered her naught but an animal with his swaggering about like some predatory beast, cold and brooding, lusty and demanding, all at once. She was to bear his child and here she stood, awash in emotional havoc, beside Shane Morgan, a rather irritable and stoic Shane Morgan, whose thoughts seemed elsewhere. This didn't arouse its typical miffed response in Phoebe, the feeling that perhaps she was being ignored, of all things, so engrossed was she in her own troubled thoughts. Thus, when Shane's hand suddenly shot out and flicked in front of her just as she raised her cup to her lips, she nearly jumped from her skin and managed, in the process, to spill the entire cup of very pink, very sticky punch all over her bosom and down the length of her ivory bodice.

"Oh, good heavens!" she cried, leaping back a pace and fanning her sodden, stained gown. "What the devil were you doing?"

"Didn't you see it?" Shane asked, graciously removing the empty cup from her trembling hand. "A moth or a beetle. Right in front of you. I got him, though."

"I should certainly hope so!" Phoebe huffed. "Oh, good grief, what the devil shall I do?" Shane's insistent hand upon her elbow propelled her along toward the terrace doors. "The ladies' salon, perhaps...yes. Oh, good heavens..." With cheeks flaming and eyes averted, she reentered the ballroom and ran smack into Jace's chest. She knew without even glancing up that it was him. No man in the world but he felt like that, even through layers of sodden silk and fine white linen. His hands were upon her before she could think, grasping her about the shoulders, and oh, how she wanted to slip her hands inside that topcoat.

His voice rumbled deep and resonant from somewhere far above her. "What the hell . . . ?"

"An accident," Shane muttered rather brusquely, exerting a persistent pressure upon Phoebe's back. "She was on her way to clean up."

Phoebe stared at the line of mother-of-pearl buttons adorning Jace's shirt, pinioned against him by the weight of her limbs gone limp beneath the heady scent of him, the heat, the palpable current between them. His hands moved with bold familiarity over her shoulders to encircle her neck, and she could do naught but shudder with pleasure when his thumb brushed over the pulse beating at the base of her throat. "I'll take you home," he muttered very close to her ear, and she swayed toward him.

"I don't think so, McAllister," Shane growled, yanking rather roughly upon Phoebe's arm until she slipped from beneath Jace's warm hands. "The lady came with me an' she's gonna leave with me, ain't that right, honey? Now go on."

"Stay where you are, Peaches," Jace murmured for her ears alone, his tone indicative of an impending brawl even more than the untested power of his clenched fists.

Blast it, but this wasn't at all how she'd planned it! She should be reveling in the murderous glower permanently affixed to Jace's brow. She should be rejoicing in the success of her childish plan to bring him to his knees with jealousy. Instead, she simply opened and closed her mouth several ineffectual times, muttered something about the salon and, clutching at her skirts and reticule, brushed past Jace and through the crowd. Her pace slowed only once when she encountered a pinched and pursed Henrietta Witherspoon lingering outside the women's salon, looking in desperate need of a cool drink. With an impatience fostered by the challenging and disapproving glare Henrietta leveled upon her, Phoebe pushed past that fortress of formidable woman and bumped headlong into another woman just exiting the salon. Such was the force of their impact that Phoebe landed soundly upon her rump with a startled cry.

"Oh, do forgive me," the woman murmured, assisting Phoebe to her feet and retrieving her dropped reticule as Phoebe smoothed her skirts. "'Tis my fault, of course. So very silly of me, you know."

As the woman pressed the reticule into her hands, Phoebe glanced up with a curious frown, attempting to meet the woman's elusive gaze with her own. She was met with naught but a cloud of rather peachy-colored hair. "You're English," Phoebe stated flatly.

The woman murmured something unintelligible and apologized again, then, with a hesitant wave of her hand, hurried down the hall without a backward glance. Musing on this, Phoebe entered the salon, only to stop short. There, alone in the salon, slumped upon a red velvet wing chair, was a recumbent Adelaide Prescott, sound asleep.

Or so Phoebe thought at first, until she ventured closer and knelt beside the elderly woman.

The woman's breathing came in tortured little gasps, her lips moving restlessly, her parchmentlike skin eerily pale, tinged with the merest hint of purple. A fat vein throbbed at the woman's temple and Phoebe stared at it for one agonizing moment and then the salon door flew wide.

"What the hell's going on?" Dalton Pryce surged through the door, followed all too closely by Henrietta Witherspoon, who erupted with a horrified gasp and nearly swooned at the sight that met her eyes. Frantically fanning her face, she sank into a nearby chair and began panting like an overfed puppy.

Any fleeting sense of disquiet aroused in Phoebe by Dalton's timely arrival was banished beneath the force of her concern. "Oh, thank heavens! 'Tis Adelaide! She's ill or...I don't know." She clutched at her reticule, watching helplessly as Dalton knelt beside the old woman. "I found her like this...sleeping or...oh, Jace, thank heavens!"

"What the hell...?" Without hesitation, Jace brushed past Phoebe to Adelaide Prescott, seeing to her in a manner that made Phoebe wonder if he'd tended to ailing people before. And the way he and Dalton Pryce worked together, almost as if they'd done so at one time before.

Jace lifted Adelaide's eyelids then pressed a very large bronze hand against the base of her powdered neck. "I think she's been drugged."

Pryce's head snapped up. "Drugged? How the hell...?"

"Maybe the punch." Jace stared at the old woman, his tone flat, unemotional. "I've seen this before. She'll come out of it in a minute or two. Potent stuff, but fast acting. A drug common among thieves." His eyes rose and locked with Dalton Pryce's, and then both men turned and fixed their gaze upon Phoebe.

She forced a smile, which wavered beneath their unflinching regard. "She's going to be all right, isn't she?"

Jace stared at her as if he hadn't heard her, as if he delved to her very soul. He'd never looked at her in that manner before, a cold, detached manner, too distant and unforgiving. A chill raced up Phoebe's spine.

Her chest heaved with her sudden shortness of breath. "Jace...what is it?"

His jaw tightened, his eyes bleak and barren until he averted his gaze to Adelaide Prescott, who suddenly moaned, deep and guttural, and began a fevered thrashing about. Jace spoke to her in a low and soothing voice, which brought an ache to Phoebe's throat, a memory of him soothing her. This seemed to calm Adelaide, for her moans became soft whimpers and her hands rested finally against her throat.

"Th-thank you, Sterling McAllister," Adelaide murmured, one veiny hand reaching for Jace's sleeve, her eyelids fluttering. "A fine young man, I always said. Never believed a word about Madeline and..." Her eyes flew wide and she suddenly clawed at her bare throat, then her ears, and began a woeful moaning that brought Phoebe to her knees beside the woman.

"Jace, what...?"

"My jewels! My precious diamonds!" Adelaide wailed, clutching now at Jace's sleeve. "Gone...they're gone. Oh, my dearest Williard shall never forgive me! Stolen, they were! Dear heavens! What shall I do? Oh...."

Cradling the woman in his arms, Jace murmured something to her then lifted a gaze seething with fiery emotion. "Get the hell out of here, Peaches," he snarled, his lip curving in a sneer. "Go... before... How damned stupid can you be?"

"Jace, what are you doing, man?" Dalton Pryce grasped Phoebe's wrist before her world ceased its confused spinning and he unceremoniously hauled her to her feet. "Not so fast," he muttered harshly, a tone she could well imagine he employed with his most hardened of criminals. So why the devil...?

"Dalton Pryce, release me!" she cried, attempting to wrench free. "What the devil is the matter with you two? You're behaving as if my behavior is suspect!"

Jace looked away from her as if the mere sight of her sickened him. "Go, Peaches," he growled. "Damn it, woman, you're mad..."

"What?" Phoebe shrieked, aware that Henrietta Witherspoon perched on the very edge of her chair. "Me?"

"Give me your bag, Peaches." Without ceremony, Dalton snatched her reticule from her fingers and tossed it to Jace. "Open it, my friend. I have a feeling I'm going to owe you one hell of an apology."

For the span of Phoebe's hammering heartbeat, Jace stared at the ivory satin reticule lying in his palm, then lifted it as if weighing it in his hand. "Peaches..." he murmured softly. "Why...why now? Couldn't you have waited? Let her go, Pryce."

Dalton Pryce blinked with astonishment. "What? You really are in love with her, aren't you? Have you forgotten an oath taken, my friend?"

"To hell with oaths," Jace growled, crushing the unopened reticule in his hand. "Let her go."

"Jace. Think, man. There's Henrietta here, remember? And Adelaide Prescott. Open the bag, Jace."

Jace moved so quickly Phoebe could barely draw a breath. And then her world went black at the sight of the brilliant diamonds slipping like fat chunks of ice from the satin to nestle with grim finality upon the red-carpeted floor.

Chapter Sixteen

Phoebe's humiliation knew no bounds. She stood stiffly on the stone veranda of the Prescott mansion, staring blankly at her hands bound before her by the length of Dalton Pryce's silk cravat, awaiting her doom beside the stoic constable Dalton Pryce had planted firmly at her side while he retrieved his curricle. Around her welled the now muted sounds of revelry, tempered of course by the fast-spreading word that a thief had boldly lurked in their midsts, brazen or foolish enough to attempt to prey upon old Widow Prescott by lacing her misplaced punch glass with some potent drug. And failing, thanks to the swift thinking of Dalton Pryce. His name tumbled from everyone's lips, followed by a stream of praise and high hopes that he would become the town's next mayor. A political career seemed inevitable for one so keen, so devoted to justice.

Their voices swirled around the foggy recesses of Phoebe's consciousness, which had long since ceased to function. So numb was she, she'd been capable of nary a sound, her hopes, her every dream scattered and crushed beneath Jace's solid footfalls as he disappeared into the night. A weight like none she'd ever known settled about her heart, knotting in her belly and swelling like sour grief into her throat. Betrayed... by the man she loved. Deserted and left for the hangman's noose by the father of her unborn babe. How the words had ached to be spoken to him this eve. How she'd yearned to run to him with the news poised upon her tongue, only to bitterly swallow those words upon spying Flossie.

A chill shivered through her at the slight breeze. So many questions, so many words unspoken. Dalton Pryce had told her to keep quiet, lest she further incriminate herself. No one would listen to her pleas of innocence, least of all Jace. Dear God, he'd looked at her as if he'd suspected her capable of such a ghastly notion all along! And she'd loved the man!

"Oops! Oh, there she is . . . the thief!"

The hoarse whispers and rustling of taffeta directly at Phoebe's back stiffened her spine and she yearned to spin about and claw those catty women's eyes from their heads. Instead, she focused upon the cobblestone drive and willed a dull roaring to fill her ears, anything to mute the purposefully shrill voices.

"Henrietta thinks Jace McAllister was in on it with her."

"But I believe Dalton Pryce. He says she acted alone, the tart! Why, Jace wouldn't stoop so low."

"Did I ever tell you I thought I saw Jace McAllister on that Mississippi riverboat I traveled on about a year ago? Only he wasn't going by Jace McAllister. His name was Sebastian Monroe and he was a riverboat gambler!"

"No!"

"Yes!"

"Are you certain it was him?"

"He wore a mustache then and ran with a wild bunch and all manner of loose women. I even saw him pull his gun out so fast one man dropped his false teeth right there on the poker table! But, honey, a man never looked so good in his trousers. Trust me, some things a girl never forgets."

"Do you think they'll even bother with a trial or will they just hang her?"

"Hanging or lynching. Either will suit her fine. Hussy! Looks like a whore with her dress all stained and her bosoms coming out of her gown like that! She looks just like those tramps on Widebottom Street and—why, hullo, Charlotte! You must be awfully pleased to be all but betrothed to the town's next mayor, hmm?"

Charlotte's skirts rustled crisply as she paused. "Hortense, my dear," she crooned too sweetly, the mere sound of her voice threatening to dissolve Phoebe in a heap of tears. "Did you enjoy the spinach soufflé?"

"I . . . I . . . yes, Charlotte, very much, though dinner was several hours ago. Why do you ask?"

"Because, my dear Hortense, you've a very large chunk of spinach between your two front teeth. Ta, ta!"

"You're wicked," Phoebe murmured, swaying against her friend as Charlotte clasped a strong arm about her shoulders. "And I love you for it."

"They're beasts," Charlotte hissed, smoothing the hair from Phoebe's damp brow and shooting the constable a withering glower. "Dear God, Phoebe, I just heard. This is entirely too dreadful. The things people are saying. Why, it's spreading like wildfire. What the devil happened?"

The tears finally slipped from Phoebe's eyes, splashing on her bound hands. "Your D-Dalton believes I'm a bloody thief!"

"Dalton?"

Phoebe caught her trembling lower lip between her teeth. "And J-Jace... Oh, God, Charlotte... They found Adelaide Prescott's stolen necklace in my reticule, that's why!"

"Phoebe! You didn't!"

Phoebe's disbelief knew no bounds and she stared horror-stricken at her friend through a blur of unshed tears. "Charlotte! Blast you! This is no time for foolery! Someone put that necklace in my bag, don't you see?"

"Some of the guests say they saw you follow Mrs. Prescott into the powder room."

Phoebe hung her head, her shoulders drooping beneath the weight of her fate. "Dear God, even my best friend won't believe in my innocence. Do you think your fine upstanding Dalton shall? Or some hanging judge somewhere? I've no proof of anything! I'm going to jail, Charlotte! I may die! Oh, good heavens, you'd best tell Shane Morgan. The man will..."

"He's gone."

"Gone? Already? Without a final word to me before I am delivered to my doom? Bloody arrogant outlaw!"

"I saw him leave long before this all happened." Charlotte's arm tightened about Phoebe's shoulders and she seemed to pause with indecision before she spoke again. "I... uh, well, Phoebe, I believe he was with another woman, a woman with orange hair."

Phoebe closed her eyes and shook her head with utter disbelief. "Fickle, to boot. Men. A bloody useless lot on the whole, don't you agree, Charlotte?"

"I don't believe that matters much now, Phoebe." Charlotte's slender fingers kneaded Phoebe's wrists beneath her bonds. "The rumor is that you're Peaches St. Clair, a much wanted, highly sought-after jewel thief from England."

Phoebe's mouth sagged and her eyes flew wide, an ominous ringing beginning in her ears. "Peaches," she whispered, suddenly too terrified to confront the truth looming before her. "Only *he* ever called me Peaches, and I allowed him to. He thought I was this thief all along. He must have. But why, and..." Her head spun with the implications of such a thought.

"The idea!" Charlotte huffed. "Dalton can't possibly believe such a thing."

"He does indeed," Phoebe croaked, attempting to stifle fresh tears. "Your bloody fiancé shall escort me forthwith to yon jail, Charlotte. Dear God, send word to my father."

"Of course, first thing tomorrow," Charlotte crooned, attempting to arrange Phoebe's tumbled excuse for a coiffure. "You're a mess. I'll get you fresh clothes, and I'll talk to Dalton, Phoebe. I'm certain I can get the man to see reason. In fact, if I employ my newest little trick..."

Phoebe couldn't help her dramatic gasp of shock. "Charlotte, *my* Charlotte, employing tricks with a man? Oh, do tell!"

Charlotte clucked her tongue and smoothed Phoebe's gown. "I would only disappoint and bore you, Phoebe. 'Tis no doubt something you've practiced on your beaux from the very start. Now stop sniffling and crying, you goose."

A tiny smile trembled upon Phoebe's lips. "You sound like me."

"Good. You always knew how to whip me into shape. And don't fret, Phoebe. 'Twill be but one night and you shall step freely from that jail, trust me. Oh, here comes Dalton now. I'd best disappear." Charlotte gave her a fierce hug then slipped into the night, leaving Phoebe to face a stony-faced Dalton Pryce, feeling very much alone and utterly terrified despite Charlotte's words of encouragement.

* * *

Something very long and spindly crept across Phoebe's bare foot. With an agonized croak, she clawed at her foot until the skin bore fresh welts, just like those upon her arms and legs, ghastly testament to the horrors she'd undergone through the wee hours of the night, locked in this rancid excuse for a cell. Her head lolled against the damp stone wall at her back, and she clasped trembling arms about her bare shoulders, hugging herself against the chill permeating the dirt floor beneath her legs. Another tremor shot through her at the thought of the hairy, spindly legged creatures venturing from every damp, foreboding crevice in these walls, eager to sink their tiny jaws into perfumed flesh. With a muffled sob, she drew her legs tight beneath her and cowered farther into the corner, her eyes wide, darting feverishly about her tiny keep.

Sometime during the night she'd thought she'd gone blind, so pitch-dark had the room become before her terrified eyes. Only now, with the merest hint of light filtering through a tiny window high above her, could she distinguish the iron bars of her prison. A sound not unlike the droning of a sleeping man came to her from down the narrow passageway and her stomach heaved and roiled.

That man…that jailer…Glute, Dalton had called him. And a more filthy, putrid-smelling, foul excuse for a human being, Phoebe had yet to encounter. Awash in the excesses of flesh and three-day-old sweat, he'd leered at her as if she were some dainty morsel he wished to sink his rotting teeth into, then licked the spittle from his lips and held a grimy hand to her cell as if he invited her in to dine with him. Her hesitation and any beseeching looks she'd flung Dalton's way were soundly ignored, though he did mutter something that seemed to infuriate Glute and set the jailer mumbling and grumbling and belching the night away over a bottle of whiskey. But he did indeed leave her alone, despite the key ring dangling from his pocket, keys that would gain entrance to her cell. She was his sole prisoner, subject to his every twisted, vile whim, her only salvation from such a fate the invisible hand of Dalton Pryce.

Tears slipped from her eyes unheeded, streaming down grimy cheeks, over parched lips, which had seen neither food nor drink since early last eve. She stared blankly at the wall opposite, willing the threat of nausea aside, her mind numb from the incessant mulling over of the disaster that had once been her life. A rather carefree life, indeed, for a girl whose sole preoccupation to date had been the supremely time-consuming and taxing search for adventure and big powerful men. And how miserably she'd failed at that.

The bile rose in her throat, her belly convulsing, and she choked on a sob. Dear God, the unfairness of life! She'd rather die than retch into that fetid chamber pot Glute had so graciously provided. She licked her lips and felt her mouth watering ominously. No...no, she couldn't...she mustn't...

A scraping of wooden chair legs against the floor startled Phoebe from her plight, as did the muffled sounds of voices and the swishing of a woman's skirts. Charlotte! Phoebe's heart leapt and she stumbled to her feet and against the iron bars, her fingers wrapping feverishly about the grimy metal, her tear-stained cheek pressed tightly to the bars, unheeding of the smudges left in their wake. And then her heart flipped and sank to her toes and she retreated a step, hastily brushing aside the last vestiges of her tears as Madeline's crisp black bombazine skirts filled the narrow corridor. In an instant, she loomed before Phoebe, starched and coiffed and far too smug-looking for so dreadfully early in the day. She nodded brusquely to a bleary-eyed Glute, who plucked some pesky thing from a hairy ear before ambling off with a grunt.

Phoebe drew herself up as best she could beneath Madeline's severely raised brow, all too aware of her dishevelment, yet far too proud to cower, even when the corner of Madeline's tight lips curved ever so slightly.

"Aren't we a sight," Madeline drawled with a disparaging flick of her eyes beneath the slanted brim of her stylish black hat. "You don't look much like an heiress, or a jewel thief, for that matter." With a sniff, Madeline drew a gloved hand beneath her nose as if she found some odor offensive, which only strengthened Phoebe's resolve to remain impassive, stiff and unyielding. "I must say, you look every bit a whore. Fitting, wouldn't you say? Oh, before I forget..." From beneath her arm, Madeline drew forth a cloth satchel and held it between the bars. "Delilah sent you something—how did she so delicately phrase it?—something to chase away the sickness that comes when one is with child. Eat up. It may very well be your last meal."

For the very life of her, Phoebe couldn't resist snatching the satchel from the witch's grasp, yet found a strength of will to refrain from tearing the thing open, clutching it, instead, to her roiling belly. Dear God, something smelled divine.

"So tell me, Phoebe, or Peaches, or whatever your name is, whose bastard child sleeps within your whore's womb?"

White-hot anger exploded in Phoebe's brain, yet she drew but one heaving breath and lifted a defiant chin. "Were you not entirely certain of the babe's father, you wouldn't be gloating before me so dreadfully smug, Madeline, as if you wished to make certain that I am indeed jailed." Phoebe's lips curved wickedly. "Perhaps 'tis jealousy that goads you, eh?"

"Brazen hussy!" Madeline hissed, her lips curling over bared teeth like a rabid canine, her fists clenching crisp bombazine.

"Brazen?" Phoebe purred, shivering delicately within her silken sheath and arching a delicate brow, determined to explore the depths of Madeline's simmering rage. "Oh my, yes, that and more, my dear Madeline. Ever since the day Jace first took me to his bed. Perhaps 'tis why the man has sought me every night thereafter, eh? But hussy? Me?" Phoebe laughed low and smooth, as silky as her gown despite the trembling in her throat. "Surely you jest, for 'tis you, Mistress Maddie of Philadelphia, who has a corner on that market, isn't that so?"

Madeline moved forward so quickly, with such an expulsion of venom, that Phoebe nearly shrank into the corner, cowering from those talons gripping the iron bars with white-knuckled fury. Madeline leaned close to the bars, her words spat with hatred, fueled by Phoebe's unflinching resolve. "You scheming little bitch! Jace doesn't love you. He never will."

Something primal flared deep in Phoebe's belly, pride and something more, a fierce determination to best her foe, to prove this woman wrong, no matter the cost. Thus, she squared her shoulders and gave Madeline a cool sweep of her eyes, summoning a husky, all-too-confident drawl. "Oh, but he does, Madeline, and well you know it. Even if I hang, Jace will never be yours."

Madeline gave a harsh laugh, a shrill cackle that raised the hairs along Phoebe's neck and sent a chill of dread racing along her spine. "I fear, little tart, that you are dreadfully mistaken." An evil flame flared in the depths of Madeline's dark eyes and her lips twisted into a self-satisfied smirk. "Jace belongs to me, he always has, since the day I bore his child ten years ago, which is something you, my dear little British floozy, shall never do."

"Don't bet Pine Grove on it," Phoebe murmured, her gaze flickering over Madeline's hands trembling upon the iron bars, the glazed eyes, the hat slipping precariously from its perch atop gray-streaked hair. Phoebe seized opportunity, praying mightily that her ploy would indeed work. "Spare me your brokenhearted delusions, Madeline, your idle threats and grim prognostications, for 'tis the stuff dreams are made of." The hammering of her pulse grew deafening in Phoebe's ears, yet she couldn't stop, she wouldn't. If only wishing so would make it true. "Jamie is not Jace's son, Madeline. Jace knows...about the blackmailing, about Gideon Goare and your dark secrets. He knows you've been selling off parcels of Pine Grove to keep those secrets, and he intends to thwart your every effort." The blood draining from Madeline's face filled Phoebe's voice with a low rumbling of confidence. "'Tis you who should wish for my fate, Madeline, over that which awaits you beyond yonder door."

"You lie," Madeline croaked savagely, her hands shaking uncontrollably upon the bars, her eyes wide, devoid of all glimmer of reality. "You lie. He doesn't know...he cannot. I'll prove it to him!" With a maniacal laugh, she lifted her skirts as if she meant to beat a hasty retreat then paused, her eyes flickering distastefully over Phoebe, her voice dripping with contempt. "The day you hang, my dear, shall be the happiest day of my life." With a final swish of bombazine, she strode down the hallway, leaving Phoebe to collapse upon the dirt floor in a silken heap, clutching the satchel to her breast and giving free rein to the tears burning for release.

"Oh, dear God, look at you!"

Phoebe opened her eyes and groaned as she attempted to move her neck, as stiff and resisting as the joints in her legs and arms, as the entire length of her back propped against the stone wall. She'd slept, her solitary haven, something she'd never sought as escape before. How she wished to keep sleeping.

She ventured a lame smile and closed her eyes upon Charlotte's stricken visage and the brilliant sunlight streaming into her cell. Sweat trickled over her temple, between her breasts, unheeded. "Give me a moment, Charlotte, will you? You know how dreadful I look before my daily toilette."

"It *is* you," Charlotte breathed, her voice as taut as the muscles in Phoebe's neck. "Dear God, what have they done to you?"

"Drawn and quartered," Phoebe muttered, rolling her head from side to side along the stone wall to loosen the joints. "Tomorrow, the stockade."

"Have you eaten?"

Phoebe couldn't help the grim curve of her lips as she struggled to her feet. "Madeline was kind enough to bring me some of Delilah's tarts, and some cheese and bread. A dear, delightful woman, that Madeline."

"I brought you some of your clothes. Those blasted bicycle bloomers and a comb for your hair and . . ." Charlotte fished inside one deep pocket, casting a furtive glance down the passage toward Glute. "I also brought some of this," she whispered hoarsely, stuffing whatever it was into the mound of clothing she thrust through the bars.

Phoebe frowned at the tiny blue bottle she drew forth from the rumpled clothing and read the scrolled label. "Ayer's Fast-Acting Sarsaparilla, for soothing nerves and other ailments too numerous to mention."

"Just in case you find sleep elusive. 'Tis said to be extremely potent, so take just a little," Charlotte informed her in so sincere a manner Phoebe hadn't the heart to laugh, nor the inclination. The day she imbibed some much-touted soporific peddled by an utterly phony medicine man . . .

"Thank you, Charlotte," she murmured, stuffing the nostrum into her breeches pocket. "So when is Dalton releasing me? Soon, I hope. I need a bath and . . ."

"You . . . uh . . . you may want to take a swallow or two of that," Charlotte advised rather grimly, biting her lip in a manner that made Phoebe's heart plummet to her toes. "I . . . uh . . . I've some rather distressing news, and though I'm not the sort to say I told you so—blast it all, Phoebe, I warned you!"

Phoebe clutched her breeches to her hammering breast. "I don't want any bad news . . . please."

" 'Tis concerning Jace, Phoebe."

Phoebe's heart careened then stopped. "No . . . don't. I . . . he's gone off and killed someone, hasn't he? He's done something dreadful, hasn't he?"

Charlotte gulped and gave a hesitant nod that set Phoebe's heart in ice. " 'Tis indeed dreadful, Phoebe, though he hasn't killed anyone, at least not since last night. And I don't think he will because he's . . . well, he's . . ." Charlotte bit her lip again, drew several unsteady breaths, and Phoebe nearly went mad with the agony of it all. "He's not what he seems."

Phoebe drew herself up with renewed ire in a vain attempt to shove aside the terror trembling within her, to forestall Charlotte. "You're bloody right, he's not!" she railed. "Thinking I'm some blasted thief named Peaches? Dear God, if I *were* a thief, I certainly wouldn't go by the name Peaches! I don't even look like a Peaches! Leaves a godawful taste in one's mouth and . . ."

"Phoebe, stop . . . listen to me. Dalton told me everything and I must tell you."

"No, you mustn't," Phoebe murmured, giving free rein to the tears slipping from her eyes. "Whatever it is, I don't want to know, truly I don't. I love him, you see. I love . . ."

"Oh, Phoebe . . ." Charlotte's hand clasped Phoebe's through the bars, her own tears spilling to her cheeks. "You cannot love the man. You won't, not after I tell you . . ."

Phoebe shook her head frantically, her lips trembling with unspoken pleas. "No, Charlotte. No . . ."

Charlotte's fingers tightened with surprising strength. "Listen to me, Phoebe, you must. Jace is no outlaw. He never was. He's a Pinkerton's detective, an operative sent by Pinkerton's to Buttermilk Falls to capture this thief, this Peaches St. Clair."

Phoebe swayed upon her feet, her vision blurring. "No . . ."

"Dalton works for Pinkerton's, as well, Phoebe. But 'twas Jace, and Jace alone, who believed you to be this Peaches, even when Dalton tried to convince him otherwise. He even thought at one time that I was in cahoots with you! Phoebe, 'twas Jace who saw you into this jail, and Dalton says that unless we can find the real Peaches, I . . .'' Charlotte shook her head helplessly and erupted with a choked sob. "Dear God, Phoebe, this awful woman simply must be apprehended or . . . Phoebe. *Phoebe!*''

But Charlotte's words were lost amidst the rushing of mighty waves in Phoebe's ears, waves that banished reality into the blackest of voids and set Phoebe adrift in a sea of brilliant light.

The sky was on fire, aflame as the sun slipped beneath a distant stand of tall, proud hemlock pines on a knoll that marked one border of Pine Grove. Jace paused midstride to drink in the display, odd for a man who'd moved woodenly through his day, all but consumed by a hollow, painful ache that had burgeoned into a numbing and consuming self-loathing and contempt. Like a man possessed, he'd wielded his ax, chopping mercilessly until his every muscle burned for some reprieve. Yet he'd provided none since rising from his bed before sunrise. He'd hauled timber, stacked logs, driven teams of sweating horses beneath a relentless hand until most of the timber had been transported to Abel Brown's mill and boat scaffold, where it would be sawed and stacked or assembled into rafts and loaded for the trip downriver. When the flood came, if it did, the timber was, finally, ready.

One half of Pine Grove's timber felled with the aid of his industrious lumbermen. When the second flood came in the September rise, the other half would still be jutting majestically into the Pennsylvania sky, never to see his ax.

Jace's throat tightened and he swallowed over a painful lump, his gaze sweeping about and settling upon the house, looming grand and glorious in the glow of sunset. The feeling welled again in his chest. Pride in honest toil and hard work. Pride, something peculiar, foreign to him, as foreign as his feelings for *her*.

He shoved a hand through his rumpled hair and balled his shirt in one mighty fist. Pine Grove would never be home, no matter how many trees he felled, how many verandas he painted, porch steps he repaired or shingles he laid . . . no matter how damn good it felt to call it home, to walk its diminishing boundaries, to sleep beneath a roof his father had built.

The sun sank low and disappeared, spurring him on with a surge of something akin to anticipation. Soon, very soon, darkness would fall, his ally indeed through the past several weeks. His strides lengthened, his heart hammered anew despite the day's gruesome toil, and he paused only once, upon entering his stone quarters.

That's when he saw Madeline.

"Jace..."

She stood beside his rough-hewn bed, one trembling hand resting upon the night table as if she'd stood thus for some time, staring at the bed in the dim glow of the sole candle nearby. Its glow cast her in shadows mostly, though the burgundy silk of her dress shimmered with a richness all its own, more vibrant even than the woman it sheathed so impudently. Low cut, with the merest cap of sleeves, looking freshly starched as if Delilah had labored over the thing since noon, the dress displayed far too much to tempt, Madeline's all-too-obvious intent. The woman should have been wearing black until a year and a day after his father's death. Not silk. Burgundy silk. A burgundy silk evening gown constructed for a woman ten years younger and twenty pounds lighter.

She'd loosened her hair and it fell in waves about her round shoulders, deceptively dark and glossy in the dusky light seeping through a lone window. Her eyes shone, a glimmer that he'd never before seen. Desperation... in the set of her mouth, the tightness of her voice, the hand reaching to him.

"Jace..." She took one step toward him and he gritted his teeth, wishing to God that he'd been wearing his damned shirt. Her eyes were all over him. One faded pair of denim pants and dusty black boots, bare-chested, sun-baked and smelling of the woods. Just the way Madeline had always liked him. Hadn't she told him so, ten or more years ago?

With one swift movement, he shrugged on his shirt and strode past her to the washbasin, where he liberally splashed his face, his neck, with day-old water, then dunked his head. He surfaced, sputtering and shaking the excess from his hair. Grabbing a towel, he buried his face in the soft cotton and something about the elusive scent of that cloth reminded him of Peaches.

"Get out," he growled, looping the towel about his neck and fixing her with a chilling glare. "Now."

"Don't do this to me," she choked, her voice wavering, catching, and he wondered if she even realized what she was doing. Something wasn't quite right about her. "I need you, Jace, please. Now we can be together..."

He gave a harsh laugh meant to elicit the painful wince she made little effort to hide. "If I wanted a whore, Madeline, I'd seek Flossie, then perhaps one of French Kate's girls, or any of the doxies down on Widebottom Street. But never you, Madeline. Now get the hell out."

She seemed to sway on her feet, her voice barely audible within the stone walls. "How did you know about James? How could you have known you weren't his father?"

He gripped the towel about his neck with such force it cut into the back of his neck.

"Did you see me with Gideon? In the barn? Or in that tenants' cottage? Which time was it, Jace?"

Goare. Goare was Jamie's father. All that time not knowing...

She moved yet another step closer. "Is that why you don't want me? Is that why you ignore me for the favors of some two-bit English whore-thief?"

Like a striking snake, his hand shot out to encase her wrist, twisting her arm painfully behind her. "Still your tongue, viper," he snarled through clenched teeth. "Peaches has nothing to do with my lack of feeling for you, deceitful bitch. Did my father ever know the truth, Madeline? Or did you let him die thinking his son had cuckolded him, eh?" His teeth ached, so bitter was his anger. "It killed him, didn't it? Living with a whore killed him."

Her head shook frantically, her eyes wide, deep voids. "No. Fever killed him, I swear it. But, Jace, I couldn't tell him the truth!"

"Of course you couldn't, Madeline," he growled, wishing for one fleeting moment he was the lowliest, the most depraved of men, who could strike a woman and claim dire provocation. His fingers bit into her wrist. "He would have thrown you out, and you knew it, so much so you didn't care about the price he paid, the idle talk he endured, the incessant speculation and rumblings as to why Carson McAllister's son ran off at the precise time Madeline became pregnant." He ignored her pleas, the tears she'd summoned, the trembling of her limbs. "People aren't as stupid as you think, Madeline. You and I were the subject of much speculation. But then again..." His eyes narrowed on her as if indeed seeing her clearly for the first time, and his voice seethed with rage held fiercely in check. "Maybe that's what you wanted, wasn't it?"

"Oh God, I did," she moaned, sagging wantonly against him, burgundy silk and bared bosom penetrating through his bared chest. "Oh God, Jace, if you'd had me but once, just once, it would have all been different. Why did you fall asleep? Why?"

He shuddered with revulsion and shoved her away with a muffled curse. "And here I'd thought all along that I couldn't remember because you were so easy to forget."

She clutched one hand to her heaving breasts and bit the other, choking on her sobs. "Cruel...so cruel. Why, God, why? All I've ever done to you is love you."

"The truth, Madeline, would have been a good way to show it. Letting me live a damned lie for ten years, thinking I'd..."

"I'm telling you the truth before it's too late. Before..."

"It's been too late for ten years," he muttered, kneading the aching muscles at the back of his neck. "It's over, Madeline. The whole damned mess. Over. Now get out. Go mewl at Goare's doorstep. I think you deserve each other."

"No, you can't. You're..." She sucked in a tremendous wheezing breath and gripped the table at her back. "God, no...you're going to get her, aren't you? You can't leave me. You can't love her...love that..." Her features twisted grotesquely, such was the depth of her hatred. "*She* knew. How did she unless you told her...unless you...? But how?"

He leveled a steady gaze upon her, his voice flat. "I didn't know the truth until I stepped through that door tonight, Madeline. And Peaches only guessed at it."

Madeline sagged against the table, her eyes blazing fire. "She...she..."

"Tricked you," he muttered, his fingers working on the buttons of his shirt, his desire to flee growing nearly unbearable. "I never thought of you as the gullible sort, but then

again, she's good, very, very good. Has been from the beginning." Shoving his shirttails into his pants, he turned to the
bureau and retrieved his revolver, tucking it into his waistband. "Get out, Madeline. And don't worry, your secret's still
safe. Neither Peaches nor I will give you another moment's
thought. Trust me."

He shoved a hand carelessly through his hair, plucked his hat
and buckskin coat from a nearby chair and strode to the door.
He turned toward her, somewhat taken aback by her utter lack
of movement or emotion, as if she were frozen in time. Something akin to pity surged through him, only to be crushed beneath the weight of the burden both he and his father had borne
because of this woman's treachery. "I've provided for the
money from the sale of the timber to be put in trust for James.
Dalton Pryce will handle it. And don't try to double-cross him,
Madeline. He's less forgiving than I."

And with that, he turned and walked into the night, his heart
lifting unburdened into the starry sky such that he did not hear
the mournful wail echoing in his wake.

Chapter Seventeen

Again, the inevitability, the terror of darkness descended from the sky.

Phoebe huddled in her corner, shivering despite the oppressive heat of the night and the weight of her breeches and cotton shirt. Since Glute had doused his meager lamp what now seemed like hours before, she'd crouched, staring blindly into the blackness, whimpering like an abandoned puppy and feeling far worse.

The night sounds welled around her. Tiny scratches... squeaks...claws scraping against stone and dirt. And that faint swishing sound made by slithering creatures, spiders... centipedes...worms. Her state did not allow her pause to consider that perhaps terror magnified or indeed created these sounds and her conviction that her cell swarmed with all manner of pest and rodent.

She clawed at her breeches and bare calves with mounting panic and choked sobs and then she heard it, and a moan caught in her parched throat. The creak of the jail portal.

Wide, fathomless eyes groped for light in the darkness and she feverishly licked swollen, cracked lips. Someone...not Glute...no, not Glute, for he snored in his chair. Then who?

"Hey! What the...?" Glute's gravelly voice echoed through the jail, accompanied by several thumps and scuffling upon the dirt floor. "Ya son of a bitch..." And then a muffled whoosh and a heavy thump, like the falling of a very large body upon the earthen floor.

Phoebe's teeth chattered uncontrollably and she cowered further into the corner as the jangle of Glute's key ring echoed down the passage. Lynching. She'd heard the tales of those frenzied mobs bent upon meting out their own brand of justice by hemp. Not even the local sheriff could stop them, nor a man like Dalton Pryce. Mad, uncontrollable mobs, determined that justice be done despite her innocence. They wouldn't listen to her pleas. They'd simply hang her from some tree, leaving her as fodder for vultures. A lynch mob wielding a dim lantern and the key to her cell, moving with all the stealth of a lone man down the passage toward her. Closer, the light was coming so very close now.

"Dear God, no!" she wailed, doubling over with her grief, her arms clutched protectively about her. "Don't take me...dear God, please, don't. I'll do anything, please..." Through the blur of her tears and a tangle of hair she saw the lamp and the shadow of a large figure poised before her cell for but one moment, then a low, muffled curse and the inevitable slicing of the key in the lock rent the air.

"No!" she wailed, burying her face into the mildewed corner, clawing and half-climbing the stone walls, seeking any haven from this fate, and she screamed when the iron bars swung open with a deafening creak. She'd fight them. She'd... And then powerful arms swept about her, turning her, and she was crushed against a steely chest, and a deep voice murmured soothing words into her tangled hair.

His scent engulfed her like his arms, the feel of him beneath her raw, bleeding fingertips penetrating the ghastly fog into which she'd descended, and for one heavenly moment, she sagged weakly in his arms. Then, as if a bucket of icy water had been dumped unceremoniously over her, she jerked violently against him, shoving and clawing against unresisting brawn, twisting and straining for an escape he had little intention of providing. With a growled curse, he lifted her from the floor, sweeping her into his arms before turning about and striding purposefully from the cell.

"Damn you!" she shrieked, her fists pounding uselessly against his chest, her legs thrashing wildly. "I'm not going with you! Deceitful cur! Lying lummox! You left me here to die! I shall kill you with my own hand, beast! I shall—!"

"I take it you're not too pleased to see me," Jace muttered, stepping agilely over Glute's prone and bloated body lying motionless upon the floor. The keys landed with a harsh clang beside the jailer's beefy hand and then the door banged open beneath the force of Jace's booted foot.

"You killed him!" Phoebe gasped, her gaze probing the shadow cast by his hat beneath a clear, moonlit sky. Only the chiseled line of his cheek and jaw were visible beneath that shadow, a harsh, foreboding countenance indeed, until he grinned, a dazzling flash of white that flipped Phoebe's belly.

"Not with one knock on the back of the head, I didn't," he drawled, his boots crunching upon the gravel as he strode around the perimeter of the jail.

Phoebe struggled with the tangle of her hair a moment, then wriggled anew within the prison of his arms. "You lying, cheating lout! Where are you taking me? To some bloody hanging judge, the better to see justice done? Or to some particularly sordid hovel Pinkerton's spies employ to torture prisoners?"

He muttered something under his breath that sounded like a snarl, and then she found herself shoved against the stone wall of the jail house and her breath caught in her throat. He loomed above her, so very tall and dark, broad and seething, muscles straining against every fiber of his clothing. "I'll gag you, damn it all, if you don't keep your mouth shut," he growled. "Unless, of course, you'd rather we were caught and you were left in Glute's capable hands. You seemed to be weathering his methods well enough."

His tone had suddenly softened, almost to a caress, belying the harshness of his words, and then his hands were in her hair, smoothing the tangles, then upon her face, tracing the contours, his thumbs brushing with infinite tenderness over her swollen lips, and it was all Phoebe could do to keep her legs beneath her, despite her every reason to hate the man. Her traitorous eyes sought his in the darkness, so close above her, and then his lips were upon hers, so very tender at first as he gathered her close.

"Peaches," he groaned against her mouth, his hands sweeping boldly over her hips.

With a moan of frustration, she shoved against him, twisting her head away. "How dare you?" she shrieked in a voice that echoed off the stone walls, all venom and fury, her fists pummeling his shoulder. "You used me! Made a bloody mockery of me again and again and I shan't have it! No more! Do you hear me? Do you . . . h-h-h-h-h-h—"

Her mouth was suddenly full of a rag that tasted distinctly of Jace, and before she realized, her hands were bound before her. She attempted to scream through the gag but the wind was driven from her lungs when Jace slung her unceremoniously over his shoulder and anchored her there with one very large hand cupped possessively beneath her derriere. She squirmed and huffed and pounded his back with her bound hands, and through her impediment called him every foul name she'd ever heard and some she hadn't, but to no avail. He strode along undaunted and paused only once, and that was to sling her like a sack of potatoes over Zack's back. He mounted swiftly and only then did he speak.

"You can ride like that until your belly's raw or you can sit upright in front of me." His tone was so very bland, as if he discussed the blasted weather. "You will, however, have to be a very good girl."

Phoebe grimaced at Sam the wolf-dog, panting and looking very bored seated docilely at Zack's feet. Twisting her head about, she gave Jace her blackest look through several clumped tangles of hair. How she despised the man, sitting on his blasted horse so arrogantly, heaving her about as if she were . . .

Where was he taking her?

He tipped his hat back upon his head and she could have sworn his eyes glittered with moonlight as they lingered upon her. "Are you going to sit like a lady and not attempt to squirm off?"

How the mocking tone suffused his words! How supremely self-assured a beast he was! As if she had any alternative! Where the devil was she going to squirm off to? As proudly as she was capable and as imperceptibly, she nodded. Before she could draw a breath, he lifted her clear of Zack and set her soundly before him, facing him, his arm wrapping like a steel band about her waist to imprison her against his chest.

"If you're good, I might even remove the gag." His warm breath stirred the tendrils at her temple and sent a shiver coursing through her, as did the deep rumbling of the chest looming just inches from her nose. Anger—so bloody elusive, and fleeting, slipping out of her grasp with but one touch of those powerful hands. "But first, Peaches love, we need to have a talk."

Talk? With a gag stuffed in her mouth?

Anger seethed anew within her as he reined Zack about and headed away from town, toward the dense woods surrounding Buttermilk Falls, away from civilization and Glute and Dalton Pryce and lynch mobs to a far worse doom? Somehow, she thought not.

She relaxed ever so slightly against him and nearly died when her bound hands slid brazenly against his groin, a tumescent groin from what she could feel of it before she snatched her hands away. She shuddered with profound embarrassment and felt her cheeks flame with far more than fury when his voice murmured low and seductive against her temple.

"Have a care, Peaches. I would indeed risk capture and the hangman's noose just to feel you beneath me in some moonlit copse. I don't need any temptation, trust me." He muttered to Zack and urged him into a smooth, undulating lope, crushing Phoebe against his chest with one flex of his arm. "Relax. We need to get as far away from here as we can by daybreak. Even then, Pryce is no fool. He'll be hot on our trail, as will every damned operative in a three-state range."

With a dawning realization, Phoebe stared into the darkness of dense forest all about them, listening to the steady drum of Zack's hoofbeats and the thumping of Jace's heart beneath her ear. Dear God, but hadn't she sensed all along that he'd rescue her? Pinkerton's and Peaches be damned! He *must* believe in her innocence! Somehow, he'd known she could never be a jewel thief! 'Twas the reason he had rescued her, before the lynch mobs could get her! He knew!

With soaring heart, she melted against him, laying her head upon his chest, full of a yearning to be as close as she could to this man . . . this arrogant beast of a man. He'd rescued her, believed in her, had indeed fallen prey to her as much as she had to him. The joy!

As if sensing her need, or perhaps due to some impasse, he reined Zack to a halt and looped the reins about the pommel. Her eyes lifted to his in a silent plea, her body moving of its own will beneath his hand stroking her spine.

"Wanton witch," he growled, loosing her manacles then slipping the gag from her mouth. He drew her hands to his lips and kissed her fingers, his eyes like twin flames boring into her soul. "Besotted and possessed, I am, and will be for the rest of my days. I trust you intend to make it all up to me somehow."

"Somehow," she murmured, then gasped as his mouth moved like a flame along her palm then over her wrist. And then her arms slipped about his neck and she arched up against him, her lips seeking and finding his, clinging and parting with a passion reawakened. With wanton delight, she rubbed her breasts against him, rotated her hips in an age-old method that elicited a low growl from Jace. He cupped her derriere and lifted her hips against him, making her entirely aware of the force of his restraint.

Phoebe spread fevered kisses along his throat to the vee of his shirt, tasting and nibbling, her trembling fingers fumbling over the buttons until his fingers wrapped about hers, stilling her quest.

"You'd tempt a damned saint," he murmured, pressing her hand close against his heart, his breath short and ragged upon her brow as if he struggled for control as much as she.

"I don't want a saint," Phoebe whispered, slipping her hands about his lean waist and snuggling against him. "I want only you." And then her fingertips met with the cold steel of his revolver tucked into the back of his waistband, and a chill coursed through her. "Surely you don't intend to use your...your...?"

"It's called a gun, love, something I have found of great use in finding dinner—like a fat rabbit or two."

Phoebe shuddered. "I'd prefer a bloody fish."

Jace laughed. "In the middle of the prairie, rabbits are a hell of a lot more plentiful than willing fish."

"Where are we going?"

He grasped the reins, urging Zack forward with a soft command. "West." The word sounded like a caress upon his lips, as if he savored it.

West. She liked the very sound of it. "Where will we catch our train?"

He gave a harsh laugh that echoed through the surrounding forest. "The nearest train to Buttermilk Falls that travels west is in Sweetwater, a good day's ride. We should be passing pretty close by come morning, but, Peaches love, the first place any agent will look for us will be the nearest train depot. It's the fastest way out West, and the most dangerous. Perhaps further along, once we make Ohio or Kentucky. Less chance for them to spot us if we hop aboard in some small town."

"West . . ." Phoebe smiled whimsically. Adventure, indeed.

"How does Colorado Territory sound? Snow-capped mountains and icy-cold springs. The bluest sky, the freshest snow, land just waiting to be claimed. I'll build you a house and we'll get a cow . . ."

A cow? Why the devil . . . ? Phoebe couldn't have cared less about the bloody cow. She burrowed closer and nearly purred. "Divine," she murmured.

"No, two cows," he said softly, and his mouth brushed over her temple then against her ear, his voice laced with a passion that lapped like an incessant tide at Phoebe. "But first, I'll build us a very large bed."

"Mmm," Phoebe cooed, closing her eyes like a contented kitten.

"And I'm going to make love to you day and night until you beg me to stop," he murmured huskily.

"Never," she breathed, her eyes slanting up. Set against a starry sky loomed the one visage forever to set her heart aflutter within her breast, the man with whom she'd spend the rest of her days, for he believed in her! He loved her! He'd bloody rescued her! Thoughts of furry rabbits and dry parched prairie, the danger lurking . . . all fled.

"So wonderful," she murmured, snuggling close for the ride, and her last thoughts, before sleep claimed her, were of the babe nestled in her womb.

She stirred in his arms, the softest of sighs escaping her lips before one slender hand slid down his belly, slowly, in a torturous manner befitting a slumbering seductress. And then her hand paused, resting with excruciating serenity atop the throbbing length between his legs. His eyes flew open and he stared at the first streaks of dawn through the branches overhead, then shifted her, reluctantly drawing that inquisitive little hand about his neck and nestling her against his hips. His chin rested against her hair, which smelled of dew and pine, smoke and sweat, a heady aphrodisiac indeed for a man besotted. She was covered with grime, smudged and tousled and, to his eye, perfectly bewitching, irrepressibly ravishable.

He should have broken her out of that damned jail before she'd spent even a night within those stone walls, bloodying her fingers, breaking her nails, clawing deep welts and gouges into her skin. Yet the timber had to be hauled, and somewhere, in the deepest, most cynical recesses of his mind, he'd wanted her to pay for the hell she'd put him through, a little honing up on the stuff fine characters are made of and all that.

Hell, he still should have broken her out the night before.

He closed his eyes again, content to listen to her breathing and dawn breaking through the forest, his hands stilling upon the winsome curve of her buttocks. A man strangely at peace, he was, despite the enormity of his situation, the unanswered questions begging to be asked of her. He'd forsaken every vow, his life's work, his personal vendetta, his family's home, for the sake of one little jewel thief, and all he could do was grin like a damned fool. He'd become what he'd despised and he couldn't imagine feeling any better about it.

A bird screeched from the elms nearby and she stirred, moving languidly against him, and he settled her high upon his chest and bent his lips to hers, which parted with a soft sigh. She tasted of sleep and the night, warm and inviting, yielding beneath his tongue and his hands molding her to him. She moaned and drew away, smiled sleepily and peeked at him like the most innocent of virgins through a tumbling golden mass and sweeping lashes.

"Good morning," she murmured, snuggling close and laying her cheek upon his shoulder. Her fingers delved into his shirt and stroked idly through the hair covering his chest. An innocent caress indeed, so very early in the morning. If only his skin didn't flame at her touch, the mere feel of her pressed soft and supple all over him. If only her hips didn't nestle so provocatively, so damned snugly against his. He was swollen, as full and heavy as a man could be, and she seemed only too content to practice her witchcraft torture upon his chest and awaken ever so leisurely.

The questions would have to remain unanswered for just a few more minutes . . . or hours, if he had anything to say about it. Something piqued the back of his mind, even as he drew her beneath him with one swift movement, eliciting a gasp of delight from her. They should have been moving on again with the first eerie gray of dawn, their bellies full of rabbit and hot coffee. They should have been miles farther west by now. They should have . . .

Her shirt, her breeches, dissolved beneath his seeking hands, finding the grass with but a whisper of sound, and his followed until the two of them lay, limbs, tongues entwined, bathed in the first rosy glow of sunrise. She flowed like molten honey beneath his hands, soft, pliant, so responsive it was all he could do to restrain himself.

"I could do this all day," she murmured, arching up to his mouth as it taunted the thrusting peaks of her breasts, her nails raking down his back.

His mouth closed over one nipple, eliciting a husky moan from her and a thrust of her hips, and he all but went out of his mind with wanting her. "I can't," he growled, rolling onto his back and drawing her with him, though his impatience had little to do with avoiding capture. His hands anchored her hips to his, his gaze roving over her poised in all her tumbled blond splendor above him. "So beautiful," he murmured, cupping her breasts, his thumbs moving over the peaks. "So full. Even fuller . . ." His hands swept over the curve of her belly, the fullness of her buttocks, rocking her against the entire length of pulsing manhood. "So damned lush, you are, like a sweet flower."

"Jace . . ." Her palms pressed against his chest but he paid her little heed, lifting her hips, his fingers seeking, delving. She clutched at him, breathing his name. "Please, Jace, I must tell you something . . . so wonderful."

"Tell me what, love?" Flattening his palm against the curve of her lower back, he drew her to him, tasting of the dewy scent along her throat, her shoulders, his fingers working a gentle torture between her parted thighs.

"Oh, Jace, I must tell . . ."

"Tell me you love me."

Her head fell back beneath those insistent strokes, her sweet lips parting with the softest sigh. "I love you."

"Like I love you, like I need you...want you, always, like no other woman, my lovely Peaches." And then he lifted her hips and entered her with one sweet thrust.

Words were banished to the dusky pink sky as he claimed her again, drawing her to the very heights of her passion before finding his own release deep within her. And slowly, like the dawning of the day, awareness crept over them.

"Marry me."

At first he thought he spoke the words too softly into her hair, or perhaps just imagined he'd spoken them, for she remained unmoving, having collapsed into his arms with a contented sigh. Yet her breathing seemed to quicken, and he stared into enormous amber pools above passion-swollen lips that trembled and parted and found his with unrestrained joy.

"Oh, Jace...oh, Jace..." was all she managed, and he tasted her tears and her hair as she hugged him fiercely.

"Is that a yes?" he murmured, rolling her onto her back and grinning from ear to ear like a well-fed lion.

She cradled his head to her breasts, a loving gesture indeed, only he found himself abandoning gallantry in favor of ravishment, his manhood swelling to life within her at the feel of her breasts pressed close. She seemed oblivious to all this, idly stroking his back, weaving her fingers through his hair, and too damned bent upon conversation of a sudden.

"Yes...oh yes, your wife. How lovely," he heard her murmur. "But first, Jace, I must tell you something. 'Tis of some importance, you see. I must..."

"It can wait," he muttered, his hands moving with bold intent over her waist. "Later."

"No, Jace, really...you are too much! We've a lifetime, you know. For heaven's sake, you'll grow bored and..."

"Never." He peered up at her, his hands stilling upon the full swell of her breasts. "Listen, love, I know what you want to tell me and it doesn't matter."

"But how could you know?" A hint of a frown puckered her brows. "It doesn't matter?"

He focused his concentration upon one pale pink nipple. "I want you for my wife, forever at my side, in my bed, no matter what, do you understand? Your little secret has no bearing on all that."

She squirmed enticingly in his arms. "What? I should certainly hope my 'secret,' as you so blithely label it, has some bloody bearing on it!" She shoved at his shoulders, attempting to wriggle from beneath him, until he stilled her quest with one sweep of his leg.

"What the hell are you talking about?" he muttered, capturing her flailing arms and rising above her, chest to chest, hip to hip.

She looked like a spitting little kitten, her eyes flashing dangerously. "How very gallant and noble of you to want me in spite of it! You're nothing but a rutting oaf determined to avoid responsibility at all costs!"

His eyes narrowed upon her, a nagging irritation mounting with his every breath. "Responsibility? You want responsibility? What about the burden I'll forever bear for breaking you out of jail? What about forsaken oaths, all for the love of a jewel thief?" He scowled at her, at the brazen distress written all over her lovely features. Even now she taunted him with the knowledge of her identity. "Cease the pretense or any heartfelt confessions, for I've managed to rationalize it all in my mind, somehow, Peaches. I can't seem to live without you, thief and all. So start making my becoming a wanted man worth it, woman, and kiss me...now." He crushed her beneath him, his mouth swooping over hers, his hips moving rhythmically. He ignored her squeals of protest, her pushing against his shoulders. "Damned foolish woman," he muttered against her throat. "I should have thrown you in jail the first time you pawned your spoils. Instead, I'm going to take you as my wife and...ow!" He jerked from her, clutching his shoulder, his shock knowing no bounds. "What the...? You bit me!"

Seizing opportunity, she shoved hard against him and wiggled agilely away, drawing her shirt and breeches about her as meager protection. "You're bloody right, I bit you!" she shrieked, her eyes wide and glazed with far more than fury. "And I'll bite you again if you come near me! And as for becoming your *wife*—" She gave a wry laugh despite the tears shining in her eyes. "That role, Jace, you shall never thrust upon me."

Those amber eyes narrowed suspiciously upon him when he bent to retrieve his pants. "I don't know what the hell's the matter with you, Peaches ... perhaps one night too many in a cell."

"What?" she screeched again, yanking on her clothes with little regard for the tempting display she provided Jace, who watched through lowered lids. "Tell me, Mr. Pinkerton, why on earth you rescued me if you thought me guilty of my crimes all along? You, who all but shackled me in that jail with your own bloody hand!"

He stared at her. "I love you. It's that simple. I don't give a damn what you're guilty of."

She shook her head helplessly, her fingers stilling upon the buttons of her shirt. "If you loved me, you'd know I wasn't Peaches! I'm Phoebe. You must know this! Dear God, I thought you knew. I thought that was why you came, why you wanted to marry me."

With a scowl, he thrust his legs into his pants and drew them about his hips. "Isn't it enough that I've sacrificed everything of worth in my life for you, woman? Isn't it enough that I love you, that I want you as my wife?"

She shook her head again, and fresh tears sprang into her eyes, yet she shrank from him when he took one step toward her, reaching for her. "At one time, perhaps it would have been. But not now ... not when I'm ... when we're going to ... Oh, blast."

He balled his fists at his sides, his frustration knowing no bounds. "I thought you women wanted only one thing, damn it all." He ground his teeth, all the questions looming suddenly. By God, he'd make her prove it to him. "Tell me, Peaches, how did you hook up with Blades?"

"Who?"

He nearly shook with his frustration. "Damn it, woman, your Shane Morgan, your Rudy Blades, the most wanted outlaw by Pinkerton's, a man I've been chasing clear across the damned continent for the past three years. He murdered my best friend, Aaron, and don't try to bluff me, Peaches. I know you only too well. Was he also planning to break you out of Glute's jail after your little scheme went awry? Was he to spirit you off with him to Dodge City and hide out awhile?" A thought blazed across his mind, nearly blinding him with sudden, irrational rage. "Were you in love with the man?"

"You thickheaded mongoose! How dare you think me the type to tarry with another while I sleep with you! You, who flaunted your floozy so boldly before my eyes, who pretended to be some bloody outlaw! I know of no man named Rudy Blades nor did I ever conspire with such a man!"

Of a sudden, the burden of the truth weighed heavily about his shoulders. He shoved a hand through his hair and kneaded the muscles at the base of his neck. "Yeah, yeah. It doesn't matter now, does it? I foiled his plans, no doubt, and he's probably halfway back to Dodge City by now, where he'll hole up for a while. And you know what, love? I don't give a damn." Their eyes met for one long moment and he glimpsed something chilling in those amber depths before she turned about to tend to her clothing, apparently resigning herself for the moment.

"I'll make coffee," he heard her mutter, and couldn't resist the slight curve of his lips. The girl probably didn't know the first thing about making anything but sweet passionate love.

"We don't have time to make a fire, Peaches," he said, rolling the rumpled blanket still warm from their bodies. He stared at her profile, the determined lift of her chin, the tilt of her nose. "You can get us some water...there, in the stream." He reached into his saddlebag. "Here. Take these." Tossing her the aluminum cups, he watched her as she made her way through the clearing and found himself marveling at her stubbornness. Perhaps she didn't as yet trust him. He had, after all, lied to her about his own identity, and then there was Flossie, and God knows what a woman's mind could do with that. He stuffed the blanket into his saddlebag, his eyes still upon her as she bent by the stream. Give her a few more days, and nights, and she'd come around. Once she believed his intentions to be entirely honorable, they could put the past to rest once and for all.

She walked slowly toward him, the sun catching at the tumble of blond ringlets cascading about her shoulders, her eyes low, as if purposefully avoiding his. When she was but two paces from him, he slipped his arm about her waist and drew her unyielding frame tight against him, resting his chin upon the top of her head.

"Peaches love, you're not the first criminal I've chased and apprehended, you know. I've done this for seven long years, ever since Aaron recruited me into the spy business. And in all those seven years, I've never once been wrong. Call it instinct. Hell, I knew who you were pretty much from the very start." He tipped her chin up and stroked a wayward curl from her cheek, his eyes probing hers. "What I didn't count on was falling in love with you, and for that reason I didn't turn you in when I should have. When Pryce or any other operative would have. I kept it all from him, from Pinkerton's, even when Blades showed up, because I didn't know what you would do if you found out I was an agent. Hell, I had every intention of asking you to come away with me, and then you had to pull that stunt with Adelaide Prescott. If I'd gotten to you first, you never would have seen the inside of that damned jail." His thumb brushed over the full curve of her lower lip. "Lay it to rest, love. There's nothing that could convince me otherwise." He gave her a lopsided smile. "Unless, of course, you can somehow produce from thin air some woman claiming to be the real Peaches St. Clair."

She stared at him so intensely for a moment he had to force a laugh. Taking the cup of water she offered, he drew it to his lips. "I'm just kidding, sweetheart." He drained his cup in one gulp then grimaced at the bitter aftertaste. "Foul-tasting water for these parts."

Those twin amber pools held him captive for several long moments until he grew dimly aware of a dull buzzing in his ears, a wavering of his vision. "Peaches . . . what the . . . ?"

He felt her hands clutching at his arms, her warbling voice from some great distance, her tears falling upon his hands, his arms, then along his face as she pressed her cheek to his. But how could she . . . ? And then the earth gave way beneath his feet and he slumped. She cradled him close, her sobs echoing through the din in his ears, her lovely face drifting into and out of his vision. And he heard her, the soft pleas . . .

"Jace . . . oh, dear God, it worked! Charlotte said it would calm me but . . . I'm so sorry! I have to . . . for us . . . for our unborn babe. Dear God, maybe I shouldn't have used the entire bottle! What if I killed you?"

Before he succumbed and slipped down that yawning preci-
pice into the void of black, a cool, calming void, he knew only
one dreadful truth: she'd drugged him.

Chapter Eighteen

She took his horse, his gun, his bloody hat and only a handful of the money concealed in the saddlebag. After all, even a man as resourceful as Jace would require a coin or two to help him along back to Buttermilk Falls, where he would be waiting when she returned with all the evidence required to prove her innocence. Unless, of course, he chose to follow her...

Allowing herself scant opportunity for second thoughts, she reined Zack in what she guessed was a southerly direction, guiding him through tangled brush along a winding stream and into a valley that meandered through sloping green hills dense with pine. Their pace was slow, due to the thickness of the underbrush and Phoebe's distracted state. She chewed at her lip, staring blankly through Zack's pricked ears, her concentration wavering whenever her belly rumbled ominously, bringing with it the threat of nausea. The air grew thick and heavy beneath the relentless sun, beads of perspiration gathering along Phoebe's brow and running in irritating rivulets along her temple, down her neck and between her breasts. Her hair lay like a suffocating shroud about her shoulders and she paused to stuff it beneath Jace's hat, which she slung low over her eyes as she had seen him do countless times.

Shoving aside the memories looming enticingly in her mind, she gritted her teeth against the watering in her mouth, the roiling of her belly, and attempted to focus her concentration upon her dire straits.

After a moment, she sighed with resignation. "Stubborn man!" she huffed, flicking a swarm of gnats from her face with a wave of her hand. "Never wrong, ha! Bloody good-for-nothing instincts landed me in jail, and him in the bloody woods with no horse." She slapped a bothersome fly from her arm and let out a groan of despair. "When I needed him most to help me, to believe in me, there he stood, awash in his infernal male ego, totally blinded to the truth even if it had bitten him in the bloody arse."

The truth...lurking out there amidst all the clues, all that had happened, and of which, at the time, she had been entirely unaware. "Too bloody hungry, I was, for that man, too eager to see the trap even he laid for me."

Someone had set her up, of this she was certain. As to who, she had more than a fleeting notion this Rudy Blades had had a hand in it, as did the woman with the orange hair, the woman with whom he'd beat a hasty retreat from the Prescott affair. Orange hair... orange hair...

Flossie? She grimaced at the thought and thrust it aside. Hardly likely that Flossie had ever quite recovered from her bout with the night creatures to cleverly lend a hand. Then who? And how? How on earth had Adelaide Prescott's jewels found their way into her reticule? She'd kept tight hold upon it all evening, except when she'd blundered into that poor Englishwoman and dropped it.

Phoebe's heart careened to a halt. *Englishwoman? With orange hair! Smelling vaguely of a peach! The real Peaches, in Buttermilk Falls, with her little hands all over her reticule!*

"No!" she breathed aloud. "It couldn't possibly be. But why? Why me?"

And then Jace's words echoed through her mind. *Unless you can somehow produce from thin air some woman claiming to be the real Peaches.*

To hell with the reasons why. What truly mattered was apprehending this Peaches, and Rudy Blades. And Phoebe suddenly had a very good idea where she would begin looking.

A sprinkle upon her nose drew her from her thoughts and she peered about with a growing unease, wondering how the sun had managed to slip so stealthily behind a burgeoning mass of blue black clouds. They advanced upon her from the west, spurring her on with a distant rumble of thunder and the promise of nature's fury unleashed. With an unsteady hand, she reined Zack along a new path farther into the forest, urging him on at a reckless pace through tangled brush, over fallen trees. And then the rain began to fall...softly.

What good was a quest to prove her innocence if death awaited her in the bleakest, most deserted regions of forest and meadow? Tears momentarily blurred her vision, and she brushed them hastily aside with a swipe of one grimy hand. A fool, she was, to have left the man she loved. Truly, couldn't she have found it within herself to let the man believe what he would? She had, after all, grown accustomed to the manner in which he called her Peaches. And what of their babe?

An anguished cry escaped her lips, yet she spurred Zack onward with a dig of her heels, her heart racing at the memory of another storm and her mount's terrified reaction to the advancing lightning and thunder. Through trembling lips the soothing words tumbled forth, though she doubted very much that the stallion could hear her over the mounting roar of rain upon the canopy of trees overhead. And then with one mighty heave, Zack plunged through a dense wall of tangled branches and suddenly they were upon a dirt road, a wide, winding thoroughfare, the sight of which brought a cry of joy from Phoebe's lips, a cry swallowed by the downpour. And then she paused, drawing up on Zack's reins and squinting through the rain in either direction.

"Which way now, adventuress?" she muttered with sinking heart, then nearly whooped with joy when she spied a horse-drawn wagon rumbling toward her. Some measure of instinct made her adjust the hat lower over her eyes and cross her arms over her bosom, the better to be mistaken for a lad by the driver hunched over the reins.

In a matter of moments, he pulled his wagon to a stop before her, peering up at her through the rain running steadily from the brim of his straw hat. A grizzled old man, he was, unshaven and unkempt, huddled against the elements in dingy work clothes with naught but a swaybacked mule to pull his empty, rickety wagon. He spat upon the ground then fixed a leery gaze upon Phoebe.

"Hey, boy!" His voice rose above the roar of the downpour. "What the hell're ya doin' blockin' the damned road, eh? Outta my way 'fore the mountain slides away!"

Phoebe tucked her chin under and summoned a deep, throaty drawl. "I'm lookin' fer Sweetwater."

The old man grimaced and his eyes narrowed suspiciously. "Whatcha been smokin' out here, boy, that ya don't know where Sweetwater is, eh? Turned ya 'round, did it? Or'd ya meet yer girlie out here, eh?"

Phoebe felt his eyes upon her, assessing perhaps, and for one painful moment filled only with the sound of the rain, she thought he would discover her true identity. She drew her arms tighter over her sodden and no doubt increasingly transparent shirt, thrusting out her chin defiantly.

The old man jerked his head. "Sweetwater's 'bout a mile down the road. Ya can't miss it."

Phoebe nearly yelped at her good fortune. Instead, she muttered a gruff thanks and spun Zack's head about, then dug her heels into the horse's flanks, setting the mud churning beneath his hooves. They had a storm to outrun before any capturing of outlaws could be accomplished.

"Damn, but you're alive. Now I'm going to have to kill you myself, you bastard."

The sweat ran into Jace's eyes, blurring his vision, and he blinked, then ran his forearm over his brow. He tried again, opening his eyes one small measure, only to encounter Dalton Pryce's scowling visage looming close above him. He closed his eyes again and averted his face, only then feeling the rain upon his skin. Not sweat, just cool rain.

"Oh God," he groaned, wondering how he could have heard Pryce correctly over the drums pounding incessantly in his head. And then there was the pain behind his eyes, a throbbing ache. "Then kill me now, man," he rasped through a parched throat. His tongue felt thick and lifeless, refusing to move. "Be merciful, will you, and do it fast."

"You don't deserve it, you dumb bastard." Pryce grabbed him about one arm and attempted to haul him to a sitting position. "C'mon, Jace, damn it, sit up. You're too damned big and heavy for me to haul around."

Complying as best he could, Jace regarded his friend with one eye, then hung his head into his arms, where they rested upon his knees. "Where is she?" His voice rang as hollow as his heart.

Pryce laughed, harsh and bleak, a contemptuous slicing through the thick air. "Who, Peaches? My friend, she's nowhere to be found."

She's gone.... "She drugged me." *Just like she drugged Adelaide Prescott and that poor old sot in Boston.*

"What a surprise, eh? Didn't she take too kindly to being rescued by the local Pinkerton's agent? You do realize what you've done, don't you? Conspiring with a known criminal... God, man, where the hell was your head?"

My head had nothing to do with it. "She's with Blades."

"She's with who?"

"Blades. That guy...the guy she was dancing with." *The guy I'm going to kill with my bare hands.*

"*That* was Blades?" Pryce swore mightily. "Now I *am* going to have to kill you. Damn it, Jace! How long has this been going on, man? Why the hell didn't you tell me?"

"I was going to get him myself, this time. Before anyone else could bungle the job."

"Well, you did one hell of a job bungling it, my friend. One hell of a job. Why the hell would he come all the way to Buttermilk Falls? Can you tell me that?"

"At first I thought it was revenge."

"Damn, not that word again. Against who? You?"

"You're damned right. He must have found out about my little liaison with his girl in Laramie and came out here to make my life miserable by using Peaches. Only now I'm not so sure that they weren't hooking up together somehow, or maybe decided to throw in their lots together." He winced as pain shot through his head. "Hell, it doesn't matter much now. He traced me through Sam. I didn't cover my tracks too well when I left Laramie. A little preoccupied with Pine Grove and Madeline and all, I guess."

Pryce coughed uncomfortably and his voice lost every last ounce of contemptuous bite. "Uh, Jace...uh, about Madeline."

Something in Pryce's manner brought Jace's head up from his arms, brought his bleary gaze to lock with that of his friend. "What about Madeline?"

"I went looking for you after I discovered that Peaches had been broken out, and Glute was certain it was you who pulled it off, though I wasn't, damned fool that I am. I should have seen it coming. And you called *me* a love-struck half-wit. Anyhow, I got to Pine Grove and . . . hell, Jace, I don't know what the hell happened out there, but Gideon Goare was lying dead in the foyer, shot once, right through the heart, and we found Madeline—" Pryce swallowed heavily "—floating in the lake. Suicide. We found a note and . . . God, what a mess."

Jace stared unseeing at his friend for several long moments, aware only of his complete lack of feeling, a numbness seeping through his limbs that had little to do with somnolent drugs. "Where was Jamie?"

Pryce let out a whoosh of air. "With Charlotte, in town, thank God. They're at my place until we can get the place cleaned up. A mess—God, what a mess. And some note, I'll tell you. I got it right here, Jace." Pryce tapped his shirt pocket. "She confesses everything about Goare being Jamie's father, and that she shot him because of the blackmail . . . and why she killed herself. She mentions you."

With a scowl, Jace shook his head and averted his eyes, fighting the bile rising in his throat. Guilt, Madeline's final quest to ruin his life. By God, he wouldn't let her do it. Without Pryce's aid, he struggled to his feet, lifting his face to the pouring rain as if to cleanse himself of all that had gone before, as if seeking coherent thought. Shoving his hands through his hair, he cast a glance about for his hat . . . and his gun . . . and his horse.

"Damned woman," he muttered, sweeping his shirt from the ground and shoving one corner into his waistband.

Pryce loomed before him, one hand resting just above the revolver slung low about his hips. "Where the hell do you think you're going?"

Jace glowered at his friend and pushed past him, striding determinedly to Pryce's horse. "Don't play lawman with me, Pryce."

"Hey!" Pryce hurried after him. "Hey, that's my saddle you're unbuckling there. What the hell are you doing, Jace?"

"What are *we* doing," Jace countered grimly. "We're going after her, both of us, on this horse."

"Oh no we're not."

"Shut up, Pryce." Jace slid the saddle from the horse's back and heaved it into a tangle of brush. "She's with Blades, remember? I'm going to need you as my second."

Pryce gaped at him. "Your *second?* Not on your life, you bastard. She's a thief, a damned criminal! Hell, I've got operatives in a three-state range looking for her!"

Jace grinned devilishly. "All the more reason to find her before they do. Do you have another gun?"

Pryce nearly handed Jace the additional gun in his holster before he caught himself and ground out a curse. "Why the hell do you even want her? You've got an unblemished career. Hell, you could write your damned ticket with Pinkerton's. Why the hell would you sacrifice all that? Go home, Jace. I'll cover for you, pay off Glute, whatever it takes. Nobody would ever have to be any the wiser. And we'll catch up with Blades, somehow. Why do it this way?"

The rain suddenly fell in torrents, blinding Jace momentarily. He clenched his fists at his sides and gritted his teeth. Admitting weaknesses had never been something to which he'd aspired. Especially admitting weaknesses to friends. *"Why?"* he bellowed above the roar, thrusting out his chin defiantly. *"Why?* Because I love her, that's why. Because I've never asked another woman to be my wife, and damn it all, she *will* be my wife, whether she wants to be or not. Quit gaping at me like a fish, man, and mount! Now!"

Pryce's shoulders sagged and he shook his head helplessly, shoving the gun into Jace's hand. "Damn it all, you're going to ruin my damned life, and I'm letting you," he grumbled, allowing Jace to assist him aboard. "I've got Charlotte, a fine law practice, everything to live for, and I'm risking it all, my very life, chasing the most vicious outlaw of our time, all because my best friend was stupid enough to fall in love with a thief. Hey! Oh no, *I'm* in front."

"The hell you are," Jace grunted, heaving himself in front of Pryce and grasping the reins. "How far are we from a main road?"

"About a mile, why?"

"How far from Sweetwater?"

"Sweetwater? Another mile or two further. But why the hell . . . ?"

"The Pennsylvania Railroad's line to Chicago runs out of Sweetwater, connecting with the Union Pacific's main line out West, am I right?"

"Yeah, but in this weather there won't be any trains to be had, my friend. Deer Creek will be running too high, maybe even flood the tracks right around Turkeyfoot Run. No way they'll let the train run."

Jace's lips curved into a wry smile. "A damned shame," he drawled. "A damned shame."

"One way to Dodge City, please."

Phoebe shoved the necessary coin at the ticket man, her eyes beneath the low brim of her hat purposefully averted. Her toe tapped impatiently upon the wooden platform, the claw of anxiety writhing in her empty belly.

"No trains today, boy."

Phoebe's head snapped up. "But it's only ten in the morning!"

The ticket agent peered at her over the rim of his spectacles and adjusted his visor with one gnarled hand. "Rain's done washed away part of the track down by Turkeyfoot Run. Yup, could be another two days or so till we get it fixed."

"Two days?"

The ticket agent bent his attention upon the stack of papers before him. "Yup, or longer if it keeps rainin'. Not that we don't need the rain, mind ya."

Phoebe's eyes darted about the deserted train depot, into the pouring rain, and she nibbled upon a fingernail. She'd scarcely enough money for train fare, much less for two days' worth of meals, accommodation. "When did the last train leave for Dodge City?"

The man squinted over his spectacles. "Two days ago the Chicago-bound train passed through. The 9 a.m. On time, she was. Yup, an' full up, too. Serves all points west, yup."

Phoebe contemplated this, her brows knit furiously, until the ticket agent piped up from his work. "Sweetwater's one hotel's jest 'round the corner, boy, if it's lodgin's ya need. Rooms might be hard ta come by, but ol' Gussie'll find a place for ya.

Yup. No way outta Sweetwater today. Roads all washed out, mud slides an' rivers floodin'. No train. Could be an interestin' stay at ol' Gussie's tonight, eh, boy?"

With a resounding lack of heart, Phoebe thanked the ticket agent, pocketed her money and turned about to seek Zack. Stranded, in Sweetwater, for two bloody days! Someone was sure to find her. Then again, if *she* was stranded, so were other travelers seeking passage to the West. Perhaps even Blades and the real Peaches? If only her luck, or dreadful lack of it, would hold.

As if to reassure herself of her plan, she slipped her fingers beneath the elastic band at the knee of her breeches. There, beneath that coarse wool, tucked inside the lace edge of her stockings, was Jace's revolver. It mattered little at the moment that she'd never even held a firearm before today, much less given thought to pulling the trigger. Desperate circumstances and all that. If the situation called for it, to bloody hell with fear. After all, how difficult could it be to fire a gun? Then again, hitting one's target was an altogether different proposition.

As inconspicuously as she could, she tethered Zack before Gussie's hotel and, with hat pulled severely over her eyes and her arms crossed tightly over her chest, she entered the establishment. The raucous sounds of revelry echoed about her and she risked a hesitant glance from beneath the rim of her hat. She'd entered a common room, one designed for dining and drinking and lingering, or so she assumed as the place bulged with patrons doing the very same. Much to her relief, in such a crowd, with the air billowing cigar smoke, she was hardly noticed and managed to shuffle her way to the front desk without drawing more than one or two glances.

"Uh... how much for a room, please?" she muttered in her throaty voice to the woman behind the desk, Gussie, she presumed. Several painfully long moments passed, during which panic rose again within her, bringing her eyes up with unspoken questions.

Gussie pursed her puffy, rouged lips and fingered the black felt patch upon her double chin. Phoebe was aware only of those all-seeing eyes beneath hooded, kohl-covered lids, and a sweep of yellow hair. "Take off yer hat, boy, an' lemme have a look at ya."

Phoebe's hands gripped the edge of the desk with white-knuckled intensity and she opened her mouth then snapped it shut. Why the devil hadn't she thought of this? She'd have gladly shorn her hair to avoid detection. For all she knew, hidden amongst this crowd of rabble could very well be an alert Pinkerton's agent or two poised to pounce upon her.

"I . . . I . . . please," she stammered, spreading her hands in supplication, feeling tears stinging the backs of her eyes. Blast this sudden penchant for tears at the most inopportune moments! "I just need a room . . . and some food, dreadfully. I don't believe I have enough money . . ."

Gussie leaned forward until her pendulous bosom lay upon the desk. With a wink, which to Phoebe's eye seemed destined for some brawny lawman looming just over her shoulder, she twisted her lips and drawled, low and throaty, "Won't take yer hat off, eh? And I know why, 'cause ya ain't no boy, is ya?"

The room spiraled, cigar smoke filled Phoebe's lungs, choking her on that fetid stench, drawing her very life's breath from her. Somehow, some way, Gussie knew. Her life was over . . . lynching . . . she would hang . . .

Gussie's voice penetrated the mounting din, and Phoebe shook her head to rid herself of those words, clutching at the desk to keep herself upright despite the crumpling of her legs beneath her.

"Yep, ol' Gussie knows why ya won't take off yer hat. Hey! Hey, sister, you all right? Ya look kinda funny . . . hey!"

And then Phoebe did the most conspicuous thing she could have in that crowded hotel lobby: she fainted, dead away.

Above the clamor of the cooks busy at work over kettle and hearth came the crisp rustle of Gussie's petticoats and the staccato of heels tapping upon wooden flooring. Phoebe bowed her head over her empty bowl and drew the coarse woolen blanket about her sagging shoulders. Such humiliation. She'd expected to awaken trussed and gagged, bound for the nearest hanging tree. Instead, she'd been given food, a blanket, and spared any questions.

"Hey, sister, ya ate that soup up real fine." Gussie drew the bowl from Phoebe's grasp and settled beside her upon the sagging cot tucked into a dim corner of the bustling kitchen. "Ya feel any better, sister?"

Phoebe studied her muddy shoes and nodded. "Yes, thank you. I..."

"Save it, sister. It don't matter to ol' Gussie why ya wanted to go 'round lookin' like a boy, though I can tell ya, sister, with them knockers o' yours, ya weren't foolin' the ones what can see straight."

Phoebe flushed scarlet and hung her head in her hands, her unbound hair slipping over her shoulders.

"Now don't ya go cryin' on me again." Gussie shoved a plump elbow into Phoebe's side. "I got ya a deal I think yer gonna like, sister. Ya need a bed an' a disguise, am I right?"

Phoebe closed her eyes and nodded.

Gussie chuckled, jiggling and wiggling the entire cot. "An' I needs me a saloon girl fer a couple days. Ol' Nellie went an' had her baby on me jest as the rain come pourin' outta the sky."

Phoebe's eyes sought Gussie's and the words trembled upon her tongue. "I can't. I've never worked..."

With a dismissing grimace, Gussie patted Phoebe's hand. "It don't matter what ya can or can't do, sister. The men'll love ya anyway." Gussie's dark eyes narrowed upon Phoebe thoughtfully and she tapped a scarlet nail against her chin. "A name...hmm. How's 'bout Sundae?"

Phoebe frowned. "Like the day?"

"Nope, like the ice cream, sister. The men'll jest eat that one up!" Gussie's throaty laugh bounced off the kitchen walls. "Now, c'mon, honey. We gots ta git ya all dressed up real fine."

Phoebe gulped, allowing Gussie to haul her from the cot and through the entire length of the kitchen to a back door, which opened upon a shadowed hall. "But I...someone might recognize me and..."

"Honey..." Gussie's voice drifted through the narrow wooden staircase they climbed, her skirts swishing hypnotically before Phoebe's eyes. "When I'm through with ya, ain't nobody gonna recognize ya. Trust me, sister."

* * *

Gussie, as it turned out, had remarkably dreadful taste. The disguise she concocted for Phoebe consisted of a brazenly low-cut white batiste blouse with a frilled collar that perched precariously upon Phoebe's bare shoulders and cap sleeves that left the entire length of slender arm exposed. A richly embroidered silk corset of the most shocking scarlet hue cinched her waist, and from beneath this flowed much abbreviated white silk pantaloons, hoisted to the very tops of her thighs by two enormous scarlet silk bows. White silk stockings reached to just above her knees, leaving a grand six-inch expanse of leg entirely bare between the silk pantaloons and the lace trim of her stockings. Obscenely high-heeled scarlet silk shoes, complete with enormous bows, matched the feather protruding from Jace's black Stetson, which perched rakishly atop a tumble of golden ringlets. Her eyes were darkened with kohl, her cheeks and lips rouged, and a black felt patch sat impudently just above the bowed corner of her mouth.

She looked like the most brazen of floozies, the most bawdy of bawdy-house queens, the most soiled of doves, and absolutely nothing like herself or any Peaches St. Clair on the run. She had to wonder, as she poised nervously in the doorway leading to the saloon, if even Jace would have recognized her.

Another saloon girl sashayed past, her ensemble as garish and provocative, if one could call it that, as Phoebe's. She breezed through the patrons, wiggling between tables, her tray held overhead, swatting at overeager hands with but the most innocent of giggles. Phoebe stiffened her spine and drew a deep breath. If *that* woman could do it, then *she*, with all her fine breeding, all her desperation, all her need for a warm meal and a warm bed, indeed, she could do it. Slanting her hat lower over one eye, and with a last glance about, she strode determinedly into the saloon.

With a scowl, Jace swept his fingers over the unresisting brim of his new hat, attempting to situate it just so over his eyes. Damn thing wouldn't bend just right. New hats never did. He shifted his shoulders within his buckskin jacket and scowled again, fingering the gun tucked into his waistband. Even his weapon wasn't his own. Damned woman!

"This is it," Pryce muttered, pausing along the wooden sidewalk to peer through one of the hotel windows. "Crowded, but I don't see any of our guys... at least the ones I know."

Jace grunted and pushed past Pryce, shoving the door open with a tad too much fervor for a man wishing to remain inconspicuous. Pryce muttered something at his back and followed, continuing to grumble and mumble when Jace paused to scan the lobby. His eyes beneath the low brim of his hat darted about, seeing all with one sweep of the room.

"The saloon," he ground out, heading for the sounds of revelry emitting from the dimly lit room to the right of the lobby. A boisterous crowd had apparently settled in for the afternoon, filling every chair and table in the enormous room with a glass-hoisting, card-playing mumble-jumble of clientele. They ranged from top-hatted gentlemen garbed in the finest of silks to the mangiest of farmhands, all intent upon keeping dry and happy until the train ran again. Being confined together was an unlikely occurrence, indeed, and the crowd was growing more restless with each drink imbibed.

A saloon girl swaggered past, her generous hips weaving expertly in and out of tables and groping hands. Hurdy-gurdy gals, he knew well. They drank their watered-down tea with anyone who could afford their company and would even dance for a buck. None were ever particularly pleasing to look upon, though to this crowd, he could well imagine anything in skirts would be worth at least one good long look or a fondle.

He ordered two whiskeys from one particularly frisky-looking gal and settled himself into a shadowed corner with the best vantage of all angles of the room. Pryce was seated at his elbow, still grumbling like a wounded bear, morosely sipping his whiskey.

"You're getting soft, Pryce," Jace muttered, draining his whiskey, his eyes flickering from table to table, probing each and every patron's face.

"I'm soaked to my damned drawers, I'll have you know!" Pryce rasped, his rigid countenance looming before Jace.

"Keep your eyes on the room, Pryce, not on me. I'm not the outlaw, remember?"

"The hell you're not! Springing a criminal out of jail, detaining an officer of the law, forcing me to look the other way, so to speak, while you run off with a wanted woman. Hell, in some states you'd be charged with kidnapping me!''

Jace flashed a devilish grin. ''Now there's a thought. Bound and gagged, wearing only his sodden drawers, and found tied to some hurdy-gurdy gal's bedpost.'' Jace frowned as if deep in thought. ''Poor Charlotte would never forgive you for that, I wouldn't think.''

Pryce gritted his teeth and clenched his fists and looked entirely beside himself. ''Why the hell did *you* of all people, have to be my best friend? Can you tell me that . . . see there you go again. We're here to find the woman you supposedly can't live without and you can't keep your damned eyes from some saloon girl.'' Pryce shook his head and gave a wry laugh, turning about to see what it was that had captured Jace's unwavering regard. ''You've got the fickle heart of an outlaw, Jace. I can tell you . . .''

''Shut up,'' Jace muttered, his eyes narrowing upon the bobbing scarlet feather, the all-too-familiar black Stetson, *his* Stetson, damn it all, that plump little backside, those long curvy legs. Only one woman looked like that, walked like that and felt like that from clear across the room. Something fiery exploded before his eyes when she turned, avoiding a paw with a dainty little shimmy and a giggle that sent the blood churning dangerously through his veins. His eyes feasted on her, all of her, finding her garish display too irresistible for sanity, yet shaking with the overwhelming desire to wring her little neck, and that of every damned man in the place.

''It's Peaches,'' he managed in a strangled voice.

''Wha—''

Before he even realized, Jace had taken three long strides toward her, shoving chairs aside, his intent focused, his every thought upon what he would do to her. And then, just as she paused near the doorway, still a good fifteen paces away, fingering her bottom lip in a manner that set his groin throbbing, a broad-shouldered shadow filled the doorway. The man moved one step into the saloon and beneath a dim lantern such that the light flamed over long blond hair, a black duster . . . and the peach-haired woman at his side.

Jace nearly doubled over from the force of the unseen fist slamming into his belly. His vision blurred, yet he could still see her, that woman with the orange hair, the same woman at Adelaide Prescott's ball, the woman who'd smelled like a peach, the woman who had so graciously summoned both him and Dalton Pryce to the ladies' lounge to assist an ailing Adelaide Prescott, the better to find Phoebe with the jewels. It all suddenly made perfect sense, the pieces fitting together so damned easily, and he wanted to run to Phoebe. *Phoebe...* English. Then his eyes locked with those of Rudy Blades.

Chapter Nineteen

"McAllister. Damn, but I'm gonna kill that son-of-a-bitch."

The words were borne on an ominous growl that reverberated through Rudy Blades's chest and sent a chill of terror piercing Phoebe's heart, as did the barrel of a very large black revolver that suddenly seemed to fill her vision. She whirled about, dropping her tray, scattering glasses and liquor and money, clutching a hand to her heart, when her eyes locked upon Jace poised not ten paces away. He simply stared at her with that unreadable countenance, as if he knew not the danger. She must have screamed his name, tried to run to him on her blastedly high-heeled shoes and managed only to stumble with a helpless cry and fall to her knees upon the filthy floor. And then she was lifted by her hair and something jabbed her painfully in her ribs.

"I got yer girlie, McAllister," Blades taunted close to Phoebe's ear, his gun digging into her ribs and bringing a cry to her lips. He held her imprisoned against his chest by the force of one brawny arm. "Don't ya come any closer or she'll get it, right in the head."

At the feel of cold steel pressed against her temple, Phoebe nearly swooned. "Jace...don't..." she croaked, holding her hands before her as if to keep him at bay. Through a blur of tears she watched him clench and unclench his fists, his eyes twin sapphire flames boring into hers. He stood stoic, immobile, as if alone in the room, all others having taken calm refuge beneath tables and behind the bar as if this were indeed an everyday occurrence.

"Ya ain't as stupid as I thought ya were, girlie," Blades crooned wickedly. "Or'd ya come lookin' fer ol' Rudy 'cause yer man over there cain't give it to ya good anymore, huh?" With brazen aplomb, Blades's hand slid slowly over her belly to cup one breast.

Phoebe nearly choked on the revulsion welling in her throat and squeezed her eyes tightly closed upon Jace's stony visage.

"She's mighty fine, McAllister. I don't need ta tell ya that I thought a' takin' her myself many times." Blades's fingers tightened around one nipple and tugged, eliciting a sob from Phoebe and something akin to a savage growl from Jace. "Ya see how much she likes me already? An' I can tell yer real mad, McAllister. Ya look like ya want ta kill me. Yep, yer real mad, jest like I was real mad an' ready ta kill ya when I found out you was fornicatin' with my girl in Laramie." Blades spat upon the floor. "Damned woman couldn't stop talkin' 'bout ya, an' when she weren't talkin' 'bout ya, she was cryin' 'cause ya left. With that dog of yers. That's how I traced ya. Come all that way, I did, ta pay ya back by stealin' yer girlie, only I thought of a better plan, ya know. Got yer girlie close ta hanged and got me an' Peaches a way out. I's got smarts, girlie," he drawled, smearing vile lips against Phoebe's neck, the gun pressing with uncompromising intent into her side. "An' I know ya likes smarts, even though ya hooked up with some two-bit outlaw I never heard of, some dumb ass what thought you was Peaches. Ha! Now don't that beat all?"

Phoebe shook her head feverishly, her words catching in her parched throat, fear momentarily paralyzing her. "N-no...he's not." She swallowed heavily, her eyes seeking Jace through the haze of her torment, and she thought for a fleeting moment that he muttered a tight, "No, English."

"Please," she croaked, shuddering with repugnance at the boldness of Blades's hand traversing the entire length of her bodice with infinite leisure. "Please stop...he's a Pinkerton's agent. He'll kill you."

Blades jerked so violently he nearly cracked her ribs with the force of his snapping arm. "What the hell...a *Pinkerton's...*?"

Phoebe nodded vigorously despite the gnawing feeling that she had done something atrocious, for Jace closed his eyes as if in pain and shook his head. Perhaps if she explained.

"He's been chasing you for three years...revenge for the murder of his best friend. You shot him."

"Damn" was all Jace muttered, with a cold finality that encased Phoebe's heart in ice.

Blades let out a hollow bark of a laugh. "A Pinkerton! Don't that beat all? Three years, eh? Ya musta wanted me real bad, huh? That's why ya were in Laramie, ain't it?" Blades's voice suddenly dripped with cold calculation, as if his thoughts had taken a different turn. "It was *you* what got me thrown in that jail in Laramie, ain't it? You was the one what found my hideout, wasn't ya? You was usin' my girlie ta get ta me, weren't ya? *Weren't ya?*"

His voice rang shrilly through the silent room, dying into a stillness broken only by the steady drum of rain upon the wooden sidewalks. The rain...the very reason they were all here, that this was all happening.

"Let her go, Blades." Jace's voice, so steady and strong, deep and resonant, sent a surge of warmth and hope through Phoebe, almost as if he'd wrapped her within his arms. "This is between you and me, Blades, no one else."

"The hell it is!" Blades roared, jerking Phoebe against him and shoving the gun into the tender spot just beneath her ribs. "Ta get me, McAllister, I can promise ya yer gonna have ta step over her dead body. Only I's gonna have my fill of her first, yup. An, mister, I never gone back on my word."

"Dead men can't keep promises, Blades," Jace snarled in so savage a tone a chill prickled along Phoebe's spine, despite the revulsion clenching her belly at Blades's horrid proclamation.

Blades laughed wickedly and took a step backward, toward the doorway, dragging a resisting Phoebe. "Yer nothin' but a two-bit Pinkerton, McAllister, an' I been outrunnin' you guys fer years. An' havin' a good time killin' ya, too. I was only gonna make ya suffer, ya know, maybe cut off yer fingers or sumpthin' fer what ya did with my girlie. But now..." His maniacal cackle filled the room and sliced through Phoebe. "Now that I know who you really are, I think I'm gonna have ta kill ya."

"No!" Phoebe's wail rent the air, only to be cut short by the stab of the gun.

"Yep," Blades drawled with a nonchalance well suited to discussing the weather. "Now drop yer gun, McAllister, the one ya got in yer jacket there."

To Phoebe's horror, Jace complied and a revolver dropped like a lead weight to the floor at his feet. She felt his eyes upon her, so bleak, a vast emptiness like that filling her heart. She'd written his death sentence with her own words! Would this indeed be the last time she looked upon him? Grief twisted in her belly, and she would have doubled over had Blades not had such a viselike hold upon her.

"Now sit down, McAllister. Right there, that's it. And you . . . yeah, you there, hidin' under that there table, you with the fancy green coat. I like it. Real highfalutin lookin'. Go on, tie him up with that thing around yer neck. That black thing. That's it. Real tight."

Phoebe watched helplessly as Jace's hands and feet were tied securely to the chair, yet he seemed so casual, so very certain of something that was entirely beyond her realm. His gaze was fixed steadfastly upon Blades, a cool, unyielding gaze that revealed nothing of his intent. He looked so big, so invincible within his broad-shouldered bulk despite his bonds, so very capable of rescuing her. Yet how could he? He must. They had a lifetime to share, after all, a cow or two to purchase, a house to build and legions of children to raise! Certainly one insignificant outlaw like Rudy Blades couldn't prevent all that? Certainly Mother Nature wasn't to play such a cruel trick upon them all. Now that Jace finally believed her?

"Say goodbye to yer man, girlie," Blades drawled evilly as he leveled his revolver directly at Jace.

Phoebe's eyes widened with unmitigated terror. No . . . not cold blooded murder. No! She opened her mouth and . . . nothing.

"So long, Pinkie," Blades drawled, and Phoebe could have sworn she heard his finger tightening upon the trigger. She required little else.

With all the fervor of a woman's rage unleashed, she lunged against Blades, pushing backward and away from him, then slicing one potent heel into his groin and driving her arms in an upward slash toward the revolver. The gun discharged, belching powder and flame, momentarily blinding her. She heard a crash, like a body falling in a wooden chair, and for one horrific moment she knew she'd rather die than live without Jace. And then she realized she was free of Blades, and she spun about and crashed right into him.

"Damned bitch, I'll get you!" he sneered, one beefy arm swiping at her with a force bent upon leveling her, only she ducked, swerving out of his path, stumbling into a table and a man, then another. The room was a swarming, uncontrolled mass. And then she saw Dalton Pryce, with Peaches the thief firmly in tow. And through the blur of faces she saw Jace, on the floor, his eyes closed and blood all over his shirt.

Phoebe froze, the enormity of it all paralyzing her for one dreadful moment too long, for a callused paw wrapped about her wrist and twisted, sending talons of pain clawing up her arm. Yet she was barely cognizant of this, so numb was she at the thought of Jace dead. And for one endless moment she allowed Blades to haul her with him, toward the door... away from Jace... toward her doom. No... *my baby!*

With a shriek, she twisted her arm and collapsed her legs beneath her. Blades spun about with a vile curse, allowing her all the opportunity she needed to slip one shoe from her foot. Summoning every last ounce of her strength, she struck the heel of her shoe against the side of his head with a dull thud. Once was all that was necessary to stun him sufficiently, and his hold upon her momentarily slipped. With a cry of exultation mixed with mind-numbing terror, she lurched to her feet and stumbled past him, aware even through the blur that was once her consciousness that he lunged after her, one arm catching at her silk stockings. She reacted without thought, or perhaps with but one thought, and that was to get Blades away from Jace, a wounded Jace—*not dead... no... not dead... needed medical attention, that was all...* Indeed, with this one thought, she staggered through the saloon doorway into the lobby, through the hotel doors and into the driving rain.

She dared one terrified glance behind her and spotted Blades, lurching through the lobby. Without a moment's thought, she untethered Zack, a rather skittish Zack—after all he'd spent the better part of the day weathering a rainstorm—and attempted to haul herself aboard, a feat indeed when one had no saddle horn, no stirrups and no convenient tree stump. Shoving aside her tears of frustration, the mounting panic, she summoned some measure of her sanity and glanced hastily about. Just as the hotel door banged open beneath the force of Blades's boot, she hoisted one trembling foot onto the hitching post, thankful in some distant part of her mind for her lack of confining skirts. Using the post as leverage, she hauled herself aboard Zack and spun him about with a cry poised upon her lips, only to croak with renewed terror when Blades heaved himself half onto the stallion's back with a grunt.

Phoebe dug her heels into the horse's sides and Zack sprang forward at a full gallop, yet Blades, amidst all his twisted fortitude, summoned the strength to hang on. Phoebe leaned over the stallion's pumping neck, offering little guidance, for the rain and her tears and the wind robbed her of her sight. The stallion wove an erratic path, swerving and lunging at breakneck speed, and still Blades hung on. Phoebe swiped at him with one hand, a useless tactic, which elicited naught but a hoarse grunt that sounded far too sinister for a man clinging for his very life to a horse's back.

The town passed by in a gray blur, followed by trees and brush, and Zack's pace began to slow, perhaps due to the mire beneath his churning hooves, and Blades began to inch his way onto the stallion's back.

Higher and higher he'll pull himself until he'll be sitting upright, yanking the reins from my grasp, controlling my fate...a cold-blooded killer...

Without a moment's hesitation, she hauled back and up on the reins with all her might, driving her heels into Zack's sides. Just as he'd done the many times they'd practiced in the paddock, Zack skidded to a halt and reared high up on his hind legs, not once but three times, maybe four. Phoebe would never know, for Blades, with a howl of rage, slid from the stallion's back into the quagmire. He rolled over once then sprang to his knees, and Phoebe found herself looking down the barrel of his revolver yet again.

He grinned, an idiotic, maniacal grin that tore asunder every hope she cherished for herself and her unborn child nestled snugly within her womb. A bullet would outrun a stallion un-

der any circumstance. She was to die, in a field of mud, on a
rain-soaked, gray afternoon in June.

And then for some reason, Blades's gaze faltered and he
turned toward the muffled sound of hoofbeats rising above the
rain. Seizing opportunity, she slipped from Zack's back and
lunged for Blades's revolver, successfully knocking it from his
grasp just as another horse descended upon them . . . and another rider. With arms outstretched and fingers reaching feverishly, she dived toward the revolver, sliding several feet on
her belly through thick goo just as Jace passed before her eyes
in a blur, moving purposefully toward Blades.

She cried out to him, only the sound came out as a hoarse
croak past the tightness in her throat. It mattered little, for he
couldn't have heard her above the rain, falling in sweeping
torrents now, and above the sound of fists meeting fists, and
flesh, and wounds.

Phoebe crouched low in the mud, hanging on to the revolver as if for dear life, her eyes piercing the gloom, searching for Jace amongst the tangle of limbs rolling over and over
in the muck. She spotted him, identifying him solely by that
crimson patch upon his shirt, which spread like an evil thing to
cover his shoulder, half of his chest, so vivid despite the goo
covering him from head to toe. He was wounded.

She bit her knuckles to keep from crying out, but she must
have, for suddenly she didn't know who was who, so drenched
in mud were they. And one of them was indeed winning this
fight. His mighty fists met belly and ribs, jaw and nose, again
and again, until blood spurted everywhere and Phoebe was
certain she heard bone splintering. He sent the other man
sprawling upon the mud with one savage fist to the jaw and
leapt upon his chest, pinioning his foe with the force of his legs,
raising one bloody fist high into the air as if to finish the job.
Averting her eyes momentarily, Phoebe cringed with revulsion
at the force of such violence, such a raw, animalistic display.
Why was it so damned necessary?

Yet he paused, perhaps because the man lay prone and defeated, unmoving, bloody pulp, nothing more, sprawled two
inches deep in goo. The victor rose wearily and turned toward
Phoebe, and by God if she could only have recognized him, for
he was as bloodied, as covered with grime! With trembling

hands she raised the revolver, leveling it squarely at the broad chest advancing upon her with purposeful intent—murderous or loving, if only she could tell! And when, dear God, would it be too late if it were indeed Blades?

Her finger tightened upon the trigger and she squeezed her eyes tightly shut . . . and then she heard it, above the din of the rain and her hammering pulse, his voice.

"English . . ."

Her eyes flew open, yet what met her gaze wiped the smile from her face and sent her heart plummeting to her toes. Behind Jace's back, Rudy Blades lay, propped up on one elbow with a gun poised, cocked, ready to fire upon Jace. At such close range, despite Blades's slack, wavering grasp, the bullet couldn't possibly miss its mark.

Phoebe adjusted her aim and pulled the trigger. The world exploded before her eyes and then she landed, skidding a good foot or two backward in the muck, soundly upon her backside. With an anguished cry, she flung the gun aside and scrambled to her feet, slipping, sliding, falling to her knees, even crawling for several yards through the acrid smoke, seeking in the gloom with wide, terrified eyes. Surely she hadn't hit Jace.

And then, just as she gave full vent to her tears, powerful arms swept about her, crushing her against a chest that had never felt so good. Her fingers burrowed in mud-caked hair. Her lips pressed feverishly against his temple, his beard-roughened cheek, then met his lips and parted with a sob of joy as the two of them sank to the ground.

"You killed him," Jace rasped against her mouth.

"I killed him," Phoebe sobbed, tasting her tears and perhaps his, then collapsing against him. "I killed him."

"You saved my life." He cradled her in his arms, burying his face against her neck and shoulder, crushing her to him as if he never wished to let her go. "Twice."

Phoebe closed her eyes, gulping in huge breaths, allowing the rain to bathe them. He was warm, vital beneath her hands despite his wound. "You saved my life, as well, but you're wounded. We must get you back."

He held her fast in his arms, stilling her movements. "The bullet only grazed my shoulder. It can wait. Now tell me." His hands cupped her face, drawing her eyes to his, her mouth just a breath beneath his. "Tell me, love."

"I love you," she whispered, arching up against him, her arms slipping about his neck. "I love you."

His hands swept over her back, about her waist, and met over her belly. His eyes lowered to his thumbs rubbing tenderly over her stomach. "Tell me the other part."

A fluttering sensation filled her as his eyes, brimming with far more than unspoken emotion, met hers. "Tell you what, my love?" she murmured, caressing that lean, ruggedly handsome face.

His lips found hers. "Tell me the part about the baby."

Phoebe's eyes met Dalton Pryce's as he closed the door softly behind him and joined her in the dimly lit hall. He gave her a lame smile and fingered his bearded chin in a manner that left her wondering why he seemed so bloody uncomfortable.

"What is it, Dalton?"

Pryce raised bushy copper brows and sighed heavily. "He's...uh...rather...uh...cranky. In a blasted foul mood, to be perfectly honest with you."

"His shoulder?"

Pryce nodded. "The doc just left with strict orders that he keep to his bed for a good several days. I don't think he took too kindly to that news, or to the medication the doc left. That bullet cut a nasty path through his shoulder, so don't let him try to tell you otherwise...like he's going to ride out of here come morning." Dalton scratched his head and patted his belly. "If the rain keeps up, we could all be in Sweetwater for a couple days. I'd best go see what Gussie's cookin' up for us, now that we're the local heroes."

Phoebe found her hand encased in his and knew quite suddenly why her friend Charlotte would want to marry such a fine man. Fine, indeed. "Dalton, I..."

"Save it, Miss Sinclair. I just want to apologize for all the misunderstanding." He flushed clear to the top of his starched white collar. "I behaved...badly. I never should have had you thrown in that jail. I should have followed every lead, seen the frame for what it was, known Blades at first sight..."

"Shh." Phoebe pressed a finger to her lips and ventured a smile. "Please . . . 'Tis merely history now. I fear we all played a hand in it, me especially." She squeezed his beefy fingers. "I shall never harbor the slightest ill will toward you, Dalton Pryce, especially since you shall soon wed my dearest friend."

Dalton puffed out his chest and flashed a wide grin. "Indeed I shall, Miss Sinclair, as soon as the blasted weather clears. If she'll have me, of course."

Phoebe smiled. "Oh, I don't doubt that for one moment, Dalton."

He bowed low over her fingers then sauntered down the hall, whistling a cheery tune. Phoebe contemplated the heavy oak door, musing on the man contained within that room as she smoothed about her hips the peach silk gown Gussie had so graciously provided. Daringly low cut, it hugged her bosom, thrusting it high to perch precariously upon the very edge of the plunging neckline. Her waist was cinched so tightly she knew Jace could easily span it with his hands. She smiled to herself . . . but not for much longer. She'd washed her hair thrice over and arranged it simply, caught high at the back of her head to fall in tumbling ringlets to her waist. She'd bathed for a good hour in lilac-scented soap and had applied the same lilac scent to her wrists, her throat, her cleavage and *there,* God help her, and had even managed to locate a pair of teardrop pearl earrings.

She looked as good as a woman could and she bloody well knew it.

"Cranky," she purred, hooding her eyes and puckering her full lips. "Foul mood . . . ha! One look at me and the man will melt. How delicious—confined to his bed. This will indeed be a two-day stay that my strapping lover shall never forget." Her tongue swept over her lips, moistening them one last time, and she pushed the door open.

He lay in the shadows, the room itself a shadowy dim to the drawn shades, the heavy velvet hangings draped about the enormous four-poster canopy. He'd apparently doused every last candle any well-wisher had lit for his convenience but one, perhaps the one he couldn't reach from his vantage, the one burning low upon a table beside the windows. She bit her lip.

This would not do. The man had to *see* her, and see her well, if her ploy was to work.

She took several steps into the room and closed the door softly behind her, then nearly jumped from her skin when a savage bark filled the air.

"Get your damned ass out of here!"

Cranky? Foul mood? The man was a raging beast. A smile teased her lips and she moved closer to the bed, close enough that she could make out the brawny shadow that was Jace, recumbent and grumbling upon the pillows. He'd flung one arm over his eyes and raised one knee such that the white sheet draped rather provocatively over his hips, baring him from neck to a good two inches below his navel.

And he was quite naked.

Phoebe's eyes probed the sheet, directly at a spot between his legs, then swept upward. He looked like some proud, bronzed beast, his densely furred chest impossibly broad and powerful looking despite the stark white bandages wrapped about one shoulder. His ribs were lean, corded muscle upon muscle, his diaphragm a ridge of sinew. The arm closest to her lay upon the sheet, and Phoebe found her eyes caressing the entire length, stilling at his hand, so very large, his fingers, so very long, tapering, capable of caressing her very soul from her.

She quivered with her passion, wondering how the man had managed to seduce her before she'd even had an opportunity to speak. Swallowing past a parched throat, she moved to retrieve the lone candle then approached the bed once more.

"Jace," she ventured softly, poising directly at his side, her eyes drinking in his chiseled profile, the magnificent mane of blue black hair.

"Leave me, woman," he growled, his arm remaining soundly over his eyes.

A frown puckered her brow as she bent the flame to the taper upon the bedside table, then set the candle in its brass holder beside it. Tentatively, she lifted one hand, laying the very tips of her fingers upon his arm resting upon the sheet. "I merely ventured to see how you're faring."

"As you can see, madam, I'm faring. Now go. Pester someone else."

" 'Tis only you I wish to pester," she murmured huskily, her fingers sliding ever so slowly over his forearm. He flexed his arm, capturing her hand in the crook of his elbow.

"You've come to gloat, haven't you?" he snarled from beneath his blasted arm, his hold upon her hand only tightening when she tried to free her fingers. "To gloat because you saved my worthless ass, and not only once, damn it all. Because you were right and I was wrong, because I fell for every trick you used, because I'm a damned worthless excuse for an agent or an outlaw or a hero...because I bungled a lame excuse for a mission because of *you*, and how well you know it. God, look at me."

"Indeed I am," she purred, resting her hips against the side of the bed, just a hairbreadth from his arm.

"A miserable wretch, I am," he muttered, apparently unaware of her intent. "Confined to a damned bed because of some insignificant little wound that I wouldn't have gotten had you not shoved at Blades's arm, I'll have you know. I had every intention of falling aside to avoid being hit, but *no*, you had to step in and get me nearly killed!"

Phoebe's eyes widened and she nearly clawed the man's bloody eyes from his inflated head. "What? You blame *me!* Dear God, you're a buffoon! Indeed, a worthless buffoon! I wished to save your bloody hide!"

"Save it!" he bellowed, flinging his arm aside as he half rose in the bed to bend a heated glare upon her, at last. "By telling Blades I was a Pinkerton's agent, by—" He blinked at her, his gaze dipping to her bosom, then lower, then up again, then lower yet again, his mouth snapping shut with a click. "Good God, woman," he whispered, his gaze locking with hers. "Look at you."

Phoebe drew herself up and glowered mightily at him. "I gloat fashionably well, do I not?"

Oh, how the man's intent could change. "Come here." His eyes, sapphire flames in the soft candlelight, flamed over the high curves of her bosom with bold appreciation, his hand reaching for her. "Now."

"Don't order me about, Jace," she sniffed, turning the plunging back of her dress upon him and swaying her hips ever so saucily as she strolled to the windows. She peered unseeing through the lace curtain. "I've need of a word with you."

"You're torturing me," he rasped.

"And well I should!" she huffed, fixing blazing amber eyes upon him. "Torture you as you torture me with your words, which, I might add, are naught but grand delusions of your insufferable ego! How you cannot bear it that I killed Blades to save you, stealing your revenge from you with one pull of the trigger. I suppose you and all your conceit would have rather died than be saved by a mere woman. And how it must pain you to admit to being wrong. I'm of a mind that you'd rather you had been right all along!"

He stared at her from that bed, looking as masculine, as bold and sensuous as a man could, cloaked as he was in all his infernal wounded pride. "Part of me does indeed wish that, I'll admit it, though only because I knew I would have you in spite of it. But damn it all, woman, it's a hell of a bitter pill to swallow when a man can't even do his damned job!"

"Ha! Then lick your wounds, lummox, for I've no desire to be shackled for the rest of my life to a man who believes himself invincible."

"*I am invincible!*" he roared, shoving the sheet aside and swinging his feet to the floor. "And I'm going to prove it to you every damned day you're shackled to me." His voice rumbled ominously in his chest despite the wince furrowing his brow. "Now, get over here, woman, before I come after you, and don't think I won't. Wounded and all, I can move a hell of a lot faster than you can in that . . . that . . ." His eyes feasted upon her. "Take it off before I tear it off. And hurry. You don't want me bleeding to death, do you? To whom, madam, would you then spend the rest of your life shackled?"

Something in the tone of his voice, the defeated look in his eye, the sudden pallor, drew Phoebe toward the bed without hesitation and dissolved every last vestige of her anger. She paused only when she'd reached him, and he pulled her between his naked thighs, his hands about her hips, his face poised not a breath from her décolletage.

"Do you know what it's like for a man to confront his one true weakness?" he rasped harshly, his eyes seeking hers. "And what it's like when he realizes that one weakness is a woman he can't live without? Phoebe . . . this egotistical lummox, this insufferably thickheaded lout, this tortured, much maligned, all-too-vincible man couldn't spend another day on this earth if you don't consent to be shackled to him for the rest of his days. God help me, woman, but you've bewitched me. I can't function unless I have you . . . unless . . ."

"Shh . . ." she whispered, drawing his head to her bosom, reveling in the feel of his mouth, hot and passionate upon her breasts, his hands claiming every inch of her hips and thighs. "However long it takes, my love . . ." A gasp parted her lips when nimble fingers released her breasts from her gown. "However long to heal those wounds . . . I shall indeed be your wife . . . for all time." A shiver quivered along her spine when her dress fell in a silken heap at her ankles.

"Good God," he whispered at the sight of her completely naked before him. "Even now, no undergarments . . ." His palms claimed her buttocks and delved between her trembling thighs, seeking.

With a throaty laugh, she pressed a hand against his chest, easing him onto the bed and against the pillows despite his initial resistance. "Rest, love," she breathed with a teasing smile and a brazen sweep of his entire, masculine length. "The good doctor prescribed a heaping dosage of the Sinclair touch, I believe he called it." As sleek as a cat, she slid her supple length against him, stilling only when her hips nestled against that hot blade looming between his legs.

His hands spanning her waist lifted her, spread her, until he filled her and she gasped with pleasure and rotated her hips gently against him. "Heal me, woman," he muttered against her throat.

And heal him, she did.

Chapter Twenty

Late in the afternoon two days hence, Zack finally lumbered to a stop along Pine Grove's cobblestone drive. Despite his bandaged shoulder, the confounded sling the doctor and Phoebe had found so necessary and the talons of pain that shot through his torso at the most inopportune times, Jace assisted Phoebe from the saddle and accompanied her toward the house. They managed only three or four strides before a flushed and flustered Charlotte bounded down the veranda steps with a shriek of what Jace surmised was joy, for she flung herself into Phoebe's embrace and proceeded to sob uncontrollably against her shoulder.

"Oh, dear God, you're alive! I thought...no...I can't tell you what I thought! 'Tis dreadful about Madeline...Gideon Goare...dear God..."

"I know. Jace told me...dreadful."

And in a matter of moments, Phoebe joined wholeheartedly in the sobs of relief, causing Jace to roll his eyes heavenward in a silent plea before he cast Dalton Pryce a knowing glance. What men had to endure for the love of a woman.

And then Charlotte was upon him, blubbering like a fool about his being a hero and attempting to embrace him without touching him, so entirely aghast was she at his sling and all those bandages. Finally, and only when he made his presence known by forcing a cough, Charlotte noticed her fiancé and, with a breathless cry, hurled herself into his arms.

Slipping his arm about Phoebe's waist, Jace drew her against him, burying his mouth in her hair. "It's finally over," he murmured, crushing her to him with a flex of his arm. "Now when, woman, are you going to marry me?"

Liquid amber pools dark with emotion lifted to his. "Tonight...this very moment..." Her lips parted and he couldn't have resisted for his very life tasting of her. She yielded beneath him the way she always would, molten honey that seeped into him as if he were a starved man, and never, ever, could he imagine having enough of her. Two long glorious days and nights she'd tended to him in Gussie's hotel, displaying again and again a wanton passion that never failed to stir his deepest yearnings, and he wanted her again, now, in his crudely thatched bed in the servants' quarters, where he had lain many a night, dreaming of doing that very thing.

"Come," he murmured against her lips, catching her hand in his and pulling her along behind him.

"Jace...where...?" She gave a throaty giggle as they moved around the house and headed directly for the smaller stone dwelling. "Dear God, but you've a mind for but one thing...and I need a bath desperately."

His eyes flamed and he drew the useless sling from about his neck. "We can take one together...later."

"And I'm awfully hungry..."

"Me, too." With one booted foot he kicked open the door to the cottage, drew her inside and into his arms. His lips found her throat and his fingers the delicate buttons of her shirt, moving with haste to rid her of this garment and her damned britches. "I want you naked," he rasped, his mouth finding the high curves of her bosom beneath the parted shirt.

Her fingers had spread his shirt wide, her hands venturing over his chest, yet she resisted, ever so slightly. "Jace, someone might be looking for us, for goodness' sake, and..." She drew a quick breath when his thumbs teased the peaks of her breasts through the thin cotton of her shirt before he slipped the garment from her shoulders, laying her bare to the waist before his eyes.

"So beautiful," he murmured, his mouth hot upon her breasts. "So exquisitely turned to nurse a babe...and a starving man."

Phoebe sagged in his arms, clinging to his shoulders when his tongue encircled one thrusting nipple, teasing, tormenting, driving away every thought but one, and then he suckled her, slowly, ever so leisurely. She tasted of sweet warm lilac and eager woman, and he knew she would...everywhere. He ignored her breathless pleas that they should stop, knowing full well that the hands parting the buttons of his shirt and tugging at those containing his swollen manhood were eager. He bent to spread his hands over her softly curving belly, his mouth following, until he laid his cheek against her and allowed her to cradle him there for several moments.

"Jace, I'm so happy."

"And I," he replied, his fingers suddenly itching to tear her britches from her saucy hips, and he would have done just that, had a resounding bang upon the half-open door not brought him erect with a grunted curse. Dimly he was aware that Phoebe uttered a frightened yelp and tended to her disheveled state with trembling hands, though he was of an entirely different mind and merely flung his parted shirt wide and left the top button of his pants undone.

With three long strides he reached the door, thrusting it wide with a snarled, "Pryce, damn it, man, go find your own damned bed and leave me to mine!"

Only it wasn't Dalton Pryce poised on the opposite side of that door. No indeed, but a man Jace guessed to be about ten years his senior, a man of his own height and breadth of shoulder, garbed elegantly in black trousers and topcoat, and wearing a look of such murderous intent in those smoky gray eyes that Jace had to wonder what had inspired such wrath in so complete a stranger. Jace met him glower for glower, eye to eye, the air crackling between them despite the lack of spoken words.

Finally, Jace narrowed his eyes and crossed his arms over his chest. "Who the hell are you?"

The newcomer raised a lofty russet brow that bespoke centuries of fine breeding. "Jace McAllister, I presume?"

Damned British with all their pomp. Jace opened his mouth but found his words catching in his throat when Phoebe uttered a strangled cry and brushed past him with a breathy "Father!"

Jace closed his eyes, feeling like a very large fool and flushing to his damned boots. He gritted his teeth and tended to his shirt with a sudden startling lack of skill before he turned his back and buttoned his pants, then spun about again to confront the man. Yet again, his damned libido had nearly proven his undoing. Several moments later and they would have been thrashing about, sans clothing, upon that bed.

He shoved his hand at this "Father," who eyed him rather suspiciously over his daughter's head before grasping his hand soundly. "Alec Sinclair," he muttered in a tight voice before he bent his head to Phoebe's. "Outside, Phoebe, now...where we can talk properly, shall we?"

With head held remarkably low, Phoebe cast Jace a side-long glance then skittered through the door, whereupon Alec Sinclair cast a wary glance about the cottage, and Jace, before following his daughter's hasty retreat. Jace was left to follow, around the house and onto the veranda, where Delilah set about serving tea around a large oval table. Charlotte and Dalton Pryce were remarkably unaccounted for, and Jace found himself hovering uncomfortably behind a high-backed wooden chair, his fingers gripping the chair, his heated gaze fixed upon Phoebe. She'd settled herself opposite him, looking positively demure as she lifted her teacup, offered her father a wavering smile and never once looked Jace's way. Uncomfortable, entirely ill at ease, she was. Damn it all, why?

"What the hell's going on, Phoebe?" Alec Sinclair muttered, leaning forward in his chair. "I received word from the dean of Wellesley College that you had quite suddenly decided to take some teaching position in some exclusive Kansas boarding school." Sinclair drained his teacup and added in an ominous tone, "Knowing, as I do, that Kansas boasts of many a cattleman, and many a saloon, but not one exclusive boarding school within a five-hundred-mile radius, I surmised right off that you had departed Wellesley under less than favorable circumstances, am I right?"

A scarlet-cheeked Phoebe nodded and fingered her sterling flatware. "I...I was to be expelled, terminated, so I left...before that blasted Priscilla Snodgrass could laugh in my face! 'Twas pride that made me do it, Father."

Jace couldn't resist the slight tug at his mouth at the thought of his Phoebe dreaming up some entirely unbelievable tale simply to avoid expulsion. He could only imagine what she'd done to bring such a thing about. At the thought, his eyes narrowed upon her with an altogether different intent.

"What, dear daughter, did you do now to bring upon such wrath, may I ask? Oh, and by the bye, Charlotte rather graciously informed me it had something to do with a midnight rendezvous?"

Finally, Phoebe's eyes lifted to Jace, eyes full of remorse, unless he'd guessed wrong. "Midnight rendezvous" evoked one image for him, by God, and his hands clenched the chair.

"I . . . I was found dallying with one of the . . ." Her cheeks flamed and she threw up her hands. " 'Twas a foolish and infantile pursuit of adventure, 'tis all, nothing more, though the dean would not have viewed it thus, especially after hearing its much embellished version from one bitchy Priscilla Snodgrass." Her hand sought her father's. "It matters naught now! You found me here, safe . . ."

"Ha!" Sinclair's bellow rent the still afternoon air and he rose to his feet and began a measured pacing about. "You've your friend Charlotte to thank for that. Apparently she had less faith in your scheme than you, my dear, and saw fit in all her wisdom—wisdom, dear daughter, that you lack—to notify Wellesley of your whereabouts. Thus, upon arriving in Boston forthwith, I knew precisely where to find you. And up to no good, by the looks of it." He cast Jace a glower that Jace returned unflinchingly, despite the bite in Sinclair's words. "And is this Jace McAllister, the man with whom I found you half-naked in that damned stone hut, is *he* the man who mistook you for some bloody thief, the man who had you thrown in some rotting jail, the man who nearly got you killed by some outlaw?"

Jace clenched his fists, gritting his teeth against the rebuttal that ached in his throat for release, and by God he would speak, only Phoebe chose that moment to leap from her chair and throw her arms about his waist, stilling his movements.

"Oh, *yes*, Father, he is . . . all that and more," she purred. Amber eyes slid to his and a soft smile spread her lips. "I love him, you see, and we're going to . . ."

"Your daughter has consented to be my wife," Jace interrupted smoothly, his level gaze upon Sinclair. "We would already have been married had she not drugged me."

Sinclair gaped at his daughter then shook his head. "Do you do this sort of thing to all the men you love?"

"I've loved only one man, Father," Phoebe quipped.

"And a lucky bastard he is, by the sounds of it," Sinclair said wryly.

"Indeed, I shall bear his baby seven or eight months hence."

"Good God," Sinclair growled, shoving a hand through his unruly russet hair and scowling stormily at Phoebe. "Then be about it, damn it all." He waved a dismissing hand before him. "Wed on the morrow, or sooner, for God's sake."

"We intend to, Father. I fear we cannot wait!"

Sinclair regarded them beneath furrowed brows. "Nor I. And not a word of your—" his hand waved in the general direction of Phoebe's belly "—your condition to Elizabeth, do you hear me? She'll string me up and quarter me for raising you in so lax a manner. God knows, the woman will somehow find a way to blame *me* for all this."

"She's here?" Phoebe cried, drawing her hands to her bosom. Wide amber eyes met Jace's. "'Tis Elizabeth—Father's wife—the woman he stole right from beneath her fiancé's nose. She's not my mother, of course. *She's* off somewhere in Italy or Spain, I believe. They divorced some time ago, of course."

"Of course," Jace muttered, casting the less than saintly Alec Sinclair a curious look. British pomp and centuries of breeding be damned. A man was a man.

Phoebe literally bobbed up and down on her toes, such was her excitement. "And the babies? Did she bring them?"

"Of course they're with her, blast it all. The woman can't bear to leave them, and she wasn't about to let me go chasing you clear across the Atlantic all by myself," Sinclair muttered with a scowl. "Some balderdash about men fouling up the simplest of projects. She's inside."

Jace had to wonder if Phoebe even heard him, for she uttered a cry of delight before scurrying into the house, leaving Jace to confront the brooding Alec Sinclair alone on the sun-dappled veranda. He stood his ground as Sinclair paced about for a moment then paused directly before him, looking him squarely in the eyes. Jace tensed, anticipating something . . . he knew not what, the man was so damned unreadable.

"McAllister, I've waited a long time for this."

Jace lifted his brow, though his fists were clenched at his sides in anticipation of a sharp punch in the belly. After all, any father worth his salt would feel Jace had it coming. The man had just learned Jace had gotten his daughter with child, which certainly implied that the little scene he'd interrupted in that "stone hut" had occurred at least once before, if not many times. And Jace had indeed been responsible for every damned disagreeable thing that had happened to the girl since she'd first stepped foot in Buttermilk Falls. He only hoped the man didn't punch him in the shoulder. He tensed again, everywhere.

And then Sinclair was pumping his hand, heartily, his grin wide and unabashed, his manner congenial, his tone brimming with glee. "Damn it man, I've wondered if my daughter would ever meet her match, and by God, she did. She needed to grow up, learn a little about life, and you were just the man to do it, to my eye. A handful since the day she was born, she was, but your responsibility now, McAllister, a burden I gladly bestow upon your broad shoulders."

"Thanks," Jace replied with a wry smile. "She's well worth it."

"Indeed, she is." Sinclair clapped him upon the back. "So tell me, McAllister, I hear you're a lawman of sorts, some sort of spy, aliases and all that. I'd like to hear all about it. I'd like to see your place, too. Fine looking, I tell you, from what I've seen of it. You're in lumber, I hear. A damned profitable business from what I've read. May come in handy that I'm in shipping, with many a line across the Atlantic, eh?"

Jace returned the man's smile. "Certainly worthy of some consideration if you'd like to discuss it while I show you Pine Grove. Tomorrow I could take you down by the mill, show you some of the tracts we have."

"A damned fine idea!" Sinclair replied with gusto. "Oh, and don't worry about the women. They'll be planning the damned wedding until well after midnight."

With a lopsided smile, Jace nodded and the two men walked slowly down the veranda stairs.

They'd just rounded one corner of the barn, their tour of Pine Grove nearly complete, when Jace spotted something crouched in one shadowed corner deep in the barn. He muttered something about feeding the horses and sent Sinclair on ahead, back to the house, then entered the barn. Dusk had begun to settle, promising to banish all light within minutes, though whatever it was that crouched in that corner seemed oblivious to this, so engrossed was it in its task. Jace strode past the horses' stalls muttering softly to the steeds and idly stroking Zack's seeking muzzle. His boots rustling in the hay were sure to rouse every last rodent that called this barn home yet refused to draw even the slightest response from the tiny huddled form. Not until he stood directly at the boy's side did Jamie glance up with a wide-eyed start and a stammered "Oh!"

Jace's chest tightened painfully at the sight of the boy, tumbled and dirt-streaked, looking as if he'd spent the day as any boy his age should. He was garbed in play clothes, a diminutive version of Phoebe's bicycle ensemble, something she and Charlotte had managed to come up with in spite of Madeline's protests. The child had come full circle since Jace had returned, in many a goodly way, though now he was without anyone to call parent.

A guileless smile lit the boy's cherubic face and he bent his fierce attention upon whatever he had buried inside a shallow hole. Jace focused upon the gold-spun hair, his throat constricting at the thought of taking the boy into his arms and begging his forgiveness for many a curt glance, terse response and decidedly cool manner, all forged by the mistaken notion that he had fathered the boy. Jace swallowed heavily, balling his fists at his sides. As if ignoring the boy would have rendered his parentage null and void. The irony of it all. How he wished to heap upon the child all that affection held grimly in check, now that he knew Jamie had not sprung from his own deceitful loins. A damned blundering fool, he was, a damned fool.

He dropped to one knee beside Jamie and peered into the hole, which contained a wooden box. "What have you got there, Jamie?"

Jamie's tiny hands moved reverently over the box then lifted the lid. "Buried treasure."

Jace smiled. "Treasure, eh? And are you a pirate?"

Jamie's wide eyes met his, his tiny mouth forming an unspoken "oh." "A pirate . . . yeah, I'm a pirate. Do you want to see my treasure?'' Without waiting for a response, Jamie began to dig through the contents of the box. ''See, I have play money....''

To Jace's astonishment, the child pulled forth a thick stack of greenbacks, *authentic* greenbacks, upon closer examination, for he blithely plunked them into Jace's lap.

''Lots of play money,'' Jamie grumbled, apparently none too pleased with this. After all, what good was play money? Several more thick stacks found their way into Jace's lap, and several more after that, until he had ten or more stacks filling his lap. A small fortune, by his account. Who in God's name had buried them here? Not Madeline, a woman driven to suicide over blackmail, something she could have bought her way out of with a mere fraction of the money Jace held before him.

With a curious frown, Jace leaned over the boy for a closer look. ''What else did the pirates bury in there?''

''Pictures,'' Jamie replied, thrusting several yellowed photographs at Jace.

And then he knew who had buried this box, for the pictures were of his own mother, Ann Sterling McAllister, and of his father, as well, shortly before his mother's death. Jace stared at the photo, his heart constricting with unspoken grief.

''And some letters I can't read.''

Letters his mother had written his father before they were married . . . keepsakes of a sentimental old fool. Jace held up a fat envelope, as yet unopened, and his vision suddenly blurred and he blinked several times before he could decipher the faded scroll on the front of the envelope: *Jace*.

His head slumped back against the side of the barn and he stared at the rafters above, uncertain as to why he hesitated in opening the damned thing. Perhaps he didn't wish to confront his father now, knowing the truth, something his father had not known, thus forever believing him a coward, a deceitful excuse for a son, a traitor of the worst kind. Yet some deep-seated need to speak with the man just once more stirred potently within him, even if doing so would slice open his every wound.

His fingers tore at the envelope and then his eyes moved over the sprawling words, written with a less than steady hand.

Forgive a selfish old fool of a man, but I couldn't take it all from her, return her to what she was. I loved her too damned much, you see. And she was like a child in so many ways. Maybe someday you'll understand that I needed her. God help me for being a lonely, weak man, but I took a vow to love her for better or worse and that I did. Knowing that you'll read this one day lightens my heart because I know somehow you'll find it within you to forgive, because, Jace, I knew the truth and I lived a lie, condemning you unjustly to life outside this home and myself to a lifetime of knowing it. That was my penance, I suppose, and having to look upon James and know that he wasn't even blood of my blood, but that of a man I'd long trusted, and foolishly at that. You were a better man than I, Jace, even as a lad of barely twenty, facing a father like me with squared shoulders and a steady gaze. A braver lad I've never known. They say you're dead and, hell, I don't believe it. You'll be back to this house, the home your mother envisioned, and when you find this I want you to know the money's for you and for Jamie in case Madeline doesn't manage the place quite right after I'm gone. I was wrong, Jace, and too damned proud to face it, even ten years later. Pride can be a damned destructive thing. Enough advice from an old fool. Oh, one more thing: Don't ever love a scheming woman. You'll sacrifice your life for her

Jace closed his eyes and hung his head. Sacrificing everything, even a son, for the love of a woman, in spite of what she was and all that he'd believed she'd done. No, he knew nothing of that, or stubborn pride.

"I forgive you," he whispered to the hay-strewn floor, the rough planking momentarily blurring. Only when Jamie's tiny voice intruded upon him did he hastily brush his shirtsleeve over his eyes.

"See what I buried in here, Jace? A fish." With obvious pride, Jamie cradled in his palms a small, very dead bluegill. "I caught it all by myself."

"I didn't know you fished," Jace replied with a crooked smile.

"Phoebe taught me. She even bought me my own cane pole. It doesn't have a reel or anything fancy, but she says I don't need one because little boys catch little fish."

Jace lifted a bemused brow. "Is that what she told you? Well, just between you and me, a woman doesn't know the first thing about fishing."

Jamie stared at him, obviously aghast. "Oh no, Jace! Phoebe knows everything! She even told me that herself."

"Oh, she did, did she? Well, we'll have to prove her wrong just this once, because you and I are going fishing, first thing in the morning, even before the sun comes up, and we're going to catch some very big fish, fish we can fry up over a fire."

Jamie's eyes widened. "We will?"

"Of course we will. I wasn't planning on going because I needed a second."

"A second?"

"Sure, a second is your right-hand man, your best guy, someone who helps you along. Do you want to be my second?"

"Oh, boy!" Jamie squealed, flinging himself into Jace's arms and giving him a fierce hug. As if suddenly self-conscious, Jamie withdrew and cast Jace a sideways glance. "Are you going to be my daddy now, Jace?"

Jace studied the child's bent head, the protruding lower lip. "Do you want me to be your daddy, Jamie?"

Jamie seemed to ponder this a moment, his tiny mouth scrunching to one side. "I want to live with you here, and eat dinner and breakfast with you." He stroked the dead fish in his palm. "And fish with you . . . and I want you to read me stories before I go to sleep at night, like my daddy used to."

"If that's being a daddy, then I'd love to be, Jamie." Jace furrowed his brow and rubbed his chin thoughtfully. "There's only one hitch. I'm planning to marry Phoebe tomorrow."

"Oh, boy! That means she'll be my mommy!" Jamie squealed again, though his bright smile suddenly dipped at the corners and his voice dropped to a soft murmur. "She's going to be my new mommy because Dearest got sick like my daddy and went to heaven. Aunt Charlotte told me that."

Jace nodded stiffly, finding himself at an atrocious loss for words faced with the boy's melancholy air.

Twin blue orbs, wide and filled with a certain dread, captured Jace in their depths. "You and Phoebe aren't going to get sick like Dearest and go to heaven, are you?"

Jace's heart lurched and he found his hand upon the child's knee, so very tiny and fragile beneath his callused fingers. "No, Jamie, we're going to be here with you for a very long time. Now, tell me, how did you find this pirate's treasure?"

Jamie swallowed, averted his eyes and looked very guilty, indeed. "I...I...some man came yesterday and brought something for you. He left it here in the barn. It was all covered up and I wanted to see it. He told me not to touch it but, Jace, I just wanted a little peek! And it fell over and broke a hole in the barn floor. That's how I found my treasure."

"Where is this thing?" Jace rose to his feet and glanced about, his hands upon his hips.

"There." Jamie shoved a dirty finger toward a large pile draped with muslin, then raised twin saucers to Jace. "It's a monster, Jace. Be careful."

Jace tempered his smile and moved to the pile, then swept the muslin to the floor. "It's not a monster, Jamie, it's a bicycle." Jace righted a reconstructed Mabel and bent down for a closer look. "The man who brought it was Charlie the blacksmith. He's the nice man who fixed Phoebe's bicycle for her. She rides it in those britches of hers. And I think," he murmured half to himself, "yes, I think she's going to be surprised."

Jamie perched hesitantly at Jace's elbow, apparently still wary of this contraption. "Is it her birthday?"

"No, Jamie, it's her wedding day. Now listen..." He swept the muslin over Mabel once more and crouched low before Jamie. "Not a word of this to Phoebe. We want her to be surprised and—"

"Not a word about what?"

Both Jace and Jamie spun about with wide eyes and guilty grins at the sound of Phoebe's voice echoing off the rafters. Jace straightened and eyed her swaying hips appreciatively as she sauntered toward them, then stopped and folded her arms over her chest. She looked too damned delicious glancing between the two cohorts with a raised brow and pursed lips, tapping a toe with decided impatience upon the floor.

"Well?" she mused, her eyes fixed relentlessly upon Jace. "What the devil are you two cooking up in here?"

Jace exchanged a guileless glance with Jamie and shrugged. "Who, us?"

Her lips pressed together and she clenched her fists at her sides. "Jace McAllister, if you think you can hoodwink me ever again . . . why, I won't marry you, I tell you. I won't!"

Jamie tugged at Jace's sleeve. "I think you better give it to her, Jace. She's mad."

Jace's hooded gaze fixed upon a fuming Phoebe, though a smile tugged at his mouth. "No, Jamie, she's not really mad, she's just a scheming little woman." He caught her flailing arms behind her back with one hand and drew her close, grinning like a devil into her flashing eyes. "Did I ever tell you how much I've always wanted to marry a scheming woman?" he murmured, then glanced at Jamie and jerked his head toward Mabel. His hands spanned her waist and his mouth found her ear. "I am, of course, counting on being thanked in an appropriate manner, woman. A few midnight rendezvous might be a good way to start."

Phoebe eased from his arms and peered haughtily down her nose. "We'll see, beast." And then her eyes flickered past him and widened, and she gasped and clutched her hands to her breast then flung herself into his arms with a breathless "Oh, Jace! It's Mabel!"

"I think she likes it," Jamie observed with a grin, then bent over Mabel for a closer inspection.

"Oh, you're wonderful," she choked into Jace's shoulder.

"I know," he replied with a smile, drawing her closer against him. "You'll have to wait another nine months or so before I'll let you on that thing."

She pushed against his chest and gaped at him horrified. "Wha—" And then she dissolved into a smile and pressed a hand to her belly. "Oh my, of course . . . yes." She turned in his arms, nestling her head under his chin and pressing his palm over her belly. "I'm so happy here, Jace."

He stared out the barn doors at the brilliant pink hues of the sun setting over a distant growth of tall pine, pine that would need felling before September, land that would require nurturing, a house that needed a loving hand and children to fill its every room, just as his mother had envisioned. "You wouldn't mind if we didn't go to Colorado Territory just yet?"

She shook her head and snuggled back against him.

"Good." He crushed her against him and rested his chin atop her head. "Because this is home, English, with you, Jamie, our babe. Finally...I'm home."

* * * * *

ROMANCE IS A YEARLONG EVENT!

FEBRUARY
S	M	T	W	T	F	S
				1	2	3	4	5	6

MARCH
S	M	T	W	T	F	S
1	2	3	4	5	6

APRIL
S	M	T	W	T	F	S
1	2	3

JULY
S	M	T	W	T	F	S
1	2	3

AUGUST
S	M	T	W	T	F	S
1

SEPTEMBER
S	M	T	W	T	F	S
1	2	3	4

OCTOBER
S	M	T	W	T	F	S
1	2

NOVEMBER
S	M	T	W	T	F	S
1	2	3	4	5	6
7	8	9	10	11	12	13
14	15	16	17	18	19	20
21	22	23	24	25	26	27
28	29	30

Celebrate the most romantic day of the year with MY VALENTINE! (February)

CRYSTAL CREEK
When you come for a visit Texas-style, you won't want to leave! (March)

Celebrate the joy, excitement and adjustment that comes with being JUST MARRIED! (April)

Go back in time and discover the West as it was meant to be . . . UNTAMED—Maverick Hearts! (July)

LINGERING SHADOWS
New York Times bestselling author Penny Jordan brings you her latest blockbuster. Don't miss it! (August)

BACK BY POPULAR DEMAND!!!
Calloway Corners, involving stories of four sisters coping with family, business and romance! (September)

FRIENDS, FAMILIES, LOVERS
Join us for these heartwarming love stories that evoke memories of family and friends. (October)

Capture the magic and romance of Christmas past with HARLEQUIN HISTORICAL CHRISTMAS STORIES! (November)

WATCH FOR FURTHER DETAILS IN ALL HARLEQUIN BOOKS!

CALEND

Harlequin® Historical

THREE UNFORGETTABLE KNIGHTS

First there was Ruarke, born leader and renowned warrior, who faced an altogether different field of battle when he took a willful wife in *Knight Dreams* (Harlequin Historicals #141, a September 1992 release). Now, brooding widower and heir Gareth must choose between family duty and the only true love he's ever known in *Knight's Lady* (Harlequin Historicals #162, a February 1993 release). And coming later in 1993, Alexander, bold adventurer and breaker of many a maiden's heart, meets the one woman he can't lay claim to in *Knight's Honor,* the dramatic conclusion of Suzanne Barclay's Sommerville Brothers trilogy.

If you're in need of a champion, let Harlequin Historicals take you back to the days when a knight in shining armor wasn't just a fantasy. Sir Ruarke, Sir Gareth and Sir Alex won't disappoint you!

IN FEBRUARY LOOK FOR *KNIGHT'S LADY* AVAILABLE WHEREVER HARLEQUIN BOOKS ARE SOLD

◈ HARLEQUIN ®

my Valentine *1993*

The most romantic day of the year is here! Escape into the exquisite
world of love with MY VALENTINE 1993. What better way to celebrate
Valentine's Day than with this very romantic, sensuous collection of four
original short stories, written by some of Harlequin's most popular
authors.

**ANNE STUART
JUDITH ARNOLD
ANNE McALLISTER
LINDA RANDALL WISDOM**

**THIS VALENTINE'S DAY, DISCOVER ROMANCE
WITH MY VALENTINE 1993**

Available in February wherever Harlequin Books are sold.   VAL93